End Game

MICHAELA JEAN TAYLOR

END GAME

Editor: Britt Tayler

Cover Designer: Michaela Jean Taylor

Formatting: Michaela Jean Taylor

*For those who silently suffer,
may you find the strength to break free.*

Author's Note

This book contains on-page scenes with mature subject matter including discussion of physical and emotional abuse and an on-page attempted assault and is intended for mature audiences.

Chapter One

"Uh . . . hello? Ma'am? Can I get some help over here?"

Blowing out a breath, I ignored the man standing on the other side of the bar—standing, might I add, shoulder-to-shoulder with dozens of other patrons who'd been waiting patiently for a drink *much* longer than him. He'd sidled up to the wooden countertop only minutes ago, and if he thought he was going to get my attention that quickly, he was sorely mistaken.

Focusing on the task at hand, I added Crown Royal, apple schnapps, and cranberry juice to my ice-filled stainless steel mixer before capping the top and shaking the contents around. The cold mixer dripped with condensation from the ice, and I had to wipe my hand against my thigh before I could pop the cap back off. The sticky-sweet smell of the apple schnapps wafted through my nose, and I wondered if my own sticky-sweet treat would be stopping by tonight. I hadn't seen Charlea in almost a week, hadn't felt her soft curves beneath my hands in too many nights—and after another busy shift like this one, I needed to blow off some steam.

Now that I thought about it, I hadn't heard from Charlea at all since the last time I saw her. Which was . . . five days ago? And even though I'd told her—repeatedly—that my interest in her was of a strictly non-exclusive nature, I'd gotten used to her texts every day. She'd become a real friend. Just . . . with some sexy benefits.

Shit. I hoped she was okay. Making a mental note to text her when things slowed down, I poured the Washington Apple shots into three glasses and pushed them in front of a birthday girl and her two friends.

"Ohmigod!" Birthday Girl squealed as she tucked her shot close to her chest. "I love theeeese." Her lime green birthday sash was backward and falling off her shoulder, reflecting offensively under the neon pink lights that swirled around the bar in time with the dizzying beat of the music.

I frowned, looking at the friend closest to her with narrowed eyes. "How drunk is she?" I asked, giving her a look that said *Don't bullshit me.*

The friend shrugged. "Drunk enough that this should be her last one?" she answered sheepishly.

I nodded, pushing down the irritability that flared in my chest. This was a bar, after all. People came here to drink. That was good, right? More money in my pocket, that's for sure. "Yeah, I'd say so. I'll bring you ladies your tab. You have a ride home?"

The other friend chimed in. "Yep! I just texted Rosie's brother," she nodded toward Birthday Girl. "He's on his way."

I nodded again, and that should have been the end of it. I didn't know these girls, and I wasn't responsible for them. I should be able to trust that they were capable of getting themselves home. But still, I couldn't resist the next question from spilling out of my mouth. "This brother of hers . . . he's sober tonight? You guys will be safe?"

Both of Rosie's friends nodded vigorously from where they stood on either side of her. "Oh yeah," the first one said, "he's been waiting at home for our call to pick us up. We're solid."

All three of them stared at me as I mulled over their response. And I realized they hadn't taken their shots yet, that I was inadvertently interrupting their fun with my . . . "mothering," as Frank called it. "Let me grab your tab," I repeated as I turned around to face the small computer behind me.

I navigated through the touch-screen system to find and print their tab, and heard Man Child's voice again from just down the bar. "Yo! Could you please slide that fine ass down this way when you're done? Jesus . . . I don't want to keep begging for a fucking drink." This time I let my eyes snap to him, taking in the rogue blonde curl falling into blue eyes surrounded by thick, long lashes.

He was . . . pretty. But I knew those good looks were trouble. He probably lived a charmed life with easy access to most of the things he wanted—typical, really, for a lot of the guys who came in here, used to being fed by a silver spoon. They expected instant gratification after throwing out a *Please* and a sultry wink. But at my bar, that kind of shit didn't fly.

Larkspur was a busy downtown nightclub that hosted hundreds of people on any given night, and tonight was our monthly ladies' night event that only made things crazier. The club was swarming with women who got to enjoy free cover at the door and discounted drinks. And where there were women, men would come—they never seemed to mind having to pay to get in. Even with three bartenders behind the bar, we were more than outnumbered.

"I see you," I called back to him with a firm tone. "I'll get there when I can."

His eyes narrowed as he scoffed. "What the hell does a guy have to do to get a beer in this place?"

Rolling my eyes, I ignored his childlike display of impatience and turned back to Rosie and her friends, sliding their tab toward them. Rosie looked up at me—well, her gaze made it up to my chin—and said, "Thank you for making this the best birthday *ever*."

I smiled. "I literally didn't do anything. But thanks?"

Each of her friends slipped a credit card into the book and pushed it back to me. "Can you split it down the middle?"

I nodded. "Sure thing." Turning back to the computer, I nearly ran into my newest bartender. "Shit, sorry!"

Nora looked at me over her shoulder, grinning from ear to ear. "It's so fucking busy tonight, Mar."

She was a special kind of freak who thrived on being in the weeds. It was one of the reasons she'd quickly soared right up my list of favorites—especially considering that, until she started working here, she'd never bartended a night in her life. "You doing okay?" I asked.

"Hell yes!" she yelled before booking it back to her end of the bar.

I laughed at her bizarre excitement, closed out the tab for the birthday girl and her friends, then brought their receipts back to them. Just as I turned to greet a smiling couple and ask them for their order, the gremlin shouted out again. "For fuck's sake, woman, I have money I'm trying to spend!"

The man and woman standing in front of me frowned at the attention-seeking display of testosterone leaning on the bar ten feet away. I looked back at the couple and whispered an apology, putting a finger up to indicate I'd be right back.

I turned to my right and made eye contact with Frank, our head of security. We had guys stationed all over the club, but Frank always took the position at the end of the bar, keeping watch over all transactions. I gave a little head-jerk to the side, toward my current bane of existence—a sign he knew well. He nodded, pushing off the wall to head this way.

Frank was our head of security for a reason. He may have a handsome, boy-next-door face, but he also had a body like a linebacker and a mean streak when it counted. I watched as his eyes scanned the rowdy patrons, readying himself for anything.

Knowing he'd be here within seconds, I turned and walked toward Blondie, smiling at him as brightly as I could. "I'm so sorry, sir. Please forgive my *blatant* disregard for your needs."

He tilted his head and peered down at me, that blonde curl bouncing against his forehead. A crooked grin tugged at his mouth as his eyes raked over my body. "That's more like it, sweetness. I was hoping you'd bring me a beer—I'm getting thirsty over here."

"Thirsty?" I smiled wider, winking. "Thirsty for a good time, I hope?"

His eyes flicked to my chest, to the skin exposed from my low-cut Larkspur shirt, before he raised his chin. "What do you know about a good time?"

Fluttering my eyelashes, I looked to where my hands rested

on the bar, feigning bashfulness. "Well, I know that for you," I teased, looking back up at him, "it's not here."

His grin faltered, and his eyes dulled in confusion. "What?" he asked.

My own expression shifted to a glare. "You don't disrespect me, you don't disrespect my staff, and you certainly don't disrespect our other customers with your entitlement issues. Whatever you're looking for, *sweetness*, it's not here." I pointed to the door on the other side of the building. "Get the fuck out."

Just as his face twisted in anger, Frank grabbed hold of his shoulders from behind. "All right, pretty boy, let's go."

"What the fuck?" Blondie spat out.

"Bye bye!" I waved as he disappeared into the crowd behind him, Frank keeping a firm grip on his shoulders. The people who'd been standing close enough to hear his tantrum clapped. While I had everyone's attention, I took the opportunity to shout out a friendly little public service announcement. "Listen up, folks! We're so happy to have you here at Larkspur, but make no mistake, if you treat this bar, my staff, or each other with disrespect, you can join Goldilocks out through that front door. We clear?" Cheers erupted again, this time from even more patrons who'd leaned in to hear what was going on.

Content with my point being made, I headed back to the couple I'd left hanging, finding them smiling again. "I'm so sorry about that. What can I get for ya?"

THINGS DIDN'T SLOW down until well after one o'clock, and even then, "slowed down" was a stretch. Still, Nora and

Sam had practically kicked me out from behind the bar, assuring me that they had things under control for the rest of the night.

I usually liked staying until closing time, but I'd closed the last eleven nights in a row, and I would be lying if I said I wasn't exhausted. I hadn't actually taken a day off in more than three weeks—but Larkspur was my life. Since starting here two years ago, on the heels of the most terrible season of my entire existence, I'd thrown my heart and mind into the nightclub and welcomed the distraction with open arms.

After closing myself out for the night, I stuffed my stack of cash tips—over three hundred dollars' worth—deep into my belt bag and pulled out my phone. I typed out a quick text to Charlea to ask her what she was doing, even though I knew it was late and that she was probably already sleeping. Even still, I wanted to check in and show some effort from my side of our little arrangement, even if neither of us owed the other anything like that.

She was a kindhearted girl, and she deserved to be thought of.

I returned my phone to my purse before slinging the strap over my shoulder and making my way to the back of the building where a small locker room existed, a reminder of the old community center that used to exist in this space. There was a single-stall shower inside, and while I normally didn't bother with it before heading home each night, tonight's shift had been crazy enough to have more than one drink spilled on me.

Making quick work of showering and throwing on some extra work clothes from my locker, I headed toward the front of the club to leave. I said a quick goodbye to Ethan and Mikey, the bouncers who worked the door, on my way out. There were only a handful of people waiting in line to get in, and I smiled at them all as I walked past.

"Oh shit, look, it's Mara!" I heard someone call out. I was used to being recognized here—I'd built a pretty large social media presence advertising Larkspur on my personal accounts, promoting the events that we hosted alongside candid shots of me working behind the bar. My social media accounts had become one of the driving forces behind the growing popularity of Larkspur as I carved out a digital presence that otherwise wouldn't have existed.

The current owner, an older, long-time investor named Robert, was much more old-school in his business approach. He preferred traditional marketing strategies, like buying advertising space in our local newspapers or paying for billboard spots throughout the city. When I started working here, I'd asked him if I could take the dive into online spaces, and though he didn't think it would amount to much, he let me have at it. Luckily for both of us, it worked.

Robert promoted me to bar manager and marketing director a year ago, and though I was still a core bartender at the club, I'd also worked to develop a huge digital presence that made both of us a lot of money—his in the form of an overall increase in revenue, and mine in bonuses and tips like I'd ever seen before.

It was October in Denver, which meant temperatures were beginning to drop considerably during the late-night hours. A chilly breeze swept around me, goosebumps spreading across my arms and neck, so I pulled my favorite black hoodie over my work shirt and yanked the drawstring tight around my face. My bare legs still shivered thanks to the spandex booty shorts I was wearing, but I did my best to ignore the bite.

My apartment was only a twelve-minute trek through the downtown city streets—a path that I could walk in my sleep at this point. Unhooking my pepper spray cartridge from my bag, I tucked it into the front pocket of my sweater. Though I took this walk home every night—usually later than this—I was still aware of the risks a big city posed. I promised myself long ago that I would never let anyone make me feel unsafe in my own skin again.

Five minutes into my walk, my favorite late-night convenience store came into view. Rudy's Market was open around the clock, offering scattered grocery options, over-the-counter medications, and fresh sandwiches and pastries from a small deli in the back. Rudy himself worked the night shift, while his younger brothers covered the early morning and afternoon shifts.

I started stopping in to get a post-shift sandwich years ago. My routine was getting it to-go, then stuffing it down at home before crashing until the next afternoon. At some point, though, I'd begun eating my sandwiches in the shop while visiting with Rudy. He was twenty years my senior and loved to reminisce about his teenage years spent in Cuba—all of which were hilarious if not borderline unbelievable.

While it was admittedly a bit unconventional, I considered Rudy to be a friend. I didn't have many of those these days, and he was kind and considerate enough to make me feel comfortable anytime I was in the store. It certainly helped that, while it wasn't technically on his menu, he had a habit of making me strawberry milkshakes.

I decided to stop in and say hello . . . I *was* off early tonight after all. Plus, I hadn't eaten anything since I garbled up some leftover boneless wings on my way out the door earlier this afternoon. Taking a second to look both ways, I crossed the street and bee-lined it for the front entrance.

The soft chiming of a bell sounded as soon as I opened the door, and Rudy's voice came from somewhere in the back. "Oh, what luck for me—is that Mara, I see?"

I smiled. "Hey, Rudy!" Rounding a display of greeting cards, my eyes landed on where he stood behind the deli counter. He was wearing a navy polo and jeans, his chocolate-brown hair combed over to the side and his smile bright against his russet skin. "How's it going over here tonight?"

Rudy shrugged. "Not too bad, I've had a few customers every hour. Most of them to buy beer."

I smiled wider. "Well, it's a good thing you and I both profit nicely from people who like beer, isn't it?"

"You more so than me, I'm sure." He chuckled and then nodded toward the fridge behind him. "You hungry?"

Nodding eagerly, I rushed out a "Yes, I am," just as my stomach rumbled. "Can I have a turkey and provolone please?"

Rudy chuckled. "Coming right up, *chiquita*."

There were three tables set in front of the deli counter, each with two chairs. It was cramped—there wasn't enough room in here to provide any more seating than this—but I wiggled myself between two of the tables and squeezed into one of the tiny metal chairs. I watched as Rudy pulled out meat, cheese, and veggies from the industrial-sized stainless steel walk-in. "Do you ever get scared of getting trapped in there?" I asked the question before I could think better of it.

Rudy quirked a brow. "No...?"

"Oh, so you're normal then?" I laughed. "Sometimes when I have to change a keg at the bar, I get worried that someone will accidentally lock me in and I'll freeze to death."

His dark brown eyes swam in amusement. "I highly doubt you guys keep your walk-in cold enough to freeze, or you'd be pouring beer slushies from the tap."

Hm. *Not a bad idea.* I was just about to tell him as much when the bell chimed again.

Rudy lifted his head. "Hello, welcome!" he called out.

I couldn't see the front door from where I sat, but I heard the low, baritone voice that responded. "Good evening, sir." It cut through the air like butter—smooth and rich as it drifted along my senses, sensual and teasing like a long overdue vice. "I was curious if you sell champagne?"

Rudy's brows pulled ever-so-slightly, but he quickly wiped the confusion away with a smile. "Uh, yes sir—one second and I'll show you our options." He rubbed his palms against the apron he wore around his waist and moved toward the front door.

I ducked my head to catch a glimpse of the new arrival through the chip shelves on my right, but only managed to catch a fleeting glimpse of a light gray business suit and large olive hands before they disappeared down another aisle.

"We unfortunately don't have many to choose from," said Rudy, his voice traveling from the other side of the store, "but what we do have is right here."

"Which one is your most expensive?" the man asked. I almost snorted.

"Uh, that would be this one, sir. It's seventeen dollars."

"Mhm." That voice rumbled out a low, pleased hum. I felt

the sound somewhere in my limbs, like a spark igniting. "It's perfect, I'll take it."

Sounds of feet shuffling moved back this way before Rudy came into view, carefully holding a bottle of champagne in both of his hands. He made his way behind the register and scanned the barcode.

The man trailed behind, pausing on this side of the counter. He was wearing a three-piece suit, the light gray material looking almost silver under the fluorescent lights. The white collar of a dress shirt peeked from the back of his neck, and soft chestnut waves cascaded around his head, just long enough for the ends to drape over that collar.

From the back, he looked . . . promising. His stature alone called for attention, and I realized he certainly had mine. Which was odd, considering I hadn't felt genuine attraction for a man in a very long time.

How long has it been? I wondered. *Two years?* Maybe longer. Not since Logan . . . but I didn't even really count him. He'd been a soft landing after the worst days—or more accurately, *months*—of my life. Plus, he was technically an ex-boyfriend, the guy I lost my virginity to when we were both sixteen, so our reconnection had been more like the comfort of muscle memory than a new, whirlwind attraction.

"Do you need anything else, sir?" Rudy asked, bringing me back to the too-bright shop.

The man reached into his suit jacket and propped a leather wallet on the counter. "No, thanks. This'll do just fine."

Rudy nodded. "Your total is eighteen dollars and thirty-six cents."

I heard the swipe of a card followed by the *ting* of the

register slamming shut. "Thank you so much for coming in, sir." Rudy smiled brightly. "We hope to see you again soon."

The man nodded, his waves rustling with the movement. "Yes, of course. Thank you for all your help." He turned around clutching the bag, but his eyes snagged on where I was sitting in the cold metal chair and as soon as they landed on me, his feet stopped moving.

Chapter Two

His dazzling blue eyes scanned me, from the green and purple streaks in my hair to the septum ring that hung from my nose. He was a handsome, sharp, clean-cut man —all business. But his eyes were soft as they appraised me, and on closer inspection, his tawny hair was wild and unkempt. It suited him . . . helped to balance the severe businessman vibe he was giving off.

My focus moved back to his eyes as they swept down my body and up once more. I tensed, bracing for the immediate judgment that men so often graced me with. One look at me and they usually either wanted to fuck me or move on like they never saw me. I was hot enough to catch their short-term interest, or *just* edgy enough to scare them away. But this man . . . he was looking at me in a whole new way.

"Oh, hello," he greeted me. Like we'd just stumbled into each other at the park on a warm sunny day, and not in a cramped twenty-four-hour convenience store well past midnight. His full lips curled into a bright smile, showing off perfectly straight white teeth. "I didn't notice you there," he said simply as his blue eyes sparkled under the harsh lighting.

His words caught me off guard . . . I almost looked over my shoulder to see whether he was speaking to someone else. Instead, I gave him a polite smile and said, "Hello."

His mouth curved higher, eyes crinkling along their outer edges. One dimple flashed below his cheek, and I couldn't help but wonder how often it made an appearance. "What's your name?"

I angled my head as I considered whether to appease him with an answer or tell him to go ahead and fuck right on off. Normally I had no problem shoving away unwanted attention with a sharp bite . . . but the normal reflex to do so hadn't yet risen. My defense mechanisms stood down.

If anything, I was *more* perplexed by my lack of bristling. Something about this man, about the smile on his face that appeared to be reflecting sincere curiosity, didn't trip up any of my guards. So I decided to go with it, to be nice. "Mara," I said back.

He nodded, repeating my name in his velvet-like voice: "*Mara.*" And then another hum vibrated from his chest. Hearing my name *that way* stirred something awake within me, something that'd been slumbering with such finality that I never thought I'd feel it again: *want*, in its rawest form. He didn't avert his gaze as he lifted the brown bag in his hands, the paper crunching from the pressure of his long fingers. "Do you like champagne, Mara?"

A smile rose on my own face, and I tucked a strand of hair behind my ear, clearing my throat. The truth was that I wasn't much of a drinker—being around it so much at work didn't make it very appealing. But . . . there was a thrumming in my chest as my blood roared to life. "Depends . . ." I trailed off.

His eyes twinkled. "On?"

I shrugged, feigning nonchalance. "What's the occasion?" His brows cinched together, and he looked at me with confusion. "You just bought Rudy's top-shelf bottle," I mused. "Seventeen whole dollars of bubbly." My eyes traced the length of his suit. "And you're dressed like *that* in the middle of the night. There must be an occasion."

A deep chuckle rumbled out from him, instantly lighting up my nerve endings. My heart pounded hard in my chest in response. He finally broke our eye contact as his eyes dropped to his feet for a moment before raising back to mine. "There's a celebration to be had, and I find it rather serendipitous to find you here in my pursuit to have it. I'd love it if you'd join me."

He was already counting me in, as if it were inevitable. It was confident . . . almost cocky of him.

And I was thrilled.

"Hm," I hummed, smiling so wide an ache pulsed in my cheeks. A handful of heartbeats passed between us. I looked over his shoulder at Rudy, who was standing behind the counter, watching our exchange. "Rudy?"

"Yes, dear?" Though my own defense mechanisms were . . . nowhere to be found, the look on Rudy's face screamed that he was unsure about this turn of events, that he already didn't like what I was about to say. And I was thankful for it—I really was. But, there was a shift happening beneath my skin, a vibration that I hadn't felt in so damn long. I knew I would regret not taking the chance to follow it through, even if it broke almost all of my rules.

Hell, I might even get an orgasm out of it.

So, I gave him my best *I've got this* nod. "Can I have a raincheck on that sandwich?"

He looked at me for a few seconds before saying, "Sure thing, Mara. No problem at all."

My eyes jumped back to Mystery Man who was practically glowing with amusement. I stood up from my chair, the metal legs scraping against the linoleum floor with effort, and then maneuvered myself back out until I was standing right in front of him. "Well, then?" I teased.

Though he hid it well behind his smile, I heard him suck in a breath. His eyes dropped to my bare legs for a moment, their skin raised from the cool air in the shop, and when they met mine again there was the smallest trace of hunger that zipped down my spine.

And still . . . I didn't bristle.

I was no stranger to the art of a one-night stand. I'd had plenty with complete strangers over the years—but all of them had been with women. Charlea started out that way before we eventually hooked up again and made it a regular thing. The last *new* man to ever get inside my pants was He-Who-Must-Not-Be-Named. And, until now, I'd been fairly certain he ruined me for all other men—but not in a sexy way. More like a *Broken and scared for my life* kind of way.

I'd known since high school that I "swung both ways," as my friends back then liked to call it. But after my last relationship went to absolute hell in a handbasket, I figured my time with men had come to an end. At least for the foreseeable future. It wasn't that I'd shut the idea down with totality—but I hadn't had much of a reason to open that door again, either.

Until tonight.

Because this man was looking at me like I could be his late-night meal. And I wanted to serve it to him on a silver platter. Wanted to enjoy the spoils that a man could provide in the bedroom.

He hugged the brown bag into his chest and held the elbow of his free arm out for me to take, grinning when I obliged. As he tucked me close to his body, I could smell his rich, woodsy scent and wondered what he did for a living, why he was dressed so nicely after midnight, and what news could have possibly prompted this errand to Rudy's for champagne.

As he pushed through the door and led me into the brisk night air, I planted my feet into the ground and stopped walking. "Wait," I said as he turned around to face me. His blue eyes were as bright and bold as a shooting star in the jet-black sky. "You never told me your name."

He grinned out the side of his mouth—an expression that was boyish and unwound. The sight of it made my toes curl. "Leo," he said, gently pulling me forward by the arm still laced into his. "My name is Leo."

"So, where are you taking me, Leo?" I asked lightly as we continued across the downtown street.

"You'll see," was all he responded with.

I laughed, still waiting for fear or discomfort to flare within me, but there was nothing but a crisp buzzing. "Are you always this mysterious?"

His grin widened. "I think you might be the first person to ever call me that, so . . . no." He chuckled. It was the first time I heard the hint of an accent—something northeastern. Definitely not native to Colorado. "I've also never brought a beautiful woman home after only minutes of knowing her, either."

"Home?" I asked, feeling a flush in my neck. "You're taking me home?"

He shot me a look, eyes wide, before saying, "Not like that —I just meant my building. The roof, to be precise. It's my favorite place in the city—the perfect setting for a celebratory drink."

I stared at him, then nodded, even more perplexed.

Even more intrigued.

"Here," he said quietly as he gestured toward the entrance of a gleaming building. It was the tallest on this street, a building made up mostly of glass I knew to be full of luxury condos. If Leo lived *here*, he definitely had money.

We walked along the front entryway toward double doors trimmed in gold. Even at this late hour, a concierge stood just inside, pushing the door open to greet us with a warm smile. "Good evening, Mr. Callahan!"

Leo dipped his head. "Georgie, always a pleasure."

Georgie took a quick look behind us as we stepped across the threshold. "No valet service tonight, sir?"

"No." Leo shook his head with a polite smile. "The car is still in the garage. I decided to enjoy some fresh air with a walk tonight."

Georgie coaxed the heavy door closed behind him with white-gloved hands. He dipped his head again with a renewed smile. "Good evening, ma'am."

"Mara," Leo looked at me. "This is Mara. And Mara, this is Georgie, the best concierge in all of Denver." He leaned in close enough for me to inhale more of that intoxicating woodsy scent. "Just don't tell Roger I said that."

Georgie huffed a laugh. "Very good, sir. Enjoy the rest of your evening."

Leo grinned. "You too, Georgie. Be safe." He tightened his hold on my arm—as if on some distant instinct—and led us toward a polished gold elevator. After he pressed the button to go up, I felt his breath skate along my neck as he murmured softly, "I need to make a quick stop at my apartment, but then we'll head up to the roof. Okay?"

His blue eyes shimmered down on me underneath the warm light of the lobby. From this close, I saw the faint lines etched into the skin around his eyes, and I wanted to see them deepen again like they had at Rudy's. I wanted to see him throw his head back with a rumbling laugh. "Okay," I said. I couldn't help the stupid smile still plastered on my face.

It was like slipping on a mask—though it wasn't disingenuous. I didn't have to force it. If anything, it felt like an old version of myself coming to the surface. One that I thought I'd lost so long ago, like an old favorite sweater in the back of my closet. I felt . . . giddy. Excited for whatever adventure this night was leading to.

The elevator doors opened with a chime and we both stepped into the car. Leo pulled a black card from his jacket pocket and pressed it against a sensor before pushing the round button that sat at the top of all others, a black PH displayed across the glowing background. *Holy shit, the penthouse?* We both stayed silent as we rode the elevator up, the only sound the thrumming of his fingers against the paper bag still clutched close to his chest. There was a rhythm to the way he tapped, like a song stuck in his head. I noticed that, even when standing, Leo's body never stayed completely still. As his fingers danced along the brown paper, his body swayed with the slightest movement.

It took a couple of full minutes before the elevator chimed again, and when the doors opened, I gasped.

The foyer's white marble floors stretched into the distance where a black leather couch sat in what had to be his living room. Straight ahead were floor-to-ceiling glass windows, and even from all the way back here, the city lights glowed brightly from below. Directly in front of the elevator was a round polished-chestnut table adorned with a black vase bursting with flowers.

It was . . . beautiful wasn't the right word. It was *extraordinary*.

My eyes snapped up to Leo, who hadn't moved from his place next to me. He was already looking at me, a small grin curling from the corner of his mouth. "This is home," he said casually, as if it wasn't the most stunning place I'd probably ever seen.

My gaze moved back to the penthouse before me. "Wow," I breathed.

"I'm just going to the kitchen to grab some champagne flutes," he murmured into my ear. "Feel free to take a look around."

I shook my head to decline the invitation. "Thanks, but I think I'll just wait here." It wasn't that I was getting cold feet or that I was second-guessing any of this . . . but I was a grungy bartender wearing sticky converse and a hoodie I knew damn well hadn't been washed in over a week. I had no business poking around in a place as nice as this.

Curiosity bloomed in Leo's eyes as he looked back and forth between mine. Then he nodded and pressed the button to hold the doors open, adding a low "I'll be right back," before stepping out and disappearing down the hallway to what I imagined was the kitchen.

As soon as he was out of sight, I doubled over in shock, hands on my thighs and my jaw slackening as it fell wide. *What the hell had I gotten myself into?* I stood and scrubbed a hand over my face, and when I opened my eyes again I almost jumped out of my skin at the discovery that I was no longer alone.

A bright orange tabby cat sat right in front of me, tail curling into the elevator as it looked up at me with golden eyes. Assessing. Judging. Leo had a cat—I almost laughed, picturing their life here. One severe, focused businessman and one fluffy orange cat orbiting around each other in a bougie penthouse like this.

In the distance, I heard ice being poured and the clinking of glasses. Bending down so I was sitting on my own heels, I reached a hand out. It eyed me warily before slowly craning its neck forward, its nose and whiskers twitching as it sniffed me. I startled when it let out a long and loud meow before scampering off around the corner, in the direction Leo had gone.

"Oh, hello Dolly," I heard him say. Another meow sounded, and Leo's warm chuckle soon followed. I felt a wave of . . . something . . . in response. Something warm yet foreign.

Not a minute later, Leo reemerged from around the corner holding a metal ice bucket with the bottle of champagne nestled within. Two flutes were gingerly clutched in his other hand. I noticed the knot of his tie had been pulled loose, and the sight of it made my stomach roll in anticipation—I wanted to pull it off him completely, wanted to unbutton his shirt to expose the skin beneath.

He paused when he saw me, his eyes flicking down again to my bare legs, then used the hand holding the glasses to grab a blanket that had been folded and draped over the back of his couch. He looked back at me and smirked. "Ready?" he asked as he joined me in the elevator. That woodsy scent wrapped around me like a sensual embrace.

Something tightened in my chest. *Ready?* "Yes." I nodded. "Please."

His expression darkened for a moment before he blinked it away, pressing the button that would take us to the roof. He inhaled a deep breath, letting it out with a low hum as he stared straight ahead, watching the elevator doors close.

I felt gravity press down around us as the elevator rose, dinging only seconds later as we reached the roof. My eyes held on to the vertical line where the two doors came together, eager for them to open again. When they did, I let out another gasp that had Leo's head snapping in my direction.

It was . . . stunning in an obscene way. Artificial grass surrounded large concrete squares where various patio furniture sets were placed—the trendy rattan kind, with upholstered cushions and soft pillows in creams and beiges. Edison lights were strung along the outer walls of the building as well as along the walls of the balcony, blanketing the entire roof in a soft, warm glow.

And the *view*.

At thirty-five floors up, I could see more of Denver than I thought possible. My feet carried me toward the nearest ledge before my brain even registered what I was doing, but I was drawn to the beauty that lay before me. The city streets stretched far and wide, their sparkling lights radiating against brick buildings and tall trees.

Despite the light pollution below, the stars were more than visible. I looked up and felt the vastness of the world around me in a way I hadn't felt in a long time. Not since I last went hiking, I supposed. I was usually so tucked into the city spaces I frequented that I tended to forget how much of the world was actually beyond me.

I felt the warmth of Leo's body as he stepped into place beside me. "It's beautiful, isn't it?" There was genuine wonder in his voice as he took in the same view I was lost in.

I let out a sigh, feeling a profound contentment in my soul. "It's incredible," I whispered.

Chapter Three

"COME ON," HE SAID WARMLY, "LET'S GO SIT." Pushing his body off the edge of the low brick wall, he moved toward the lounges closest to us, setting the bucket of champagne onto the table. I watched as he placed the two glass flutes down before he looked back at me. He held the blanket up for me earnestly, a crooked smile brightening his face. "This is for you . . . it's a bit chilly out tonight."

He was right. I'd put the hoodie on for my walk home, but my plan for when I was back inside my own apartment had been to throw on some warmer sweatpants over my bare legs. With this adventurous turn of events and our now thirty-five-story-high celebration, the crisp late-night breeze was chilling me straight to the bone. I followed him over and took the blanket from him. "Thank you."

He nodded as I sat down, pulling the fleece over my legs. It was heavier than it looked, providing instant warmth and allowing me to relax into the cozy cushion. Leo gave me a small smile as he picked up the bottle of champagne and removed the foil from the top, exposing the cork beneath. He popped it with one quick flick of his honey-toned wrist and looked at me with gleaming eyes, his broad chest puffed with pride.

"You never told me what we're celebrating," I remembered, hoping to dissect Leo's joy a little bit, to understand how a man like him ticked.

He poured a generous amount of champagne into each flute and handed me one before he spoke. "I closed a deal," he explained, his smooth voice curling around me, heating my blood up a notch. Or two. "Maybe the most important one of my career."

I'd had a hunch it would have something to do with business, an early judgment based on the way that he was dressed. I imagined he was a man who invested in stocks, who had a 401k and a high-yield savings account. "A big one?"

His shoulders lifted in a small shrug. "Actually, not a very big one. But an important one all the same."

It was pretty late in the night for him to be closing deals. "What kind of business do you do?"

Leo simply looked at me, hesitating. And I wondered why . . . it should have been an easy answer, right? "It's a little complicated. The 'professional summary' section of my résumé includes various buzzwords"—he grinned at me, like he knew exactly how he sounded but was confident enough to own it— "like executive leadership for struggling companies, acquisitions and mergers, flipping businesses for hefty profits . . . Essentially I ensure that any business I work with performs well and exceeds profit expectations."

"Oh." My thoughts instantly turned to Larkspur and my dream of buying it. "That's pretty impressive."

He gave me a sheepish smile that didn't quite reach his eyes, his shoulders noncommittally lifting and falling. "It's a family business. My father is much more impressive at it all than I'll ever be." I narrowed my eyes at him as his face flashed with what looked like resentment before he wiped the expression clean altogether. His father, I gathered, was a sore subject.

"So did you buy a business? Or sell one? Or . . . lead one?" I asked, steering the conversation to safer ground.

Amusement settled back over his features as he smirked playfully. "Bought one. Though it's not one that would normally fit my firm's portfolio." He sighed. "Anyway, I'm confident in its potential." A clump of dark brown hair fell into his eyes as he tilted his head to look at me, and I watched eagerly as he ran his free hand up to push it back.

I lifted my full champagne glass, stretching my arm out to meet his. "Cheers to your success, Leo." My mouth pulled with a smile. His returning grin was devastating as he reached forward with his own flute to clink it against mine. We both took long sips, our gazes locked together. I wondered what might come next, after we finished our drinks. Would we end the night, or would we have another? Would I end up in his bed, like I was starting to hope for? "Aren't you going to sit down?" I asked as I put my glass back down. It was cold, and I thought he might want some of this blanket, too.

Plus, with his body closer to mine, I could throw out a few signals to see if he took the bait. It would be nice to be touched by a man again.

Leo's eyes ping-ponged between the seat next to me and my face. If not for the sudden fixed intensity in his expression, as though he could read my thoughts, it might've been comical. He moved around the rectangular coffee table and lowered himself down next to me, instantly warming my side. "So," he husked, "you know why I'm celebrating. Now it's your turn. What were you doing out so late? Middle of the night sandwich craving?"

I laughed. "No, I just got off work—I'm a bartender. Rudy's is on the way home, and I stop in sometimes after my shift when I haven't had dinner."

Concern flashed across his face. "You didn't eat dinner?"

I took another sip of my champagne before answering. "No."

"I'll make you something," he said quickly.

"Oh . . . no, it's okay. Really. I'm not even that hungry."

As if on cue again, my stomach rumbled audibly. Leo narrowed his eyes. "Mara, I'm going to make you something, and you're going to eat it."

The command made my heart falter, and I knew there was no getting out of this. So I made a show of rolling my eyes in protest before giving in, not wanting to come across as too easy for anything he might be dishing out tonight. "Okay, okay. I'll eat your food."

He hummed into his glass as he downed the rest of his champagne, his eyes never leaving mine. I felt the loss of his warmth as he stood, grabbing the bucket as he circled the table. "Let's go," he said, nodding toward the door that led back to the elevator.

"Wait," I objected. "Now? We just got up here . . ."

"Mara," he countered. "You're hungry. And I can't in good conscience continue to pour you Rudy's top-shelf champagne knowing you're drinking on an empty stomach. Come on," he said, a touch of urgency slicing across his face. "We can resume this celebration downstairs."

My gaze shifted to the edge of the roof, and I greedily took in the way the buildings glowed in the dark from the city's lightshow below. A small wave of disappointment fluttered within at having to leave this incredible place, knowing I'd likely never be back. But I didn't want to reveal those cards to Leo, didn't want him to know how entranced I was. So with a small sigh I stood, clutching the blanket in one hand and my half-empty glass in the other.

Once we'd both stepped into the elevator's heated car, Leo hit the PH button. As the elevator began to descend, he turned to look at me. "Is there anything you're allergic to?"

"Antibiotics," I answered.

"What?" It was clear I'd caught him off guard with that. "You're allergic to antibiotics?"

I nodded. "Yeah. Gave my mom a real scare with my first ear infection when I was five. My throat closed and I couldn't breathe—I was purple by the time I got to the ER."

He stared at me for a long while, only speaking again after the elevator chimed. "But no food items?"

"Nope. No food. Just potentially life-saving medicine," I teased, eager to smooth out the intensity on his face.

The doors opened, and this time there was a smaller cat with black and white fur waiting on the other side. Leo's smile was instant. "Hey, Swift," he cooed.

The cat—Swift—meowed, looking up at us with interest.

Leo stepped into his apartment. "Come, Mara. Swift won't bite . . . She's friendly. Though," he hedged, looking back at me with a twinge of embarrassment, "Dolly might."

"Oh," I breathed, eyeing the small cat as she rubbed her neck against my ankles. "Okay, good." I shook myself free and caught up to Leo as he rounded the corner back into his kitchen. As soon as I turned the same corner, *another* loud gasp burst out of my mouth.

Leo's nose flared as his eyes darkened to smoke. "You really should stop doing that." His voice was quiet and careful.

Heat pooled in my stomach. "I'm . . . sorry." But I couldn't help it. The kitchen was breathtaking. Sleek black marble with flecks of gold and white topped the counters and island, the cabinets climbed all the way up to the ceiling, and the appliances were so fancy they looked like they must have cost more than a full year's worth of rent on my own apartment.

But the kitchen was only in my periphery now because my gaze was fixed on Leo. On the way his bottomless blue eyes roamed over me with hunger. On the slope of his neck, corded with muscle, to his broad shoulders and chest contained only by his crisp white dress shirt.

I wanted to see what he looked like without all the finery. I wanted him naked as he let me explore him with my fingertips and tongue.

Clearing my throat with a twinge of embarrassment at my obvious eye-fuckery, I forced my gaze to the stainless steel fridge, doing what I could to balm over the moment with something steadying. The gleaming silver surface was spotless, not a smudge or fingerprint to be found. "You must have quite the cleaning crew."

Heat was still heavy in his gaze as the right side of his mouth tugged. "Yes, Vanessa is . . . thorough." I nodded, drinking more of my champagne as I wondered if Vanessa was also a target of his . . . charms. "Red or white sauce?"

"Huh?" I asked, still reeling from that fiery exchange.

His mouth curled higher, smug and satisfied. It was clear the effect he had on me. "Red or white sauce, Mara?"

I loved how often he said my name. Like he wanted to keep rolling it off his tongue. "White, please."

"Good choice," he said through that grin as he moved to the fridge. He pulled out a carton of heavy cream and a wedge of Parmesan cheese before stepping over to a built-in pantry where he grabbed a bag of flour and some seasonings.

"Wait," I started. "You're not making something from scratch, are you?"

His gaze caught me over his shoulder. "I said I was going to make you something, Mara. And that's what I intend to do."

"Oh, you don't have to do that, really, it's not worth the trouble—"

His scoff cut off my words. "Why is it not worth the trouble to feed you? You're hungry, you need to eat. Let it happen." His eyes flashed like lightning as they fell to my mouth. Fell further to sweep along my body with a confidence that told me he knew exactly where to apply the kind of pressure that would make my limbs dissolve. He looked at me like he'd make sure I enjoyed it. "Trust me, it's worth the trouble to feed you something."

It felt like being hit by a bus, the dominance and insistence of those words. I watched, utterly captivated, as he shrugged himself out of his jacket, folding it and tucking it into one of the tall stools at the center island. His tie soon followed, and then his thick fingers were unbuttoning the top two buttons of his dress shirt and rolling his sleeves neatly up to his forearms.

The sight of his tan arms made me dizzy. They were long and toned, dying to break free from the restrictive cotton they'd been trapped within. "Come." His voice broke me out of my daze. "Sit down here." He indicated to the empty chair beside the one holding his pile of discarded clothing. I forced my feet forward and folded myself onto the soft cushion, eyes fastened on those arms the entire time.

Leo threw a kitchen towel over his shoulder before placing a small pot on the cast-iron stove and flipping the heat on. He added a few tablespoons of butter to the pot before gracing me with a wolfish grin. A laugh burst out of me at the sight. "This is pretty impressive," I said, my brows climbing up my forehead.

He shrugged. "It's just a simple Alfredo sauce. I'm going to use store-bought noodles, so the meal isn't completely home-made. Do you eat meat?"

"Yes," I responded as a whoosh of air left my lungs at the thought of other things I might taste tonight.

Leo nodded, adding a flat skillet to the stove top and moving back to the fridge to pull out a deli-wrapped parcel. "You like a little heat?" Mischief had joined the hunger in his eyes.

"Yes." I smiled.

Another grin as he grabbed a thick cutting board from beneath the island, setting it on the marble surface. His confidence in navigating around his kitchen was . . . hot. I'd have thought a man who lived alone—especially in a place like this—would have a personal chef. An expense that probably wouldn't even graze the sum of his accounts.

Settling deeper into the stool, feeling the fabric rub against the backs of my exposed thighs, I watched how Leo's shoulders stretched out wide through his shirt, rolling as he moved. His movements were fluid, his body poised for action—like he'd have the ability to curl himself into any space with ease, despite his impressive height and build. He was probably a good dancer.

Probably a great lover.

After seasoning the chicken, Leo moved the breast to the skillet. There was a satisfying sizzle as the meat hit the steel, and he let out a pleased hum. I wanted to feel that hum vibrate against my skin. My desire was winding its way up my spine, sinking its claws in deep. It was heady, edging on the verge of need. To have a man like him on top of me, inside of me, where no man had been in almost two years—it was all I could think about as he focused on my meal.

We stayed quiet while he continued to display his prowess in the kitchen: boiling salted water in a pot for the pasta; adding seasonings and cheese to the cream-based sauce; flipping the chicken to browned perfection. He didn't measure any of his ingredients, didn't have to pull out a recipe to follow—he was comfortable and assured in every move he made.

I was so focused on his hands that I didn't notice he'd turned his attention back to me. "Mara," he rasped. My eyes lifted to his, finding them dark and hungry once more. Something told me it wasn't in response to this meal he was preparing. "If you keep looking at me like that, I won't be able to stop myself from bending you over this island and giving you what you want."

His cheeks were pink with the traces of a flush I was sure matched my own. "What?" I feigned innocence, but I knew he had me. The directness of his words only aroused me further.

Leo stared at me for a long moment before his attention was captured by the bubbling pot of sauce at the stove. "Shit," he mumbled, turning his body away from me to stir it and turn down the burner.

After draining the noodles in the sink, Leo pulled a black ceramic plate out of a cabinet and scooped the pasta and sauce onto it. He sliced the crisped chicken breast and added it on top of the pasta before sprinkling some red pepper flakes over it all and pushing the plate in front of me. The food smelled incredible. "Wow, this looks amazing, thank you," I said, smiling as I picked up my fork from the setting he'd handed me earlier.

He wrapped his fingers around the neck of the champagne bottle and refilled my glass. "You're welcome. Please"—he nodded toward the plate—"enjoy."

"You're not going to have any?"

"No, I ate dinner at a normal hour with the rest of the world."

I made a show of rolling my eyes again, and his eyes darkened as they dropped to my mouth, the potency of his expression back in full force. I ripped my gaze away from his, forcing my gaze down to the food in front of me. I took a bite and couldn't help the small moan that escaped from the back of my throat. "Oh my god," I said through a full mouth, "this is so *fucking* good."

Leo grinned, satisfaction evident in those lips that were the perfect shape for biting.

As I tore through the whole plate of food, Leo stood next to me with his hip leaning against the island, sipping from his glass of champagne. It only took me a few minutes to eat every bite—I'd been much hungrier than I let on. But it was also a testament to Leo's skills in the kitchen . . . the food truly was so fucking good.

When I finished, Leo swiped the plate and fork away and moved to tuck them into the sink before turning to look back at me. There was still an intoxicating energy in the air, thick and all-consuming. I squirmed in my seat under the heat of his gaze—though I couldn't deny the excitement beneath the surface. "Thank you for dinner," I said as my heart pounded in my throat.

He smiled but didn't say anything. He gripped the edge of the counter behind him, as if holding himself back—from what, I wasn't sure. But it thrilled me all the same. Eventually, whatever war he was waging in his mind transitioned into a firm decision. I saw the confidence return to his gaze, along with those obvious traces of desire.

He stalked toward me, rooting himself into the ground by my chair. "Mara," he murmured as his eyes roamed my face, "was a champagne toast all you wanted from me tonight?"

My lips parted and my mouth went dry again. I didn't know how to answer his question . . . so I simply stared up at him.

He lifted a hand, gently running his fingertips across my jaw before letting them flutter down my neck. "Hm? Mara?"

He wanted me to say it. To admit that I wanted more.

Fine. I could be bold, too.

Taking a deep breath, I said simply, "No."

His pupils blew wide as he pressed his lips together. "Mm," he hummed. "What else? What else do you want?" His fingers curled around my shoulder, slipping through the opening of my hoodie. He kept his pressure featherlight, a mere whisper of a touch, and I shivered.

I strengthened my resolve and finally answered. "You."

And before I knew it, he was everywhere, his mouth claiming mine with an explosive fury.

Chapter Four

Leo's kiss was slick and needy, fast and hungry —the kind that happened in the middle of fucking, when two bodies were simultaneously climbing higher and anchoring down into each other. When things became a frenzy of skin and teeth and tongues and hands.

His mouth was dirty, his tongue hot. His fingers were greedy as they explored the topography of my body, taking what he wanted like it was already his. His confidence was potent, and I didn't mind it one bit. Not like this—this was the one place in my life I was willing to relinquish control— though most of the women I'd slept with over the past few years had been more content to let me take charge.

I'd happily give Leo the power tonight . . . even if I would never let him have it anywhere else.

"I don't do relationships," I said into his mouth before he lifted my hoodie over my head and threw it to the kitchen floor. He needed to know before we went any further that this wouldn't lead to anything more than a good, hard fuck, *especially* now that it seemed I needed to spend some time readjusting my stance on intimacy with men.

"Okay," he breathed, his tongue curling along my top lip before he dove back in. One of his large, rough hands cupped my breast over my shirt, squeezing with the most delicious pressure. With what seemed like very little effort, he pulled me from the stool and lifted me onto the island as he thrust his hips between my thighs, bracing himself on either side of my hips and pinning me in place.

The next time he came up for air, I forced more words out into the shared breath between us. "Just a onetime thing," I whispered as his hands splayed over my waist, the stretch of his fingers easily surpassing the length of my shorts. "You might never see me again," I added before groaning at the feel of him sucking the skin below my ear. *Thank god* I'd taken a shower before leaving the bar.

A chuckle rumbled from his chest, shaking through my own. "Okay," he said again—though, it sounded like he was just placating me.

"I'm serious," I insisted, ripping my mouth away from his. The sight of him nearly rendered me speechless, nearly tore every thought right out of my head. His lips were pouty and swollen, slick from my tongue. And his hair was falling haphazardly around his face—I wanted to pull it, to wind my fingers through it. But I forced myself to think through this drugging haze. "I can't commit to anything more than this."

His blue eyes softened as they looked back and forth between my own. He reached a hand up to my face, lightly grazing my jaw with the backs of his knuckles. The amusement fell from his expression, replaced by something heavier and more sincere. "I hear you." He nodded. "Just tonight. Nothing more." Chills ran up my spine at his touch. My hand tugged at his collar, pulling him back into me with force. I was delighted when he grunted into my mouth in response. But then he pulled back again, his face more determined. "We don't have to do anything more, Mara. This wasn't what I—" He paused, resetting. "I have no expectations. We can stop this now."

The thought of stopping made me almost frantic. I shook my head, the "no" spilling out of my mouth without second thought, and his returning grin was so eager it made my chest squeeze. With both hands, he cupped my ass and hoisted me up, turning to take me somewhere beyond the kitchen. I reached between us to unbutton the rest of his shirt, my fingers moving clumsily as they tried to make quick work of each one, anxious to get to the body underneath.

"Fuck," Leo muttered into my neck, pressing me against a wall as my hands slipped up the white T-shirt I discovered beneath the collared dress one. His stomach was hard, and I could feel the wave of abs rippling beneath his skin. He darted a hand down to where my legs were wrapped around his waist and quickly found the apex of my pleasure, swirling his fingers above the spandex of my shorts, as if to reward me for finding the treasure of his bare skin.

I gasped at the feel of it, at his warm pressure, *there*.

"Fuck," he groaned again, eyes glazing as he pulled back to look at me, "that fucking sound." And then his mouth was consuming mine again as he carried me further down a dark hallway.

There was something exhilarating and *just* this side of dangerous about not knowing the floor plan of his apartment, of never having been here before and not knowing where he was taking me. The slipping awareness that I'd just met the man whose hands were gripping my body with fervor—and that I'd likely never see him again after this—made me feel like I was floating outside of my own body.

My skin came alive as my own need unraveled. The inferno between us was growing rapidly, setting out to swallow us whole. I couldn't wait for the burn. I wanted it. Wanted to feel the sting of it for days and days after. Wanted to chase this pleasure, to let instinct take over and take flight with the gorgeous man holding me like I was his prize.

Leo kissed me deeply, and though my eyes were closed, I sensed we'd walked into a dark room. He wound my ponytail around his fist before pulling it to force my face to the ceiling, exposing my neck for his mouth to skate across. I liked how firm he was with me, that he somehow knew I could take it.

"Take off your shirt," he urged into my skin, his breath warming my collarbone. I tugged at the hem of my shirt, almost laughing at the thought of the words printed on the back: I CALL THE SHOTS. Right now I didn't want to. Not one bit.

I pulled the shirt over my head and let it fall to the ground. Opening my eyes, I found Leo's gaze scouring over my chest in the dim light, his line of sight curving along the black lace that hugged my breasts. Beneath my spandex shorts I was wearing the matching thong—it was a set I bought recently at a lingerie shop when I'd wanted to spoil myself after a night of insane tips. I'd assumed it would be Charlea who'd find the lacy material during one of our romps, but the way Leo's eyes fastened on the see-through material made me glad it was him.

"Your turn," I whispered, and his eyes jumped up to mine, dark like liquid smoke. He set me on my feet and let me slide his dress shirt down his arms before I pulled the undershirt over his head. My eyes nearly bulged at the carved lines of his bare chest, at the wide planes of muscle beneath his skin. And his stomach—it was an incredible work of art, fit for a magazine cover. *Damn.*

Leo grinned, and I wondered if I'd accidentally said it out loud. His eyes moved up to the top of my head. "Take your hair down," he whispered, his pulse thrumming wildly beneath the skin of his neck.

I reached up to pull my ponytail out of the elastic, letting my blonde hair cascade around my neck and shoulders, the bright green and purple streaks more exposed now. As Leo's eyes roamed the colorful tendrils, my throat constricted with a sudden onslaught of nerves. Leo clearly had fine taste and easy access to pretty things. I was a bartender with a septum ring and colored hair. Maybe this was too much for him—I wouldn't blame him if it was.

But that doubt was swiftly discarded when Leo's gaze moved down my body, not touching me with anything but the heat of his blazing blue eyes. "You're so beautiful," he murmured, his throat working with a swallow, a sign of his sincerity. And it pierced me right in the chest, inflated me like a balloon.

My eyes stung as an unexpected flare of emotion bloomed at the compliment. I'd spent so much time building up walls to keep myself safe from everyone around me, but sometimes I desperately missed the vulnerability that came with letting someone get close. Something about tonight, about this chance encounter with Leo . . . I felt more exposed than I had in a long time. Like the carefully curated veil was gone, and I was suddenly bared wide open.

After my last long-term relationship ended, my self-confidence and self-worth was trashed. Eventually, I'd found the ability to create a persona for Larkspur—a tough-as-nails, badass bartender who didn't take any shit. It came with the short shorts and tight shirts that helped earn great tips. My social media page was filled to the brim with comments from complete strangers telling me how "hot" and "sexy" I was and, if given the chance, what they'd like to do with me. And I'd forced myself to exist inside that persona in *all* aspects of my life. I'd even grown to like it, for the most part. It was a battle suit, and I wore it well.

But hearing Leo call me beautiful—seeing the truth of it in his eyes—was enough to make me second-guess everything in the span of seconds. My defenses had been down with him from the beginning, and I realized I wasn't Larkspur's Sweetheart right now. I was here, in Leo's penthouse, unflinchingly giving him the real me. Needing to be seen by him . . . to be enough.

That was okay, right? At least for one night?

Confidence blazed through me as I pointed to his pressed pants. "Off," I said.

He laughed. "Not so fast." He stepped closer, his hands falling back to my hips, his fingers pressing divots into my skin. "You first," he whispered, kissing me deeply. His tongue curled into my mouth as his fingers slipped beneath the hemline of my shorts. He licked across my jaw as he slid them down my legs, his mouth following a similar trail on my neck and chest.

When his tongue flattened over the black lace that covered my nipple, I sucked in a sharp breath through my teeth. "Oh god," I whispered as my eyes fell shut, and he hummed with satisfaction as he dipped his mouth further toward my hips.

My shorts fell to my ankles, and he gripped my thigh as he lifted my leg, my foot escaping from the material as his tongue teased along my panty line.

He pulled back to appreciate the thong that matched my bra. "I like those," he said, more to himself than me. His eyes were glazed, heavy with desire. "I think we should leave them on for now." He pulled my other foot out of my shorts and rose back up to his full height, caging me against the wall with his arms, crowding into my space. Bright, blue eyes punched into mine. "What do you want, Mara?" He bent down to nip at my chin, grazing my skin with his teeth. "Hm? Show me what you want."

As he bent down to suck on the point of my shoulder, my gaze landed on the large bed in the center of the room. It was unmade, the thick white duvet pushed down toward the foot of the bed, exposing soft gray sheets. I imagined him drilling me to the mattress with his hips, rolling into me as the muscles of his back danced.

He stood tall, piercing gaze assessing. The warmth of his breath ghosted my cheek as his chest rose and fell, heart pounding against my hands, his fingers dancing a quiet path along my stomach. "Mara," he spoke again, his tone firmer.

My gaze snapped from his bed to his eyes, finding them so full of need it made me shiver. "Yes?" I whispered.

"Show me what you want," he begged, before he captured my lip with his teeth.

I fought through the nerves swirling in my belly.

Show him, my body sang.

So I did.

Reaching out to grip his wrist, I pulled his hand toward me and pressed it firmly between my legs. Instinctively, his palm cupped me with eye-rolling pressure as his finger swiped along the fabric of my underwear. Where I was already so wet for him.

He groaned, a deep guttural sound escaping from the back of his throat as he swiped his finger against me again. Pressing his lips against mine, he spoke into my mouth. "So needy for me already, aren't you?"

My eyes fluttered closed as I nodded, chasing his tongue with my own. The sensation of his finger between my legs splintered through me. "Yes," I breathed.

The heel of his palm rounded against me, driving friction where I needed it most. "What a good girl you are," he rasped as his other hand wrapped gently around my throat, the pressure ultra-light, testing to see how I might react to it. And though I half expected my self-defense tactics to kick in from a touch like that, they just *didn't*. I wanted more.

I stared right into this near-stranger's eyes and realized how deep my trust ran with him. Even as he brazenly tested my boundaries, he did so with an obvious care, attentive in the way he moved and slowly enough that I could stop him at any point. But I didn't want to—I wanted to give him everything. "Harder," I begged. "Please."

Leo smiled with his whole face, his eyes blown wide with lust. And then the hand on my throat gripped tighter as the one between my legs pressed harder, driving slow circles with the heel of his hand as his fingers curled against me. The increased pressure rippled a shudder down my spine, and my legs began to tremble from the pleasure building.

His fingers continued their assault between my legs, the fabric of my panties sinking deeper and deeper as I rocked my hips against his hand, chasing for a sweet release. Leo's gaze bounced from my eyes to my mouth before falling down to where I was grinding against him, and he let out a trembling breath. "I love how eager you are for this."

"Yes," I hissed. His hand rounded against me harder, his pace quickening as he helped me chase what I was desperate for. I closed my eyes tight, so damn *close* to tipping into a blinding release. The hand around my throat squeezed a little harder, and I was mere seconds away from ecstasy . . .

But then he was gone.

My eyes snapped open to find that Leo had taken a full step back. Both of his hands were hanging at his sides, no longer working my body into a sweet oblivion. His gaze was hot as I whined in frustration from the loss of them.

"Why'd you stop?" I demanded, my chest heaving.

A smirk spread across his lips as he stepped forward again, his face coming within inches of mine. "Mara," he murmured, "when you come, I want your eyes on *me*." His tongue darted out to lick his bottom lip. "Do you understand?" His gaze fell to my mouth, bright and hungry. "I want to feel your body explode against mine. I want to hear you cry out as pleasure courses through you. But I want to see it in your eyes when it happens. Yes?"

I sucked in a deep breath. The way he looked at me . . . it was like coming up for air after years of being under water. His gaze was filled with heat and lust, yes—but there was so much more in the depths of those blues. I could see a longing that matched my own, a mirrored reflection of the deepest parts of me that ached to be seen.

His eyes caught mine again, and I nodded.

He lurched forward until he was caging me again, his hands gripping my waist as he thrust his hips between my legs. His mouth pressed eagerly against my neck, and I felt the sting of a bite below my ear before he caressed the mark with his tongue. "I think I'll have fun with you like this for a while," he whispered against my skin, sending goosebumps cascading along my shoulder and arm. "How long do you think I can tease you for?" he rumbled. "How many times can I bring you right to the edge without letting you fall?"

"Leo," I moaned as his hands gripped my ass.

"I know, baby." He kissed my jaw. "I'm right there with you. Can you see how fucking crazy you're making me?" He lifted me again with his strong arms, catching my mouth with his as he raised me up to turn and move us to his bed.

I wrapped my arms around his neck, pressing myself against him as much as I could. I wanted to feel him on every square inch of my skin, to mold his body to my own as he brought me higher and higher. I'd never felt anything like this in my entire life—this raw, primal need for *more*. It was electrifying. Invigorating, as if I'd somehow stumbled upon exactly what I needed to wake me up from the dull haze of my life, to *feel* again through the careful constructs of my existence.

He lowered me onto his bed, stepping back again to look at me. His gaze snagged on my chest, my stomach, on the thong I still wore.

"Look at you," he rasped. And god, it was my own undoing. "I'm not going to be able to control myself if—if we do this." His hands were nearly trembling with restraint as they slid up the length of my legs with featherlight pressure. "I bet you're so sweet and tight, aren't you?"

"Oh, we're doing this," I said quickly, making him laugh. "I want it to be good for you," I added, my voice soft in the quiet room.

"It's already the best sex of my life, and we haven't even had sex yet." His dimple flashed, and I wanted to sink a finger into it. But instead I focused on his hands as they rose to the elastic band of my underwear, peeling them off and dropping them to the ground. And then those fingers landed back on my thighs, pressing down until they gripped my ankles and pulled them apart, spreading me open for him. Every touch was careful and deliberate, pulling on the thread of desire deep in my belly until it was so taut that a mere whisper might snap it free.

"Fuck," he groaned, his eyes glued between my legs. "Fuck, Mara."

And then he lowered his head.

I cried out as his tongue flattened over me and dragged up up *up*, hitting that bundle of nerves as stars filled the room around us. My hips bucked against him, grinding along the slope of his nose, and I nearly came right then.

But Leo pulled back again, looking at me from just above my hips with a glimmer of triumph in his eyes. His mouth glistened with my arousal, and it sent me to the moon. "I fucking love how bad you want this."

I whimpered again, newly frustrated at how close I'd just been. "You're toying with me," I moaned.

His eyes flashed. "Oh yes," he confirmed. "You're the first woman I've had in my bed in a *long* time, Mara. Trust me when I say I plan on making this last."

My laugh was swallowed by a moan as Leo swiped his tongue along me again, and my body came alive at the feel of it. My gasp morphed into a cry as his fingers dug into the flesh at my waist, holding me in place and forcing me to take the pleasure head-on. His tongue dipped inside of me, sparking pure magic as I felt myself begin to dismantle. "Leo," I begged as he licked me again, circling me with his lips before he began to suck. "Please let me come." I was so close, *so close.*

He raised his eyes again, and this time they were dark and dangerous, heady with want. I shuddered as he moved to crawl over my body, engulfing me with his sheer size until his face hovered right above mine. He caught my mouth in a delicious kiss, and I could taste myself on his lips as his tongue pressed into my mouth. Pulling back again, he whispered, "I want to come with you."

I sucked in a breath—my skin was so hot I half expected to see flames. "*Yes,*" I insisted.

Leo groaned, moving to stand from the bed. He walked to a sleek black dresser that stood against the opposite wall of the room and rifled through a drawer. I heard the unmistakable crinkle of foil before he shut it and turned to face me.

His eyes were black as he unfastened his belt and pulled it from the loops, dropping it to the floor. And then he undid his pants, pulling them down his legs and off his body. He was left in only a pair of boxer briefs, his hard length straining against the front. Dark shadows of a tattoo curled along his left thigh, and it nearly killed me.

That was, until he took those off, too, and I got a good look at him.

My mouth watered as he came back to the bed, tossing two condoms onto his nightstand before tearing the wrapper of the third. My eyes followed his movements as he sheathed himself, his deft hands making quick work of the task. Then his knees hit the mattress and he crawled over me, nestling his hips between my legs. "Are you sure you want this, Mara?" he asked, holding himself up by his forearms planted on either side of me. "Tell me now if you want me to stop."

I was desperate for him to do anything *but* stop. "No, I want this," I said. I was almost embarrassed by how much I wanted this.

He hummed out his satisfaction before his mouth lowered next to my ear, warming my skin. "If things get too rough, tell me to stop. You understand?"

I shuddered. Fucking hell, this was so *hot*.

"Tell me you understand," he urged, a finger lightly skimming my throat as I swallowed.

"Yes," I breathed. "*Please.*"

And then he sank himself deep inside of me in a single thrust.

Before I could adjust to the feel of him, before I could even catch my breath, he'd pulled himself out and pistoned into me again. I heard the slap of his hips against my thighs, and felt the tension within me beginning to reverberate.

Leo groaned as he captured my mouth again with his, pushing the lacey cup of my bra down so that my breast spilled out for him. And then he ducked lower to take my nipple between his teeth as he slammed into me again.

"Oh my god," I breathed, feeling the edges of my vision start to blur.

He continued to move inside of me as his teeth sank into my soft flesh again before he soothed the mark with a kiss. My eyes fluttered closed at the pure ecstasy of it, at the pain and the pleasure and the tension winding so unbelievably tight within me.

"Eyes *on me*, Mara," he roared, driving himself harder and setting a faster pace as he lost himself to his own pleasure. I snapped my eyes open, finding his gaze fixed on me with pure lust. He wrapped his hand around my neck again, his palm pressing gently against the column of my throat. And then lowered his gaze to where we were joined and groaned again. "Look at how beautifully you're taking me." And when he curled himself into me again, he squeezed against my throat, and I detonated.

I cried out as my orgasm ripped through me, and Leo caught my scream with his mouth. Pleasure rocked through me with such intensity that I temporarily lost feeling in my fingers and toes—it was unlike anything I'd ever felt in my entire life. Leo kept his hand around my throat as he sank into me again and again and again before he, too, was ripped apart from his own release.

It was the most intense orgasm I'd ever had. My body trembled with pleasure as my heart pounded chaotically. It was minutes before I could put my mind back together, and still all I thought of was Leo's dirty mouth and the way he made me come. "Holy shit," I breathed out when I could finally form words.

His hand lifted from my throat as he peppered soft kisses against my neck. "Yeah," he rasped through his own staggered breathing. "You're incredible, Mara."

"*That* was incredible. That—that was insane."

Leo laughed softly against my chest. "It's called edging," he murmured, pressing his lips to my chin. "And it suits you."

I knew what edging was . . . I just never knew it could feel like *that*.

He trailed an electric path of kisses down to my chest before he gently lifted himself off me and stood from the bed. "I'll be back in a minute. Don't you dare go anywhere," he said, then he disappeared into what I assumed was his bathroom.

I couldn't go anywhere if I tried. My limbs felt so loose and relaxed, I doubted I'd have the strength to get up from this bed anytime soon.

Leo reemerged less than a minute later, the condom no longer wrapped around him. He was still hard, though, and a shameless smirk spread across his face. "You said I only have one night, Mara," he husked, his eyes bouncing over my sprawled position on the bed. I caught a flicker of something more serious in them, but before I could get a better read on it, his expression had darkened once more. "I intend to enjoy it to the fullest. Get on your hands and knees."

Chapter Five

I would never admit it to Leo, but last night was by far the best sex I'd ever had in my *entire* life. It awoke something inside of me that I didn't even know existed, something electric and vibrant that I wasn't sure would stay sated for long.

I spent the night tangled in his bed, even though I'd had zero intentions of staying overnight. My apartment was only a five-minute walk from his building and I'd originally planned on quietly slipping away after he'd fallen asleep—it was usually much simpler that way. But after Leo shot me to the moon and stars the first time, he'd barely slept. As if something was awake inside of him too—a hunger that seemed to match my own.

His body sought mine out the entire night. A warm thumb swiping lightly over my bare chest as he sighed, bent around me and content; a heavy leg thrown over both of mine, caging me into the soft mattress as if to never let me go; a cocooning of his hips as they curved around my own after I turned to my side and closed my eyes. Each shifting touch and graze had my heart pounding harder in my chest. It was like my nerve endings were live wires, dancing and sparking at the feel of his skin, at his breath as it hummed into my neck.

Three more times in the light of the moon, we found ourselves in the throes of each other—hands gripping tight, bodies moving in earnest, teeth grazing skin. It was too good. I couldn't get enough of him, and it was clear he had the same frantic urge to hold me, to move over me and inside of me as he made me come again and again. It made me anxious for the morning sun to rise and our bubble to pop, but I allowed myself to be wholly his, blanketed under the stars that winked down at us through the wall of windows in his bedroom.

A few hours of pretending, of living in another dimension where maybe this penthouse was *ours* and Leo cooked dinner for me every night and always looked at me like I was a treasure —and he never, ever hurt me or degraded me or made me feel small—wouldn't be so bad.

But even as naturally as they bloomed in my mind, those thoughts scared the shit out of me. Because beneath the whimsy of it all were scars that ran deep, wounds that had never quite healed, and I didn't trust that Leo wouldn't pour salt directly into them if given the opportunity. I wouldn't even know where to begin with trusting again, not after what I'd been through.

Now it was seven thirty in the morning and the sun had been up for far too long for me to still be in Leo's arms. I'd been trying to convince myself to slip out from underneath his warm embrace, to quietly dress and sneak out his door without another look. But with every internal five-second countdown, I found myself rooted in place. I listened to the comfortable rhythm of his breathing while his forehead rested against my chest and his heavy arm snaked around my waist. My eyes traced along the edges of his back as I continuously restarted that countdown—making it to zero at least a hundred times without so much as budging.

It had been so long, so fucking *long* since I'd felt . . . safe. Since I felt like I could exhale next to someone else like this. And Leo had done just about nothing to earn it, aside from making me pasta and giving me more orgasms than I could count on one hand.

That scared me even more.

I couldn't explain the ease I felt with his body around me, or the burning curiosity to know more about him. Even now, as I battled tooth-and-nail to rip myself away from him so that I could propel myself back into the real world, I nearly regretted my words last night.

I don't do relationships.

Just a onetime thing.

You might never see me again.

Now they felt like a lie, because as my fingers grazed through the ends of Leo's hair, the only words blazing inside my heart were, *What if?* I sighed, and it came out louder than intended. Leo stirred, his face pressing further into my chest with a rumbling, happy groan.

Shit.

I stilled, freezing my hand where it hovered just above his head. But it was too late. Leo was awake, and he was pressing soft kisses up my chest toward my neck. I shivered at the feel of it.

"Morning," he whispered before his teeth nipped my collarbone. He palmed my hip, squeezing with gentle pressure.

I couldn't help the smile that pulled on my lips. Couldn't help the joy bursting in my heart because he woke up still wanting me. "Hey."

"How'd you sleep?" His tongue darted out to lick the sensitive spot behind my ear, and my eyes fluttered closed.

"Sleep?" I rasped. "I'm not sure we slept at all."

Another low, throaty groan slipped from his mouth, and I felt it on my lips as he kissed me. There was renewed urgency in the way his fingertips dipped into my skin, as if he was feeling the imminent end of this, too. Like if he could just hold on, he'd be able to keep me for a little longer. But if he was as anxious as I was, it was only revealed through that fervent touch. His gaze was steady, roaming where he pleased.

He lifted himself up onto his elbows and settled his hips between my legs as he deepened his kiss. When his hand lowered beneath the covers and found me already wet for him, he lazily slipped two fingers inside of me while his tongue matched the movement in my mouth.

His dizzying strokes were unhurried, like we had all day to do this. To be together like this. And I found myself gliding out of the bounds of my fantasy and into the reality that it was daylight and we were still here. Still fucking like we didn't know how to stop.

I didn't want to stop.

I didn't want this feeling to ever go away.

But I also couldn't let myself tip into the undercurrent of whatever this was—couldn't justify the ruination of everything I'd worked so hard to build. All the things that kept me safe.

So after he made me come *again,* after he found his own hard release inside of me while his mouth was fastened to my sweat-slicked shoulder and his hand was pressed against my heart, I finally forced myself out of his bed.

Leo was silent as he watched me pull my shorts over my legs and wrap myself back into my hoodie. I stuffed my work shirt in the front pocket and looked around for my socks, increasingly aware of the ongoing silence and the weight of his gaze. After I found them underneath the bed, I stood up to face him.

He looked devastating, the sheets mussed from our transgressions in a tangle all around him. I watched his mouth form a relaxed grin, but his eyes gave him away. Twin edges of disappointment.

"I stayed way too long," I breathed. At least it was honest.

He shook his head once, firmly. "You haven't stayed long enough." I sighed, and his eyes moved to my mouth. "Please let me see you again. Let me take you out somewhere. Properly, this time. Whatever you want—wherever you want."

My heart raced in my chest as it screamed at me to say yes, but I shoved the word down. Locked it up tight. "Leo," I groaned, suddenly feeling defensive. "I said this would be it." The words came out colder than I'd meant.

"So, say you've changed your mind," he countered, his expression growing harder. The line etched between his brows almost cracked through my restraint.

I felt the hot sting in the corner of my eyes that told me I needed to get out of here and quick. "I can't." It came out in a whisper. "I'm sorry." I turned around and walked out of his room, out of his orbit. Out of this haven that had soothed my fears all night.

Dolly and Swift were both lounging in the golden sun-filled living room, draped over opposite ends of a black leather couch.

They looked at me like the imposter that I was. Just as I rounded the corner and caught sight of the elevator that would bring me back down to earth, I heard Leo's voice call out from his bedroom. "Mara, wait!" Something banged, followed by a muffled "*Shit*!" and I hurried my steps, pressing the single, opaque button to call for the elevator. "Mara," Leo bellowed, footsteps sounding closer, "Jesus, just give me a second to walk you downstairs."

My heart was in my throat as the elevator chimed. The doors opened and I quickly jumped through them, pressing the button with force to take me out of here. As the doors began to slide shut, Leo's striking form came into view, and the last thing I saw before they snicked together was the wreckage on his face.

IT TOOK me hours to calm my racing heart. After finally making it to my quiet and lonely studio apartment—a stark difference from the sparkling penthouse I'd just left—I carved a narrow path into the old hardwood floor with my pacing. My skin was bursting with anxious energy, my chest ached with a loss I didn't quite understand, and my mind was caught on repeat with visions of teeth and tongues and the kind of magic that could only be made in the dark.

By ten o'clock, I'd decided to shift that energy into a six-mile run around the city so I didn't implode from the inside out. I hadn't been running as much as I used to these last few years—I preferred to run in the early morning, but the hours I kept at Larkspur made that near impossible. Lately, I spent time moving my body with a daily yoga practice and twice-weekly Muay Thai training at a gym a couple of blocks away. But today I just needed to *run*. I needed to lay everything out on the pavement, to pound it out of my heart.

After changing into cropped leggings and an oversized T-shirt, I pushed myself out the door and into the busy streets of downtown Denver. Autumn had firmly set in in Colorado and the air had a bite to it that would soon lead to bitterly cold days. But for now, it was still warm enough to get by without a jacket during the afternoons—especially while running—and the changing leaves and early festive lights were the perfect setting to submerge myself into. A few miles in, my lungs burned from the effort, so I forced a deep breath all the way down into my belly while I stayed focused on the world around me and the pace of my steps.

And *finally*, I found some relief.

I circled around the city and hit six miles about a block away from my building. Instead of going straight home, I stopped at a local coffee shop for the largest Americano they had and a bagel to-go, carrying both back to my apartment where I was now stuffing my face with carbs like the world was ending. Between the sexy all-nighter and this morning's exertion, my body was quite literally starving for sustenance. I finished off the bagel in record time before stripping off my sweaty clothes for a scalding hot shower.

Though it hurt somewhere deep inside of my chest to do so, I spent my shower scrubbing away all the evidence of last night. I could still feel Leo everywhere on my skin, still felt his presence around the corner of every thought, and knew that it wouldn't be easy to fully wrestle him away. Knowing he lived just down the street didn't help—I was terrified of bumping into him again. What would I even say?

I'm sorry for running after spending what might have been the best night of my entire life with you, but the feelings that came with it were way too intense for me to face?

I scoffed. God, I sounded like a lunatic. So what if the sex was mind-blowing? So what if a perfect stranger was able to cut right through my defenses and look at me in such a way that he might have actually *seen* me? I couldn't explain the sadness I felt, couldn't explain the anxious trembling in my fingers. How did I justify the wild thoughts that Leo was someone I could fall for if only I allowed myself to get to know him? I wasn't ready for anything like that. But walking away from him had been harder than anticipated.

Though I hated to admit it—hated to even let myself think it—I knew I was lonely. The iron walls I'd built so fiercely around myself had created a wide chasm between me and the rest of the world. I kept everyone in my life at a safe distance because I *had* to, not because I liked it. I never imagined this life for myself, but everything I did was out of necessity. I would never put myself in a position that could lead me down that dark path again. I'd been too weak to stop it from happening the first time, and I wasn't sure I trusted myself to be strong enough now—so better to avoid it altogether.

As I ducked my head beneath the hot stream of water to rinse out the silky conditioner coating my hair, I heard my phone ring from somewhere in the apartment. Frowning, I tried to think of who would be calling me. I spoke to my parents every Sunday afternoon before work but today was only Thursday. The staff at Larkspur would text me before they'd ever call, and it wasn't like I had many friends.

The phone eventually stopped and I finished my shower, turning off the faucet when it ran cold and pulling a towel around my body. I dried myself off roughly, noting the places that were sore from Leo's urgent and desperate touches.

Not that I minded. I loved the way he'd been just as unmoored as I was, just as caught up in the moment and aching for more than soft and tender. Except now the small bites of pain were reminders that the whole thing wasn't just a fever dream. It made my chest squeeze again.

Shoving down the emotion, I pulled on my green bathrobe and padded out to the main room of my apartment. My bed rested in the far corner of the rectangular space, pushed against the wall with the biggest window. Closer to the bathroom was a small pastel pink couch I'd purchased as soon as I moved in. It was plush and velvet and felt feminine in a way I'd never known furniture could be, and I loved it.

Laying on the glass coffee table in front of the couch was my phone. I picked it up and saw the missed call was from Robert Thatcher, the owner of Larkspur. After reading his name on the screen for the third time, I frowned. Why would Robert call me? I hadn't seen him in almost three months— he'd spent the summer on the Amalfi Coast with his husband, Alessandro, and decided to stay a little longer. Maybe he was back in Denver?

I plopped down on the couch and swiped my thumb to call him. He answered after two rings. "Mara, darling! There you are!"

His voice was loud and bright, and there was no indication that anything was wrong. I let my shoulders relax. "Hi, Robert! How's it going?" I quickly calculated the time in Italy—it would be around dinner time right now. If he had an impor-tant update, he would have called hours ago. Which meant—

"It's good, sweetheart. We got back to the city a couple of days ago, though I don't expect we'll stay long. Ale is already trying to whisk me off to the Maldives." He chuckled, and I could hear the rasp from his expensive cigar indulgence. "Lis-ten, I was hoping you could meet me at the club in an hour? I have something important I'd like to discuss with you."

His words reverberated through my body, and I was instantly sweating. "Uh, sure!" I kept my tone casual as I looked at the digital clock on the microwave. It was currently one o'clock. Larkspur opened at four, which meant Robert wanted to meet two hours before we opened—well before any other staff would be in the building—which *meant* this would be a private conversation.

Whatever he wanted to tell me, it must be . . . big.

"I'll be there at two," I confirmed with a tone so breezy it rivaled the Santa Ana winds.

"Thank you, Mara!" he sing-songed. "See you soon—ciao!" I could hear the rumble of another man's laughter in the back-ground as the phone disconnected, and I sucked in a deep breath.

Could it be?

Two years ago, after I'd long-proven my success and dedica-tion to Larkspur, I sat Robert down in a spurt of bravery and told him I wanted to buy in. That I wanted to own a piece of the business I'd worked so hard to help build. Though he was —at best—*amused* during the conversation, he was sincere in his response: he gave himself five more years before he'd be ready to retire. Five years, and I could buy the whole thing if I wanted to.

Since that day, I'd been stashing as much money as I could in preparation. I didn't know how much I'd need, but I knew it would be a lot. Larkspur pulled in huge revenue and business was only continuing to grow. I was fully prepared to apply for loans if I had to, but wanted to have a decent amount of savings at the ready. Worst case scenario—if I didn't have enough—I would find someone to partner with. But if I *could* swing it, I wanted it all to myself.

According to Robert's timeline I still had three years left, but my chest heaved at the thought that Robert might be trying to push that deadline up. He and Alessandro had spent almost the entire year traveling, and I was practically running Larkspur by myself. What would happen if he laid the opportunity at my feet now? Could I be ready?

I sighed. There was no use getting wound up about it until I knew for sure, but I hated feeling unprepared. As I hurried to my closet to pick out my most professional outfit—something that said *I'm a savvy businesswoman who could* totally *buy this bar*—I shoved aside my worry and put my game face on.

Chapter Six

I walked into Larkspur with ten minutes to spare, praying I didn't look as nervous as I felt. Or as sweaty—the temperature outside had taken a bizarre turn with some out-of-season warmth, and walking a mile through the city in business slacks wasn't exactly without effort. Still, I made it, and whatever this conversation was about—whether good or bad news—at least I was close to knowing.

The backdoor had been unlocked, which meant Robert was already here. As I walked through the dark stockroom, careful to avoid tripping over the stacked cases of liquor from the most recent delivery, I called out for him. "Robert?" My gaze jumped to the left, where the office door was still shut tight.

"Out here, Mara!" he bellowed from the front. I shifted my attention forward and pushed through the black-painted batwing doors that led to the front-of-house, opening to the left of Larkspur's wooden bar top. Only half the house lights had been turned on, and they cast a dim glow throughout the space. It was always a little eerie to be inside the club during the day when it was empty like this. Almost like its soul was missing.

Robert was sitting at the bar in a loud blue button-down shirt, left open at the top to display a smattering of sun-bleached chest hair. He was obnoxiously tan, the gold chain around his neck shining brightly against dark, weathered skin. A tan line from his glasses shined brightly on his face and I had to bite back a laugh. This . . . this was what a rich white man looked like on the cusp of retirement. I couldn't have imagined it any better if I tried.

"Hi, Robert," I greeted as I rounded the corner of the bar. I noticed an expensive bottle of whiskey sitting in front of him, flanked by two lowball glasses. The bottle looked like it had been pulled from Robert's personal collection out back—it was way too swanky to be served here at Larkspur.

One of the glasses was already filled with two fingers of whiskey while the other sat empty in front of the stool next to him. My nerves swelled with anticipation as I approached, sliding into the stool with as much poise and grace as I could. "It's so great to see you." I gave him my best thousand-watt smile. "How was Italy?"

Robert's dark brown eyes examined me before a grin curled on his face, and I felt a fraction of relief in the casualness of it. "It was incredible—so good that it was nearly impossible to drag Alessandro back to the States. We had a lovely time, Mara, thank you for asking. How have things been here?" His eyes swept around the empty club, and I hoped he was pleased with what he saw. I hoped he could feel the vibrance of success that pulsated in this room.

I'd given everything I had to Larkspur. Every ounce of my energy went into making sure this nightclub ran as smoothly as possible. Sure, we had the occasional hiccup: a drunken brawl in the middle of the dance floor; people getting a little too frisky with others, willing or unwilling; a couple of terribly incorrect liquor shipments that had to be quickly fixed so as not to run out of our more popular drinks. But overall, things had run like a well-oiled machine, and I realized I desperately wanted Robert's approval. It had been over three months since he was last here, and I kept it all up without fail.

I faced him with an open chest, showing full-engagement with my response. "Everything's gone *really* well. We have a handful of new staff on board, and we're seeing an increase in revenue each week . . . I've been sending you those reports—"

Robert nodded. "Yes, thank you. The numbers have been looking great."

I smiled, knowing there was a compliment there. "This place is flourishing, Robert. Truly. And I'm so happy to have your trust in running it while you're away."

Robert gave me a small smile as his eyes softened. And I felt it—the static hum of something coming. A coiling inside of my chest. "I appreciate that, Mara. Your dedication here has certainly not gone unnoticed. Because of you, I've been able to hold off on my retirement while still having the opportunity to make Alessandro happy with his insatiable need for adventure. But . . ." He hesitated, his posture going a bit rigid as he sat up straighter. "We aren't getting any younger. And Alessandro wants my full attention. He wants to see the world, and I love him. I want to give that to him. So, the time has come for me to fully step away."

I took a moment to let the words sink in, bracing myself for what he'd say next. Except he stayed quiet, and the silence was sharp as it fell around us. When he still hadn't spoken after a full minute, I forced the question burning on my tongue. "You're going to sell?" It came out softer than I'd meant, almost a whisper.

And then I saw the smallest grimace. It was so subtle that it would have been easy to miss if I wasn't hanging on his every move, desperate to know where this was going.

"Wait," I said, feeling panic slide through my limbs like ice. "Robert, don't tell me you already sold."

He let out a heavy sigh as his eyes moved somewhere past me. After another excruciating moment of silence, his gaze met mine. "I've sold the business, Mara." His words hit me like a sharp slap in the face.

My shoulders slumped as my eyes moved to the floor. I willed the tears to stay at bay with every ounce of control that I had. I wouldn't cry here—not in front of Robert. Not until I was alone, where I'd undoubtedly fall into ruin on the floor.

How could he do this? How could he sell Larkspur without even saying anything about it? This was my dream, and I'd worked *so* hard for it.

Somewhere in the distance of the loud clamoring of my mind, Robert continued to speak. "I ensured a few contingencies as part of the sale. The first of which is that you will remain the club's most senior manager. The buyer doesn't seem to have any interest in making major organizational changes, and he knows the impact you've had here—I made sure of it. I'm certain he will not get in your way as you and Larkspur both continue to thrive."

I let out an errant snort. *He.* Of course he sold the club to a man. "You sold the bar to someone else, Robert. That sounds pretty 'in the way' to me." The bite in my tone was unmistakable, and I *almost* apologized. Almost. I'd never spoken to Robert like that before . . . but my insides were screaming, boiling with rage at him, at this stupid buyer, at the goddamn patriarchy of it all.

Robert knew how I felt about this club, and he *knew* I wanted it when he was ready to retire. I'd poured my literal blood, sweat, and tears into this place. And *still* he never gave me the fucking chance.

Was it because I was *just a bartender* and made the majority of my money from tips? That I didn't have the financial backing of most investors? Or was it because I had no problem showing a little skin in my professional environment, especially to help drive more energy into the machine that was this club? We all knew it attracted more patrons, and more patrons meant more money—for me and *certainly* for Robert. He'd never had a problem with my professionalism before . . . but could that be why he overlooked me for this?

Fuck that.

My gaze moved up to meet his as I spoke again, my words laced with an anger I didn't care to hold back. "What else?"

Confusion marred his brow. "What do you mean?"

"You said you ensured a few contingencies, but you only named one—me. What else?"

"Oh." He sat up straighter again, his eyes roaming the bar's surface in front of us. "Well, Larkspur will remain a nightclub. Nothing will change in that regard. Staff will stay on payroll for at least a two-year term unless any individual issues arise that would otherwise interfere with their employment contract. I kept everyone protected to the best of my ability, I promise you. Nobody's roles will change unless the change is mutually agreed upon."

My heart pounded in my throat, even though there was an undeniable relief in knowing no one would lose their job because of this. Robert pulled a handkerchief from his pants pocket and blotted it against his forehead. "Look, Mara, he's a good buyer. I trust he'll be exactly what Larkspur needs to keep momentum going. He'll be what *you* need, if you let him."

I had to swallow down another scoff before it burst out of me, brushing my hair behind my shoulder as I fought the fresh burn of tears. "What makes you think I need anything, Robert? You haven't even been here. I sent you detailed reports every week . . . you know how well things are going. Why didn't you come to me first? Why didn't you give me the chance?"

Robert's eyes dropped to my neck, and a hint of amusement danced in his otherwise-serious expression before he wiped it away. My hand instinctively reached up to feel for something amiss, but all I felt was clammy skin. He cleared his throat, looked at me with sincerity. "You could benefit from a little more experience, Mara."

And that was it. That was all he had to say.

I stared at him for a long moment before I heard a door shut somewhere in the back—someone else had come in through the unlocked door. I sat up and turned to face the doorway that led to the stockroom.

Robert shuffled in his stool next to me and I heard him gulp down his whiskey. I snapped my gaze back to him as dread pooled in my belly. "Who's that?"

His eyes flashed toward the door. "That," he responded in a careful tone, "is the new owner. I invited him here as well . . . to introduce you."

My head spun at a dizzying pace, and I had to shift in my seat so I didn't fall off the stool. My limbs were heavy with the weight of disappointment and frustration. I felt . . . trapped. Forced into this interaction I had *no* interest in being a part of. Whoever this man was, I already wanted to make him disappear forever. This was *my* bar, *my* nightclub. And dammit, I would find a way to make him wish he'd never bought it. I'd find a way to run him out, to force him to sell it to me.

My eyes clung to Robert's face as I heard the soft *swoosh* of the batwing doors. Slow, confident footsteps paced against the concrete floor as the new owner approached. I closed my eyes and took a deep breath, willing my face into a neutral expression in the final moments I had before I was forced to face him.

"Good afternoon, Robert," the man said.

And that voice slithered into my soul like a venomous snake.

I teetered on the edge of a knife as my brain slowed down, focusing on the familiar timbre. Robert's gaze hovered just above my shoulder, on the man who now stood only a few feet behind me. "Hello, Leo," Robert replied warmly, and ice spread through my body at the confirmation.

Leo bought Larkspur? Leo, my fucking one-night stand?

This couldn't be happening. I sat frozen, unable to turn around to face him.

Did he know who I was last night? That I worked *here?*

Oh my god—he was *celebrating*. He was celebrating a business deal, and I celebrated right there with him. I drank seventeen-dollar champagne on his roof and ate his stupid pasta and let him do unmentionable things to my body—and the whole time, the sneaky fucking viper was stealing my bar!

Shame bloomed up my neck. I'd let this man in and

allowed him to get close to me. So close that I daydreamed what it would be like to actually let him into my *heart*. And now . . . now he was my *boss*?!

This *really* couldn't be happening.

"Leo." Robert's voice cut through the torturous train of thought sounding off inside my mind. "I want you to meet Larkspur's extremely talented bar manager, Mara." He gave me a confident smile, but after a long moment of me staring at him with what I was sure was wild fear in my eyes, his brows pulled together. He gave me a pointed look that said *Turn around and say hi*, like a parent scolding his child, and I knew I couldn't stall any longer.

Taking a deep breath, I closed my eyes and willed myself to step down from the stool, turning in the direction of where Leo stood. Electricity prickled along my skin as I counted to three, and when I finally found the resolve to open my eyes, I nearly fell to the ground.

Leo.

It should have been a *crime* how good he looked in this moment of wanting to pulverize him, wearing a black suit that was clearly custom-made to fit his body. My grip on control slipped as an onslaught of memories from last night flooded into me—what his skin tasted like, the sounds he made when he came.

This was some sort of cruel, karmic joke.

I watched his eyes nearly bulge from their sockets and his brows jump up in a surprised arch. His mouth fell open and snapped shut before falling open again as he scanned me up and down.

So he didn't know, then.

Honestly, that almost felt worse. Because it meant he

hadn't been out to take advantage of me. Last night was a *real* accident . . . and there was a heavier loss of something in that truth. Something that might have been real between us.

But it would have been lost anyway, right? I mean, I walked out this morning with no intention of letting him find me. If not for this twist of fate, I never would have seen him again.

"Hello," I croaked, watching the deep rise and fall of his chest as his stare turned intense.

His eyes searched my own, as if trying to be sure that it really was *me* standing in front of him. His mouth fell into a frown, and it was like a punch to the gut, how similar it looked to the expression he made this morning as he watched me disappear behind those elevator doors. I had to push down a sharp yearning to reach out and touch him.

"Mara?" he asked.

Behind me, Robert sucked in a breath. "It seems you two already know each other?"

My eyes never left Leo's face as a quiet, incredulous laugh escaped from my throat. His gaze fell to my neck, to the same place that Robert's had moved a few minutes ago. I opened my mouth again to speak, but Leo beat me to it. "Yeah, you could say that." His voice was low and dejected.

I heard Robert shuffle off his stool, taking this awkwardness as his cue to leave. "Listen, I have to go. Alessandro is waiting for me at home—you know how it goes." He huffed a laugh. When neither Leo or I shifted our attention to him, he continued. "I'm going to leave the whiskey here. It seems as though you two may need it. Leo, please let me know if you need anything. I'll be around for another couple of days before I'm overseas again. Of course, you can always reach me by email if needed once I'm gone."

Leo nodded once, a sharp dip of his chin. "Sounds great."

My eyes narrowed on him as the facts continued to press themselves together.

Leo bought Larkspur. Leo was my *boss*.

Robert never gave me a chance, and my dream of owning this place was in the rearview.

I felt a warm hand wrap around my shoulder before Robert spoke again, keeping his voice low enough that I wasn't sure if Leo could hear him. "Go easy on him, Mara. I know you're disappointed, but it has nothing to do with him."

I frowned. If only he knew.

He squeezed my shoulder before walking toward Leo to shake his hand, finally forcing Leo's gaze away from me. I took the moment of reprieve to gulp down a few shaky breaths, closing my eyes as I clutched at the tightness in my chest. My blood was roaring in my ears, the room spinning. I tried to shove the emotion down—the last thing I needed was to start sobbing right here in front of Leo, but it took everything I had to keep my tears contained.

Eventually, I felt a soft touch on my cheek, and I opened my eyes to find Leo standing right in front of me. Concern laced through his features. "Mara," he said firmly. "Mara, take a deep breath."

My chest rose and fell rapidly with shallow breaths, and I realized I was on the cusp of a panic attack. I averted my eyes from his face, because seeing him like this was overwhelming. This was too much—this was all too much.

"Mara," he said again, his fingers now gripping my jaw. "Look at me." But I kept my gaze on the ceiling above us. "Jesus," he murmured, letting his hand fall away from my face. He turned toward the bar—*his* bar—and grabbed the bottle of whiskey, pouring some of the amber liquid into the still-empty glass before holding it in front of me. "Here," he said. "Drink."

On this, we could agree. I took the glass from him and tipped the whiskey into my mouth. It burned the entire way down my throat, causing me to cough and force in a few deep breaths. I held the glass out and whispered, "Another."

Leo didn't hesitate to pour me another shot, watching intently as I threw that one back, too. He replaced the cap on the bottle and set it onto the bar, sighing as he planted his hands on his hips. "Look, Mara," he started, his eyes falling down to the ground between us. "I understand this is completely unexpected—"

"No," I cut him off, shaking my head. "No. I can't do this." I could *not* have this conversation right now. I set the glass down on the bar next to the bottle, and without looking at him, I ran out of the club.

Chapter Seven

I stared at the ceiling above me as I lay on my bed, letting the tears roll down the sides of my face and onto the comforter beneath me. Larkspur's doors would open to the public in a little less than an hour, but I was scheduled for the closing shift tonight. I technically didn't need to get there for another few hours, which was convenient because the thought of stepping through those doors again—knowing who would be inside—had my stomach twisting fiercely.

After running out on Leo for the *second* time today, I contemplated never stepping foot in Larkspur again and what that would mean for my future. With the decent chunk of money I'd saved, I knew I could take a pause, reconsider the current trajectory of my life and possibly adjust the target to something brand-new. At the very least, the money would allow for me to take a little breather and let myself *really* process through some of the things I'd been putting off— namely the shit that came before I ended up at Larkspur.

But then I thought about how hard I'd worked, how much I'd sacrificed for Larkspur's success, and the idea of giving up made me feel small. It made the time feel insignificant, like it had meant nothing. I mean, the embarrassing reality was that it *had* meant something, just not in the way I wanted it to. I'd lined Robert's already-deep pockets with even more wealth and turned his business into an attractive opportunity for another rich man to swoop in and take.

Larkspur had been ripe for the taking, and I'd been too trusting and naive to realize Robert might actually go behind my back with a sale. At the end of the day, he didn't owe me anything—I knew that. There was never a contractual agreement between us that said I'd have first dibs at ownership if he were to retire. But he'd told me to hang on, and I believed him. I'd taken him at his word.

His word meant shit, it seemed.

But still . . . I'd worked hard to make Larkspur the success it was today. I used my personal social media accounts to promote it, I developed theme nights and exciting events to drive more business, and I'd been managing the bar staff for the better part of two years. Larkspur was my baby, there was so much of *me* in it. Was I really going to give it all up because of a man?

Leo, unfortunately, was the curveball. Without it, I might've been able to figure out how to navigate through this mess, but the added twist that the new owner was *him* was nearly incomprehensible. Closing my eyes, I let out a long sigh. Of course this would happen. Of course the second I allowed myself to be vulnerable, to let my guard down with something that felt real, it all went to hell in a handbasket.

But I was strong. I'd already proven I was a fighter.

Opening my eyes again, I felt a sense of calm determination wash over me. A sense of knowing that, even though this all felt hard, I could and *would* overcome it. I didn't build this life for myself just to see it all thrown away because of my own insecurities. My reluctancy to be vulnerable.

I'd already done that, and I wouldn't let it happen again.

I wouldn't give Leo—*or* Robert—the satisfaction of bowing out. Leo may have bought the club, but he didn't know what he'd gotten himself into because that club was *mine*, and I wasn't going to give it up so easily. I sat up in my bed, wiping away the remaining tears from my cheeks. The time for crying was over. Now it was time for a fight.

I jumped out of bed and toward my closet, sliding it open to sift through my assortment of branded Larkspur shirts. Despite the brisk October temperatures, the club was always pretty warm from the hundreds of bodies swarming the bar, so I opted for a tank top. It was one of my favorites—soft black cotton with the words *THIRST RESPONDER* printed across the chest in a bold, neon green font. The added benefit of showing off some cleavage while I knocked Leo down from his new-owner pedestal certainly didn't hurt.

I grabbed my smallest pair of spandex shorts and a pair of nude tights from the dresser, as well as a matching neon green bra, knowing it would peek out a little from beneath my shirt. I'd finish the outfit off with some white crew socks and sneakers.

Laying everything out on my bed, I smiled. It was still early, but if I started getting ready now, I would have plenty of time to crimp my hair to the heavens and apply my favorite set of fake eyelashes. So, I bounced toward the bathroom and flicked on the light, renewed with fresh energy and the desire to take back what was mine.

In the bright light of the bathroom, I turned on the faucet for my *second* shower of the day before I focused my attention on the mirror, scanning over my face. I needed another round of scaling heat against my skin to wash away the evidence of my heartbreak. My eyes were red-rimmed and puffy, my hair crumpled from lying on my bed while I sobbed—but both of those things would be remedied soon.

As I pulled my fancy black blouse over my head—the one I'd worn earlier to meet Robert and had since cried all over— something dark and purple flashed in the mirror. Bobbing my head out of the shirt, I squinted toward my reflection and found an angry purple hickey on my neck.

A *hickey*! On my fucking *neck*!

I hadn't noticed it . . . Not after my run when I'd showered the first time, and not when I'd gotten dressed for the meeting. Admittedly, I'd been in a bit of a fog, but the mark of color was a stark contrast to the paleness of my skin. I had to have been blind not to see it.

Oh my god. I catapulted myself toward the mirror, looking at it more closely as I remembered how Robert's and Leo's eyes had flashed to my neck at Larkspur this afternoon. It was because they'd seen this . . . this *monstrosity* of a bruise on my neck. A mark that Leo had left last night. I breathed through my mouth as the waves of embarrassment crashed through me.

Robert would have thought it unprofessional. And as I stood there, angry at him for his betrayal, I'd been parading this proof of my inadequacy. And Leo . . . He would've known he was the culprit. *Did he think it was funny?* I scowled. I bet he'd been laughing inside at the entire fucked-up situation.

I backed away from the mirror and quickly noticed another hickey on my chest, just below my collarbone. It, too, was a dark shade of purple, left by Leo's mouth. I shucked off my pants as fast as I could and twirled around, searching every inch of skin. There was another one on my left hip, and a deep one inside of my thigh.

Tears stung my eyes, threatening to break free again. Seeing my body riddled with bruises like this was . . . unnerving. Though my rational mind knew that they were hickeys, marks of passion that had been consensual, my irrational mind was screaming that I'd been hurt again. That I'd been used again. And the swell of that familiar emotion was almost too much to bear.

Steam from the shower filled the small bathroom and ripped my reflection from the mirror, so I forced myself into the scalding water where I could scrub myself clean—again.

Two and a half hours later, I left my apartment and headed in the direction of Larkspur. The sun was beginning to set in the mountains to the west, and the sky was arranged in fragmented color—pinks and oranges shaped by the scattered clouds hanging loosely in the sky. There was a light scent of rain in the air, though it didn't look like it would come tonight. I breathed in deep, filling my lungs with it as I set off with sharp focus.

I wore my faithful hoodie—the same one I'd worn last night—to keep myself warm during my walk. My hair was crimped into large waves by my trusty three-barrel iron, and it bounced along my shoulders and back in a cascade of blonde, purple, and green. I went all-out with makeup tonight, the smoky purple shadow and false lashes making my naturally green eyes look bigger and brighter.

I knew I looked good. I'd taken a quick selfie in the glowing light of the sunset from the biggest window in my apartment before I left, posting it to social media with an invitation to come and see me at the bar tonight. If it wasn't already going to be a busy night, I had a feeling it would be one now.

It took me twenty minutes to walk to the club, and instead of going through the back door I decided to enter through the front. I wanted to see how long the line was to get in, and I also wanted to check in with the bouncers to make sure they were okay. Of all the staff at Larkspur, the bouncers held a special place in my heart. At a busy, vibrant nightclub like this, safety was *so* important.

Especially to me.

Ethan stood at the small podium near the front door, dressed in a black button-down shirt and black dress pants. His bright blue eyes were crisp in the fading daylight as they landed on me. I watched his mouth curve into a lazy grin as I approached, but I could see the worry set in his face. "Mara . . . man, am I glad to see you."

My brows cinched. "Why? Is everything okay?"

He nodded, taking a quick glance at the line in front of him before returning his gaze to me. "Yeah, but word on the street is there's a new boss in town, and people are worried."

I sighed, feeling the sharp stabs of guilt as they pierced through me. I should have been the one to break the news to the staff. Or at the very least, I should have been here while it happened. In my knee-jerk reaction to run out of here this afternoon, I'd forfeited the opportunity to announce the change and simultaneously help everyone else navigate it.

Ethan studied my face. "Based on your lack of shock, I'm assuming you already knew?"

I rolled my lips between my teeth and exhaled. "I found out this afternoon. What has everyone been told?"

He shrugged. "There was a new guy at the bar when we all got here, drinking expensive whiskey like he owned the place—literally. He asked us all to sit down and told us he was the new owner, that we should go about our work tonight as normal and to let him know if we needed anything. And then he poured everyone a shot. It was . . . odd."

I scoffed, rolling my eyes. Leo was going to get Larkspur's liquor license revoked if he thought it was okay to feed the staff shots before their shifts. Didn't he know that? "I'm sorry you found out that way," I said with sincerity. "The whole thing is a little fucked but . . . we'll get through it."

"Yeah?" he asked, his brows rising in question. "Should we be worried about anything?"

"I talked to Robert earlier today. He assured me everyone's safe."

Ethan's expression flooded with relief. "Good." His gaze snagged on a pretty woman near the front of the line, watching as she wiggled her hips to the beat of the DJ's music that was bleeding from inside.

"I better get in there. You okay out here? Need anything?"

"Nah." He smiled, eyes flashing back to me, notably lighter after hearing his job wasn't in jeopardy. "We're rocking out here, baby. I'm good, thank you."

I couldn't help the smile that bloomed from my own face. Ethan's charisma was infectious when he turned it on—it was why he was so good at the door. Sometimes people had to wait nearly an hour to get in, but they were still happy to be here because of how fun he made the experience. "Okay, I'll check on you in a bit."

He shot me a sly grin before his eyes moved back to the girl with interest. I almost let my chuckle bubble to the surface— he was the epitome of a shameless flirt. But I didn't have it in me to mind because he never let it get in the way of his job.

Working my way through the doors, I found the club bursting at the seams. There was a palpable energy, a *vitality* in the air, like the club was revealing its soul tonight. It was my favorite thing about this place—the *life* in it. I thrived on it in the early days, let it sink into my own soul and bring me back from the hell that I was in.

My eyes swept around, scanning the faces and bodies and movements of everyone in here. The DJ was moving chaotically to the beat of his music, entranced by the effect he had over everyone. Behind the bar, Nora and Sam were flushed and focused. Surrounding the bar was a swarm of patrons eager for another drink.

I blew out a breath—I didn't see any sign of Leo, but I knew that he was here. I knew it in my bones.

It didn't matter, though. Not really. I had a job to do, staff to support and customers to serve. Whether Leo was around or not, I already knew I would lose myself to the work. Lose myself to the magic of this place, just like I did every night.

Working myself out of my hoodie, I started toward the bar. There was a small cutout on the side near the doors that led to the stockroom for staff to duck under. Frank stood tall and stoic against the wall between both access points, ensuring that no customers were able to get through either of them, should their curiosity dare them to try.

He gave me a curt nod as I approached, eyes continuing to scan all around us. He was the head of security, and he took his job seriously. Of everyone here, he might've been the only one who had me beat in the desire for safety. "Hey, Frank—you good?"

"Yes, ma'am. Anything I can do for you?"

His response was all the indication I needed that this wasn't the right time to discuss any changes in our club politics. I figured as much—he was busy. "Nope." I shook my head. "I'm here for the rest of the night, so let me know if anything comes up."

"You too, Mara," was all he said in response.

I smiled and dipped my chin before ducking beneath the bar. I hadn't even raised back up to my full height before Nora came barreling into me.

"Oh shit, Mara—I'm so sorry! I didn't see you down there . . ." Her eyes were wide as she looked down at me. Even standing straight up, Nora towered over me.

I threw my hands up and waved her off. "Don't worry about it. You good?"

"Yeah." Her shoulders rose an inch in a small shrug. "Mostly. But everyone's a little freaked out. I've been waiting for you to come in so we can talk, but it's way too busy right now." She looked around at the crowd of customers surrounding the bar, unease stretching across her face.

I hated thinking anyone was worried. "We'll talk later tonight, but everything's fine. Okay?" I might not have fully believed it, but I'd make damn sure the rest of the staff felt at ease. I owed them that, at the very least.

Nora smiled. "Okay," she breathed out, then reached past me to grab three pint glasses from where they were stacked, turning toward the beer taps on the far wall. I glanced over at Sam at the farthest end of the bar. He was our newest bartender, but he had years of experience and fit right in with us like he'd been here from the beginning. His eyes darted my way as he worked a shaker in front of his chest, and I forced confidence into my smile as I waved hello.

I could see the tiniest smidge of tension lift from his shoulders—as the newest employee, he was probably the most worried about the change in ownership. And he and his new wife had a kid at home.

I sighed as I tore my gaze away from his, terrified he might see me crack. *What a clusterfuck.*

I shoved my hoodie and my belt bag in an open space underneath the bar, making quick eyes at Frank to show him where I'd stashed them so he could help keep an eye on it. I would normally never keep my personal belongings out here, but I was too afraid to go back to the office—*my* office—and find a potential unwanted guest. Even *if* said guest might look like delicious sin in a tailored suit.

It would make things ridiculously easier if I hadn't spent last night with the man wearing that suit. If I'd decided to have a one-night stand with *anyone* else.

If he hadn't made me feel like the entire experience was . . .

I choked the thought down before it could fully manifest, because no *way* was I going to let myself acknowledge how special it had felt. That was a truth worth burying deep, deep down—so deep it never saw the light of day.

Chapter Eight

Four hours later, Larkspur was busier than ever. It seemed that my impulsive social media post had yanked people from their hidey-holes, and in addition to the usual Thursday night turnout the place was packed. I'd thrown myself into the fast-paced rhythm of the bar, making drinks and processing payments for hundreds of customers. And while it was easy to keep my focus on the crowd in front of me, there was an undercurrent of anxiety lapping at my gut the longer the night went on without laying eyes on Leo.

I *knew* he was here—I just didn't know where.

After closing the tab for a group of guys who'd bought their third round of beers, my eyes swept over the liquor bottles on the back wall, noting that more than a few of them were almost empty. Someone would need to get to them—and soon. I glanced at Sam and Nora, finding them both in the center of their own hurricanes as they hurried to make drinks and serve customers at their respective sections of the bar.

I knew the right thing to do was to restock the shelves myself. There was nothing worse than reaching for the liquor you needed and finding the bottle empty. My gaze fell on the batwing doors, and I felt a wave of apprehension rip through my chest. Leo had to be back there somewhere.

Sighing, I pushed my hair behind my shoulders and ducked under the bar in my pursuit. Frank gave me a loaded look as I passed him, and I caught the smallest of grins before he turned his attention on the bustling crowd.

Just as I was about to push through the swinging doors, Leo surprised the hell out of me by walking through them from the other side, his mouth morphing into a wide smile when he saw me. "I was just coming to look for you," he said cheerfully.

I took a moment to look him up and down, finding—to my severe annoyance—that he *still* looked incredible. He was wearing the same black suit from this afternoon, except the black tie he'd had on earlier was gone and the first two buttons of his shirt were undone. My gaze snagged on his exposed throat, remembering what it tasted like beneath my tongue and — Nope.

I could *not* go there.

I forced my eyes up only to find him fixing me with the same gluttonous intensity, his gaze moving from my hair down to my legs. Something wafted into my nostrils then, warm and nutty, and it took a second for me to place the smell before my eyes dropped to his hand, zeroing in on the source.

"Where did you get that?" I asked, glaring at the coffee in his hand.

He looked down to the white cardboard cup secured with a black lid. "What, this?"

"Yeah, *that*."

"I made it."

"Made it where?"

Leo's eyes caught on Frank, who was standing somewhere behind me. A small sigh escaped from his mouth, though he still looked a little amused. "In my office."

"*Your* office?" I scoffed. "I'm quite certain there is only one office in this building, and it's *mine*."

Leo's eyes snapped back to me. "Yours?"

"Yes. Mine. As in, that was *my* hazelnut coffee you stole. *My* coffee maker you used with your greedy little fingers."

An even wider smile spread across his face. "You know better than anyone that I don't have little fingers, Mara." His eyes flashed as they dropped down to my waist. "Though, they may be greedy . . . I'll give you that."

My cheeks were instantly aflame, and I heard Frank clear his throat from where he stood against the wall.

Fucking hell, I could *murder* Leo.

I *should* murder him.

I grabbed the sleeve of his stupid expensive suit jacket and pulled him into the stockroom where it was still dark. The switch to turn on the light was out of my reach, so I didn't bother with it as I turned around to snarl at Leo. "Where the *hell* do you get off saying shit like that in front of my staff?"

Leo chuckled, and the sound rippled through me like a wild current. "Jesus, Mara." His voice was low and dark, teasing against my senses. "I'm sorry, it just came out. I mean, have you seen the way you look tonight?"

I scoffed. "Put a filter in that mouth of yours, Leo, because in case you haven't noticed we're not in your fucking penthouse anymore. We're back in reality where, through some deranged cosmic joke, *you're* my new boss."

Leo sighed, and though I could barely see his face, I knew it had grown serious. "For what it's worth, I had no idea you worked here."

I knew he didn't—I could see the genuine surprise in his eyes when he saw me standing at the bar with Robert this afternoon—but it didn't stop me from wanting to rake my nails against his skin in exasperation. "I was wearing a Larkspur shirt. How could you miss it?"

"You were wearing a sweatshirt!" he flared. "And then . . . and then I wasn't really paying attention to what was on your shirt, Mara, because I was more concerned about taking it off!" He blew out a breath. "Look, obviously this isn't the most ideal situation. But I can't say I'm upset to see you again." His voice was softer as he reached a hand out to trace a finger along my jaw. "Why did you run away from me this morning?"

I jerked my chin away, and his hand dropped dramatically against his thigh. "I told you. *One* night. It shouldn't have been a surprise that I didn't want to stick around." The words tasted foul on my tongue, because the truth was I *hadn't* wanted to leave. But I couldn't tell him that—not now. Decidedly not ever. "And in case you haven't put it together yet, you *stole* my bar. So I'd say any intimate adventures between us are firmly off the table at this point, wouldn't you?"

Again, Leo sighed. "I didn't steal your bar, Mara." He paused, shifting on his feet. "During negotiations, Robert told me about his bar manager—that she was an incredible asset to the club and had expressed interest in buying it in the future, but that . . . that she wasn't ready and he couldn't wait. He brought it up because he thought you should still be given the chance to continue to lead and run things. He was very clear about ensuring your place here. I'm not trying to get in your way. This is still as much your bar as it is mine, okay?"

I closed my eyes through the lick of pain. His words were laced with pity, and I hated it. "No, Leo. You may have dropped some serious cash to write your name on the paperwork, but this isn't your bar and it never will be, so don't hold your breath."

I twisted away from him so I could turn on the light, but Leo's arm darted out, his warm fingers wrapping gently around my arm. "Mara, please," he tried, "don't walk away from me again."

"What am I supposed to say?" I retorted, turning back to face him. Frustration reared through my chest like a fire igniting. "What the hell am I supposed to do in this situation? Do you want me to *thank* you for keeping me around?" My voice shook as it rose. "I've spent the last two years building this club into what it is today, and I deserved more from Robert. I deserved a fucking chance—a *conversation* at the very least— before he sold it. And to find out it was *you* who bought it? Do you know what that feels like, after what we did last night? I have a fucking hickey on my neck, Leo. You marked me, you've been *inside* of me, and now you're my boss! Do you want me to crawl right into your bed again and pretend that none of this is compromising?" I squeezed my eyes shut so that the tears didn't fall, hoping he couldn't see my raw emotion in the dark. "This whole thing feels impossible." It was the most honest thing I could say.

Leo didn't speak for what felt like a full minute, but when he did his tone was gentle. "Mara," he murmured. "I know you have no reason to, but I need you to trust me."

I almost laughed. *Trust him?* Yeah right. I didn't trust *anyone*, and I wouldn't be starting now. Not like this.

A tear ran down my cheek, and I quickly wiped it away with my free hand. Leo would never understand how much this meant to me, how much of my heart was in this building.

How could I expect him to?

"I have to get to work," I said, pulling my arm away from his grasp.

He didn't say anything as I turned on the light and began to collect bottles from the shelving unit against the wall. But he didn't leave me, either. I could feel the weight of his gaze as I took what I needed, delicately tucking the bottles into my arms before I made my way toward the front, never once looking back at him.

THE REST of the night moved quickly. Nora and I cut Sam around midnight, letting him go home to his kid since he'd been the first one here today. I would've normally let Nora go too since I was the one closing, but it was still busy. Plus, it didn't seem like she was ready to leave—I knew she had questions about what was going on.

Leo didn't make any further appearances from the back. I wasn't sure if he'd retreated into the office or if he'd left for the night. I wouldn't blame him if he did—not after our heated exchange. His words still hung heavy in the air around me as I worked, the reality that Robert said I wasn't ready to own Larkspur. I knew it wasn't Leo's fault, but it hurt all the same.

The thought of having to establish a new normal with a

new boss scraped uncomfortably against my ego, because for so long I genuinely thought I would be the next owner. Robert had been perfectly content leaving me alone to run things, so what the hell made him think I wasn't ready? It frustrated me beyond belief.

Again, I knew I couldn't blame Leo for Robert's actions. And maybe if I hadn't spent the night with him last night, I would have it in me to make nice with him, to show him what a good bar manager I was. But last night *did* happen, and that on top of everything else felt way too heavy.

As closing time approached, the crowd finally began to thin out, and after cashing out an older couple who looked adorably awkward enough to possibly be on a first date, I made my way to the other side of the bar where Nora was pulling a pint of beer from the tap. Her boyfriend, Andre, sat at the far corner of the bar, watchful of the crowd with a bottle of beer in hand.

"Hey, Nora—have a second?"

She turned to face me, strands of her long blonde hair falling loose from her braid and framing her face. "Yeah, let me just serve this beer real quick." She turned to drop it in front of a younger man who looked like he'd only recently become of drinking age, and then came back to where I stood. "'Kay, what's up?"

I took a deep breath. "Look, I'm sorry I wasn't here when you got in today. I know everyone was blindsided by the news of a new owner, and I should have been here to help mitigate everyone's worry. So, I apologize . . . truly."

Nora waved a hand in the air like it wasn't a big deal. "Don't worry about that. I just want to make sure you're okay —I imagine you were probably more blindsided than we were."

I scoffed. "You have no idea." My gaze caught on a man who was taking a seat at the bar, his faded Broncos bomber looking a little worse for wear, like he'd been wearing it every day for the last decade. He was alone, and something about the way his eyes scrutinized the other patrons put me on edge. "I was hoping it would slow down enough to talk through things a little more, but I just want you to know everything's okay and everyone's jobs are safe. I was assured of that."

Nora smiled. "Well, that's a relief. I think Sam was pretty worried—"

"I'll call him," I interrupted. "Tonight, when things slow down. I don't want anyone to worry."

I sensed a shuffling in my peripheral vision, and my gaze snapped in the direction of the man who'd just sat down. He was trying to talk to the group of women seated next to him, but I could tell from their body language that they weren't interested. Turning to look over my shoulder, I saw Frank in his usual position. Hopefully I wouldn't need him, but you never really knew when something might pop off.

Facing Nora again, I found her regarding me closely, her brows pulled together. "Something wrong?"

"No . . . I don't think so. Hey, you should go. We're closing soon, anyway, and it's starting to slow down. I'll be all right."

She tilted her head. "You sure . . . ?"

I forced a bright smile. "Nora, your man has been sitting there all night patiently waiting for you." Nora's own smile grew wide on her face. "Go. I'll be fine."

She threw her arms around me in a warm hug. "Thank you!"

I laughed, secretly relishing the comfort of her embrace. "Get out of here."

Nora cashed herself out at the computer as I jumped in to help customers, purposefully avoiding the man who'd just sat down. I wanted to keep an eye on him for a beat to see how he would handle rejection from the women around him before I started serving him any alcohol. *Just* in case. I couldn't explain the way his presence had snagged my attention, but I'd learned to listen to that intuition over the years—it usually meant something.

Thankfully, he seemed to have gotten the hint and stopped trying to infiltrate their conversation, eventually focusing his attention on the DJ booth. I worked through drink orders for a handful of other customers down the line of the bar before I decided I'd let him sit long enough.

As I approached, his gaze jumped from the DJ booth to me, his eyes more than obvious as they swept down and back up my body. It didn't necessarily bother me when men looked at me like that—I knew what I was doing when I wore these clothes to work. But still, something about the lack of emotion in his eyes gave me a dirty feeling. "Thanks for your patience," I called over the loud music, ensuring a smile was present on my face. "What can I get for you?"

"Beer's fine," he muttered. His eyes moved to my hair.

"Sure thing. We've got a special on Bud bottles tonight. Or do you prefer a draft?"

He shrugged. "Bud'll do it."

I nodded, pretending it wasn't a little weird that he didn't care what he drank. It made me wonder what he was really doing here.

Maybe he likes the music?

I tried not to let my own preconceived notions take root, tried not to judge him until he gave me a firm reason to. It was habit for me to always look for the bad in people—it's what'd helped keep me and others safe in this job for so long. When shit went down with an aggressive or unruly patron, I usually already had my eye on them. But I'd also categorized plenty of completely normal people as potential assholes, and I knew they didn't always deserve it.

So I bent down to one of the many below-bar fridges we had and pulled out a bottle of Bud. I flipped the top off with the bottle-opener I kept in the waistband of my shorts and slid the beer in front of him. "You wanna keep an open tab or should I close you out?" I asked.

He eyed my chest before he shrugged again. He hadn't once looked me directly in the eye. "Close it."

Alriiight. I spun back around to the computer and printed a bill for the beer, tucking it into a black book before setting it down in front of him with a polite smile. And then I turned my attention to the group of women beside him who wanted to order another round.

It only took me about five minutes to make the four lemon drop shots they'd ordered, but once I'd served them, I realized that the man was no longer seated in his stool. The black book had been pushed up the bar, so I reached for it and flipped it open. The tab for the beer was still neatly tucked inside, but there wasn't cash or a card anywhere to be found. My eyes snapped up, scanning the dwindling crowd of the club for any sign of him.

I didn't see him anywhere.

Well, he wasn't the first customer to walk out on a tab, and he wouldn't be the last. At least the damage wasn't major.

"Mara," sounded a deep voice behind me, and I nearly jumped out of my skin.

"Shit," I breathed, turning around to find Leo standing behind me. His eyes were blue steel outlined by dark lashes as they bounced around my face.

The corners of his mouth turned down. "I'm sorry—I didn't mean to scare you."

I made it a point to look away, to make a sweep down the line of customers to see if there might be someone who needed something from me—anything to get me out of another conversation with Leo.

Unfortunately, everyone looked content.

I sighed, turning to face the computer screen instead. "Can I help you?" I asked rather curtly as I pulled the disappearing man's tab back up so I could void it out and mark it as a loss.

Leo stepped closer, and I sucked in a breath from the feel of his arm lightly brushing against my shoulder. I breathed in a trace of what must have been his cologne—he smelled like the mountains, like pine trees and damp earth. Like the Colorado air. And it suited him. I realized it may not have been cologne at all . . . That maybe it was just his natural scent. "I was curious how long you'll be here tonight?" His voice was low, the timbre of it dancing along the skin of my neck.

My brow furrowed as I swiped my manager-access card into the machine, approving the void on the lost tab. "Why?"

His tone changed. "Did someone walk out on their bill?"

I spun around with a glare. "Yeah, actually, someone did. What's it to you?"

His eyes narrowed. "Well, considering this *is* my business, I find it more than appropriate to question the possibility of a lost transaction." There was something about the way the words rushed out of him that revealed that slight accent again. Leo was *irritated*.

Looking back at the computer screen, I tried to quell the simmering fire beneath the surface of my skin. "It was a three-dollar tab in a club that's pulling in close to six-figures tonight. I'd hardly call it much of a 'lost transaction,' *sir*." In all honesty, the loss irked me as much as it seemed to irk Leo. But it irked me *more* that Leo was even here to be irked in the first place. I watched his face fall further, and despite my frustration, I didn't like the way his expression made me feel. "Look, I'm sure you mean well. I'd just rather not be chastised over three measly dollars. The guy was a creep anyway."

"I wasn't trying to chastise you . . . wait, what do you mean?"

I shrugged. "It was only three dollars. It's really not that big of a deal."

His nostrils flared. "No, the other part. The guy was a creep?"

"Oh." I finally looked back at him, catching the way his jaw clenched in rapid succession as his eyes fastened to mine. "He put out some weird vibes. Wouldn't look me in the eye, leered at the women next to him like they were pieces of meat. I wish I could say it's not common, but in a place like this it's pretty normal." I paused, noting that Leo's teeth were practically grinding together. "If it's any consolation, I think he was a 'generally safe' kind of creep. I had my eye on him for a while before I served him."

"Mara," Leo retorted, his tone sharp enough to cut glass, "are you telling me that it's *normal* for customers to disrespect you here? To make you feel uncomfortable?"

Something about the way he said it—like he was on the thinnest edge of unraveling from a reality that was common-place for me—made my stomach curl in on itself. "This is a nightclub," I said. As if that was all the reason in the world to accept the danger that often lurked in the corners.

"I don't give a shit," he growled.

And . . . *wow*. I mean, he was right. It was unfair to have to deal with the blatant misogyny that thrived in a place like this. Wasn't that *exactly* what I fought so hard against? From the day I first walked into this place, I'd wanted to make sure anyone who came through the door felt safe enough to do so. And yet, I'd still somehow grown accustomed to how grimy customers could be—especially when alcohol and an entitlement to "fun" were thrown into the mix—that I'd begun to hold bad behavior against some arbitrary rating scale. Like, maybe tonight's creep wasn't so bad because at *least* he kept his hands to himself.

I inhaled a deep breath, taking Leo's words right on the chin as I nodded. "Point taken."

Twin lines carved out space between his brows. I forced my gaze back at the computer screen, clicking around randomly under the heat of his glare. "That's it? 'Point taken'?"

My defenses were falling again, just as they had last night. I had a deep urge to reach an arm out, to brush a finger along his jaw and soothe out some of that frustration on his face. But I couldn't . . . *wouldn't* go there with him again. So, instead, I played the business card. "We're closing soon, and I have a lot of people to start closing out. Is there anything else I can help you with?"

Again, he frowned. "This conversation isn't over, Mara."

I forced a smile. "Whatever you say, *sir*."

Chapter Nine

I slept like the dead, waking only when my phone's alarm blared its assault against my unconscious bliss at eleven. Between staying at Larkspur until nearly three in the morning to close up and the near all-nighter with Leo the night before, I was *beyond* exhausted. I was too tired to even stop for food last night—I jumped in the shower as soon as I got home and immediately crawled into bed and passed out.

Heavy clouds covered the sky outside my window, and all I wanted to do was stay wrapped in the comfort of my warm blankets until my shift tonight. But I had things to do. Twice a week, I attended an early afternoon Muay Thai training class at a gym about twelve blocks away from my building, and I also needed to get into Larkspur early to do some admin work. A liquor shipment was due to be delivered that I'd need to process into inventory, and I had to post the staff schedule for the next two weeks and ensure payroll was up to date.

A small part of me hoped a certain tall, rich, and devastatingly handsome new nightclub owner wouldn't show up today, but something told me he wasn't going away that easily. His words from last night had been tumbling through my mind since I'd woken up, sinking their way deeper and deeper into my psyche.

This conversation isn't over, Mara.

I blew out a breath. At some point, I *knew* I was going to have to face Leo. I was going to have to be a big girl and navigate my way through an honest and productive conversation with him to figure out how we were going to work together. That was the only way to move forward—we were both adults, and neither of us could change the current circumstances.

Sure, we may have seen each other naked. We may have done things together that were *well* beyond the boundaries of a typical boss/employee relationship. Like, a lot of *really* dirty things. But we didn't know what we were getting ourselves into that night, so the right thing to do was to accept the reality of the situation and move on with as much dignity as we could find.

And maybe—if I could swing it—I'd eventually convince him to sell *me* the club.

But first: damage control. Though Leo stayed at Larkspur last night until after I left, he didn't speak to me again. After the last of our customers had been let out and Frank locked the doors, I pulled the registers and found the office open and empty for me to process through the day's revenue. As I counted the cash at the large wooden desk, my eyes kept bouncing to the coffee machine that sat on the far corner, and I thought about Leo using it to make himself his little hazelnut treat.

Maybe I'd reacted a bit too harshly. It's not like he knew that coffee was my own personal stash.

Bleary-eyed, I logged the sales figures into the system, stuffed the money in a cash bag, and locked it away in the safe. When I poked my head through the doorway to the public space in front, I found Leo and Frank chumming it up at the bar, each with a bottle of beer in hand. I called out that I was leaving and turned around to walk away before either of them could get a word out, choosing to ignore the fact that Frank was flirting pretty heavily with the enemy.

Today, I would try a *little* harder.

I forced myself out of my soft bed and into an all-black athletic ensemble for training. In the bathroom, I brushed my teeth and washed my face before pulling my hair up into a high ponytail. My green eyes were bright against my pale skin, which reminded me to throw on a little sunscreen before I made the almost two-mile trek to the Muay Thai gym. I decided I would jog there—it would be a good warm-up, and by the time I got myself out the door I was running a little late anyway.

Outside, the October air was colder than it had been in months—a sure sign that winter weather would be here soon. The trees that lined the city streets were beginning to turn yellow and orange, transforming downtown Denver into a beautiful autumnal vision, and it seemed likely that we'd have rain today or tomorrow. Tucked into my thick fleece athletic jacket, I stuffed my AirPods into my ears and turned on some nineties hip-hop before I began jogging at an easy pace.

I felt a burn in my lungs only five minutes in—but I pushed through. I loved throwing myself into physical activity. With my body being preoccupied with movement, I was able to work through the tough shit going on in my life. My daily yoga practice was for quieting my mind, whereas I let my thoughts flow freely during other kinds of exertion, processing through problems in a more nurturing space. It was my own personal form of therapy, of meditation.

Today, I had plenty to focus on.

There weren't as many pedestrians out as was typical for a Friday afternoon, but with the brisk temperature it made sense. People were likely staying cozy inside their homes, or enjoying the warmth of a nearby coffee shop. Soon it would be much colder than this, but even in the dead of winter, I still loved to run outside.

Since there was less of a crowd out today, I found myself looking at each person's face as I passed them, offering a polite smile to anyone who's eyes caught mine. Just over halfway to the training facility, my bouncing gaze caught on a pair of familiar, bright blue eyes. Eyes that grew wide with recognition, just as mine did.

Leo.

He looked like a dream in a white long-sleeved thermal shirt and black athletic shorts, jogging in the opposite direction that I was. Wavy locks of hair bounced along his forehead with each long stride, natural and free from any product as they danced along the tops of his eyebrows. The ends were slick with sweat, as was his forehead and neck. He wore expensive-looking black headphones over his ears.

I couldn't help my gaze from dropping down to scan his entire body, momentarily fastened to his torso and the way it twisted back and forth as he ran. And then lower, where a hint of his thigh tattoo peeked out from beneath the hem of his shorts. God, his legs looked too good to be true, his muscles taut with effort as he moved—but I knew better. I knew how real they were, how they felt pressing down between my own. Seeing him like this, in clothes far more casual than the suits he'd been in the last two days, stirred something eager inside of me.

Heat rose to my cheeks despite the cold air, and I forced my eyes back up to his as we both slowed to a stop. We stared at each other for what felt like a full minute, other pedestrians meandering around us as we disrupted the flow of foot traffic.

"Mara?" Though his face still held his surprise, there was an obvious trace of delight in his features. I didn't know what to make of it, because while it was surely a treat for my eyes to see him, it was anything *but* for my mind and heart.

I pulled out my AirPods and peeled my tongue off the roof of my dry mouth. "Hey, what are you doing out here?"

He made a point of looking down at himself. "It would appear that I'm in the middle of a run," he teased, the corner of his mouth lifting higher, "and it would seem you're doing the same?"

I shrugged, feigning nonchalance at this whole encounter. As if him being here right now wasn't sending me into inner chaos. "I'm headed to training. Figured I'd warm up with a run to get there."

Curiosity flashed in his expression. "Training? What kind of training?"

"Muay Thai," I said simply.

Leo huffed out a sound of astonishment. "No kidding?"

I stared at him blankly. "Nope. Not kidding."

He schooled his face into neutrality, clearing his throat. "Right. Okay. Well . . . be safe? Please. And I'm sure I'll be seeing you later today?"

I did my best not to let my disappointment show,

managing a small smile that I hoped didn't look too forced. *Try harder, Mara, remember?* "Yeah, I'm sure you will. I'll be in a little early today."

Leo nodded. "Okay, sounds good. I'll see you then." He looked at me for another moment before clearing his throat again, pushing himself off the concrete and back into a light jog, keeping a solid few feet of distance from me as he passed.

Pushing my AirPods into my ears, I let Tupac's "Keep Ya Head Up" drown out the surge of apprehension that rippled down my spine as I thrust myself onward.

My limbs still felt like Jell-O as I unlocked the back door to Larkspur. Today's Muay Thai class had been more brutal than normal with an extra emphasis on kicks and shin-work. I'd been paired with a man for the sparring segment of class—there were only two other women in attendance, and both of them were beginner-level. The instructor thought that, of the three of us, I'd be best-suited to be paired with a man.

Not that I minded. That was the whole reason I practiced Muay Thai in the first place. I wanted to know that I could defend myself if anything ever happened to me. And if I *were* ever attacked, it probably wouldn't be by someone who matched my smaller size.

After turning the lock, I heaved the door open and slipped inside the dark stockroom. No one else was scheduled for a couple more hours, but the inventory shipment would be here soon, and I had things to take care of.

I moved toward the small office so I could set my things

down, and just as I found myself at the door, I heard a *clank* coming from somewhere at the front of the building, followed by a muffled, "*Shit!*"

Instantly, I was on guard. No one else was supposed to be here. *Had someone broken in?* I crept toward the quiet but obvious noises coming from somewhere in the front of the building.

As soon as I reached the swing doors, I pushed myself up as far as I could onto my tip-toes and strained to peer over them, finding a man in a dark gray work shirt standing on a ladder.

"You okay?" a second person below him asked. My gaze dropped down to a second man who stood next to the ladder, dressed in a sleek navy suit.

Of course—Leo.

"Yeah, yeah, no problem." The man on the ladder waved a hand toward Leo as he refocused on the small black orb that he was drilling into the ceiling.

Pushing my way through the doors, I cleared my throat.

Leo turned his body toward the bar, his eyes finding mine. His face morphed into a bright smile. "Mara, you're here!"

My gaze flitted to the man on the ladder before returning back to Leo. I raised my eyebrows in question. "What's going on?"

He hiked a thumb toward the ladder. "Oh this? Ah . . . we're installing a new security system. State of the art . . . a real good one." He looked back at the black orb with an obvious sense of pride, as if he'd constructed it himself.

"A security system?" I asked. "Why?"

Leo stuffed his hands in the pockets of his slacks and strode toward me, his long body closing the wide space between us in no time. "I was hoping to have everything installed before you got here—I wanted it to be a surprise." He sighed. "That's okay though. I'm glad you're here. You can help me determine the best location for the camera above the bar."

I blew out a raspberry, exasperated. "Why are you installing a security system, Leo?"

He cocked his head as he stared back at me. "For security," he said simply.

I rolled my eyes. "Seriously? Why do we need a security system? We have a whole security *team*. How much are you spending on all this?"

His eyes grew more serious as his tone darkened. "We need a security system because there was a 'creep' at this bar last night who walked out on his tab with you. And that doesn't sit right with me, Mara."

The sudden flash of anger behind his words made my stomach flip. "It's a busy nightclub. Sometimes assholes walk out on their tabs—it's part of the gig. We do our best to stop it, but it's inevitable that some of those assholes slip through the cracks." My eyes bounced back to the expensive-looking camera being fixed to the ceiling. "Please tell me how much you're spending on all this."

"It's not cheap, but we can certainly afford it."

I knew he was right. There was no way a security system cost more than what the club pulled in on a single night. But truthfully, I didn't like that a decision like this was made without me. It felt like my control was already slipping, and control was the *one* thing I thrived on.

I must have been showing my frustration, because Leo added, "Look, it shouldn't come as a surprise that we're extremely profitable—something I'm sensing has a lot to do with you. If it bothers you this much for the business to pay for the system, then I'll pay for it myself from my own private reserve of funds. But Mara, this is non-negotiable. I will *not* have you in danger here."

Oh. "Well, I . . . ." I stumbled over my words, having been struck right in the chest. "I just want to be a part of decisions like this. I've been running things here by myself for a long time, Leo."

He nodded. "Noted. I apologize that I didn't consult you first." He paused. "I suppose I should also tell you, then, I'm planning on bringing in a new security team."

My mouth went dry in a panic. "*What?*" I screeched. "You can't do that!" My mind immediately jumped to Frank and Ethan and the rest of the team who worked so hard and cared so much about our safety here. I would burn this place to the ground before I let Leo mess with my team. "Robert said you couldn't affect anyone's employment like that—"

"Mara," he interjected, holding his palms up. "Slow down. I'm not touching your team. They can function as normal. I'm hiring a different kind of team. One that's more . . . executive-level team, whose goal is to remain unseen. They'll blend in with the rest of the patrons—you won't even know they're here."

I opened my mouth to argue out some sassy retort . . . but my jaw snapped shut again when I realized I didn't have one. He wasn't doing anything that would affect the current team. If anything, additional security would benefit it. Especially if they were secret eyes. We could certainly use that.

I sighed. "Fine. But you're paying for them, too."

He smirked. "Done."

Shaking my head, I turned on my heels and marched back toward the office. The door was unlocked—Leo must have already been in here today—and when I walked through the door I found a brand-new bag of hazelnut coffee from a local coffee shop I'd been loyal to since first walking in years ago. There was a ruby-red gift bow stuck to the top, and a sticky note pressed to the front of the bag.

Mara, I apologize for taking what wasn't mine. I hope this can serve as a truce?
Enjoy, Leo

I blinked as I stared at the bag, feeling both genuinely pleased and deeply annoyed. Trying to settle my nerves from battling with him, I decided that a cup of coffee sounded really great, actually. So I moved the new bag to sit beside the one that was currently open before I brewed myself a cup in my favorite green Larkspur mug and sat down at the desk to finish up the upcoming staff schedule.

There was a pile of papers at the center of the desk—a work order for the security system currently being installed. It listed Leo as the main contact. Well, it listed Leopold Callahan.

Leopold.

A grin grew wide on my face at the clear ammunition.

I shuffled the paperwork to the side, clearing a space for myself in front of the computer, and got to work.

Chapter Ten

I'D ONLY BEEN AWAKE FOR APPROXIMATELY FOUR minutes, and I was already rolling my eyes from where I was burrowed in my small but absurdly comfortable bed. The time-stamp showed the text came in two hours ago, at seven-thirty this morning.

Does the man know what sleep is?

We left Larkspur at the same time—it was nearly four in the morning before we got things cleaned up and prepped for another long night—which meant Leo either only caught a couple hours of sleep, or he never went to bed at all. The thought of Leo going to bed sent my mind tripping into visions of him sprawled out in his king-sized bed, of soft gray sheets draping over the olive skin of his hips as he traced lazy circles on my shoulder with his fingers.

Fuck.

I hastily typed a response and sent it before I could think twice.

> I'm not sure how you got my number, but I suggest you lose it.

I watched as a little text bubble appeared before swiftly disappearing, only to reappear again moments later.

212-555-1024:

> Hello, Mara. Your phone number is part of your employee records, just as it is for everyone else on staff. I'd like to politely stress the urgency of this required conversation. There's a coffee shop on the corner near my building called Blue Sparrow Cafe. Would you please meet me there? Soon? Looking forward to it, Leo

I frowned as I reread the text. Required conversation? What could possibly be so urgent, and why wouldn't he have brought it up last night? Sighing, I tucked my phone to my chest and rolled over in bed, pulling the comforter up to my chin.

I could get a coffee with him, right?

It wasn't like it was a date or anything. It was probably work-related, though he didn't exactly offer any hints as to what this mysterious-yet-urgent conversation would be. But it *had* to be about Larkspur, right? I'd been pretty firm with him that anything between us going forward would need to be strictly professional.

I brought my phone back up in front of my face.

> Fine. I'll be there in an hour.

At the very least, he could wait until I got through my yoga practice. I'd already missed it yesterday morning after sleeping in too late, *and* I'd missed it the morning before after scurrying out of Leo's penthouse. I could always feel the effects on my mental health when I didn't get in that stretch time—anxiety and stress would creep in through the cracks of the mental foundation I worked tirelessly to keep strong. Wrestling myself out of bed, I groaned from the throb of my sore muscles after yesterday's training as I stretched my arms above my head.

Yoga was *definitely* needed this morning.

Grabbing my rolled mat from where it leaned against my nightstand, I laid it out on the hardwood floor behind my couch before grabbing a sports bra and leggings to change into. After syncing my phone to my Bluetooth speaker, I turned on a meditative sound therapy playlist I liked to listen to as I practiced.

My yoga routine usually only took twenty to thirty minutes, depending on the day. If I was particularly sore or if I had a lot on my mind, I'd take a little more time to sink deeper into each pose. Right now I had plenty of things to work through, so as I stepped to the top of my mat, I closed my eyes and did my best to drown everything out. Pressing my hands together in front of my heart, I began to flow into my first sun salutation.

I am strong. I am confident.

I'd been practicing yoga religiously for the last two years—it had been one of the first things that seemed to help with my stress and anxiety after finally breaking things off with Seth. I loved the way it made me feel inside, that by simply moving my body into a flow that aligned with my breathing, I invited in a calmer and more limber physical and mental state. I could literally *feel* the tension leaving my body, and after trying a dozen odd things, including but not limited to rock climbing, roller derby, even joining a women's curling team in one of my many fits of impulsivity, I wasn't going to look a gift horse in the mouth.

I am fearless. I am . . . happy.

Even after all this time, that mantra was not as easy to believe in. Happiness sometimes felt as tangible as the mist that hung thick in the air after a night of rain—I could feel it in a general sense, but it was too obscure to really grasp and hold between my fingers. I mean, what *was* happiness anyway? I had a great job and made decent money, I had a family who loved and supported me—as much as I let them, at least—and above all else, I was *safe*. Those truths made me feel successful. Was that the same thing as happiness?

I am ready to receive.

That thought was also a little harder to process. Until now, it always elicited wonderful thoughts around the work I was doing at Larkspur . . . that one day, I would buy the club from Robert. Now that I knew it was nothing but a pipe dream, I felt silly saying the words inside of my head. As I folded over into a downward dog stretch, I wondered what, exactly, was I supposed to be receiving?

I supposed I wasn't quite ready to give up the dream of

owning Larkspur. Obviously, Leo's presence threw a not-so-subtle wrench in those plans . . . but nothing was permanent. Someday Leo would probably want to sell, too—wasn't that pretty typical of rich entrepreneur-types? Did I have the patience and determination to wait him out?

Continuing to move through my practice, I paid close attention to the stiff muscles of my calves and thighs. After a half-hour of movement, I felt much looser and more prepared to tackle whatever Leo had to throw at me. I was a strong and confident woman who'd proven herself capable of handling anything, so I had no doubt I could continue to represent myself professionally to my new boss . . . even if the occasional pesky desire for him crept into the dark corners of my mind.

It would take time . . . but I was nothing if not determined.

Blowing out a long breath as I finished my final stretch, I knew it was now or never. I was ready to take him on.

I walked into Blue Sparrow Cafe only a couple of minutes late, immediately spotting Leo at a table in the far corner. There were already two steaming cups of coffee on the table—a sight that sent my heart into a catapult—so I skipped the line to order and instead made my way directly to him. From this angle, I could only see his side profile. He looked deep in thought as he stared at the wall across from where he sat. A beautiful beige cashmere sweater stretched across his broad shoulders, the sleeves rolled up to just below his elbows, and dark blue jeans hugged his legs. He was the picture of a handsome, well-dressed man.

As I got closer, though, I noticed his wavy hair was in disarray, like he'd been running his fingers through it all morning. I realized something was wrong when he turned to look at me, noting the dark storms in his eyes. It contrasted sharply from the seemingly happy and confident man I'd left at the club last night.

But then he blinked, and it was as if those storm clouds were never there. "Good morning, Mara." His mouth stretched into a smile as he stood up from his seat, moving to the opposite side of the table to swiftly pull the other chair out for me. "I hope you don't mind—I took the liberty of ordering you a hazelnut coffee."

I nodded. "That's perfect, thank you." I tilted my head as I took a closer look at his face, mesmerized by his ability to slam his walls down so quickly. A few lines set deep in his brow were the only indication that something was amiss. "What's wrong?"

He let out a humorless chuckle as he sat back down, folding his large frame into the stiff metal chair. I caught the tic in his jaw before he opened his mouth to speak. "Is it that obvious?"

This felt like my conversation with Robert all over again—I could feel myself bracing for impact. "Is it the club?"

Shaking his head, Leo picked up his mug of coffee and brought it toward his full lips. "No, nothing has happened," he assured me, "the club is fine. There's nothing to worry about." He shuffled in his chair, sitting up straighter as he set his mug down without taking a sip. His thick fingers began to assault the table in an anxious rhythm. "Listen, I need to ask you for a favor, Mara."

I stiffened. "Okay. Regarding what?"

He grinned, and it suddenly felt like we were on opposite sides of a sparring ring. Leo was up to something, and I had a strong feeling I wasn't going to like it. "My parents are coming into town," he volleyed back.

I stared at him blankly. "Okay," I repeated, my mind scrambling to try and get ahead of whatever he might be about to drop on me. "Is that a bad thing?"

His shoulders rose in a small shrug. "It's not ideal. But I was hoping you might be able to help make it a little easier." I watched his face closely as he smiled politely up at a man who walked by our table. His voice came out a smidge lower when he spoke again. "My parents are . . . not your typical parents."

This was beginning to feel like one of those hidden camera shows. What did it mean to have non-typical parents? Were they drug lords? Pirates? Did they run a traveling circus?

And what did them coming to Denver have to do with me? How the hell could I possibly make that easier for him? Tucking my fingers into the handle of my purple mug, I lifted it to my mouth and took a sip of the still-scalding but *delicious* coffee. "Okay," I said a third time, not knowing how else to respond.

Leo studied me carefully as his fingers ceased their erratic tapping against the edge of the table. "They're . . . tough. They aren't warm and loving like some parents. In fact, I'm confident that neither of them actually likes me very much," he rambled. Still, he watched me intently as I took another sip of my coffee. "*Fuck*," he muttered, shoulders slumping. "I'm just going to say it, Mara." He looked at me intently, as if willing me to stay calm. "I need you to pretend to be my girlfriend."

I choked on my coffee, almost spit it out onto the table.

"*Excuse* me?" I gasped, grabbing a napkin to dab at the bit of hot liquid running down my chin.

Leo's returning smile was too forced. "Come on, Mara. Would it be that hard?"

What the fuck? "You're joking, right?"

His smile dropped as his brows pulled together. "Look, I know it sounds a little crazy—"

"A *little*?" I interjected with a sordid whisper-shriek.

He sighed, shoulders flexing beneath his sweater that probably cost more than my monthly rent. "This would be beneficial for both of us . . . I assure you."

I couldn't help the scoff that soared from my throat. "How exactly does pretending to be your girlfriend benefit me?"

A wry grin spread across his cheeks. "It benefits you as my business partner."

Frustration snaked its way down my spine at his words. It felt like a mockery. "I'm not your business partner, Leo. I'm your *employee*. There's a very big difference between the two."

His grin curled higher, as if I'd said exactly what he hoped I would. "You won't just be my employee . . . Not if you do this for me." I froze in place as my mind hung on the words that so casually rolled off his tongue. "I'll make you partner, Mara. Do me this favor, and I'll give you half of the business."

The entire café around us disappeared as my vision tunneled, my focus entirely on the wicked man in front of me. *Is he serious?* He'd give me ownership of the business for pretending to be his fucking girlfriend?

This felt like a massively cruel joke.

Actually, this felt like the sleazy workings of a deep-rooted patriarchal scheme. Of *course* this rich and powerful man would dangle an ownership-carrot in front of me in exchange for something as ridiculous as being his girlfriend. The shock of it alone was enough to make my stomach roil. I couldn't possibly participate in something so fundamentally immoral. Leo was certifiably *insane*.

But as I opened my mouth to tell him a firm "no fucking thank you," the words caught somewhere in my esophagus and all that came out was an odd, breathy whimper. Which only made me more furious, because how *dare* Leo put me in a position where I'd have to say no to the one thing I wanted most? How dare he offer up the *one* thing that might just be my Achilles' heel? My *unicorn*?

His eyes blazed in triumph. "Sorry, I didn't catch that."

No, no, *no!* I would not agree to something so ridiculous. The inner tapestry of my female rage wouldn't allow it. *I am strong. I am confident. I am not a toy for this man to play with.*

It didn't even make sense . . . why would he need a pretend-girlfriend to face his parents? "Why?" As soon as the words came out of my mouth, I regretted it. Because I shouldn't care why . . . I should be getting up out of this seat and walking out that door.

He frowned. "Why what?"

I glared at him. "Why would you put me in a position like this? How does me pretending to *date* you solve the fact that your parents don't like you?"

He winced, and I would have felt sorry about such harsh words if I wasn't currently mad enough to throw this mug of coffee right at his stupid handsome face. He pressed both his palms into the surface of the table, bracing himself. "I'm not sure I could put it into words."

"Try," I demanded.

Leo sighed, eyes rising to the ceiling. Like the answer might be up there, somewhere. "I told you the night we met that running companies was a family business," he explained. "My father is the CEO of a large enterprise that essentially heads a conglomerate of entities that perform various functions for high-profile companies." I must have given him a *What in the what now?* look because a grin played at his mouth before he brought a hand up, wiped it away, and continued. "And for a long time, I worked closely under his wing. He was *dutifully* preparing me to take everything over. Except, as he saw it, I was lacking in what it took to succeed, and the pressure of it all got to me.

"So about a year ago, I left home. I needed to create some distance . . . to collect myself. I came to Denver and have been keeping my head down all this time. Until a week ago, when . . . well, when I purchased Larkspur." Most of Leo's words flew right over my head . . . not because I was incapable of understanding, but because the words poured out of his mouth at rapid speed and my mind was still spinning with this insane girlfriend-for-ownership proposition.

Taking advantage of a small reprieve with a long sip of my coffee, I forced myself to focus on where this story might be going. "And in purchasing Larkspur, your parents found out where you are?" He nodded enthusiastically, as if relieved that I seemed to be understanding his predicament. But I didn't understand—I didn't understand what any of this had to do with me. "Leo, how does having a . . . girlfriend," I said the word in a hushed whisper, as if it were poison on my tongue, "possibly help anything?"

Leo's gaze clung to mine, his hands inching toward me as he leaned forward. "Look, Mara, I've had a difficult last few years. I thought I had a solid plan, that I could permanently step away from the family enterprise . . . but it turns out my dad was right. I don't think I have what it takes to create success on my own." The bright blue of his eyes dulled in an instant. "I hate to admit it, but I need my father—the family business is all I have. I was hoping I could purchase an already-successful business, make a few tweaks to drive profits even higher, and then use that experience to explain my absence to my parents.

"I pulled funds from my own trust to purchase the club, thinking my father wouldn't notice—but I was wrong. He golfs with the bank manager; I don't know why I expected anything different." He sighed, and I could hear a shaky rattle in his breath. It almost made him seem . . . *scared*. "He called me early this morning to inform me that he and my mother are coming to Denver—*tomorrow*. They'll be here for a week, and I'm not ready to face them, Mara. I haven't had time to make my mark at the club. But maybe . . . maybe falling in love would help bridge the gap. If I've been distracted because I found the woman of my dreams—they won't necessarily respect it but I think they might at least understand it."

I took in a deep breath, warring with the conflicting feelings of not wanting to get involved in anyone's family drama, but also with the uneasiness that I was beginning to feel for Leo after seeing how nervous he was. He was *this* shaken up over the concept of his own parents visiting, and that struck a nerve in me.

He continued to watch me with an expression that was almost pleading, and instead of forcing him to explain any further, I forced *myself* to think about what he was offering me: *ownership* of Larkspur.

"I want seventy-five percent," I stated with a tone firm enough to knock Leo back in his chair.

His mouth parted in surprise, his eyes glinting in what might have been awe or utter shock at the demand. "Seventy-five percent?"

I nodded as I stood up from my own chair. "Yes. And I want a contract with the terms outlined, which will include that your ownership is of an *absentee* nature. I want to run my own club, Leo. No disrespect."

Leo frowned. "Mara, they're coming tomorrow. We don't have time for—"

"I suggest you draw something up quickly then," I retorted as I turned to walk toward the door. "I'll see you tonight."

Even though I wanted to—it nearly *killed* me not to—I didn't turn to look at him as I walked out.

Chapter Eleven

"You're a *billionaire*?"

Leo whipped his head around from where he sat in the office chair to look at me, frowning. His eyes cascaded down my frame, taking in my oversized Larkspur T-shirt that fell mid-thigh and the black fishnet stockings I had on underneath. The sleeves almost reached my elbows and the neckline was higher than any of my tank tops—all things considered, this was one of my more conservative outfit choices for a shift. But as his gaze dropped lower to the combat boots on my feet, his frown deepened.

I'd gotten to Larkspur a few minutes ago, walking through the backdoor to find things were already pretty busy. I made my usual rounds to check in on everyone and then circled back to find Leo and discuss our absurd conversation this morning. After said absurd conversation, I'd spent the early afternoon executing some *mild* sleuthing on the internet to see what I could find out about Leo's family. It was there that I'd seen his father listed on *Forbes*'s list of self-made billionaires.

Leo's eyes were still scrutinizing as they rose up to my face. On the desk in front of him was a silver laptop with various spreadsheets and bar graphs displayed on the screen, demonstrating what I guessed was some sort of financial report for Larkspur. I didn't even need to get a closer look to know that whatever reporting tools he was using were much snazzier than anything I'd worked with over the last couple of years. In the last two days of Leo being here, I'd come to realize he was organized to the point of obsession.

Forcing my eyes away from the computer screen and back to Leo, I allowed myself a single moment to take in the crisp black button-down shirt he was wearing and had to shake off a surge of lust that had *no* business presenting itself. "My father is," he confirmed, suave and serious. And then his annoyingly gorgeous blue eyes narrowed. "Wait, how do you know that?"

I pressed a hand to my hip over the army green cotton of my shirt. "Google," I replied, a bit smug.

His eyes widened, the smallest trace of panic seeping into them. "What else did you find?"

I narrowed my own gaze. "What do you mean *what else did I find*? What else is there, *Leopold*?"

He shook his head defensively, and I watched his waves sway with the movement. "Nothing. Just . . ." He hesitated, running his palms over his thighs. "Do me a favor and don't go digging for any more information about me. If you want to know something, I'll happily tell you myself."

I grunted. "As if that isn't the most red-flag request to come out of a man's mouth."

He pressed his lips together into a firm line. "I'm serious,

Mara." His wide chest expanded and contracted beneath his pressed shirt. "There are things in the media that are, quite frankly, pure fiction . . . Narratives involving my family that couldn't be further from the truth." He looked thoughtfully at the floor. "*Some* things are true, I suppose. But not everything."

Hm. *Color me intrigued.* I simply stared back at him, unwilling to agree to his ask. His nervousness only made me want to google him more.

Aside from the *Forbes* issue, I'd found a few other blogs and articles that were interesting, to say the least. Apparently, Callahan Enterprises had a less-than-stellar reputation despite their incredible revenue reporting. Most of the negative rumblings had been in regards to Leo's father himself—Alaric Callahan—but Leo had been implicated in a few accusations, too, like undermining board authority and the misappropriation of funds.

Scrubbing a hand over his face at my silence, he sighed. And then he locked his eyes on me. "Mara," he nearly whispered. "Please."

For the second time today, something about his expression made me falter. It was like he was letting his veil drop to reveal an all-encompassing exhaustion, and I didn't like it. So, I decided to steer the conversation toward a subject that felt safer. "Do you have a contract for me?" I wagged my eyebrows at him, as if the question weren't completely insane.

Leo stumbled at the subject change, mumbling something under his breath that I didn't catch, but relented as he picked up a sheet from the pile on his desk. "Right here," he indicated, holding it out for me as his eyes once again fell to my legs.

I snatched the paper out of his hands and began to read it, swallowing down a sudden bout of nerves.

RELATIONSHIP CONTRACT

My stomach flipped at the sight of the bold title printed at the top of the page.

What the *hell* was I getting myself into?

This agreement ("Agreement") serves to establish a consensual relationship ("Relationship") between the following undersigned parties:
Mara Roberts
("Girlfriend")
Leopold Arthur Callahan
("Boyfriend")

My gaze jumped off the page to find Leo staring at me earnestly. "You know," I said, forcing the words out as casually as I could, "if this fake relationship happens to lead to fake children, I'm telling you now we will not be letting your parents anywhere *near* their names."

Leo rolled his eyes. "Mara," he groaned.

I smiled, satisfied, before I looked back at the paper and willed myself not to break into a nervous sweat.

The Agreement is set forth for a period of ten days, beginning on the date it is signed and therefore rendered active. Both Girlfriend and Boyfriend hereby agree to the following provisions as conditions to the Relationship set forth herein:
1. EXCLUSIVITY. *Each partner agrees to be physically*

faithful during the term of the Relationship. No other sexual partners are allowed for either party.

"I'm sorry"—the words came out in a high-pitched squeal despite my best attempts at *calmcoolcollected*—"are you contracting me to have sex with you?"

Leo's eyes bulged wide. "No!" he exclaimed. "There is no obligation to . . ." He cleared his throat as he ran a hand through his disheveled hair. "It's merely stating that we can't sleep with other people. But that certainly does not require any sort of physical relationship between *us*, Mara, nor is there an expectation of one—I assure you."

I watched him with mild suspicion, unconvinced why that point would be necessary in the agreement. "I wouldn't be your real girlfriend, Leo. Do we really need an exclusivity clause?"

He sighed. "I'm fully aware of the fact that you wouldn't be my real girlfriend. But during this . . . agreement . . . we have to maintain the image of being together for real. My father is ruthless and has been known to poke holes in my . . . affairs. If we aren't careful, he'll sniff out the lie." His eyes again fell to my legs, to the stockings that left little to the imagination. "Neither of us can be caught in a compromising situation."

I smiled. "Okay, so no more fucking customers in the bathroom during my shifts?"

Leo's eyes darkened and then blazed, coming alive with anger at the joke. His jaw clamped shut as he pulled at his shirt collar, working to collect himself. It was a long moment before he spoke. "No. Certainly not."

Nodding, I forced my attention back to this ridiculous contract. "Noted."

2. *LIVING ARRANGEMENTS.* *Girlfriend agrees to live with Boyfriend at his place of residence.*

I leveled him with a look. "Why can't we stay at my place?" As if I would ever let Leo near my apartment. It was my safe haven—I rarely let anyone through my front door. But I didn't like his audacity to assume I would just move in with him for a whole week.

He arched a brow. "My parents are staying with me, and it would be wise to allow them to see us in our . . . everyday life."

"You mean you want to show off our fake love," I countered. "Our mecca of romantic bliss."

"Well, that *is* the point of all this. If we're going to do it, we need to do it right."

"Hm," I grumbled, continuing on.

3. *NON-DISCLOSURE.* *Neither partner shall, in the proper course of their duties during the continuance of the Agreement, nor after its natural termination, disclose to any other person, or make use of for their own benefit, any personal information relating to the Relationship or to the other partner that may be discovered during the term set forth for this Agreement.*

4. *RECIPROCITY.* *If each of the above outlined terms are met for the duration of the Agreement to complete satisfaction, Mr. Callahan will yield to Ms. Roberts an active ownership percentage of Larkspur (nightclub) that is equal to seventy-five (75) percent of its current appraised value. Furthermore, Mr. Callahan will transition into a silent partner role, actively available to support the business only if and when Ms. Roberts signals for such need.*

At the bottom of the page sat two lines, side by side. My name was printed beneath the one on the left, and Leo's was printed under the one on the right. I looked back up at him, finding a molten heat of what could only be irritation still set in his gaze. "I thought you said your parents were coming here for a week."

His head dipped once in acknowledgement. "That's right."

I held up the piece of paper. "This agreement is for ten days."

His eyes snapped to the page in my hand before landing on me. "It's just a safety net. If my father deems it necessary to dig himself further into my life, he'll extend their trip here without thinking twice."

I considered his words. It seemed like there might be more to it than that—but quite honestly, I wasn't sure I wanted to know anything else. If I was really going to agree to something like this, what was an extra three days? And if his parents did leave after a week, then we could just cut the agreement short.

My heart began a wild rhythm in my chest as I stood in front of Leo. Was I really ready to do this? Could I give myself to him—or at least pretend to—for an entire week? Could I go back to that penthouse, back to his *bed*, and maintain control over my heart? I felt myself pause at that—it had been so damn hard to leave him the first time.

Would I be able to stay anchored to reality amid this whole facade?

This time would be different, I decided. It wasn't like Leo and I would actually be intimate with each other. All of this would just be pretend . . . *nothing* like our night together. As real as it may have felt in the moment, the bubble had already burst. Plus, there was really no choice in the matter, because as ridiculous as all of this was, Larkspur was the prize. And I would do just about anything to see that dream through. I could convince a stuffy billionaire of my love for his son if it meant getting what I wanted, right?

Taking a deep breath, I stepped forward and placed the contract on the desk next to Leo's computer before looking him head-on. "Do you have a pen?"

His eyes roamed my face, scrutinizing me. "Are you sure?"

I gave him my biggest, fakest smile. "How could I say no to you, *my love*?"

He didn't return my smile. His eyes only hardened further. But then he swiveled in the chair, reaching for a pen inside his black leather briefcase before holding it out between us. "After you."

Swiping the pen out of his grip, and before I could even think about stopping myself, I leaned down to sign my name in blue ink. Then I handed it back to Leo, who cleared his throat again before he, too, signed the document.

Just like that . . . I was his.

Leo tucked the contract away in his briefcase. "I'll scan this and send you a copy to your email by the end of the day." He looked back up at me with an unreadable expression. "Now, if you'll excuse me, I need to get to work."

He shifted in his seat, then turned toward his computer. He minimized the report he'd been looking at before and instead pulled up a window of what looked like security footage. The screen showed a dozen squares containing multiple viewpoints from various angles, but I could tell right away it was Larkspur. In one frame, Sam was moving behind the bar talking to customers, and in another Ethan stood at his post at the front entrance. "Wow," I muttered, feeling a little fiery from Leo's attempted dismissal as my eyes jumped from square to square. "I didn't realize you were into voyeurism. That's some kinky shit, Leo."

Though he tried to hide his reaction, his shoulders stiffened at the accusation. "Yes, it'll be a wonderful resource as I keep a close eye on my *girlfriend* this week." He turned to look at me.

I smiled. "Good to know. I'll be sure to give you plenty to look at."

He exhaled, reaching up to pinch the bridge of his nose. "This must be some kind of bad dream," he muttered.

My smile grew wider as I sat on the edge of the desk, my right leg brushing against the fabric of his pants as I leaned in close. I didn't miss the way his eyes tracked the movement. "I'm your wet dream and you know it, *honey*."

In the blink of an eye, Leo shot out of his chair and pushed his legs between mine, pressing up against me. The top of my head only reached his chest from where I sat on the desk in front of him, giving me a front row seat to the way his throat bobbed roughly around a swallow. "Be careful what you wish for, Mara." His voice was low and dangerous.

While I was determined to remain unaffected by his little display of power, I'd be lying if I said it didn't make me falter, like I might be losing grip on my own control. The feel of him so close to me like this—his strong thighs pressed against the insides of mine as his face bent down toward me—had me spinning with memories of the way this very same mind-bending pressure had led to immense pleasure only a few nights ago. I could smell his clean skin, could feel him as he breathed, and it was altogether too much. But I tried my hardest to stay neutral. "Or what?"

He smirked, his eyes sparkling with a heady mix of desire and irritation. But he didn't answer me.

I made a show of shrugging, feigning indifference. "I've already told you I'm not interested in fucking my boss, Leo. I'll pretend to be your girlfriend, but I'm only doing it for this club." I let my eyes roam across his chest as I smiled again, masking the longing to reach out and touch him. "Plus, it's not like you were that memorable, anyway."

My heart punched wildly in my chest as his nose grazed across my forehead, inhaling against my skin. "Mara," he rumbled, his voice full of heat, "we may have been thrown into a near-impossible situation, but make *no* mistake." He wound his hand through my hair, fisting a large section of it and forcing my face up. His deep blue eyes pinned me in place, and I almost shuddered. My gaze dropped to his mouth as he continued to speak. "It's *never* been like that before, for me *or* for you—I could see it in your eyes, the same wonder that I felt. This thing between us isn't over. It can't be. I don't know how, and I don't know when . . . but it's only a matter of time before we can't stand it any longer." He pulled me even closer so that my entire front was pressed against him. "I already can't stand it," he whispered into my temple, the words dripping through me like liquid gold.

The honesty of them was *unbearable*.

I sucked in a big gulp of air, squaring my shoulders while my traitorous chest heaved. He watched me for another long moment before finally stepping back to sit down and refocus his attention on the surveillance footage. "If there's nothing else, I really do need to get to work."

My god. I wasn't sure I'd ever been more turned on *and* wholly frustrated in my entire life. His reinforced dismissal was a slap in the face. This arrangement felt more dangerous now— as much as I'd been trying to ignore it, it was obvious we both still felt some of the lasting effects of our explosive night together. Because . . . What had he said? *It's* never *been like that before*.

It stood to reason that the tension he was exuding was about *more* than just his parents.

I needed to get it together. As casually as I could, I jumped off the desk and landed on my feet beside him. "I'd like to politely remind you that this is *my* office. Lucky for you, I have to get behind the bar to help Sam, so you can stay in here for the time being. But this *is* my office, Leo, just as this is my club."

"Not for another week," he gritted out between clenched teeth, his eyes locked on the computer screen in front of him. As if he might implode if he looked my way again.

"Either way," I pranced toward the door, triumphant in my ability to get under his skin. "It's mine."

Chapter Twelve

It was an hour before the shakiness in my limbs subsided. It took even longer to get our verbal spar out of my mind as I worked to help Sam catch up behind the bar, thankful for the loud music and high energy. It helped shake the want that'd been pulsing through me after feeling Leo against my body, after hearing the confession that poured from his lips. I had to figure out a way to keep myself composed, because tomorrow I'd be diving head-first into the deep end of that man's world.

After dropping a couple of dirty martinis in front of an older couple at the end of the bar, my eye caught on a familiar face. Charlea's smile was wide as her deep brown eyes crinkled in delight. I gravitated toward her from the other side of the bar, her presence already like a soothing balm.

"Hey, stranger!" she greeted, wrapping a warm hand around my arm when I reached her.

"Hi, gorgeous." I leaned over the sticky, wooden surface to

kiss her on the cheek. She was sun-kissed with a fresh tan, her white tank a bright contrast against her skin. She smelled like vanilla and citrus—like the sweetest treat—and it warmed me from the inside out. "I didn't know you were coming in tonight."

Her shoulders knocked up in a shrug, a slender gold necklace glistening from her collarbone. "I thought I would surprise you. I'm *so* sorry I didn't text you back Wednesday night." She nervously pulled at a strand of her auburn hair as she studied my face. "I've been at my parents' up in Bozeman for a family reunion and . . . it was a hectic few days."

I waved a hand. "Don't worry about it." Relief flooded her features.

Truthfully, I hadn't thought about Charlea since I texted her Wednesday night before—well, *before*—and there was definitely a little tug of guilt beneath the excitement of seeing her now. Not that either of us had anything to feel guilty about—our relationship was a strictly casual no-strings type of deal. The fact that I'd ended Wednesday night with Leo instead of Charlea was perfectly within the bounds of our arrangement.

Still, it felt good to see her. Even if I did just sign away my ability to do anything *more* than see her for the next week. She let out a deep exhale. "God, I've missed you, Mara." Her mouth twisted up in a flirtatious smirk, and though I could feel the tendrils of desire begin to snake their way through my veins, I had to be fair to us both and see it for what it was: a distraction.

Leo's words from his office were still tumbling around my head, still sputtering through my heart. The truth, plain and simple, was I couldn't imagine being with anyone else after our night together. It was going to take a lot of effort to shake that high.

"How was the reunion?" I asked, careful to steer the conversation to safer grounds.

She grimaced. "Um . . . you know . . . it was okay? My mom was practically chiseling at my soul for any update on my dating life—she's determined to find me a suitable man to marry." Charlea was from a conservative family and was dealing with the pressure that came with being a girl who was into girls. Though we'd only danced around it, I was pretty sure her parents still didn't know she was gay.

I frowned. "I'm sorry, babe. Hopefully you had *some* fun?"

Her mouth tugged up into a smile. "As much fun as someone can have surrounded by cattle and manure."

I laughed, feeling lighter than I had all night. "Do you want a drink?"

She nodded. "Yes please—the usual?"

I smiled. "Coming right up." I veered toward the backbar to grab a nice bottle of vodka—I wasn't going to serve the girl responsible for a handful of orgasms each week house liquor that smelled like rubbing alcohol—and felt my phone buzz from where I'd tucked it into my waistband. Besides my co-workers here, Charlea was really the only other person I texted, so I couldn't imagine who it might be. After grabbing the vodka and a chilled copper mug, I set both down on the rubber mat near the soda gun and pulled my phone out to find a new text notification on the screen.

I caught a quick flash of Leo's name just as Sam whizzed by, missing me by a hairbreadth. "Please tell me you have extra oranges sliced over here," he called out as he pulled the fridge's door open.

I clicked my tongue at him. "You know, if you put a little more effort in prepping on the nights you open, you wouldn't run out of your garnishes so quickly. It's Saturday night, Sam. You *know* you're going to need to have extra shit on hand."

He gave me a sheepish look as he ducked down, scanning the lower shelves. "I know, I know—I'm sorry. I got in a little late today . . . the sitter canceled at the last minute and I had to make an unexpected stop at my mom's to drop Molly off."

Shedding the attitude, I frowned. "Oh. Don't worry about it . . . I was just giving you a hard time."

Sam pulled a stainless steel container full of orange slices out and held it above his head in victory. "Jackpot!" His eyes flashed in my direction. "I'm stealing these."

A laugh fizzed out of me at the sheer delight in his expression. "Okay, but you owe me. Cut some more and replace them when things slow down?"

He nodded eagerly. "Of course! Thank you." He bent down to press a chaste kiss on my cheek as he hustled back to his end of the bar. I laughed again as I looked down at my phone.

LEOPOLD

Good evening. I find it necessary to remind you of an active contract in which you agreed to be mine. And I don't share what is mine, Mara.

My stomach flipped at the words on the screen as I read them again.

And again.

He must have seen me talking to Charlea. Not even two hours after the ink dried, and he was already pulling some territorial bullshit. Looking up, I scanned the busy crowd for any signs of Leo amongst the patrons, but didn't see him anywhere. And then, as the colorful house lights made a sweep across the room in tandem with the beat of the DJ's music, the glint from a new camera above the bar spliced through the dark club. *Of course.*

Leo was spying on me through his fancy new security system.

Just as I was about to send off a sassy retort, another text buzzed though.

LEOPOLD

For fuck's sake. Do you allow all the employees to kiss you like that?

Rolling my eyes, I threw the camera a menacing glare before returning my attention to the bottle of vodka in front of me. Sam was harmless—not to mention in a relationship—and I wasn't going to let Leo start controlling how I interacted with the people in my life. I decided not to respond to his texts, instead focusing on making a Moscow mule for Charlea. I'd just anchored myself to him for the next week, I couldn't also let him see me fluster.

I garnished the edge of the copper mug with a lime wedge, and then walked the drink over to Charlea and set it down in front of her. "On me," I said with a wink. "Let me know when you're ready for another one—I'll check in on you soon."

Her returning smile was dripping in sin. "Can't wait."

As Charlea leaned in to take a sip of her mule, I eyed the camera and gave Leo a wink as well . . . for good measure.

"Fuck you, you fucking bastard!" The words boomed across the club from the far corner, near the DJ booth. I stood up on

my tiptoes to try to get eyes on whatever was happening, but the crowd was so dense I couldn't see anything except a wave of movement as people huddled around each other. Groaning, I turned to run toward Frank, but found him already flying into motion. So were Ethan, Drew, and Cedric—all swarming from their various positions around the club.

It never ceased to impress me, the way our security team descended upon a possible threat. Frank had used his old military training to prepare the entire team for moments like this, and it was incredible to watch as they circled their target like a pack of synchronized predators. Now that I knew they had it handled, I shifted my focus to the customers at the bar to distract them from the drama playing out behind them.

Just as I turned to face my side of the bar, I caught the blur of a black dress shirt and unruly chestnut hair striding out from the back with purpose. Leo had probably seen what was unfolding through the cameras and was coming out to help.

Or he was coming out to watch our in-house team in action to make notes for the new executive group he was bringing in next week.

Suddenly my skin felt tighter than the fishnet stockings wrapped around my legs. I may have already conceded that having an additional team here would be a good thing, but it still stung that Leo was making decisions like that at all. I watched his eyes shift to the bar, scanning down the line of people until they landed on me. We stared at each other with a mixture of heat and hostility—and then he was gone, disappearing into the sea of bodies as he headed right for whatever was looming within.

More shouting sounded from somewhere to the left, and a dart of unease flew through my chest as it always did when something like this happened. It was . . . triggering. I'd dealt with enough violence to last a lifetime, but I still couldn't quite manage to face it without setting off a trauma response in my body as though the danger were imminent. My gaze flitted to Charlea, noting the concern set in her brow as she watched me. I couldn't tell if it was concern for what was going on behind her or for what she could read in my expression. Either way, I wanted to ease her mind—so, I took a deep breath and fixed a wide smile on my face.

My eyes darted down the line of customers seated beyond her, knowing I needed to keep their attention anchored on me. Frank always said the best way to help when something was going down was to keep the area as clear as possible—fights could easily escalate when wild swings or shoves affected bystanders. "Who needs a drink?" I called out, keeping my expression light.

A group of frat boys from the nearby college campus all lifted their beers and cheered, as if I were signaling a party call. I turned to direct my smile toward them, but something else caught my attention, and I realized it was the man from two nights ago who'd skipped out on his tab.

He stood looking around the club, both hands shoved into his pockets. I marked his clothes, taking note of the oversized black polo shirt and gray jeans he wore so I could report it to Frank later, after whatever else was going on had been settled. It was only a three-dollar tab that he'd bailed on, but I didn't like that he was here again and I worried he'd try to do the same to Sam.

"Excuse me?" a small voice sounded to my right, where a woman who couldn't be older than twenty-five stood in a red dress. Her eyes were wide, her neck flushed. Something about the expression on her face snapped me into movement. I recognized the shroud of fear in her eyes, as if I were looking in the mirror at a younger version of myself.

My eyes scanned her up and down as I took in the sheen of sweat on her upper lip. Maybe she was a part of whatever scuffle had just occurred? "Can I help you?" I asked.

"I'd like to order a shot," she said carefully. "A . . . a Black Panther, please."

Panic clawed at my throat. A Black Panther shot was one of a handful of "drinks" on Larkspur's secret menu, advertised in the women's restrooms as a means to discreetly ask for help from our staff. Some were a little more low-stakes, like the Purple Cowboy, which prompted us to call a cab so that someone could quietly slip out and safely bail on a bad date. A Black Panther was our most severe—it was a full-scale distress signal when someone was scared of a potential assault. It triggered us to get our security team with them quickly so that they could assess and eliminate any threats to their safety.

It more than likely meant the police would be called.

Larkspur's secret menu was a safety program Frank and I worked on shortly after I became bar manager. This was a popular nightclub in downtown Denver, and unfortunately places like ours were nefarious for trouble. I wanted every woman who walked into this club to feel like they were safe, like they could let loose and unwind without fear of anyone fucking with them. I wanted women to feel the freedom that every woman *deserved* to feel in any setting of their life. I wanted them to feel like they could have fun without the fear of being taken advantage of. Since we'd started the program, plenty of our safety drinks had been ordered, but no one had *ever* ordered the Black Panther.

I risked a quick visual sweep, looking for any obvious signs of who might be threatening her, but there was no one around her that I could see. "Okay." I nodded sharply. "Of course, coming right up. Just give me a quick second, okay? I'll be right back."

I waited for her nod before I shifted my gaze toward the door to the stockroom, letting out a curse when I realized Frank was in the middle of dealing with whatever bar fight had broken out. I looked up at the camera, mouthing the word "help" in case Leo was watching, but even as I did I knew it was useless. Leo had just left the office to deal with the commotion —there was no way he was already done.

Shit! Okay, I was determined to handle this. I turned and found Sam pulling draft beer into a pint glass and marched toward him. "Sam," I hurried out in a low voice. "There's a woman in a red dress at the bar who just ordered a Black Panther. I need you to go find Frank and get help over here as quickly as possible. I don't give a shit what else is going on, we need at least two bouncers here *now*. I'll stay with her until then."

Sam's eyes widened. "Fuck," he whispered. "Okay—on it." He set the half-full glass down and jogged down the bar line, ducking under the counter at the far end before disappearing into the crowd.

I turned back to face the woman, deciding I would bring her into the office until we figured out what was going on . . . but she was gone. Spinning on my heels, I looked all around the perimeter of the bar searching for any sign of her bright red dress. My heart pounded inside my chest as a new wave of adrenaline rolled in. I should have *never* taken my eyes off her. A flash of red danced in my periphery, and I twisted to find the woman cutting through the crowd away from the bar. I breathed a sigh of relief in spotting her—but that relief was short-lived when I realized that she was being pulled by a man in a dark polo shirt.

It was the same fucking asshole from two nights ago.

My feet hit the ground of their own accord, and I kept my eyes trained on the red dress as I worked not to lose sight of her again. Dread almost knocked me sideways—I knew better than to leave her alone. I left her right in the grasp of a potential predator.

She had been who he was looking for when I saw him only minutes ago . . . The realization made me sick.

I started to run, my combat boots thudding along the rubber mat on the floor behind the bar as I moved in the opposite direction that Sam had just gone. Without access to the under-bar crawl space on this end, I was going to have to jump over the bar top.

I didn't even think twice.

"Look out!" I shouted, just as my hands gripped the edge of the wooden surface. I hoisted myself up between two customers who swiftly grabbed ahold of their drinks. "I'm *so* sorry," I said as I swung my feet over and fell down the other side, still keeping an eye on the woman's dress as the man pulled her down the dark hallway that led to the bathrooms. She turned back to look over her shoulder, fear written all over her face as she willed anyone to help her.

But it was no use. The focus was still on the bar fight occurring in the middle of the club—it was a perfect cover. The weight of responsibility settled into my shoulders as a lethal calm kicked in. My own fear began to dislodge from where it'd clung tightly against my spine, and I felt it fall away as control locked into place.

I *had* to help her. I would do whatever it took to get her away from him.

My boots squeaked against the floor as I launched into a sprint. Everything around me disappeared, my vision tunneling so that the only thing I saw was that red dress as it slinked into the shadows. I moved my legs as fast as I could, twisting my shoulders to break through the crowd. I could hear Frank's distant shouts, but didn't know what he was saying or if it had anything to do with me. My mind wasn't processing anything intelligible other than the fact that I had to get to the woman.

Within moments I'd reached the long, dark hallway that led to the bathrooms. The door to the women's bathroom was shut tight, and I prayed like hell that the man hadn't thought to lock it. I might be dosed full of anger and adrenaline—a mix that would undoubtedly cause some damage—but I knew I wouldn't be strong enough to get through the heavy door if it was bolted shut.

Thankfully, it gave as my body slammed against it, and I nearly toppled through the other side. I quickly regained my composure, looking up to find the woman pressed up against the wall. The creep's hands were roughly palming the skirt of her dress as he fought to keep her in place. Cold rage slid down my body and I lurched forward, grabbing the man by the neck and yanking him backward.

He wasn't very tall, so even with my short stature I'd been able to effectively hook a whole arm around his neck. "Oof," he grunted, losing his balance. He turned to look at me with glassy, dilated eyes—either he was incredibly drunk or in some drug-induced haze. He shot out an arm and shoved me hard enough that I fell to the ground, pain radiating from my tailbone and up my spine. I pushed up off the cold linoleum floor just as he turned his attention back to the woman, but she'd already started running for the door, sobbing into her hands. The man was quick, grabbing her waist with both hands and pulling her against his chest.

Scrambling to get my footing, I launched myself at the man and crashed into him hard enough that he released her to brace his own impact against the wall. "What the *fuck* is your problem?" I screamed. Turning to face the woman, I yelled for her to run as I did my best to stop the man from pushing me to the side. He shot his arm out again, his fist barreling right into my stomach, and I almost puked on the spot.

Growling in frustration, I reeled my arm back before launching my own fist toward his face. My knuckles flew into his nose as a loud *crack* echoed through the small bathroom. Blood poured down his face as he groaned, and I knew I'd broken it.

"You fucking *bitch*," he snarled, cocking his fist before he shot it at my face.

As I watched his disgusting, meaty fist wind back, I felt the shift. The distant smell of cigarette smoke filled the air around me, and it was enough to shove me right back into the past. Terror crawled its way up my throat, begging to be let out in a scream. My attention shifted from his fist to his glassy eyes, and I watched in terrible fascination as their steely gray morphed into the murky brown that had haunted me for so damn long.

No, I pleaded to the universe. *I will not go down like this again.*

Lucky for me, I practiced dodging punches twice a week in Muay Thai. So as that cocked fist flung forward, I ducked to the right, feeling the air move against my skin from his attempted hit.

*Un*lucky for me, I did *not* anticipate the fierce swing his left arm would make in tandem with his punch. That left hand made impact against the side of my head with such force that it slammed me into the wall.

Pain seared across my face, and my vision blurred as someone shouted.

And then I was out.

Chapter Thirteen

THE FIRST THING I BECAME AWARE OF WAS THE warmth on my cheek. It was soft and soothing, moving across my skin with gentle pressure. I liked the sensation . . . a lot.

The second thing was a pounding headache that radiated out from my right temple, spreading its way through my brain like the intricate webs of a spider.

I groaned.

"Mara?"

I . . . knew that voice. It sounded gruff, laced with a steeliness that stirred something to life inside of my chest. It was . . . mad. Furious, even. But tender.

"Mara," it said again in a low rumble that rattled my bones. "Can you open your eyes for me?"

"Mm," I managed to grumble. The words *I'm too tired to try* streaked by, but it seemed words were hard for me at the moment.

I realized there was someone else near me, too—someone

breathing heavily, as if they'd just run a mile through mud. "Paramedics are on their way, boss." I knew that voice, too.

Boss. The word prickled at me like a cactus, making me feel . . . uncomfortable. Frustrated. "Thank you, Frank," the first voice spoke from much closer, somewhere right above me. The warmth on the side of my face suddenly disappeared before fingers traced lightly along my forehead. It felt so nice . . . I desperately wanted to fall back asleep.

But as comforting as it all was, there was an undeniable sense of *wrongness* that I couldn't quite figure out. Maybe this was all a bad dream—it would explain the anxiety thrumming through my veins. If I could open my eyes and see what was on the other side of this cool and enveloping darkness, I'd know for sure. Maybe I could try to do that, for real this time.

It took all the strength and concentration I could muster, but I finally got one eye to peel open just as that comforting warmth resumed its place along my cheek. Reflexively, I leaned into it.

On the other side of the darkness was the most beautiful shade of blue I'd ever seen. It was like a wide open summer sky, so bold and deep and majestic that I wanted to float right up into its airy layers. "Mara," the voice repeated, this time with a bit more enthusiasm. "Can you hear me?"

Yes, of course I can hear you, was what I wanted to say. But instead, what came out of my mouth was pure gibberish. I frowned . . . or, I thought I did. It was definitely a problem that my brain wasn't connecting with my mouth. *Had something happened to me?* I grunted, forcing my other eye to open—and though things were blurry, I found that the incredible blue was actually a striking pair of eyes set beneath a mess of overgrown hair.

"Leo?" I managed, finally. Because of course it was Leo—who else had a voice and a touch that could bring me such contentment?

"Hey, sweetheart," he murmured. *Sweetheart.* I definitely liked that.

Or did I? Wait a minute . . . "What happened?" I asked, just as a particularly nasty swell of pain throbbed from my temple.

"You were attacked," he explained carefully. "You chased a man into the women's restroom and stopped him from assaulting a customer." His voice trembled, as if he were suffering the same near-debilitating migraine as I was.

I didn't like the way his shakiness sent a ripple of fear through me. "Are you okay?" I asked.

A heavy sigh sounded as his blurred head dropped. "My concern is for you at the moment. Can you tell me what hurts?"

On the surface he was even and attentive, and I leaned into that confidence, allowing myself to finally come undone as the chaos of emotion swirled through me like a ravaging tornado. Flashes of a bright red dress danced in my mind, and it all came back. My brows pulled together, though the motion nearly made me black out. "My head. The . . . the right side of my head. I hit the wall . . . when he hit me."

Leo's hand gently lifted from my cheek to push my hair away from my face, and I winced. "Fuck," he muttered in a tone that dripped with anger. Was he angry with me? If he was expecting any sort of apology, he'd be waiting a very long time. "Frank, tell them she has a head wound. It's not bleeding heavily, but I can already see some nasty bruising. She might have a concussion."

"Yes, sir," Frank responded with a tone that was equally

furious. Dammit. Frank was mad at me too? Heavy footsteps moved away from where I lay on the cold floor. I could hear more people speaking quietly amongst themselves just outside the bathroom.

A sudden thought crossed my mind. "Is the woman okay?"

Leo looked down at me intently. "She's completely fine. Not a scratch on her, thanks to you."

My eyes fluttered shut again as I let out an exhale. "Good."

"*You* on the other hand—"

"What about . . . what about the man?"

Leo's thumb came up to stroke gently across my brow. "He's in police custody. They got here about five minutes ago and took him away. He's in rough shape . . . you broke his nose, and then I—"

"Paramedics are three minutes out." Frank's voice carried from the doorway.

I tried to push myself up at that. "I don't need paramedics! Call them off, *please*—I'm fine." I got myself to my elbows, but Leo's touch became firm on my shoulder as he held me in place.

"Mara, lie down." His voice was gentle yet insistent. "You were hit in the head; we need to have you cleared by medical professionals before you try to get up."

I groaned. "No, please, I—I don't have insurance. I can't go to the hospital, and definitely *not* in an ambulance. That's like a twenty-five-million-dollar car ride!" This was all becoming too much . . . I just wanted to crawl into the comfort of bed and drift away. I needed to settle this fear, needed to calm the anxiety that made my skin feel so tight that I might burst.

"Don't worry about the cost."

"Easy for you to say, you fucking billionaire. I'm a *bartender*!" I didn't mean to sound so angry, but I needed him to release me. Needed him to understand this was about so much more than just tonight. I needed to run . . . to escape this suffocating feeling.

"I'll cover it," he insisted, his tone firm.

"No!" I bit back. "I'm not letting you pay for anything because I'm *not* going. I'm fine . . . I just got, like, *mildly* knocked out. Look," I said as I tried to push myself up again, tried not to show how bad it hurt to do so. "I'm feeling so much better. See?"

"For fuck's sake," he growled. "At least let them take a look at you before you stand up, okay?" He took a deep breath. "If they say you're fine to go home, I'll bring you home myself. But if they say you need further medical attention, you *will* obey—do you understand me?" His words were sharp and smoldering, and I felt them sear, burning me from the inside out.

I scoffed, ignoring the heat in my chest. I hated to give in, hated that I couldn't push harder. But I was exhausted and weak, and I knew that I wouldn't be able to get past him.

"She's in here!" Frank's voice called out, and I groaned again as I heard what could only have been a medical team moving down the long hallway.

Leo muttered a frustrated curse under his breath.

"Is she currently conscious?" A woman's voice echoed along the tiled bathroom wall.

"Oh yes," Leo confirmed. "I'd mind your fingers—she's quite feral at the moment."

"Could you please step out of the way, sir?"

Leo's body stiffened as he hesitated. "Please . . . please be careful with her." The words were much softer as his own fear cracked through.

Something sticky and aching bloomed inside of my chest, momentarily distracting me from the pain in my head. It was the same twinge I'd felt the morning after meeting him, when I struggled to leave his bed—it felt a lot like longing. Like a craving so fierce it made my stomach twist.

Leo finally shifted away from where I lay as two people replaced the space he vacated. "Ma'am, can you tell me your name?"

A tear slid down my face as I closed my eyes. *When did I start crying?* "Mara."

"Hi, Mara, my name is Beatrice. I'm here with my colleague Carlos, and we're just going to check you out, okay?"

Another tear escaped. I couldn't bring myself to answer her, knowing if I opened my mouth I would likely let out a sob. The shock of this whole ordeal must have been wearing off, because suddenly my head pulsed harder and I felt like I might actually break.

Taking my silence as acceptance, gloved hands began to lightly prod against my face and head as Beatrice and Carlos made vocal observations that I had no interest listening to. Carlos worked to gather my vitals while Beatrice focused on my head wound, and I curled into myself, shielding my mind from everything that was happening, from everything that *had* happened tonight.

It was a defense mechanism I knew all too well—my therapist once explained that in the face of trauma, some people responded by disappearing inside of themselves, disassociating from the reality of their external environment. It was how I navigated the agony I faced at the end of my relationship with Seth, and it was easy to slip back into now.

"Mara, can you tell me what day it is?" Beatrice asked.

"Saturday," I replied. "Saturday night."

"Good. On a scale between one and ten, how would you describe your current pain level?"

"I'm fine." The words carried a lot less fervor than they had with Leo, but I was so damn tired. I didn't want to fight anymore.

"Okay. Can you define it with a number?" Her fingers pressed against the nape of my neck, feeling for any cause for concern.

I thought about that—it wasn't my first time being hit, and it was far from the worst. "Six," I responded, numbly.

"Good." Beatrice seemed satisfied. "I can see obvious signs of a cerebral edema on your right temple, which means there's some swelling. It would be wise to have you seen at the hospital to ensure there isn't any trauma to your brain. We have an ambulance outside and can take you there now."

"*No,*" I begged as my eyes opened, concentrating with fuzzy clarity on the woman's face. "Please, I just want to go home. Can I please go home?"

"Our recommendation would be to keep you under observation. It's likely you have a concussion, and there is a risk that further issues may develop over the course of the next twenty-four hours. If you don't want to be seen at a hospital, you should at least have someone keep an eye on you."

My gaze moved to where Leo stood behind her, his dark clothes a stark contrast against pale pink walls. I couldn't quite make out his face, but I could sense him shifting on his feet. "I'll stay with her."

Beatrice turned around. "What's your relationship with Mara?" I didn't miss the scrutiny in her question. I'd just been attacked after all—I appreciated her concern for my safety.

But I spoke before Leo could get a word out. "He's my boyfriend." I knew I might regret the words, but it was a much better alternative to a hospital bed.

Frank coughed from the doorway.

Beatrice nodded. "All right." She continued to speak, giving Leo careful instructions—but I tuned it all out as I settled into myself. Soon, Beatrice and Carlos were gathering their things, content to release me into Leo's care. "Let's make sure you feel okay on your feet," Beatrice said as she held a hand out. I took it, and she eased me to my feet. The transition to an upright position came with a jolt of dizziness, but I focused on keeping my spine straight as I stood. "How does that feel?"

I nodded once, feeling the throb of pain at the center of my forehead now. "I'm okay," I insisted.

A hand pressed lightly against my back as another wrapped around my elbow. "I've got it from here," Leo assured.

As we slowly walked down the hallway, I realized that all of the club's house lights had been turned on, and the bright white of them was like a hammer to my head. I squinted through the pain, moving unsteadily as I leaned into Leo's firm hold. The club had been cleared out—only a small cluster of police officers stood in wait for an update from the medical team with looks of stern yet hopeful appraisal on their faces.

"Mara!" a voice shrieked from my left. I turned and found that Charlea was still here, a truth that pierced me right in the chest.

She'd cared enough to stay.

"Charlea?"

She flung herself toward me as Leo's hold on me tightened. "Easy," he instructed gently.

"Is she okay?" Charlea asked him, her voice riddled with worry as she refrained from flinging her arms around me.

"I'm okay." I attempted to crack a smile and continued: "You should see the other guy."

"I was so scared, Mara. I saw you jump over the bar and run, and then we all heard screaming . . ."

"I'm okay," I repeated, dipping my head slightly. "Just a little banged up, but nothing I can't handle. I promise."

Leo shuffled us forward. "I'll keep a close eye on her," he confirmed a bit stiffly, though his earlier jealousy seemed mostly in check. "We need to get her home now."

Charlea eyed him warily, and I could see the hesitation in her expression. She looked at me in silent question, and I gave her a nod. *This is okay*, I told her with a look. *He can be trusted.*

Her expression shifted. Softened. "I'll reach out tomorrow to see how you're doing," she promised, pressing her hand to my arm before wrapping her own around herself.

I nodded. "Okay, I'll talk to you tomorrow."

An officer stepped toward us from Leo's other side. "Sir, we need to get statements from both of you."

"Tomorrow."

"I'm afraid I must insist. The sooner we can get statements, the more detailed they tend to be. If I could just have you . . ."

"Tomorrow," Leo gritted out. He tilted his head toward me. "She needs rest. I'll ensure that both of us are made available to your office for whatever questions you may have, *tomorrow.*" The ease with which he commanded authority in his effort to protect me was striking.

The officer sighed and held out a hand with a card pressed

between his fingers. "Give me a call tomorrow morning. And, uh"—he turned to me—"get some rest."

"Thank you," I replied on an exhale.

Leo continued to navigate us through the club, steering us toward the back entrance. I realized there was still a twenty-minute walk ahead to get to my apartment, and I nearly crumbled to the floor at the thought.

"I drove my car today," Leo murmured reassuringly at the curve of my ear, as if he'd read my thoughts.

"Oh, thank god," I mumbled. I was exhausted. I wanted to bury myself beneath my comforter and disappear for the next week.

Chapter Fourteen

It had finally begun to rain, the current downpour strong enough to have us both soaking wet by the time we reached Leo's car—a swanky black two-door Bentley that did *not* belong in the parking lot behind Larkspur. He opened the passenger door before lowering me into the seat, both hands braced around my forearms. "I'm going to ruin your car," I groaned as he pulled the seat belt across my chest and clicked it in. This was too nice of a car for me to be a sopping mess inside of, especially knowing I'd just been lying on the floor of a nightclub bathroom. The seat alone was probably more expensive than my whole apartment.

"Fuck the car," Leo muttered as he shut the door before rounding to the other side, glancing my way as he got in and put his own seat belt on. I could almost feel the hum of his anger as he took off, navigating through the downtown city streets. It was only a few minutes before he was pulling into the parking garage beneath his building, forgoing the valet and finding a spot as close to the elevators as possible.

"You brought me to your place." It wasn't a question.

He nodded. "I need to stay with you tonight, and I didn't want to assume an invitation to yours. But if it makes you more comfortable, I'm happy to grab an overnight bag and take you there, instead." Despite the anger that still rippled across his face, his words were soft and gentle.

I considered that for a moment. As much as I wanted my own bed, I didn't like the idea of Leo seeing my apartment. It would be . . . too intimate. Even through the dull ache of my current numbness, it would only take one more crack in the iron tonight before I truly shattered apart. Plus, I was supposed to start staying here tomorrow anyway—his parents were coming into town, and we still had our contract to abide by. "I'm okay staying here, but I don't have any clothes."

His throat bobbed as he swallowed, his eyes falling to my fishnets before rising back to my face. "I have plenty of extra shirts and sweats. You can use whatever you want . . . if you're comfortable with it, that is. I can also ask the concierge to pick something up for you, though I'm not sure if any stores are open at this hour."

I wrung my hands together. "No, that's okay. I'm sure whatever you have will be fine." My tongue felt thick in my mouth at the thought of wearing Leo's clothing, but I didn't have any fight in me. He helped me avoid the hospital, even though I knew he wanted me to go. The least I could do was make this easy on him.

He got out of the car before helping me out, then guided me toward the elevator with a strong but careful hold. As much I wanted to walk on my own, my head was pounding and my knees felt weak as they carried me forward, so I gratefully leaned into Leo's frame and allowed him to carry some of my weight.

When we entered his dark penthouse, Swift came running to investigate, meowing happily as she danced at Leo's feet. Dolly sat stoically on the area rug in the living room, tail twitching as she observed from a distance. I hadn't expected to see them again. "I'm not sure Dolly likes me," I said quietly.

Leo almost smiled, the ghost of it there and gone in an instant. "She's a little tougher to crack, but she'll come around —don't worry."

I'm not worried, I wanted to say. I might be spending more time here over the next week, but I wasn't going to let myself get too close to anything or anyone during my stay. It'd be better that way—this was nothing but a transactional agreement. *Business*.

We moved toward Leo's bedroom, where I'd run from only days ago never expecting to return, and my body tensed halfway down the hallway. He must have felt it, because he looked down at me with an edge of concern. "You can take my room tonight. You'll have the bed all to yourself," he assured. As though my concerns were tied only within the sleeping arrangements.

But it was more than that. The last time I was here, I spent *hours* allowing myself to fantasize about what it would be like to belong to a place like this with someone like Leo. Imagining what it would be like if this were *my* home, too. And now, I was going to have to act out that very fantasy in real life and do it well enough to convince his parents.

It seemed so . . . unbelievable.

Pressure pinched between my shoulder blades, driving

further discomfort through my body. Leo stood patiently, giving me an opportunity to argue against sleeping in his bed. But I was too tired to argue. I'd have to sleep there anyway, right? The show must go on.

"Works for me." It came out in a whisper, and I hoped he wouldn't press the subject further. But he didn't, and we began moving again toward the half-open door at the end of the hallway. "I'd like to shower, please. I . . ." I paused, finding the right words. "I need to feel clean."

Leo nodded. "Of course. You can use the bathroom in here, and I'll work on gathering some clothes for you to sleep in." He swallowed, his jaw clenching as we made our way through the threshold of his bedroom. Reflexively, my eyes jumped to the large bed. "Will you be okay in there on your own?"

A flush crawled up my neck. "Yes."

"Okay." He nodded again, though his brow was wrinkled in thought. "Take as long as you need . . . but I'm going to check in on you every few minutes, okay? If the heat from the water makes you dizzy, just call out for help. Try not to push yourself."

Worry was evident in his expressive eyes as he looked down at me—they were like windows right into his thoughts. It made my heart clench. "I'm okay, Leo," I said on a shaky breath.

He hummed, though he looked unconvinced. "Would it be okay if . . ." He paused, sighing through his nose as he looked at the floor before his eyes lifted back up to mine. ". . . if I hugged you?"

Well, I definitely hadn't been expecting *that*. "You want to hug me?"

"I just . . ." He seemed to struggle to form the words, his

deep, rumbling voice catching somewhere in his throat. "I feel like you could use a hug after . . . everything. And if it's all right, I'd really like to give you one."

There was a subtle mark of vulnerability in the way his lips pressed together, hidden under a much more obvious layer of determination. Something about it pierced me in my lungs, making it harder to breathe. "Okay," was all I could think to say back.

He moved toward me with a single, tentative step until his chin was mere inches from the top of my head. And then his broad shoulders flexed as he lifted his arms, slowly wrapping them around my much smaller frame. He held me with a gentle, careful pressure that made me feel like I was floating up and into him. Like we might be hovering right off the floor. I was so shocked by the entire encounter that I never even moved my own arms to return his embrace. Before I knew what was happening, he was releasing me, jostling my nerve endings with the loss of his warmth.

"Are you mad at me?" I blurted. I couldn't help it—I wasn't sorry for what I'd done, and I hated the thought of caring about what he thought, but truthfully I did.

His jaw tensed and his eyes hardened. "No, Mara. I'm not mad at you." Still, something wicked swirled beneath the surface of his gaze. A lock of dark hair fell against his brow as he dipped his head once. "I'll give you some privacy . . . but I'm right here if you need anything at all." And then he turned to walk out of his bedroom, leaving me alone with a new frenzy of thoughts.

I KEPT the shower relatively quick. It had taken me a while to be comfortable closing my eyes for long periods of time—it became the perfect opportunity for unwanted thoughts to creep in years ago when I was neck-deep in my fear and anxiety issues. Tonight's events brought some of those fears back to the surface, and while the hot spray felt like heaven on my skin, the time alone in my head made me nauseous with unease.

Of course—that might have also been the concussion. Either way, I didn't think staying under the water for too long was a good idea.

After slipping out of the shower and finding a fresh towel, I heard Leo at the door, his voice calm and controlled. "Mara, are you doing okay?"

"Yep!" I called out, cringing at how cheery I sounded.

"Okay, I'm leaving some clothes out here on the bed. I'll shut the door and wait in the living room while you get dressed. Will you meet me out there when you're done?"

I stared at my blurred form through the steamed mirror. "Sure, no problem!"

Quiet footsteps sounded, followed by the muffled click of a door latching. I turned the cool metal handle and peeked out into the bedroom, finding it empty. Leo had turned one lamp on in the corner so I could see better, but hadn't turned on the main light of the room. Eyeing the floor-to-ceiling window on the other side of the bed, I figured it was his way of offering some privacy. I wondered if it might also be because he knew my head was aching, and that a bright light would only add to it.

Making quick work of letting the towel drop to the floor and pulling on the gray sweats and sweater set Leo left out, I tried to ignore the warmth in my chest for all he was doing for me. I already knew Leo had a way of knocking right past my defenses, but nothing good ever came from giving away my softer parts. I was more than certain that at his core, Leo was a good man. But even still, that wouldn't stop me from holding tight to my vulnerability.

After picking up the towel off the floor, I made my way out and down the hallway to find Leo seated on his couch. He was still wearing his dress clothes, and the creases around his eyes looked etched in stone as he stared at the turned-off television screen. The lights in this room were dim as well, and I knew it for what it was—he was trying to keep me as comfortable as possible.

He heard my footsteps and looked up, his gaze meeting mine with a look of intensity that nearly sent me to my knees. "Are you okay?" he asked quietly as he stood up.

I honestly wasn't sure how to answer that. My head still pounded, but I knew that physically, I was fine. Mentally, the logistics of what happened tonight were clear and I could objectively keep the facts straight—the attack had nothing to do with me. I wasn't the intended victim; I'd merely jumped into a bad situation before it could get worse.

Emotionally, though, I felt like I was skating on pretty thin ice.

My chest felt like a vise, like it might rupture at any moment.

"All things considered, I'm okay." It was as honest as I could get.

He looked at me for a long moment before his eyes moved to my temple. "Your head?"

I shrugged. "I've had worse."

I'd meant it as a joke, as a way to lighten the tension in the room. But I could see from Leo's face that I'd accomplished the opposite. "Fucking hell," he mumbled, shaking his head as he walked toward me. When he reached me, he lifted his hand as if to check it himself, but then paused. "May I?"

I nodded, and he carefully brushed my hair away from my temple to get a better look at where my skin had ripped open. The paramedics hadn't bandaged it, instead giving instructions to Leo on how to care for it after I'd gotten cleaned up.

He sucked in a quiet breath as he looked it over. "I've got some ointment we should probably put on it."

"Okay," I agreed, and he led me to the kitchen so I could sit on a stool. It was the same stool where I'd eaten his pasta only a few nights ago, and the thought made my stomach flip.

There was already a first aid kit waiting on the counter, and as he reached inside of it, I noticed his knuckles.

"What happened to you?" I asked, my gaze stuck on the splotchy red skin that looked like new bruises around the knuckles of his right hand. I hadn't noticed it before, hadn't seen it in the car or when he brought me up to his apartment.

"What do you mean?"

"Your . . . your hand." My eyes shot back up to his. "He hurt you, too?"

He looked at me. "No, Mara." He paused, his gaze flooding with severity. "When I went into that bathroom and saw you on the floor, I . . . I lost it. He was holding his own face, bleeding from his nose, but I didn't care." He didn't say more, but I didn't need him to.

"Oh," I whispered. It suddenly felt like the kitchen was on fire.

"This might sting a little," he murmured, squeezing out a bit of ointment on the pad of his finger before reaching again to push back my hair. I closed my eyes as I felt his finger brush softly against my temple and, despite the sting, I found myself leaning into his touch. His fingers lingered before his hand slid down my face toward my jaw.

When I fluttered my lashes open again, I found his blue eyes sparking with emotion, and I almost couldn't bear it—couldn't bear for him to be so affected by this. "I'm okay, Leo. And I'm sorry you had to take me in tonight."

He shook his head firmly. "There's no reason for you to be sorry, Mara. Trust me, I wouldn't want you anywhere else."

That same ache rose up in my chest at his kindness, and it was too much. "I'm not your responsibility. Contract or not, I don't need you to take care of me."

His eyes flashed, and the corner of his mouth tugged up for only a second before his lips pressed firmly together. "You beautiful, vicious dragon," he said, his hand stroking against my cheek. "There is nothing wrong with you showing your teeth, but I'm worried about the things you keep inside this mind of yours. If you need someone to bite, I can take it. Whatever you need so that the fire doesn't eat you alive—let it out with me, sweetheart. I want to burn with you."

A flood of tears sprang forward and I couldn't stop them from leaking out. Leo tenderly wiped them away before pulling me in and tucking me into his chest. This time, I wrapped my own arms around him tightly. "Thank you," I whispered into his shirt.

After a moment, we pulled away from each other, and Leo gave me his best reassuring smile. "Let's get you into bed—you need to rest."

Chapter Fifteen

I ENDURED A FITFUL NIGHT OF SLEEP, VISIONS OF murky brown eyes and a vile silver skull ring haunting my every dream. Leo woke me up each hour with a soft nudge to the shoulder, asking me simple questions to ensure my brain hadn't turned to mush—apparently on Beatrice's strict orders as part of the deal to keep me out of the hospital. Though, I didn't mind replacing the brown eyes of my nightmares with Leo's crisp, misty blues in the shadows of his bedroom. It was a deep relief, each time.

As promised, he yielded his entire bed for me to sleep in. But he didn't quite let me loose from his watchful eye, choosing to sleep on the large chaise lounge that was tucked in the corner of his bedroom against the wall of windows that looked down upon the twinkling city. A twinge of guilt brewed within me when I saw him fold his large body into the chair, his bare feet hanging off the end under a throw blanket. But I also didn't harness the bravery to offer up the other side of the bed. I knew my limits.

My eyes resentfully opened in response to Leo's latest attempt to rouse me. He was whispering my name, skating his finger along my arm. My skin exploded in goosebumps from his touch, and I rolled beneath the heavy comforter to face him, noticing the amber light that danced along his face from the window next to the bed.

I'd made it through the darkness.

"Good morning," he said in a raspy morning voice. He was wearing a pair of black-rimmed glasses that made him look less like a wealthy business investor and more . . . human. "Just checking on you. How do you feel?"

I pressed a palm to my forehead, fighting through the fog of fatigue to take inventory of my body. My head still pulsed uncomfortably, but nothing like the pain from last night. My wrist was sore from the hit I'd gotten in, but all things considered, I felt lucky. "I'm okay," I responded honestly through my own sleepy grit. "Much better."

Leo's mouth curved in a pleased smile. "There's breakfast waiting for you in the kitchen whenever you're ready. No rush . . . if you want to sleep a little longer."

"No," I said, pushing up onto my elbows. "I'm actually starving." The corners of his mouth rose a bit higher, though his eyes kept watch over my face.

"Okay." He stood to his full height and held out a hand to help me out of bed. "Let's go get you something to eat."

Leo let me lead the way toward the kitchen, his long sweatpants pooling around my feet as I walked. I'd rolled the waistband as many times as I could, but I still practically swam in his clothes. The gray sweater he'd lent me fell down to my knees.

I could feel his eyes on me from where he followed closely behind, and I turned around halfway down the hall only to find that scrutinizing look blazing in them. It seemed he took his instructions from Beatrice very seriously. "I'm fine," I asserted. All things considered, I knew I *would* be fine. I just needed to deal with a little salt in some old wounds.

My eyes widened in surprise as soon as we rounded into the kitchen to find the island covered in various food items. I spotted pastry boxes, plastic to-go containers, and even a couple of rolled burritos tucked in parchment paper. Eyes on Leo again, I asked, "What is all this?"

He shrugged. "I didn't know what kind of breakfast you'd like, so I had the concierge run out and grab a bit of everything."

My chest fluttered, and I tried my best to stamp the feeling down. "It's incredibly wasteful." I regretted the words as soon as they left my mouth. Here was this man, going above and beyond to provide me with some much-needed sustenance after practically babysitting me all night, and I was complaining.

But Leo grinned as he leaned against the wall, crossing his arms over his plain white T-shirt. He looked like a dream in his casual clothes, slim fitting black joggers hugging his strong thighs. "I'll ensure that whatever you don't touch is provided to the staff downstairs. They can take their pick so nothing goes to *waste*."

I pursed my lips. "How about it goes to the homeless outside?" There was no shortage of people to feed who weren't as privileged as the people inside this building—I'd passed by many of them on my walks to and from work.

Something flashed in his steely eyes, his grin never leaving his face. "Okay, Mara," he agreed. "I'll make sure of it."

I looked at all the food, moving closer to inspect the contents of each container. Eyeing one full of biscuits and gravy, I pulled it toward me before reaching back out to grab a small container of fresh fruit. "This is perfect," I said. "Thank you."

Leo pushed off the wall to find a fork for me in one of his kitchen drawers, reaching to hand it over across the island. "So, I know this is probably the last thing you want to think about right now, but unfortunately my parents are due to arrive this afternoon." He placed both hands on the edge of the island, using the surface to support some of his weight as he looked intently at me. "I'm not . . ." He paused, swallowing as he seemed to collect himself. "Please understand that there are no expectations around your involvement. After last night—"

"You're rescinding the contract?" I interrupted through a full mouth of food.

He sighed. "Mara, after what happened last night, I couldn't possibly ask you to parade around some fake fairytale just to help me appease my stifling parents. It's . . . selfish. Beyond selfish. And you—"

"No," I cut him off again, before I could even fully process his words. It was like my mouth had a mind of its own. I mean, not having to follow through with that ridiculous deal *did* sound tempting, but it would mean reversing the part where I got Larkspur in the end. "I don't want to cancel it."

He arched an eyebrow. "You don't?"

"No. I'm still in. I . . ." I would never in a million years confess this out loud, especially not to Leo, but after everything that happened last night, after all of these old wounds had been reopened, I *needed* a distraction like this. Something I could exert some control over. And the deepest, rawest parts of me knew the one real truth that I didn't want to admit even to myself—I didn't want to be alone. "I would like to continue as planned. I'm fine, really. Last night was . . . a shitty thing that happened. I don't want to wallow in it."

Even as I said the words, I could feel my body flushing with an icy heat. So I gave myself a reprieve from his gaze and instead looked down at my food, shoveling a piece of biscuit and sausage into my mouth.

"Are you sure?" Leo asked tentatively, obviously unconvinced.

I didn't look up at him as I answered, focused on stabbing a sliced strawberry with my fork. "Definitely."

After what felt like a full minute, he sighed. "Okay." He sounded tired, and I knew it had everything to do with my takeover of his bedroom last night.

"I'm going to have to get some things from my place, since I'll be *living* here and all." I finally looked up at him. "I think I'm going to go home to pack a few bags and get out of your hair for an hour or two. I'm sure you'd like a little time to yourself."

"No, I'll take you."

My shoulders dropped. "Leo, you're exhausted. I already ruined your night, don't let me ruin your day, too."

He scoffed. "You most certainly did not ruin my night, Mara. While I desperately wish you hadn't run after that man and gotten hurt, I understand why you did it. And you are also not going to be the reason today is ruined, either. *That* will undoubtedly be accomplished by my father."

I sighed. "Well, what if I just need a minute to myself?"

"I'd normally give it without another thought. But so long as you have a 'probable concussion,' I'm responsible for making sure you don't drop dead from a brain bleed. You're still on my watch for . . ." He looked at the digital display on his silver microwave. ". . . fourteen more hours. Which means, you're not going anywhere without me."

I dropped my head back and looked up at the ceiling, knowing there was no use in fighting him on this, and choosing to ignore the flare of ridiculous excitement that lined my stomach. "Fine."

MY KEYS JANGLED in my hand as I worked to unlock my door, knocking against the mini-canister of pepper spray that hung from the silver hoop. Leo watched from where he stood, stiff and robotic like he was my bodyguard and not my . . . Hm. *What is he?* A friend felt like a stretch—though, I supposed if we were going to be successful with our ruse this week, we needed to convince others we were much more than that.

Still forced to wear his clothes—admittedly a better alternative to last night's skimpy work outfit—I turned to eye him warily as I pushed open the heavy door to my studio apartment. "It's small," I warned him before he even had a chance to say anything. "Not all of us can afford penthouses, and it's only me, so it's just—"

"Nice," interrupted Leo as he stepped through, looking around at my six-hundred-square-foot safe haven. He'd swapped his glasses for contacts, but had still kept it casual in his joggers and tee, adding only a half-zip athletic sweater before we ventured here. Leo had insisted on driving, but I wanted to feel the early sunlight on my face, the cold air from last night's rain in my lungs.

Leo's gaze landed on my pink velvet couch adorned with forest green decorative pillows. "It's nice in here, Mara. Very . . . you."

I felt my skin tighten around my body, compressing against my bones. No one else had been inside my apartment in over a year, and to see *him* here, scanning over my things while probably doing his best to keep a straight face—it made me feel more exposed than I would have liked to feel around him. "You can just take a seat." I waved toward the couch, thankful I'd at least had the foresight to put all my clean underwear away from where it'd been piled there yesterday morning. "I'll just be a few minutes."

He nodded, seating himself into a worn cushion as his strong legs splayed wide open. My couch looked like doll furniture with him on it. Quickly turning away from the sight, I tried to pretend like he wasn't here at all as I started pulling enough clothes for the week out of various dresser drawers, stuffing them into a beige canvas duffle as I went. I made sure to grab my birth control pills off my nightstand—an assurance I still found comfort in despite my recent lack of intimacy with men.

Halfway through my packing, my phone vibrated from where I'd tossed it on my bed. A picture of my parents appeared on the screen—a photo I'd taken the last time I saw them, my father's arm wrapped around my mother's shoulder as she looked up at him with a soft smile. I'd taken it on a whim in the kitchen one night, wanting to capture proof of their easy love so I could remember something like that was possible.

Glancing back toward Leo, I found him absentmindedly taking in the details of my apartment—the green lava lamp on the end of the TV console, a framed poster of Fleetwood Mac on the wall next to the fridge, the string of white fairy lights that I'd fastened to the ceiling. If I didn't answer this call from my parents now, I'd have to call them back later. It was Sunday, and I'd promised till I was blue in the face that, at the very least, I'd make time for them each week and provide evidence that I was still alive and kicking. Before I could talk myself out of it, I swiped my thumb to answer the call and changed the audio setting to speaker-mode so I could keep packing. "Hey, guys," I said quietly, glancing at Leo again a bit self-consciously.

"My baby girl!" My father's baritone voice rumbled through the phone, and Leo turned to find me watching him.

I quickly turned away.

"How are things going?" I asked, hoping to keep the attention on them for as much of this phone call as I could.

"Oh, we're good, honey," my mom answered. The sound of her cheerful voice always drove a nail of guilt into my chest. Both she and my dad were such happy, loving parents, and I knew how lucky I was for it. But there was a chasm between us. It was a horrible, yawning thing—full of all my secrets and shame.

Old remnants of cigarette smoke wafted around me, and I closed my eyes to dispel the ghost of my past.

Seth had ruined so many fucking things.

"That's good," I said. "Dad, you finish building the shed yet?" He'd retired from his construction job last year and was still trying to figure out how to occupy his time.

He chuckled. "Not yet, but I'm close."

"You know the other day I found him out back, furious

and beet-red, working on that thing," my mom jumped in. My father chuckled again, and it made me smile to imagine it. "I thought you were supposed to find hobbies that didn't feel like work," she kindly chided.

"I like the work just fine. I'm a man who needs to keep my hands busy." It was true—my father had always placed his self-worth in things he could make and build. He wasn't the smartest or the savviest of businessmen, but he could outwork anyone. I knew his retirement was a big deal to him, that he didn't feel ready to let that part of him go. But he was getting older, and construction work wasn't getting any easier.

"Well, I can't wait to see it next time I'm home," I said lightly, though the words instantly made me anxious.

My mother latched on. "When do you think you'll come home to visit, honey? Lord knows we miss you something fierce."

I sighed. Knowing they were a less-than-thirty-minute drive away from the city definitely didn't help on the guilt front, because lately I was only seeing them a handful of times a year. "I know. I'm just . . . busy. Things at the club have been a little up and down, and there's a few things I have to see through. But the holidays are coming up—I'll try to come home more, okay?" The lie tasted sour on my tongue.

"Maybe you'll have a nice girl to bring home with you?" Mom asked. "Or a nice young man?"

I refused to look, but I could feel Leo's eyes burning on the back of my neck. "Who knows," was all I said. After Seth, I'd built a pretty strong wall between myself and the rest of the world—including my parents. They'd known my interest these last few years had been on girls, despite never having a firm discussion about my sexuality or how I chose to define it. I wasn't even sure *I'd* known how to define it. Until Leo, I'd had no interest in any new men. Now, I wasn't so sure.

"You know, there's a nice young man who moved in down the street, where Mrs. DeSoto used to live! I think he lives alone —maybe you could stop by and introduce yourself next time you're here?"

"Leave our poor daughter alone," my dad gruffed. "She doesn't have time for men . . . or women . . . do ya, honey?" Leo snorted, and I whipped my head to glare at him. *Shit!* Things went silent on the other side of the phone line. Eventually, I could hear my father take a deep breath. "You have company with you, honey?"

"No," I blurted. "It's just the TV. I'm . . . the news is on while I clean."

"Oh," he responded, his voice considerably lighter again— thank god. "Well, we don't want to keep you too long, we know you're a busy little lady. Everything going okay? Anything you need, baby girl?" Again, the twinge in my heart, the shame that felt like poison.

"I'm okay," I assured them as best I could. "I promise. I miss you guys, and I can't wait to see you soon." I needed to visit them—I knew I needed to. There were so many things that were left unsaid over the years, and I wanted nothing more than to lay it all at their feet . . . If only I could bring myself to. They were so good to me, so supportive of me bartending even if they didn't understand it. They didn't make me feel bad about my piercings or colored hair—hell, they were just desperate for any piece of my life I would share.

But that was the problem. Because if I gave them everything—if I told them the truth about Seth, about the abuse—I wasn't sure they'd be able to handle something like that. I just . . . I couldn't do it to them.

"You know our door is always open. You don't even have to ask—just come over any time, okay?"

My eyes stung and my breaths came more rapidly. "Okay, Daddy." I wanted to slip into the body of my six-year-old self and crawl into his lap for one of his powerful hugs. I used to think I would forever be invincible with a dad whose presence was so large and formidable and protective, like nothing could ever hurt me. But sometimes the monsters under the bed grew up to be six feet tall and handsome, and you never saw the danger until it was too late.

After saying quick goodbyes and hanging up, I refocused on stacking columns of clothes in the duffle bag, ignoring the slippery slope of emotion swirling through me, the uncomfortable tension pressing into my ribs. But I wasn't alone, and there was a static energy in the room that was being directly sourced from the man on my couch. Eventually, he spoke. "You aren't going to tell your parents about what happened to you?"

I balked. It took me a moment to realize he'd meant what happened last night. "No," I answered on a shaky breath. "Of course not."

"Why not?"

I turned around and threw Leo a hard look. "What do you mean *why not*?"

He watched me carefully. "They seem like nice people. It's obvious how much they care about you. Why not let them support you through it?"

Wiping a falling tear off my cheek, I turned away from him again. "There are plenty of things I choose not to worry them with." It would break their hearts to know how much I'd suffered.

"Is there anyone you *do* allow into your life enough to support you?" he asked. "Perhaps that woman from last night?"

If you need someone to bite, I can take it.

"Leave Charlea out of this."

A pause. "Are you in a relationship with her?"

Throwing a pair of pants down on the bed with force, I turned and marched toward him. "Just stop, Leo. We aren't going to do this, okay? I appreciate you looking out for me last night, and I understand what's expected of me for the next week. But please don't get it twisted—you *aren't* my boyfriend, and my personal life has nothing to do with you. Okay?"

Leo smoldered as he rose from the couch. "You put yourself in serious danger! *Someone* should know about it. If I hadn't gotten there—when I saw that you were hurt, it was like I couldn't breathe, Mara. It makes me crazy to think about the danger you were in. How is that not just as devastating to you?"

Whatever you need so that the fire doesn't eat you alive—let it out with me, sweetheart.

My eyes welled with tears again. "It *is*, of course it is. I let my guard down. You know it was the same guy who bailed on his tab? I told you he was a 'generally-safe' kind of creep . . . I'm so stupid." I scoffed, shaking my head. "You were right to be concerned—the cameras, the extra security, you were right to bring it all in. After bartending for so long, it's like I've come to expect bad behavior. I've gotten numb to the fact that they're still everywhere, and it's *not* okay! That pisses me off more, because what gives? What's it going to take to ensure everyone who steps into the club can feel safe?"

Leo's fist closed, his fingers squeezing together. "I don't know. But you're not stupid, Mara. And you're not alone in figuring it out, okay? Don't take on this kind of pain alone. I'm here, and I'm going to help you figure it out. I promise you that."

I could tell he meant it, that last night had rocked him in a way that made him want to fight, too. And it jarred me, a little. Maybe having his support *could* help. "Thank you," I murmured from where I still stood.

He glanced briefly at the duffle bag on my bed. "One battle at a time. Let's get you packed and settled at my place. We still need to give statements to the police about what happened." He blew out a breath and rolled his jaw. "And then, we have to face my parents."

Chapter Sixteen

We dropped my things off at Leo's apartment, then took his car down to the police station to give our statements. The officers took pictures of the bruising on the side of my face, on my hands, as well as the marks on Leo's knuckles to document our injuries in support of our statements. While it was more than obvious what had happened last night, they'd explained that detailed documentation was needed in case the man—Benjamin Carroll—fought the charges against him.

It turned out there were charges stacked against him—going back farther than his visits to Larkspur. After his arrest last night, the fingerprints Benjamin had given during his booking tied him to an armed robbery that had occurred at a known drug dealer's house in a nearby town earlier in the week. His description also matched multiple reports from assault victims across the city who'd come forward to describe how they'd been forced into nightclub bathrooms and aggressively groped during their struggle to escape.

All things considered, the officers in the department repeatedly shared that it was very lucky no one had gotten more injured and that, by all accounts, Leo and I were to thank for his apprehension.

I was more upset than anything to learn that he'd hurt other women—but, as Leo gently reminded me, he'd been caught. Now we just needed to hone our efforts on safety resources at the club. Benjamin Carroll caught us during a perfect storm when a large fight had broken out on the dance floor. Frank and the rest of the security team were so focused on getting the fighters—all seven of them—out of the club, so no one noticed anything else was wrong until Leo spotted me jumping over the bar.

"Trust me when I say the executive security team I'm bringing on will be paramount to our success," he said as we drove back to his place. "They're practiced in identifying and neutralizing any risk that might present itself."

"You make them sound like a SWAT team," I muttered, keeping my gaze out the car window.

"It's a private company comprised of ex-Special Forces. Their contracts typically focus on protection services for a single party, but I put enough money behind a deal with the owner to ensure we get a handful of their best guys to use their skills in ways that will serve Larkspur."

I had to admit, I was impressed Leo had pushed for this even *before* last night. "All this because I told you a customer was creepy?" I looked at where he sat behind the steering wheel of his Bentley.

His eyes dimmed as he adjusted in his seat. "That was enough," was all he said.

I looked out my window. "What time do your parents get in?"

"Sometime this afternoon. I asked for a more concrete timeframe, but I think my father prefers I sweat in anticipation."

"Are you really that nervous to see them?"

Leo scrubbed a hand over his face. "Not normally. My father has always enjoyed any opportunity to intimidate me, but for the most part, I stopped being scared of him when I was a teenager. I just don't enjoy him—he's a brutal man, in business and in his personal life. And it's been a year since I've seen either of my parents. I'm expecting a near-vicious level of scrutiny after my little disappearing act . . . which is why I wanted to bring you in."

I considered his words. "Yesterday morning, when you asked me to do this, you said it would help explain your absence."

Leo looked at me briefly before his eyes were back on the road. "Yes," he confirmed, though there was a slight hesitation in his tone.

"You bought Larkspur less than a week ago. What have you been doing in Denver for a whole year?"

"Oh. Well . . . I attempted to get back to the basics. I mean . . ." He gripped the steering wheel tight, the skin of his knuckles going white. "I realized I didn't know *what* to do, exactly. So I spent some time on that, on myself."

"A whole year?" I asked. "Just . . . getting to know yourself?"

He flashed his eyes at me again, quick as a whip. "Mm-hm." There was definitely more that he wasn't telling me, but I didn't want to press.

Not yet, anyway.

Leo pulled his Bentley into his designated parking space and trailed close behind me as we made our way up to my new home. All things considered, I felt good. Granted, it was possible that in response to the roller coaster ride that my life had turned into, I'd finally become delusional enough to enter into a state of blind acceptance.

I couldn't help but think, though, that last night's attack at Larkspur had shoved Leo and I into a potential truce. It might've been a loose truce, built on a nearly nonexistent foundation, but as I stood next to him in the elevator on our ascent up to his sparkling apartment, I realized I didn't feel so nervous about the week to come.

NEITHER OF US were going into Larkspur tonight—it was my night off anyway, and Leo didn't go because he had to keep an eye on me, or so he said. With his parents coming, he would have been mostly absent anyway, so I didn't feel too bad about him staying home because of me.

I'd received texts from Nora, Sam, Frank, and Ethan throughout the day, all checking on me and making sure I was okay. Each one of them made the knot in my chest loosen just a little—it felt nice to have people who genuinely cared about me, as if they were real friends and not just people I worked with every day.

Charlea had also texted a few times over the course of the afternoon, and that made me smile too—though, I found myself keeping my conversation with her light enough to avoid making plans. There was no way I could explain my little arrangement with Leo without sounding absolutely insane, and it wasn't like she was my girlfriend. I'd settled on the choice to wait until Leo and I got through this week together, and then go from there.

Something told me I'd need the release that came with a sexy sleepover.

I sat quietly at Leo's kitchen island. Just like last time, his skills were captivating, and the food smelled absolutely divine. I was fully engrossed as the gorgeous man in front of me expertly sautéed blackberries and pears with a generous splash of red wine while lamb chops roasted in the oven. He was making a chutney *from scratch*, apparently. Another pan on the stove was full of seared potatoes and carrots seasoned with rosemary and thyme.

"Where'd you learn to cook like this?" I asked as my mouth watered.

He turned to face me, a cocky smirk spreading along his handsome face. "My grandfather taught me most of what I know. I started cooking with him when I'd visit him and my grandmother as a boy, and liked it so much that I took a few classes in college."

"Wow," I said on an exhale. "It's pretty amazing." My skills in the kitchen were far more frivolous, but I *could* make a mean grilled cheese sandwich. My mom was the one who always cooked meals for our family, but I was never interested enough to hang around and learn from her.

The thought sent a pang of regret through my chest.

Leo's smirk dazzled brighter as he gave me a quick wink before turning to the pot in front of him. He wore an off-white sweater that looked so soft I had to stop myself from reaching out and touching it. Soon, the elevator chimed from the front entryway, signaling it was on its way up from the lobby, and I watched his body visibly stiffen as his back grew rigid.

"Are you okay?" I whisper-shouted across the expansive island, as if the people thirty feet away and tucked inside an elevator car would be able to hear me.

He turned to look at me, the easy smirk no longer present. Instead, his face was twisted in anxiety as his eyes seemed to search mine for something. Taking in a deep breath, he nodded. "This will be fine," he said, more to himself than to me. But it wasn't very convincing.

I was wearing one of my nicer shirts, black cotton with sheer, flowing sleeves that tapered to a cuff at each wrist. Dark denim jeans hugged my waist and thighs. I'd curled my hair as well—I didn't really care about what his parents thought of me, but it was important that my being Leo's girlfriend was believable, so I wanted to give it my best shot. Especially after he'd stepped up to look after me last night.

And, *most* importantly, because Larkspur was on the line.

Leo used the kitchen towel resting over his shoulder to wipe his hands down before throwing it on the counter and marching toward the elevator doors. I stood up and trailed a few feet behind him, forcing a smile on my face and remembering the goal here—Leo and I were supposed to be in love. With that in mind, I skipped forward and tucked myself into his side when I reached him, throwing an arm around his middle. I tried not to notice how firm and muscular his torso felt. He looked down at me with a puzzled look, but I flashed him my brightest fake smile. "Put your arm around me," I said behind clenched teeth.

His face morphed into what looked like shock. But then

the elevator doors were opening, and he swung a large arm around my shoulders at the last second. We both turned to face the older couple.

The man was tall, but not quite as tall as Leo. His skin was the same deep olive tone that held a sharp contrast to the white button-up dress shirt he wore under a tailored black suit. It seemed Leo got his jaw line and chestnut hair—and fondness for luxury—from his father. He carried what looked like a large black overcoat in one arm while this other hand held a designer suitcase.

Next to him was a thin woman with jet-black hair and blue eyes the same color as Leo's, except where Leo's were bright and glittering, hers were cold and sharp as they assessed us both with a heavy look. She wore a posh blue dress and a fur jacket that was cut at the waist. Swift—suddenly appearing from behind the front entryway table—rubbed affectionately against my ankle before she let out a soft meow, and I watched Leo's mother's gaze drop down to stare at the cat as a frown formed on her face.

For a long moment, we all simply stared at each other. Leo's arm had tightened so firmly around my shoulders that it squeezed my bones against each other, but I kept the fake, toothy smile plastered on my face. Eventually, Leo spurred into movement and stepped forward to reach for his father's suitcase, his gorgeous hair slipping down across his forehead. "Here, let me—"

"Hello, son." His father's voice wasn't loud, but it commanded attention.

Leo's arm dropped to his side as he straightened again. He nodded once. "Hello, Dad."

His father's eyes trailed around the foyer. "Nice place you

have here." It sounded like a compliment, but it didn't feel like one.

Leo swiped a hand through his hair, pushing it back up and off his face. "I hope you both are hungry . . . I've got dinner almost ready in the kitchen." He reached for the suitcase again. "Here, let me take this from you." After taking a hold of the handle and pulling it toward himself, he let go of it to lean in and kiss his mother on the cheek. "Hi, Mom. You look well."

His mother's frown straightened. "Thank you, dear." Her eyes moved past him and landed on me, and it was like suddenly being under a microscope with the way she scanned me up and down. "Who's this?"

I felt like an idiot, standing here with a wide smile glued to my face. But ready or not, the performance was on. Leo turned to face me, a grin spreading on his own face. And though it was obvious how tense he was, I didn't miss the way his eyes twinkled as he moved to resume his place next to me, abandoning the suitcase. His arm snaked around me again, and goosebumps rose along my neck. "This . . ." he said, before pressing a small kiss to the side of my head. It was warm and soft and so unexpected I nearly squeaked. "This is Mara. Mara"—his eyes moved to his parents—"this is my mom and dad."

Both of his parents stared at me blankly. I felt my smile falter for a moment before I forced it back up and stepped forward, holding my hand out in front of me toward Leo's father. "Nice to meet you . . ."

"Alaric," he finished for me, taking my hand into his for only a second before he let it go. His hands were cold from the October air outside, but I wondered if he might be this frigid all the time. "And this is my wife, Christine."

Pivoting to face his mother, I found her eyes fastened to my septum ring. "It's so nice to meet you, too," I said tightly.

Christine's gaze bounced from my piercing to her son behind me, disdain evident in her features. "You have a . . . friend?"

Leo cleared his throat, pulling gently on my arm to tuck me back into his side. It was an immense relief. "Girlfriend," he corrected, sounding more confident than he had mere moments ago. "Mara is my girlfriend."

Christine's eyes widened as they snapped to me. "Oh, how lovely."

Leo smiled before pressing another kiss into my hair. I'd worn enough makeup to hide the bruising around my temple, but worried slightly that Leo might accidentally ruin it with how much he was kissing me there. "Right, okay, let's get you both settled in and then we can sit for dinner, yes?"

Alaric nodded. "Sounds great, we're starved."

Leo showed his parents to their room on the opposite side of the apartment where a small hallway led to two additional bedrooms and a bathroom, and while they got settled in, I headed straight for the kitchen to pour myself a large glass of the wine Leo'd used to cook with. I would need it if I was going to have to sit through an entire dinner like this—it was one thing to pick up on the fact that his mother didn't like me, but it was another to have to deal with it while pretending to be in love with her son.

"Mara," Leo scolded in a low voice. "What are you doing?" I turned to find his narrowed eyes fixed on the glass of merlot in my hand.

"What does it look like I'm doing?" I took a large gulp of the deep red liquid.

I thought Leo was going to swat the whole glass out of my hand with how quickly he reached forward to take it from me. "It looks like you're trying to drink alcohol when you still have a fucking *concussion*!" His voice was low but full of frustration.

My eyes rolled dramatically. "Oh my god, I think I would know if I was still in the throes of a concussion, *Leopold*." But his eyes only narrowed further.

"Is that wine?" his mother asked as she rounded into the kitchen, no longer donned in her obnoxious fur coat. She looked at the glass in Leo's hand with desperate longing.

Leo's expression morphed into one of easy confidence. "Yes," he confirmed with a small smile. "We have merlot and pinot noir currently breathing, and a few bottles of chardonnay and riesling in the wine cooler. What would you prefer to drink tonight?"

"Pinot noir sounds wonderful, please, dear."

Leo nodded, pulling a clean glass from the cupboard and heading across the kitchen, where two decanters of red wine were resting on the counter. "How was the flight?" Leo asked as his father joined us from the bedroom. He still wore his suit, as if this might all just be a business meeting.

"Ah." Alaric shrugged as his hands dipped into the pockets of his slacks, an air of haughtiness heavy around him. "We took the company plane, so it was comfortable enough."

"Long flights are always a little hard on your father's knees," Christine said, looking grateful as Leo handed her the glass of wine.

"Oh, stop, Christine." His brow wrinkled. "My knees are fine."

I made myself busy with stirring the carrots and potatoes.

"You know," Alaric continued, "we *did* meet an incredible

young man in the executive lounge before we all boarded our planes. He's a rising star in the acquisitions and mergers world, and can you believe he was on his way out to Denver, too? We talked about having dinner together one night this week—he'd be a great person for you to connect with, Leo."

Leo hummed, and I could feel the annoyance that radiated from him. "Can I get you something to drink, Dad? Scotch, perhaps?" Leo asked, changing the subject.

"That sounds fine," he responded.

"Okay. While I work on that, why don't you both take a seat at the dining room table and Mara and I will follow shortly with the food."

"You don't have a server?" Christine asked, looking around the kitchen as if someone might suddenly materialize to serve our dinner. I had to hold back a scoff.

"Uh, no, Mom. I don't keep full-time staff here. But we don't mind, do we, honey?"

I felt the weight of everyone's gaze slide to where I was still stirring the vegetables. "Not at all," I managed. Alaric and Christine hesitated for only a moment before making their way to the table Leo had set earlier while he headed for the bar just off the living room to pour his father a drink. When he returned, he set the lowball glass on the island before grabbing the towel to pull the lamb out of the oven, and I poured the vegetables from the pot into a beautiful ceramic bowl with a matching serving spoon. "You doing okay?" I whispered to Leo as he transferred the lamb to a large platter with tongs.

He shrugged. "Just hoping to get through a nice enough dinner, and then we can all recuse ourselves to opposite ends of this apartment."

I reached up to press a hand to his bicep, feeling his taut

muscles beneath the sweater he wore. "We've got this, okay?" I encouraged. "And tomorrow, you better believe you're going to pay for taking my wine away and making me do this without any liquid courage."

Leo huffed out a quiet laugh, the skin around his bright blue eyes crinkling with amusement. It felt good to see a real smile on his face. "Thank you," he said softly. "And . . . I'm sorry I've already kissed you twice in front of them, but I was panicking, and I just went for it. I can stop that if you want me to . . . We never really talked about what's okay and what's not, so maybe we broach that subject when we get the chance at a private conversation?"

This time, it was my own real smile that grew at the way he rambled. "Don't be sorry," I said, leaning into his arm a little more before letting my hand drop. It was obvious how affected and nervous he was—I hated thinking it had to do with his *parents* of all people. I picked up the bowl of vegetables and looked back at him. "And don't stop."

Chapter Seventeen

I woke early the next morning. The city beyond Leo's bedroom window was illuminated only by streetlights and a nearly full moon that shone brightly in the sky. It would be a couple of hours before the sun rose, but as tempting as it was to pull the warm comforter high over my shoulder and try to drift back to sleep, I knew I was awake for the day. Pushing myself up to a sitting position from the center of the bed, I peered over at the chaise lounge in the corner of the room to find Leo still dead asleep, Swift and Dolly curled between his legs.

We went to bed shortly after dinner. Leo's parents claimed to be exhausted after their day of travel—though I figured traveling on a private jet wouldn't be nearly as exhausting as trudging through an airport for hours to fly commercial like most people did. Still, Leo had been exhausted, too. He'd been awake most of the previous night to keep an eye on me and my concussion, after all.

Seeing his frame cover the dismal surface of the lounge chair only intensified the guilt I felt for taking his bed a second night. But despite our arrangement, we had no business sleeping in the same bed. Once this was all over and Leo gave me part-ownership of Larkspur, he would still be a professional partner for an undetermined amount of time, so we had no good reason to shove our bodies under the same blankets, even if it was just to sleep.

I wasn't sure I'd be able to handle *just* sleeping next to him, anyway—not after the night we'd shared together. The chemistry between us had been, quite frankly, *too* good. Like the brightest of fireworks exploding all around us kind of good. And despite the walls I'd constructed to protect myself, I wasn't sure I'd be able to keep up if we got any closer than we'd already had to make this arrangement work.

Though, it *had* gotten easier and easier to feign affection last night through the course of dinner. The more his mother seemed bothered by my presence, the more attentive I became toward her son: taking a break from eating to hold Leo's left hand with my right on top of the table's surface, lovingly blotting at his mouth with my napkin to wipe away a trace of chutney despite his mildly bewildered expression, even pressing my lips against his cheek to thank him for such a wonderful meal. There hadn't been much conversation between any of us, but the communication Christine and I were sharing across the table with our actions spoke volumes—and I had no qualms against playing petty-bitch-defense against a fellow petty bitch.

Quietly climbing out of Leo's bed, I unplugged my phone from the charger on the nightstand before prying the bedroom door inch by inch to pad down the dark hallway toward the kitchen. I'd noticed a coffee machine on his counter while he cooked last night, and figured I would enjoy a quiet moment to myself while I had the chance. I found fresh grounds tucked away on a shelf inside the pantry and—after googling how to work his fancy, thousand-dollar machine—set the coffee to brew.

Turning my attention to the cupboards in search of a mug, I almost tripped over a large, orange cat. "Shit!" I shrieked, slapping my hand over my own mouth. Dolly peered her golden eyes up at me, looking like she was a mere three seconds away from eating my face off. "Shoo!" I whispered, waving my hands. Dolly didn't budge. Letting out a resigned sigh, I resumed my search for a mug and, after locating one, set it on the counter as I waited for the coffee machine to finish.

"Is that coffee?" a deep voice rumbled from the opposite hallway, causing me to almost jump out of my skin. Dolly hissed before running to the living room to perch herself up on the back of the couch. *Oh, so* now *you decide to leave me.*

I scowled at her before turning to find Alaric standing in a plush black robe, his hands shoved inside the square pockets at the front. His hair was finger-combed to the side, the ends brushing along his temple, and his brown eyes lingered on the coffee machine. "Yes," I responded, swiftly crossing my arms over my chest. I'd put on a bralette beneath the tattered Madonna sleep shirt I'd thrown on before bed last night, but I still felt exposed.

His gaze bounced to me. "Is there enough for two?"

"Oh, um . . . I only made enough for myself. I didn't think anyone else would be up for a while."

The right side of his mouth ticked up. "I'm afraid, because of my business, I've lost the ability to sleep much past four in the morning. Though I do find the early hours quite peaceful."

I nodded, unsure of how to respond, considering I normally slept in until noon and didn't actually go to bed until four. "Well, I can make more once mine has finished brewing—if you want."

His eyes fell to my feet before slowly scanning up my body, taking in what felt like every minute detail. It felt . . . gross, and I was immediately set on edge. When his gaze finally reached my face again, he smiled. "That would be wonderful."

"Sure," I responded curtly, turning toward the machine.

"Thank you, darling," he drawled before slipping back down the hallway toward the guest room he and Christine were staying in.

I let out a long exhale when I heard the click of his door. When the machine was done brewing, I poured the coffee into the mug before replacing the used grounds with fresh ones for another cup. But if that man thought I'd be serving it to him on a silver platter, he had another thing coming. He could find his own damn mug.

As soon as the machine started brewing again, I decided it was probably safer to keep myself tucked away in Leo's bedroom for now—at least until he was awake and could act as a buffer between his parents and me. I knew we needed to pretend to be in love and all that, but that didn't mean I had to build any sort of foundation with either Alaric or Christine. Nor did I *want* to. As far as they would know, we'd be broken up after this little family visit.

Armed with my cup full of hot coffee, I made my way back to the bedroom, Dolly following curiously behind me.

Leo woke up almost two hours later, just after sunrise. I'd spent the majority of that time back in bed, diving down social media rabbit holes on my phone and doing my best to shake the odd encounter I'd had with Alaric. But after a while, I'd grown bored, and decided if I was going to be stuck in this room, I might as well get my yoga practice in for the day. So I'd quietly changed into a sports bra and shorts set in the en suite bathroom and rolled out my mat on the floor next to the bed.

I'd just transitioned from a table-top position to downward dog when I heard rustling behind me. Catching an upside-down sight of Leo from the view between my legs, I watched as he sat up and looked over at me, his eyes immediately landing —and staying—on my ass. Shaking my head, I lowered myself down into a plank before lifting my shoulders and chest into a cobra pose.

Leo's sleepy voice sounded from where he was more than likely still watching me. "Could you go back to that last one?" His words were raspy with a hint of teasing.

I scoffed in response. "No."

He chuckled softly as he rose from his makeshift bed before suddenly sitting down again, pulling the blanket he'd slept with over his lap. "Shit," he muttered quietly to himself.

I turned my head to look at him, feeling the muscles in my neck strain from the effort. "What?"

He looked embarrassed, his eyes wide as they lifted to mine. "Uh," he started. "I'm just going to need a minute . . . before I can get up."

I arched a brow and lowered my gaze to the blanket he clutched tightly in his lap. *Oh!* I snapped my head toward the wall in front of me, taking my attention away from Leo so he could deal with his . . . *situation* with some semblance of privacy. "Sorry for doing this in here," I mumbled as I lifted my hips and shifted some weight back into my arms for another plank. "I just . . . thought it would be more appropriate than practicing out in the living room."

I kept my eyes forward and brought my right leg forward for a lunge, breathing deeply through a warrior pose as I pretended to remain unaffected—though my skin prickled as visions of Leo moving his strong body over mine ricocheted around in my head. A heated stream of desire spread throughout my limbs, and I did what I could to will it away— even as I heard the low scratch of his voice sound again from behind me. "No need to apologize, Mara. I understand this probably isn't the most comfortable of situations for you. I'll . . . I'll do whatever I can to try ease things, okay?"

I nodded, inhaling deeply through my nose before letting the breath back out between my lips. "Mm-hm."

A happy meow sounded as Swift jumped off the lounge and bounded toward me. I was still deep in a lunge when she casually meandered to the top of my mat and sat, curiously looking up at me. When it was time to transition myself down into another plank, I bent over to plant both of my hands on either side of my ankle and brought my right foot back, lifting my hips into another downward dog to release some of the tension in them from the lunge.

Swift moved into her own downward stretch, her front paws reaching wide in front of her as her nails unsheathed and pierced my mat.

"Hey!" I whispered. "You can join me for morning yoga, but you can't fuck up my mat!" Leo laughed quietly behind me. Still not looking at him, I whined. "It's not funny." Swift rolled over, exposing her fluffy little black-and-white splattered belly.

Leo shuffled around as he got up, and I kept my eyes on the wall so as not to accidentally see something I *didn't* want to see. "She's just trying to be your friend," he murmured lightly as he walked past me and into the bathroom, shutting the door closed behind him.

I looked down at Swift's gray eyes. "Is that right?" I asked. "Are you trying to be my friend?" She meowed again, and this time I scratched her gently on the chin. Her eyes closed as she started purring beneath the light touch of my fingers. "Okay, fine, we're officially friends. I could use some in this place." She rolled again and bounced back up onto her feet, running like a crazed maniac toward the chair Leo just vacated. I turned to find her nestling in again next to Dolly, whose wide golden eyes were fixed on me.

I didn't think Dolly was ready to be friends with me yet, and I couldn't blame her. I wasn't exactly friendly toward her dad either. Still, though, I didn't like the thought of being unlikeable, so I decided I would try. "You're next, Dolly."

Dolly stared at me for a moment longer before she got up and turned to face away from me, settling down into the blanket as she looked out the big window.

I ARRIVED AT LARKSPUR EARLY, insisting I needed to handle a bunch of admin duties despite getting through most of them a couple of days ago. The truth was I needed to get out of Leo's apartment—away from him and away from his parents

—and while I thought about sneaking back to my own apartment for a couple of hours instead, I figured it wouldn't hurt to spend a few hours inspecting the bar.

The staff had a strict set of closing duties that kept things relatively organized, like washing the rubber mats, putting all dirty glassware into the dishwasher to be cleaned and dried overnight, wiping down the bar with an antibacterial cleaning solution, and mopping the floors throughout the club. We also had a cleaning crew that came twice a week for a deeper cleaning, and a bar maintenance guy named Walter who came weekly to ensure keg lines and beer taps were regularly looked at and sanitized. Still though, I liked to push up my own sleeves now and then to wipe down every door knob and handle throughout the entire club, or to soak all faucet heads in club soda to break down leftover grime, or maybe to reorganize the stock room and the office.

It helped me to feel like I had a finger on the pulse of this whole place, even as we continued to get busier. It was also another great way for me to blow off a little steam, which I was itching for, especially since I'd shut myself away in Leo's bedroom to avoid his parents for most of the morning. After an awkward, silent lunch around the kitchen island where his mother continued to stare at me with a look of aversion, I bolted, claiming to have a million things to work on at Larkspur.

Much to my surprise, Leo strolled in from the stock room only a half hour into my self-prescribed cleaning spree, wearing a beautiful midnight navy suit and a devilish grin. His wavy hair was styled, and he was freshly shaven. He looked *divine*, and the juxtaposition of such a finely dressed man inside of a nightclub like this made my blood hum beneath my skin.

I watched as he looked around before turning toward where I was knelt behind the bar with a sudsy sponge in hand, scrubbing the metal caddy that held the bottles of our house liquor. He looked so much more relaxed than he had two mornings ago when he'd summoned me to ask me to be his fake girlfriend, which was odd because when I left him this morning, he was tense as he stared his father down. "You good?" he asked, eyeing me curiously.

I realized the force of my scrubbing was a little . . . much. Giving myself a moment to take inventory, I considered. "My head feels much better. The rest is getting there. Why aren't you with your parents?" I asked.

"I enjoy the view of you on your knees." He smirked, ignoring my question, and I nearly choked on my own spit.

"You're such an asshole," I muttered, putting a little more oomph into my scrubbing.

"I'm just teasing you, Mara." His eyes danced as his mouth tipped up in amusement. "What are you doing down there, anyway?"

"What does it look like I'm doing?"

I watched as his eyes roamed over me, taking in the bar T-shirt and longer bike shorts I'd decided to wear tonight along with the sponge in my hand and the bucket of soapy water in front of me. "It looks like you're cleaning. Don't we outsource that?"

I shrugged. "Yeah, but it's never as good as doing it yourself, you know?"

His eyes pinned me into place as he leaned over from the other side of the bar, resting his arms on the glossy surface. "No, I don't. If the service is unsatisfactory, then we should find an alternative solution."

"They do a great job!" I retorted.

"I'm just saying"—he flashed his bright white teeth—"I've found that, with the right budget, you can hire people to do things *exceptionally* well."

I rolled my eyes. "Okay, moneybags, that sounds a little creepy. And also, the service we hire really does a great job. I just like to find ways to help."

Leo laughed, his face open and sunny, and it landed in my chest. "All right, point taken. I won't interfere."

I stared at him, watching his smile widen from the attention. "What's gotten into you?"

"What do you mean?"

"You look—" I waved a hand out toward his face. "Happy. And when I left, you looked like you wanted to throttle someone."

"Well, you gave me the tracks to run on, I suppose. I went for a quick jog after you left to try to release some of the tension I was feeling. And then when I got home, my father told me he made dinner reservations for all of us at NoMu Wednesday night—along with that 'strapping young man' they met at the airport before their flight."

Damn. NoMu was probably the fanciest restaurant in Denver, and it usually had a waitlist that was months long. There was no telling how much cash he'd had to throw down to wriggle into a table on such short notice. "I have to work," I said, focusing back on my task. A dinner on the town with Alaric and Christine sounded about as fun as sitting through a root canal. "And why does NoMu make you so happy? Is the food that good?"

"You'll take the night off and join me as part of our agreement," he said firmly, though still with a smile. "And I'm not sure about the food, I've never been there. But what I will say is that when my father delivered the news of our impending, likely tortuous dinner together, it stressed me out so much that I'm afraid I might have slipped right into a bit of a delusion. And then I basically did what you did and feigned a bunch of work to get to here, so . . ."

Though his words were humorous enough to laugh at, I could see his eyes dimming at the implication of trouble at the dinner. This sunny disposition he displayed was nothing more than a charade—and based on how well he sold it, I would guess it wasn't a one-off. It frustrated me, because I knew what it was like to have to pretend. "Leo, if your father stresses you out this much, why even bother?"

His smile disappeared, and he looked at me for a long moment. "It's, uh . . . complicated."

I wanted to press further, but I also needed to be careful. The deeper I got into Leo's personal life, the harder it would be to unwind myself from it after the week was over. "I really should be at work . . ."

"It's a Wednesday, Mara. How busy could things be on a Wednesday? We'll make sure the bar is covered, but I need you with me at this dinner. It's non-negotiable."

"Well, if we have to do this, I think we should try to find a way to get to know each other better beforehand." His eyes flashed, and I almost threw the wet sponge at him. "Not like that. I just mean . . . you want this relationship to be believable, right? So we should prepare."

He nodded, his expression becoming genuinely lighter. "A date, then."

The word warmed my cheeks. "Uh . . . sure. If that's what you want to call it."

"Yes, I think it's appropriate." His eyes dipped down to my legs folded beneath me as I still knelt on the floor. "Do you have a dress? For dinner?"

This time I couldn't stop the laugh from erupting from my mouth. "No." I swallowed. "I don't wear dresses . . . not *nice* ones, at least."

"Hm." He pushed himself upright and off the bar. "We'll deal with that later. Why don't you get yourself cleaned up—I've asked our new security team to start today, and they'll be here in about twenty minutes. Frank is on his way, too."

I sighed thinking back to what happened here during my last shift. If I hadn't been so motivated to get out of Leo's apartment today, it might not have been as easy to walk through the door. But I reminded myself that I was strong, that this too shall pass. And if I was *really* honest, I could admit that not having to face it all by myself felt . . . nice.

But I would never tell Leo that.

I stood up, blowing a strand of loose hair away from my face, and saluted him with as much sarcasm as I could string together. "Roger that."

He grinned before he turned to walk away, and I didn't miss the "smart-ass" that whispered from his lips.

Chapter Eighteen

Rocco Marchetti looked like a warrior. He was a giant brute of a man with a body that nearly burst out of the seams of his all-black suit, though the way his form tapered at the waist was indication that the bulk of him was made up of sheer muscle. His hair was cropped short, nearly the same length as the stubble that covered his entire jaw, and his eyes were as black as the wall behind the bar.

He looked like he'd come right off the pages of one of my favorite mafia romance novels with his menacing hands and surly attitude—though seeing a man like that in *real* life was much different than reading about one. While I was sure he'd have no problem pulling any woman (or man) he wanted, he made it abundantly clear that he was here to work tonight. I could feel the ruthlessness that exuded from him as he listened intently to Leo, who was giving him and his men a detailed tour of Larkspur's facilities.

There were five men in total including Rocco. None of the other men had been introduced to us, and none of them had said a word since they'd all arrived thirty minutes ago. It was a bit unnerving, the way they all stood stoically with mean looks on their faces. While none of them were quite as big as Rocco, each looked like they could tear Leo in half.

"Where the hell do you think Leo found these guys?" I whispered to Frank, who'd moved closer and closer to me as this little tour went on.

I heard his rumbling chuckle as we kept ourselves a handful of feet behind the rest of the group. "All I know is he went to school with the guy who owns the company. And that guy owed him a favor."

"Huh." I considered as I clocked the thick man with a ponytail who stood closest to Rocco. "Well, this is one way to cash in a favor, I guess."

"It's all for you, you know."

I felt the blood drain from my face as my thoughts sputtered around those words. "What?" My whisper came out sharper. "What do you mean?"

Frank shrugged and Leo's eyes snapped our way, so he continued to sway his arms back and forth as if he were shaking off a chill to cover the movement. And I knew then that Leo probably told him to keep whatever he was about to tell me a secret. The joke was on Leo, though, because Frank was my head of security—not his.

And that made him *my* proverbial bitch.

"He told me last week he wanted to beef up protection for the staff here, that a customer had disrespected you and he didn't like it, and that you and the rest of the team shouldn't have to worry about anyone who walks through our front door. And then Saturday . . ." Frank took a deep breath, clearly still a little shaken about what went down. My eyes flicked to the dark hallway across the club that led to the bathrooms, and I felt a fresh burst of fear roar to life in my stomach. "Saturday happened, and I think it really fucking scared him."

"Wait," I whispered, turning to face Frank. Leo was distracted as he showed his new detail the security system and cameras mounted on the ceiling—another resource that he'd brought in so quickly after taking ownership. "He said the extra protection is for the *staff*?"

Frank nodded, looking a bit sullen. "Yeah. I mean, we should have been protecting you. But there's just so many people in here, and as things get busier— We have a hard enough time keeping a pulse on all the customers that come in. I've always known you can handle yourself Mara, but I should have never left you hanging the other night. Someone should have been stationed with you and Sam at the bar. I'm so sorry."

Emotion burst through me as I reached a hand out and placed it gently on Frank's arm. "Frank, that wasn't your fault. There was a literal bar fight breaking loose, and you were needed. Don't you dare think what happened to me is your fault. That guy would have found any opportunity to try to do what he did, and we may have missed it. Plus," I said, forcing a smile, "our shot system worked. The bar fight caused enough of a distraction that the woman was able to slip away to order a Black Panther . . . It *worked*, Frank, and *we* created that."

I watched as he swallowed back his own emotion. "I'm still not going to stop being sorry." He cleared his throat, straightening as Leo turned to face us with a curious gaze.

"Frank?" Leo asked. All five of his new minions turned to

look at the man next to me. It was a testament to Frank's own strength that he didn't seem fazed by any of them.

"Yes, sir?"

"I think it would be helpful if you took some time to review the logistics of your current security team. Maybe you can go over their schedule, where you have each of your men stationed, what your standard procedures are . . . give our new friends the lay of the land in your world. Sound okay?"

Frank nodded. "Yes, sir."

Leo's eyes bounced to me, and I found myself instantly lost in their depths. Knowing he was going to these lengths to keep us safe—to keep *me* safe . . . I didn't know what to do with that information. "Mara," he said on an exhale, as if he'd been looking everywhere and finally found me, despite the fact that I'd been with him for this whole tour. I stood frozen next to Frank as Leo took the five steps needed to close the distance between us, captivated as I watched the expression on his face morph from concern to what looked like wonder. And then he smirked. "The most dangerous thing in the world is a silent woman," he said, to no one in particular. "Especially when she's smiling like *that*." He gently tapped the pad of his finger against my bottom lip.

Had I been smiling?

Shit. I quickly schooled my expression, wiping any traces of a smile right off. In fact, I went so far as to glare at him, exasperated that he would call me out for something like that in front of all these people, let alone touch me so intimately. We both agreed we'd keep everything regarding the contract quiet at work, so there was no reason for him to treat me as if we were anything more than professional co-workers. And co-workers *definitely* didn't try to make contact between their finger and another co-worker's lip.

I felt the foundation of our little truce crumble as his playful display demolished through my comfort zone. "What?" I snapped. Now wasn't the time to let him have a taste of my vengeance—but I found joy in anticipating *when* I could lay it on him.

"Oh." His smirk crawled higher up his face, and dread pooled in my stomach at what he might say next. "I wish you'd warned us that you woke up and chose violence today."

Hm, okay that wasn't so bad. Still wildly unprofessional, but at least it was more snarky and less intimate. I rolled my eyes and turned away from him and the rest of the men around us, muttering, "I don't have time for this," as I walked away.

I WAS SCHEDULED to open the bar tonight, and even though it was only a Monday, Nora arrived for her closing shift around six. We'd only recently started scheduling two bartenders on Monday and Tuesday nights. They were normally our slowest of the week, but with how much business had increased over the last few months—and after Sam got caught in a particularly grueling Tuesday night shift by himself when all of Denver showed up—I decided it wasn't worth anyone being caught on their heels. It meant the bartender who opened usually didn't make as much money as they would have if they'd had the whole night to themselves, so I usually took that shift and gave the beefier closing shift to someone else, only staying as long as we needed to ensure there'd be no surprise rushes.

Tonight was a more typical pace for a Monday: the bar seats were half-occupied, a handful of booths around the perimeter of the club had been filled, and only a few people had gotten loose enough to dance to the house playlist. On the nights we didn't have a DJ, we used my music streaming account to play an eclectic mix of both trending hits and old bangers from legends like Tupac and Heart. "Big Poppa" by Biggie was currently bumping through the speakers, and I shimmied in place to the beat of the music while prepping a new batch of garnishes. It was slow enough that I'd stopped serving customers a little while ago and was going through some of our closing duties so Nora wouldn't have to handle things alone at the end of the night.

After taking a round of beers to a high-top table near the bar, Nora sidled up next to me and watched as I cut an orange into wedges. "So," she said with an uneasy tone, "are we allowed to talk about it?"

I glanced up at her to find worry etched in her big brown eyes as she fidgeted with the tail of her long braid. She was taller than me—the top of my head only reached her shoulder—and for a moment, I had the distinct feeling that she was looking at me as an older sister, despite being a few years younger than me. And it knocked me sideways, because *I* was supposed to be the strong one in this place. I was supposed to be the one who had it all together for everyone else so I could effectively lead them. "Talk about what?" I asked, purposefully looking back down at the orange in front of me as I sank my knife into the rind.

"Saturday night, Mara." A sigh spilled out of her mouth before she lowered her voice and leaned in a little closer. "Are you okay?"

Movement caught my eye as Ethan opened the front door to let a large group of people in, and I realized I *knew* those people. Nora's boyfriend, Andre, led the pack while our mutual friends Logan, Adam, Amelia, and a petite Hispanic girl who looked a lot like Andre followed closely behind him. I looked back up at Nora, her eyes still glued to me. "I'm okay, Nora, I promise. It really wasn't that big of a deal. I was just trying to help stop something worse from happening . . . I would do it again in a heartbeat."

Her eyes blazed with concern before she wiped it away, nodding her show of support and love. I reached out to squeeze her hand in thanks before we turned to focus on the incoming group. Nora locked eyes with Andre and smiled so brightly it was like she'd caught the stars in her teeth. "Hey you!" she greeted him.

Andre's lips curved and his eyes crinkled. *"Mariposa."* Nora leaned across the bar to give him a brisk kiss, and I shifted my attention to the rest of the group, placing cocktail napkins in front of each of them.

"Haven't seen you all in a few weeks. How's everyone doing?"

Adam smirked. "Oh, how we've missed you, our small-but-mighty bartending queen."

"Mara," husked a voice from the end of the bar. I turned my head to find Leo and Rocco standing together, Leo's eyes trained on Adam.

I almost rolled my eyes before I turned back to the group. "It's good to see you all—give me a second and I'll be right back to catch up." Spinning on the heels of my leopard printed Vans, I marched toward Leo. "What?" I asked with an impatient tone when I reached him.

His throat bobbed as he swallowed down a retort, his eyes flashing toward the group before landing back on me. "Rocco is going to take Frank's usual posting for the rest of the evening. It's slow tonight, and I'd like Frank to spend some time working with Rocco's men. It'll also give Rocco an opportunity to absorb what things are like around the bar to observe and flesh out some of our weaknesses."

I glanced at Rocco, watching as he scanned the faces of each patron with a scowl. "Okay, but he stays in his corner. I don't need him scaring anyone away."

Leo nodded. "Nor do I."

"Good," I mumbled.

"Great." He smiled.

"Is that all, *sir*?"

His eyes flashed before they darkened, and I immediately regretted my feeble attempt at sarcasm. "For now," he responded, his voice considerably rougher than it had been moments ago. It sent a shiver up my spine.

I felt the need to pour a bucket of ice-cold water over whatever spark was glinting in his eye, so I rushed more words out of my mouth. "I'm almost done helping Nora with the prep work for tomorrow. I'm going to visit with some old friends who just got here, and then I'll be leaving for the night. Unless there's anything else you need?"

His brows knitted together. "Well, isn't that convenient? I'm wrapping up here too. I'll drive you home."

Home. My eyes flashed to Rocco, who was watching me with a new curiosity. I looked back at Leo, giving him a pointed look. "Thanks, but I don't need a ride."

"It's not safe out there," he countered, crossing his arms

over his chest. "And I happen to know you haven't eaten anything for dinner. We can stop at Rudy's for sandwiches. In fact, I insist."

"Oh!" Rocco sounded off with a surprised grunt, looking at me with renewed interest. "She is your woman! Why didn't you tell me?" His accent was thick, but there was no mistaking his words.

I glared at Leo before turning my fiery gaze to Rocco. "I'm not his woman."

"Well—" Leo began to say.

"I am *not* your woman."

We stared at each other for a long moment before he finally broke. "Yes, she's right. She's not . . . erm . . . we're not—"

"We're not together," I finished for him, eyes still glued to Rocco.

Rocco grinned, amusement written all over his face. "If you say so."

"Oh, I say so," I assured, eyes snapping back to Leo. "I appreciate your offer, but I don't need a ride." I could tell he wanted to interject again, but I turned my back to him and walked away—something I seemed to be good at lately.

Behind the bar, Nora had already served the group a round of drinks—everyone had a bottle of beer in front of them except Amelia, who sipped from a glass of red wine. Nora was out on the floor greeting a couple who'd just arrived at a table, so I took a moment to scan everyone else at the bar to make sure they were okay. Once I was sure everyone was topped up, I leaned against the bar's surface to talk with the gang.

Logan turned from his conversation with Andre and a smile lifted from his mouth. "There you are."

"Yeah, sorry. Duty called—you know how it goes," I laughed. "How are you guys?"

Logan shrugged. "Shop's been busy. We've all been busy, actually—I think this is the first time we've gotten together in over a month."

Adam groaned. "Finally! I swear, dude, between the shop and planning your wedding, you guys are *always* busy."

Logan blinked at his best friend. "You're a neurosurgeon, Adam. You literally have *saving lives* on your to-do list . . . I seriously don't understand how you always have so much wind in your sails."

Amelia snorted out a laugh.

Andre politely chimed in while Adam shrugged with a smug look on his face. "Mara." I turned to find his gray eyes sparking beneath the bar lights. "I'm not sure if you've met my sister yet—this is Marisela." He wrapped his arm around his sister, who smiled at me.

I held my hand out. "Hey Marisela, I'm Mara. It's nice to meet you!"

"It's nice to meet you too—I've heard a lot about you from Nora."

"I've heard a lot about you too. You and Nora are opening up a sandwich shop together—she's been keeping me updated on the process."

"Yes!" She nodded enthusiastically, and I could feel her joy radiating from her smile. "I'm so excited, we actually just found a location."

"What!" I smacked my hands together. "Where?"

"Right down the street from the auto shop, actually," she answered, beaming.

Andre tugged her closer. "We'll be able to keep an eye on

them. And I'm sure our guys will love grabbing lunch there." He looked down at her, eyes flaring with pride, and it made my chest ache.

I knew how excited Nora was these last couple of months as she and Marisela worked through the details of their new venture. They'd been meeting regularly in the mornings to develop the menu, source all the food, and to build the brand with the help of Amelia's marketing magic. Knowing they'd found a space to lease would bring it all that much closer to fruition. "I can't wait until you guys open," I said. "I'll come in and post about it on my social media channels."

Marisela's eyes lit up. "Yeah?"

I nodded. "Of *course!*"

Nora came bounding back behind the bar, an obvious confidence in her step as she looked toward her man. "What did I miss?"

Andre grinned. "Just talking about how excited we all are for the new restaurant."

Nora smiled from ear to ear, eyes zipping to me. "Oh, yeah —I have a lot to catch you up on."

I nodded. "I can't wait to see it—I'm happy for you, Nora, and I'm here for anything you guys might need, okay?" I wondered if she would have to quit working here once her new gig was officially open for business, and the thought made me sad. But it also made me feel really, *really* proud of her. From the moment she'd started working here, her passion and eager-ness to learn had been off the charts. I made a mental note to check in with her about the future so I could be prepared either way.

She tucked a fallen strand of hair behind her ear, her smile still bright. "Okay."

Logan spoke up again, an obvious curiosity in his tone. "What's with the suit? Part of your security team?" He nodded toward Rocco, who was glowering from Frank's usual post.

"Oh, um . . ." I hesitated. Was I allowed to talk about Leo's personal military, or was stealth the whole point? It wasn't like I didn't trust Logan, so I pressed my elbows against the bar, and whispered, "Kind of."

Sensing he was in on a secret, Logan leaned in conspiratorially. "What do you mean?"

"*Welllll*," I drew out, "we had a little incident here a couple of nights ago . . . a customer went berserk and tried to assault a woman in the bathroom, and I ended up getting hit in the process of trying to stop him, and Leo . . ." I trailed off. No one in this friend group—aside from Nora and maybe Andre—would know about Larkspur's little owner debacle. I sighed. "We have a new owner, and apparently he takes security seriously—which is great, don't get me wrong. He hired some new guys that will be planted all around here. They'll be mostly undercover . . . to help keep an eye on things. That"—I nodded toward Rocco—"is their boss."

Logan's golden eyes went sharp as I explained. "You got hit? What do you mean you got hit?" I could feel Amelia's attention turn toward him from where she'd been chatting with Marisela and Nora, as if she had an inner alarm in her very bones of his worry—I wouldn't doubt it, knowing how close they'd gotten since getting together.

I straightened to my full height and put my hands up in front of me. "You should see the other guy," I said with a forced laugh. "I'm fine, I promise."

Logan clucked his tongue and lifted his Rockies hat off his head before settling it back down. He looked at me for a long moment before he spoke again. "You've been through enough, Mara."

His words hit me like a freight train. Logan was the only one I'd ever told about my past . . . about Seth. And even still, he hardly knew much. I hadn't exactly intended on telling my old high school flame anything about it, but when I'd accidentally stumbled into his auto shop back then—still carrying the proof of the bruises Seth had left—I had to come clean about some of it. "I know," I murmured softly.

His lips pressed together in a firm line. He'd always been a quiet one with the ability to say more with just a look than most people could articulate with a dozen words, and he knew the inner pain and terror of abuse just as much as I did—his at the hands of his father. The look he gave me now spoke volumes, but I didn't want to hash any of it out here. *Not now*, I told myself, even though I knew the truth was that I'd never want to.

I was becoming a professional at sweeping the shit in my life under the rug, doing my best to pretend that things were okay.

I forced my gaze away from Logan, looking down the line of the bar again to see if anyone needed anything—any excuse to navigate away from the heaviness pressing down on me— but instead, I found Leo sitting alone at a high-top, scrutinizing the back of Logan's head with an intense stare. I frowned, looking back to Logan. "I'm getting out of here for the night . . . but it was great to see you all."

He gave me a long look that told me he wasn't pleased. But then he dipped his chin. I gave him a small smile before I pushed away from the bar and started toward where Rocco stood on guard, ducking through the bar's access point before beelining it to Leo.

"Stop looking at my friends like you want to rake them over coals," I muttered as soon as I reached him.

Leo snorted. "I'm sorry, what?"

"You heard me." I put my hands on my hips. "First you were shooting daggers at Adam, and now you're shooting them at Logan. Those are my friends—I've known them for a long time. And Andre, the tall one with tattoos—that's Nora's boyfriend. He's a good man. They all are. So you need to leave them all alone, okay?"

Leo shot me a narrowed glance. "You looked pretty chummy with that last one."

"Logan?" I scoffed. "Maybe a long time ago." Leo's gaze heated at the implication. "You see that gorgeous brunette sitting next to him? That's his fiancée, Amelia. They're my *friends*, Leo. And you have no business sulking about them, anyway. You're my boss, remember?"

He sucked his teeth. "We have a contract—"

"And I'm not jeopardizing any part of it," I interrupted, feeling the familiar surges of irritation that he conjured so easily.

Finally, he nodded. "Fine. Are you ready to go?"

"I meant what I said—I don't need a ride home. I can walk."

He smirked, his eyes smoldering now. "Calling it *home* already, sweetheart?"

"You're impossible," I grumbled, annoyed.

But then his face softened, the heat in his eyes shifting to determination. "Come on," he nodded toward the stockroom. "Frank will close up the bar with Nora. The car's parked in the back, and I can't show up at home without my beautiful girl-friend in tow, can I? Plus," he added, looking down at my bike shorts and then at my bare legs below, "it's cold."

I let out a deep breath as I tried not to let my heart flutter too much at his use of the word *beautiful*. "Fine," was all I said, before I followed him out.

Chapter Nineteen

BRIGHT RAYS OF LIGHT PERMEATED AROUND THE room, warming my skin like a sweet caress. Swift—who'd bailed on Leo at some point in the middle of the night to join me in the king-sized bed like a precious little opportunist—lifted her head in lazy curiosity as I rolled over, so I gave her a gentle scratch behind the ears, feeling the rattle of a purr beneath my fingertips. My eyes jumped to where Leo's prone body was practically crumpled in half, one tree trunk of a leg hanging off the edge of the cushion, his hips splayed open as his ankle bent at an odd angle against the floor. He was fast asleep, lightly snoring.

I had no doubt he was going to be sore today after his third night in a row of sleeping like that. And while he may have had the uncanny ability to riot every single nerve in my body, I was getting closer and closer with each passing night to relenting and telling him he could just sleep in the bed next to me. Maybe it wouldn't be a big deal.

But I wasn't quite ready to let go of that one frayed rope of control, holding fast to reason.

I quietly sprouted out of bed, doing my best not to jostle Swift, hoping I could sneak in yoga before Leo woke up so as not to have a repeat of yesterday morning. It had been beyond awkward to know he was watching me, but I also couldn't bear the thought of bringing my mat out to the living room where Alaric or Christine might stumble upon me. I hadn't seen either of them since before I left for work yesterday, and I wanted to keep it that way for as long as possible.

But as I reached my hand into the dark closet where my mat should have been rolled up and leaning against the wall, my fingers only grasped empty air. Frowning, I curved my body further into the closet, squinting in the dark for some semblance of the bright green color of what I was looking for—but nothing was there.

"What're you doing?" Leo's deep voice sounded from directly behind me, making me jump and trip over a forgotten cat wand with a feather and a little bell at the end. Thankfully I'd caught hold of the door jam just in time to avoid tripping over Swift and Dolly, who'd come running at the sound of what could only be morning playtime. "Shit," Leo murmured, his hand wrapping warmly around my shoulder. "I didn't mean to scare you."

"You were literally sleeping a second ago," I gasped through the adrenaline rush. "How did you manage to slither over here so quickly? You didn't even make any noise."

I looked behind me to find a goofy smile on Leo's face, his thick-rimmed glasses resting smartly on his nose. The square of his jaw moved as he parted his lips to respond. "One of my many charms, I suppose."

"Huh," I said dumbly, now distracted by the pillow marks pressed into the skin of his cheek. "I uh—I was looking for my yoga mat, in case you were wondering. I wasn't trying to like . . . pilfer through your clothes."

His forefinger tapped twice against my collarbone before he took his hand back off of my shoulder, and I turned my body around to face him. "I wouldn't mind if you *did* pilfer through my clothes—I enjoyed the sight of you in something of mine, come to think of it."

My cheeks burned. "Again, I *wasn't* looking through your things," I defended, feeling oddly embarrassed about how it must have looked when Leo opened his eyes and found me hunched into the opening of his closet. "Did you happen to move my yoga mat? It was rolled up here—it's like, a lime green color . . ."

"I did move it, actually," he said casually. "It must have slipped my mind." The curl of his smile was gone, his mouth now resting in an easy straight line, but there was an unmistakable shimmer in his eyes behind those coke-bottle lenses that had me scooching to the edge of my proverbial seat.

He was up to something.

Frowning, I pressed on. "Okay . . . where is it?"

Crossing one arm over his chest, he brought his other hand up to press a thick finger to his chin. "Hm." His eyes rose to the ceiling. "I think I put it across the hall."

I felt my brows pull in what I could only assume was a wicked scowl. It was way too early in the day for games like this. "Leo—" I started to argue, but he cut me off.

"Come on, let's go look." He didn't even wait for me before he turned on bare heels and strode toward the bedroom door.

I let out a breath before I followed behind him, distantly aware that I was wearing an obnoxious bright pink pajama set with neon yellow bananas printed all over. If Christine happened to catch a glimpse of me now, she'd probably have an aneurysm from my un-ladylike display of comfort.

Luckily, the rest of the apartment was quiet—Leo's parents were probably still tucked away on the other side of the penthouse. Leo pushed open the door across the hall, and I noticed a warm golden-pink light glowing from inside the room. As I stepped inside, the smell of jasmine and vanilla wafted around me, and I gasped as I took in the scene.

A closed piano had been pushed into the corner, and three different styles of guitars resting on stands stood in a single file next to it. The instruments had clearly been moved out of the way to make space for the meditative oasis that took up the rest of the room: my yoga mat was rolled out into the middle of the floor, ready to be used; an essential oil diffuser was perched on a beautiful wooden shelving unit that also housed various plants and a Himalayan salt lamp (the source of the golden-pink glow); and the rustle of waves crashing sounded from the far corner where a boxy speaker had been set up.

"I thought this might be more comfortable." Leo's husky morning voice trickled into my ear as I gaped at the room. "I know this isn't home for you, but I thought—"

"It's beautiful," I whispered, making a second sweep to note every little detail of this gift he'd given me. "How . . . where did you find the time to do this?" I asked. I was with him all night, and before he got to work he'd been entertaining his parents.

My eyes caught his as he answered, his expression hopeful and earnest. "I went downstairs to see Robert yesterday and explained—to the best of my ability—that I was hoping he and the building's staff could help me set up this surprise for you. A runner went out and bought everything in the afternoon, and after my parents left on their own to go to dinner the housekeeping staff came in and set things up. Is it . . ." He took a breath. "Is it okay? I know your yoga practice is likely very personal . . . I just wanted to try to help to make things better."

He was *nervous.*

"Leo." I reached out to grab his hand, anchoring myself to him and this feeling of genuine gratitude. "This is the nicest thing anyone has . . . *ever* done for me."

I could see the relief flood his face as a small smile broke through. "Yeah?"

"Yeah." I felt emotion sting my eyes, and I wondered if he truly understood the impact of this surprise. I was . . . blown away. I looked at him again . . . *really* looked at him. The indentations on his cheek were softening, but his hair stuck up at odd angles from sleep and he kept having to push his glasses up from sliding down the slope of his nose. His T-shirt was threadbare white cotton with a worn image of a bear chasing a hiker, the words SOMETIMES MOTIVATION FINDS YOU scrawled across the top. All of his usual finery and sharp corners were gone, and standing in front of me was a man who'd been dealt his own shitty cards in life. A man who was simply doing his best.

"Thank you." I squeezed his hand, still clutched tightly in my own. And I decided this would serve as a shift between us— a real truce. Maybe even a *real* partnership.

"About our date," he started, and rather than deflect from the warmth that spread through my chest by pulling my hand away, I leaned further into the moment, turning to face him head-on to give him all of my attention. "Do you have anything planned after work tonight?"

My eyes snagged on the brush of stubble on his jaw. I opened tonight, and since it was a Tuesday I'd likely be off by seven or eight. "Nothing," I answered. It came out as a whisper.

He nodded, his gaze falling to my mouth. To my parted lips. "Okay. I need to spend a little time with my parents today —I don't think I'll be going into Larkspur. But let me pick you up after your shift? Let me take you somewhere?"

My tongue was a lead weight in my mouth as that damned swirl of desire rose again. It made me want to run, to give a dismal excuse about actually needing to close the bar or visit a friend or *something* that wouldn't trap me with these feelings that I didn't know how to control. But after the lengths Leo had gone through to make me feel comfortable, he deserved more effort from my side as well. "Okay." I nodded, then watched his teeth flash in response. "Let's do it."

Leo was already waiting in the parking lot behind the building after my shift, leaning against the driver's-side door of his Bentley. He looked like an old Hollywood star with his hair mussed, his cheekbones sharp. Instead of his usual suit and tie, he wore dark jeans over brown boots and a red flannel shirt that hugged his broad shoulders. A rugged dusting of day-old stubble peppered his jawline and reached down toward his neck. I'd never seen him anything other than meticulously clean-shaven, but this was already my favorite version of him.

My cheeks flushed with embarrassment when I realized that I was frozen at the door, gluttonously taking in the sight of him, still holding the push-handle in my now-clammy palms. His mouth curved into a smile at my hesitance, and I knew I'd been caught staring. I did my best to school my face before I pushed my feet forward. "Hey!" I called out as I worked to close the distance between us, trying to tamp down the erratic rhythm of my heart.

His eyes stayed rooted on me like an anchor, but for which one of us I wasn't sure. His wide grin told me he somehow knew my heart might be racing, and I wondered if his might be, too. "Hey you," he answered, stuffing his hands into the pockets of his jeans. Under the dark sky, those eyes looked almost midnight. Full of starlight. "Ready for this?"

Live wires danced all over my skin as more nervous energy settled in, but for once it felt like the *good* kind of energy—the kind that flitted in right before something good happened. Something that could change the trajectory of an adventure—similar to how I felt the night we met. "I am, actually," I smiled through my breathy response, feeling self-conscious of the way my cheeks pulled high on my face.

Leo's eyes glinted in the glow of the streetlights as they cut a path down my body, taking in the simple black shin-length dress I'd slipped into in the locker room before coming out here. "I thought you didn't wear dresses."

"I don't," I answered. "But . . . for some reason I packed this one to bring to your place. I had a feeling I might need it."

"Ah," he said, amused. "I'm really glad you did."

Heat crawled up the expanse of my neck as I felt myself tipping back into his sticky web of magic—he'd already caught me in it once. I knew our date tonight was supposed to be the way to get our story straight before the big test tomorrow night, but I still found myself feeling giddy and a little unsteady under his sharp focus. "How do you feel about hole-in-the-wall dive bars?" I asked, forcing some levity to the conversation.

"Depends," he countered, expression growing serious. As if I'd asked him for his opinion about stock options.

"On?"

He took a step toward me, his gaze falling to my shoulder where my hair was draped over the hemline of my dress. "I'm a man of execution, Mara. Which means when I commit to something, I go all in. So if your intention is to woo me with a shitty dive bar, I want it to live up to my expectations. I want it to come with shitty beer and shitty food. Maybe a shitty band." He reached his hand out, lightly trailing a finger over the top of the shoulder he'd been eyeing, gathering my hair and dropping it so that it fell across my back. His fingertips brushed through the ends of it before he drew his hand back to his pocket.

I shivered. "Got it. Shitty first date, coming right up." I tried to suck down air as I spoke.

He laughed. "I have a feeling nothing about this is going to be shitty."

I forced my eyes away from him, forging a path down the frame of his car instead. "Speak for yourself," I said.

He shook his head, grinning from ear to ear. "You are a wicked woman. Come on, let's go." He held his hand out for me to take, and I didn't think twice before my own was eagerly reaching for his, taking it as if we did this every day.

As he led me toward the passenger door, I couldn't help the question from spilling out. "This isn't a real date, right?"

I don't do relationships.

Just a onetime thing.

You might never see me again.

Though his grin stayed put, the spark in his eyes dulled as he navigated me into the seat. "Just tonight." He repeated the words he'd said to me almost a week ago. "Nothing more."

I didn't believe him then, and I definitely didn't believe him now.

Chapter Twenty

Leo pulled into the farthest corner of The Manhole's parking lot at my behest (it was way too nice of a car to be left next to the dirty old trucks that lined the curb near the front door), and I couldn't help but shiver again at the feel of his palm sliding down my back after retrieving me from the passenger's side. He must have thought the reaction was from the biting wind because he didn't hesitate to pull out a black leather jacket from his seat to drape over my shoulders.

It smelled just like him—like the mountains—which only sharpened my desire.

He opened the door for me in true first-date fashion and steered me inside with an iron hook around my waist, caging me into his personal space. The close proximity of our bodies sent apprehension pinging through me as I took the first few steps inside the dark and dingy bar, internally praying like hell that no one from Larkspur would be here. It proved to be of little substance, though, after finding only seven other people littered about. I doubted anyone from Larkspur even knew this place existed.

I expelled a shaky breath as Leo's palm rested on my hip. His skin was unnaturally warm against the cotton of my dress, a blazing point of heat in an otherwise drafty room. He stood next to me, content to wait for me to make the first move. To take the reins.

Could he tell how nervous I felt inside?

Of the seven other people scattered around, only two of them were women. One of them, a stout woman with spiked hair and a cut-off denim jacket, took only a brief interest in Leo and me before turning back to her small group of rowdy biker friends. The other was a petite woman who looked to be pushing seventy despite her platinum blonde hair and obvious cosmetic enhancements. When she'd caught sight of Leo, she seemed to levitate right out of her chair, fastening all of her attention to him.

I couldn't blame her. Of the men here, Leo was the only one who looked like he didn't wake up this morning and immediately light up a cigarette before putting on yesterday's clothes. But still, the reflex to tuck myself closer and claim him came without thought, and I might have been embarrassed about it if he didn't reciprocate the gesture by squeezing the hand wrapped around my hip before dipping it further along the curve of my ass—like this kind of intimate affection was normal for us.

I felt him bristle next to me when he could no longer ignore the woman approaching us, but when I looked up to take inventory of his face I found him throwing her that effervescent, thousand-watt smile that he slid on so easily. Ever the showman.

"My goodness, baby," she drawled through a raspy voice, "has anyone ever told you that you look just like a young Rob Lowe? I mean, it's *uncanny*." She turned to look back at the dark-haired man she'd just left at the bar who looked as confused as I felt. "Otto, doesn't he look just like Sodapop Curtis?"

"Oh, well now—" Leo began to say, but the woman cut him off, flushed with obvious excitement.

"I swear my Otto and I watch *The Outsiders* at least a dozen times a year—it's our favorite movie. Your hair's a little lighter, but heavens-to-betsy you look just like him!" She turned to me, eyes broadening in surprise like she didn't notice me standing here before. "Is this your lady? Wow, isn't she somethin'. You better lock her down quick if you haven't already—you two would have the most incredible babies."

Heat rushed to my cheeks.

"Leave those poor people alone, Marge—you're gonna scare 'em off," Otto yelled from the bar.

"Oh hush, I'm bein' friendly!" she called.

Leo's hand lifted and I felt his fingers wind through my hair as a laugh rumbled out of him. "Thank you for such lovely and kind words—Marge, is it?" Marge nodded vigorously. "You know, the moment I saw you I thought of a young Goldie Hawn."

Marge's eyes went as wide as saucers. "Oh my word, young man, you've just made my night! Please, let us buy you both a drink."

"Marge!" Otto called again.

"What?" she hollered. "Can't you see I'm in the middle of somethin' over here? I mean, good lord almighty—look at this beautiful couple, don't they remind you of a younger version of us?"

Otto grunted, and Leo's smile brightened as he squeezed me to him. "Marge, you are too kind. And while I sincerely appreciate your offer, we'll have to respectfully take a rain check on those drinks because this is our first date, and I feel inclined to take care of everything tonight so I can give this beautiful woman next to me one for the books."

Marge gasped. "A *first date*? My goodness gracious, look at me gettin' all caught up in your business. Please just ignore this old bird and you kids have yourselves a wonderful evenin' together." Her brow furrowed for a moment as she looked at Leo carefully. "Wait, you brought her *here*? Son, there are plenty of better places than this ol' stink house."

Leo didn't skip a beat. "You know, Mara has a moral objection to chain restaurants, and I didn't want her to be too uncomfortable. Plus she's a bartender, so I figured she'd appreciate the charm of a shitty place like this."

A loud laugh burst out of me as Marge's eyes twinkled. "Aw, what a good boy you are for puttin' her needs first." She looked at me and made a big show of winking. "You caught yourself a good one, hon."

My eyes were wet with laughter. "Thanks, Marge. Jury's still out if he's relationship material, though."

Marge nodded her understanding as Leo tugged tightly on a lock of my hair, making me laugh again.

"Well, I'll let you kids enjoy your evenin'. Otto and I are rootin' for ya!"

"Thank you, Marge," Leo smoothly replied before waving his free hand at Otto. "Have a great night!"

Otto lifted his beer, tilting it toward us.

Marge returned to her man as I led mine toward an empty high-top, smiling wide as I whispered under my breath, "The charm of a shitty place like this?"

Leo finally unfastened his hand from my body to pull one of the tall stools out for me. "Only the best for my girl."

"So." Leo eyed me with a playful expression after the bartender—an ancient man who looked at us like we spoke a foreign language—dropped off a round of beers. "Tell me about yourself, Mara."

I snorted. "Okay wait, that's not honestly how you start off a first date, is it?"

His eyes sharpened. "Excuse me, I didn't realize we were doing that."

"Doing what? Asking questions?"

"Judging each other's first-date game." He threw me a pointed look.

I laughed and flicked my hair over my shoulder. "When you start a conversation with something as canned and distant as 'tell me about yourself,' it's kind of hard not to have opinions."

"It's a fair question!"

"It's boring."

"You know why I like it?" He lifted his beer to his lips and tipped the amber liquid into his mouth. Garth Brooks's "The Dance" started playing from the jukebox, and I turned to find Marge standing next to it with quarters in her hands, shooting me another wink. She'd already cornered Leo once more as he briefly left me to use the restroom, whispering something in this ear that caused him to bark out a laugh that reverberated against the walls. "It gives you the opportunity to tell me anything you want," Leo continued. "Keeps you in control when things are awkward at the beginning. It's non-specific. Low stakes. Non-threatening."

"Boring!" I quipped over the sound of the song's melody, laughing again at the fierce determination on his face.

Leo straightened, looking utterly appalled, like he'd just caught me pick-pocketing his grandmother. "You'd prefer I dive right into the potentially raw specifics of your life?"

I shrugged. "At least it's more interesting."

His eyes narrowed as a competitive edge settled over him, apparent in the broadening square of his shoulders. His lips pressed together, the pouty flesh of them tucked into his teeth. "Okay, then. You're on, you vicious little dragon. Why didn't you tell your parents about what happened to you?"

Any amusement I felt died in an instant. "Don't do that." I looked to Marge, who was now back in her seat at the bar taking a shot with Otto. I lifted my own beer to my lips and took a long pull, the carbonation burning down my throat.

When my eyes landed back on Leo, he looked smug. "Do what?"

"You know that isn't an actual first date question. If this were a real first date, you wouldn't know to ask something like that." My cheeks flushed at my own defensiveness, and I hated it. Hated feeling like I was suddenly under a microscope. Like my skin was burning.

"Maybe it is." He took another sip of his beer, eyeing me carefully. "Maybe we're friends. Maybe we've been friends for a long time, and we've only just decided to try dating. And, in the realm of keeping things interesting as your friend-turned-date, maybe I'm concerned about you." It felt like the heat from the dusty bar lights were lasering into my skin.

"Wow. You really like pretending when it comes to the women you date, don't you?" It was a low blow, but I didn't like this game. It was like he'd found a tender bruise and decided that he wanted to press into it with his thumb and swirl it around a little.

If the insult landed, he didn't let on. Instead, he wound up for the game-winning point. "You really like pretending you aren't lonely, don't you?"

I was instantly moving, pushing out of the stool. But Leo anticipated my reaction because he was right there in front of me, blocking me with his body as he wrapped his hand gently around my shoulder blades. His touch was tender, and again, I hated it. "Hey—" He cleared his throat, his expression considerably softer. "None of that. We're on a date, remember?"

I wanted to snarl at him. "Some date."

His eyes dimmed, but he didn't retreat. "Look, I'm sorry. I just . . ." He trailed off as his gaze swept around the bar. Then he looked down and cursed at his feet. "I worry about you, okay?"

"Why? There's nothing for you to worry about." I hugged my arms over my chest, the weight of his arm still draped over me acting like a tether. "I'm fine."

He stayed quiet for a long beat, his eyes the only tell of the war going on in his mind to either challenge me or let the whole thing drop. But then I watched the moment he relented, sucking in a breath and releasing it with a "Please sit." I stared at him for a long moment, feeling ashamed of myself, until he lifted both of his hands in surrender. "I'll keep the potentially raw specifics off the table until at least the third date."

"Fifth," I countered, the corners of my mouth tugging.

"Fifth," he amended.

He watched me as I sat back down in my stool before he took his own seat, resting both hands on the round table and looking at me. The quick tempo of a new song sounded from the jukebox—"Jackson" by Johnny Cash and June Carter. Leo's body seemed to unfurl when he heard it, a sideways grin growing on his face as his chest expanded beneath the flannel of his shirt.

"You like this song?" I asked, even though I knew the answer.

"I love it," he confirmed. "It's my favorite of them both."

"I wouldn't have pegged you as a Johnny Cash fan."

Leo's fingers rapped against the surface of the table to the beat of the song. "He was a brilliant songwriter. My favorite is "Folsom Prison Blues"—you know he sang that live to the inmates at Folsom Prison?"

"I actually did know that. My Grandpa Jack is a big fan."

"What's your favorite song?"

"Like, ever?" I asked. He nodded, and I hesitated before answering truthfully. "Rhiannon."

A wide smile curled on his face. "Of course." Like he'd already known, like he just wanted to hear me say it.

"What do you mean, 'of course'?"

His blue eyes flared. "Nothing. It's just . . . I used to watch old videos of Fleetwood Mac's live performances. Stevie always sang like . . . like she was on fire. It suits you."

I felt like I might spring outside of my skin. "You used to watch old videos of Fleetwood Mac?" It was my mother's favorite band—she idolized Stevie Nicks, and I grew up listening to all her records on our old vinyl player. Every Sunday we'd do chores around the house and my mom would turn the music up loud before slipping into an old orange apron and dancing while she mopped the hardwood in the kitchen. Her hair would be thrown up, strands of it falling in her face from the way the music overtook her whole body.

Leo's smile turned shy, like the admission was tied to something personal for him, too. "I've always been a bit of a music buff." He watched me earnestly. "And I've sort of always thought . . ." He let the words run off. "I thought I might want to try writing my own songs."

Leo, writing music? My eyes caught on his fingers still tapping against the table, and it made sense—all the times I'd noticed his body moving as though he were listening to a private performance. "Is that why you have those instruments in the spare bedroom? The piano and the guitars?"

He nodded, cheeks flushing pink. "Yeah. I like to play . . . or—" He broke off, tilted his head pensively. "I guess I did."

If the slight downturn of his lips were any indication, this wasn't an easy topic for him. I felt compelled to know why. "You don't anymore?"

He took a long sip of his beer and I watched the column of his throat work around a swallow. And then he shook his head. "No."

Bullshit, I wanted to say. But it would make me a hypocrite to press into his bruise.

I nearly jumped out of my seat as a loud whistle sounded from the bar. I turned to find Marge with her hands thrown above her head, grinning like she'd just won a hundred bucks on a scratch ticket. The opening song from *Footloose* played out of the jukebox, and you would have thought Kevin Bacon himself walked through the front door with how fast Leo shot from his chair. "No fucking way!" he burst, his dimples on full display. It knocked something loose inside of my chest, that ache shifting into something liquid and molten like the amber of his beer.

I laughed as he hustled to the middle of the bar where two guys were already moving tables and chairs out of the way to create a makeshift dance floor. He jumped right in without skipping a beat, pulling two chairs against the wall as Marge sashayed from the bar, coming to stand between Leo and the others from the biker group who were all definitely a little more than buzzed.

As the lyrics started, all six of them kicked into the synchronized movement of a line dance, and the sight of such an eclectic group coming together sent my heart tumbling. Leo's eyes never left mine as the tips of his boots tapped the floor in perfect rhythm with the others. Not for the first time, I felt pinned by his gaze. There was a mischievous tilt to his lips and a shimmer in his eyes as he curled his finger, beckoning me over to join them.

I waved my hands in front of me to communicate a clear *No way in hell* response.

He laughed out loud, eyes crinkling as the group jumped and twisted to face the bar, continuing the dance. Still, his eyes stayed rooted on me, brows quirking as if to say *Get your ass up here.*

Country dancing had never been my thing—I didn't have a rhythmic bone in my body—but I couldn't ignore the tug in my chest insisting I get up and join him, to follow the joy that was so clearly written all over his face. I wanted to feel it in myself.

So before I could think twice, I pushed myself off the stool and walked toward him. I didn't miss the way his cheeks widened when he saw me coming, or the incandescent fire in his eyes as he scooted closer to the ponytailed man next to him so I could squeeze between him and Marge in line.

While Leo nailed every step with surefire accuracy, I fumbled like an idiot trying to keep up, laughing so hard my stomach hurt as I kicked a foot up when everyone else leaned over and clapped. Both he and Marge tried to show me the steps as we went on, and for a handful of breaths I thought I'd caught on, only to lose all sense of it when the quicker footwork came in before the next twist. But despite my horrible execution, I felt lighter than I had in months . . . years, even.

Gone were all my bearings, all of the worn footholds into the boundaries of control I'd woven so fiercely around me. I eventually stopped trying to keep up with the dance, shimmying myself closer to Leo instead as I gulped down a real, honest-to-god deep breath that seemed to only shift his warmth into my lungs. I wanted to share in the high he was emanating, wanted to suck down his happiness like secondhand smoke, as if it were curling around me for the taking. Our eyes snagged again, and I found myself wondering how this beautiful man had ever let *anyone* steal his light.

I realized his concern for me earlier might not have been so different from the way I scrutinized him now, taking in the way he shined so brightly, in such opposition from the way he allowed dark clouds to dim his light at home. I decided I would apologize later, to make an even stronger effort of this truce blossoming between us.

But for now, we danced.

Eventually the song ended, and everyone scattered back to their places around the bar as the new slower melody started. Leo looked down at me with a longing that glittered with hope, raising a hand and slotting it neatly against my hip. He wove his other hand into mine, and before I knew it we were swaying and humming along to "I Cross My Heart." Emotion burst out of me in a wave so sudden I had to press my cheek against his chest, hoping the moisture in my eyes wouldn't wet his shirt.

"I needed this," he said, exhaling out a contented sigh over the top of my head. His honesty was like a shot of bourbon—it made me feel dizzy and alive.

I smiled into his flannel, basking in the smell of his soap. "I did too. More than you know."

"We haven't even gotten to our assignment," he remarked, and it took me a moment to place the meaning of his words, until I felt my heart deflate remembering the contract . . . the dinner tomorrow. Our fake relationship. This night was supposed to be about preparing.

But I wasn't ready to let this feeling go yet, so I started a new internal countdown—like I'd done before. I would let myself sink into this heat for just a couple more minutes before I pulled myself into the cold of the loneliness he'd just called me out on. "I think we met each other at a bar just like this," I managed to say.

Leo hummed, and though my face was still planted against his chest, I imagined he was smiling. "You, in this dress," he said, his voice low. "You were definitely wearing this dress."

My heart filled with so much need that I was floating on it. "And you, with that smile."

"You like my smile?"

My palm moved slowly down his spine as I memorized the slope. "Shitty places like this suit you."

His shoulders shook with a quiet laugh. I pulled my head back, facing up to find his teeth flashing as he beamed down at me. He was so handsome it hurt. The hand on my hip skated along my dress, winding against the small of my back until his arm was fully around me, pulling me in closer until our hips and chests pressed together.

We continued to slow dance, stuck in each other's eyes, before I felt the tip of his nose graze along mine as his face fell closer. His mouth was inches from where I wanted him most—just a small shift and my lips would catch fire against his. But he didn't close the gap, leaving the distance for me to decide what to do with.

My countdown hit zero, and I promptly started it again.

"Mara," he whispered, his eyes falling to my mouth. "Is it wrong to tell you that I can't stop thinking about you? About our night together? I've missed you so much."

I couldn't help myself as I pressed my lips to where his dimple was currently sheathed, feeling the day's worth of stubble bite against my flesh. "I hate that I've missed you, too," I admitted. His hand flexed against my back, and I knew if I didn't save myself now, I'd sink into him so completely I'd never be able to get out. Leo was quicksand—he'd swallow me whole. So I pulled away. Forcing a smile, I continued the story. "We fell in love fast," I said, certain in some other life it would be true.

His eyes glittered a striking constellation—I wanted to chart it. To tattoo it into my skin. "I've already proposed at least half a dozen times."

"Trying to lock me down, huh?" I laughed.

"Oh yes," he confirmed as he wrapped his arms around my shoulders, pressing a kiss between my brows. It was so freeing to share this moment—this honesty—of what we both imagined it might have been like. If only our circumstances were different and my heart wasn't so fucked up. "But you keep turning me down, you wicked woman."

"It's not really in my nature to make things easy, you know."

Leo's cheeks flushed crimson as he grinned wide. "I think," he said softly near my ear, "we should go home and drink expensive whiskey and watch Sodapop and Ponyboy and the rest of the gang stir up trouble in the East Side."

I laughed again, feeling drunk on the way he caged me in. The way he made me feel safe. "I've never seen the movie," I confessed.

Leo's face twisted into horror. "You're kidding, right?"

"Nope. They played it in my high school English class, but I was out with the flu. I've only read the book." I watched him pull his phone out of his back pocket, swiping on the screen as the backlight glowed on his face. "What are you doing?"

"Requesting an Uber. We're going home so we can watch the movie—I can't have my girlfriend in the dark on what is arguably one of the best movies of all time."

I smiled, leaning in closer to whisper, "Do you really think it's one of the best movies, or did Marge put you up to this?"

He huffed out a laugh, eyes dancing with mischief as they flicked up to me, his phone momentarily forgotten. "She stopped me on my way to the bathroom and told me it would 'seal the deal.'"

I gasped. "Leo Callahan, are you trying to put out on a first date?!"

His eyes went a bit hazy as his gaze fell again to my mouth, tucking his phone back into his pocket. His response was quiet. "So what if I am?" It felt like a dare. A test of boundaries.

And I wanted to give in. That dangerous yearning pulsed through me, a starseed rooting into the trenches of my heart. "I'm not sure it's a good idea," I said honestly, my gaze shifting to the jukebox. I couldn't look him in the eye, couldn't see the impact of my words on his face.

He lifted a hand to push my hair back, and I arched up to it, greedy in the way his fingers lingered in the strands as my neck and scalp exploded in goosebumps. "I know," he said quietly. "But can you blame me for hoping?"

It sounded like he meant something more than just tonight, and it was disorienting. The whispers of longing emboldened inside of me, but we were already almost halfway through the contract. All of this would be over soon.

Will I be ready to say goodbye?

My heart ached even thinking of it, and I wondered how I'd let myself slip back into such a fierce want. I could blame the date or Leo's bright golden smile or this whole damn charade—but blaming him would be a fallacy. My want for him began before this contract even started, and I was the lying traitor when I told myself I could manage it.

"Come on." He steered me gently toward the door. I could see the pain flash through his smile. "Let's go home."

Chapter Twenty-One

IT WAS ALMOST MIDNIGHT WHEN WE SLIPPED through the front door of the apartment to find it quiet and dark. Leo's parents had gone to bed hours ago, content to sleep off their day's worth of petty judgment and passive aggressive subtleties designed to chip away at their son's resolve. Just being back in the same general vicinity as them sent a rattle of anger through me. Tonight had shown me what was beyond Leo's masked charm and had let the man beneath shine through. Now I would make it an effort to keep that light of his beaming.

I hoped his parents were struck blind from it.

We'd stopped on the way home for popcorn and licorice—Leo had given the Uber driver a hundred-dollar bill to wait for us in the parking lot so we wouldn't have to request another car. I was terrified to leave the Bentley back at The Manhole's parking lot, but Leo asked the resident concierge downstairs to have a driver run and get it, handing over the keys like it was nothing. I wasn't sure I could ever get used to such access to convenience, but then quickly shut the thought down when I realized I never would. I was only in Leo's orbit for a few more days before the clock would strike midnight, and I'd return to my shoebox of an apartment down the street where no one in the building cared about me except for maybe Mrs. Buxom next door, who sometimes left me tin-foil-wrapped meat when she'd made too much for herself.

"I'm going to go make a bag of popcorn," Leo whispered as Swift glided figure-eights around his ankles, audibly purring like the seductress that she was.

"I'll make us drinks." I smiled, feeling an expansion in my heart that I couldn't name, a stretching of my chest cavity as I watched his mouth tick up into a grin and his eyes flash to my mouth before he turned toward the kitchen.

In the few days I'd stayed here, I'd hardly spent any real time in the living room, so as I moved through it to get to the mini-bar in the corner where the decanter of bourbon sat, I eyed the black leather couch and glass coffee table with interest. It wasn't the pink velvet boho faux-luxury I was used to, but it didn't evoke the cold stuffiness I would have expected from a rich bachelor's furniture choices. The throw blanket that warmed my thighs on the roof that first night lay folded over the arm of the couch, and a delicate white candle with a burned-down wick rested atop the table. I was reminded of the confidence Leo displayed in his kitchen when he cooked—he was comfortable in his home, had made it *his* in a way that made me being here feel like I'd snuck into a place I had no right being in. It made me a little uneasy, like he'd realize at any moment how ridiculous this all was—that I was nothing more than a fun bartender on a good day and barely holding myself together on a bad one. Who was I to take the role of his girl-friend, to earn a place in a penthouse like this?

My mind somersaulted into a frenzy of chaos—a telltale sign of my fears coming to the surface. I had enough self-awareness to put my finger on the issue: I was losing control of the outcome. My neat and tidy plans of how I wanted this agreement to play out were now blurred like smeared ink on wet paper, and my feelings toward Leo were slipping into dangerous territory. Knowing firsthand the kind of shit he went through in his own life, I regretted how difficult I'd been every step of the way to get here.

I'd punished him for the pain that still pulsed in my veins, pain that had nothing to do with him. I'd assumed him to be entitled and full of himself the day I'd found out he'd purchased Larkspur, assumed him to be at the helm of the some larger system working against me. But he was proving me wrong—and my misjudgments lay right there in the new yoga room down the hall, or written all over his face when he swept me into a slow dance.

I gave the crystal glasses a generous pour of amber liquid and carried them to the couch, settling into a middle cushion that cradled my body like an old friend. Leo joined a few minutes later, a bowl full of warm popcorn in hand and both cats trailing at his feet, eager for the cuddle-fest that was sure to ensue—I couldn't blame them. He sat down next to me and pulled the throw blanket over our legs before reaching for the black remote control on the table.

"Can I ask you something?" I asked before I could talk myself out of it.

His blue eyes found mine, his face glowing from the light of the turned-on TV screen. "Anything," he answered.

"Why don't you play music anymore?"

He stared at me for a moment before he moved his gaze back to the TV. It felt like a dismissal. "I can't expect to succeed in life on whimsy and foolish dreams."

I frowned. "What does that mean?"

"It means . . ." He looked back at me, his eyes sharp. ". . . that music is a distraction from the things I should be focused on."

It was a few beats before his words sank in because I was more focused on the way he bristled, on the way his jaw clenched tight and his chest stopped moving as he held in a breath. All clear signs of his defensiveness.

But it wasn't my intention to be on the offensive—not anymore. "Hey," I murmured. "Lay down your armor, Callahan."

He exhaled, and it was a long, drawn-out deflation as his frustration lost traction. "Sorry," was all he said. His eyes moved away from me, back to the TV.

But now my curiosity was piqued. "What things do you think you should be focused on? The club?"

He nodded, his gaze drifting back to me casually. "The club is a start, but yes. The family business. I was . . ." He bit his cheek as he thought about his next words. "I'm supposed to take it all over. It's what I've worked toward my whole life— what my father has been preparing me for."

His answer didn't feel right. "Is that what you want for yourself, though?"

He shrugged. "I've learned that what I want doesn't really matter. I thought it did . . . I thought I could carve out a different path for myself. But it didn't work out, so I don't have many options."

My heart ached at the way his eyes turned away from me again. Like he was ashamed, defeated. Like he didn't measure up to whatever bar he'd set for himself. I wanted to know more, wanted the specifics of his hurt so that I could figure out a way to help him overcome it. But that would be going well beyond the boundaries that I needed to hold fast to for my own sanity. I couldn't hurt myself to save another—not again.

So instead of digging into a topic that was clearly difficult for him, I chose to instead settle further into the couch and show him my support with a safe amount of physical touch as I rested my head on his shoulder. He paused his navigation through the TV's streaming menu for a moment at my crossing of this line, and I worried that he'd shift away. But then he moved his free hand to my thigh under the blanket, stroking against my dress with his thumb, and clicked to start the movie.

IT TURNED out that Marge may have been on to something, because as Leo and I pretended to watch *The Outsiders* it became more and more apparent that both of us were . . . distracted. Leo's hand hadn't left my thigh in the half hour since the movie started, and the feel of his broad palm wrapped around my leg had turned my skin into molten lava. It didn't help that his thumb was skating a dizzying path back and forth, causing the cotton of my dress to fold in on itself as it rose higher and higher up my lap beneath the blanket.

The air seemed to ripple between us—but I didn't stop him. I tried not to give any indication of the effect he was having on me, though it was becoming increasingly difficult with every swipe of that damn thumb. I took another long pull of the bourbon in my glass before chasing it with a bite of licorice, willing the flush on my neck to cool off before he looked at me again.

Because he *would* look at me again—he'd been looking at me a lot tonight, stealing glances when he thought I wouldn't notice as the movie played on. It felt like he was caught up in some internal battle, and I didn't know if it was about our conversation earlier or if he could feel the heat radiating from my body at his touch. Either way, I was content to pretend those looks weren't adding fuel to the already incendiary friction between us.

"You want some more popcorn?" Leo asked, then cleared his throat. I chanced a glance at him, finding his eyes charcoal in the dark living room.

I eyed the bowl, seeing only a few buttery kernels left. "I'm okay, thank you." I smiled.

His gaze fell to my mouth, and his eyes darkened further to match the sky outside the wall of windows. He pulled the bowl back, leaning forward to set it on the coffee table before settling back into his seat, gently squeezing my thigh before that glorious thumb made another sweep. But then his whole body stilled when he made contact with bare skin, realizing how high my dress had moved up.

I sucked in a breath, closing my eyes as he slowly and carefully used the pads of all five fingers to graze a featherlight touch against my skin. It felt so good that I wanted to melt into the couch and stay here until I could chase this feeling all the way to the end . . . to what end, I wasn't sure. But I wanted it, tried to hold on to it so it didn't slip away like a match struck just to be blown out.

"Mara," Leo rasped, "that fucking sound."

I opened my eyes to find his locked on me, glittering with feral intent. *What sound?* "What?" I whispered, glancing down to watch the movement of his hand as he made another sweep under the blanket, moving higher up my thigh.

"Do you know how incredible you look when your cheeks flush?" he asked, keeping his voice low. "Do you know how hard it makes me?"

God, my skin burned as I remembered what Leo looked like hard and hungry. My mouth went dry as I remembered how he'd tasted, how I desperately wanted to taste him again. "I think it's just the bourbon . . ." I started to say, but then a finger skimmed along my panty line and I couldn't help the gasp that poured out of me.

"Mm," Leo rumbled, his body nearly vibrating with restraint. *Is that what he'd meant?* Remembering how I'd gasped that first night when I saw his kitchen, when I'd first tasted his food—he'd come undone at my reaction then, too. And it elated me, quite frankly, to know I could get to him like that. It felt . . . powerful. "Tell me to stop, Mara. Or tell me to keep going . . . I need some guidance here."

Keep going, my body pleaded. I wanted to arch into his hand, wanted to give him all of me. Wanted to know exactly what he'd do with a slip of my boundaries. But my logical side was still fighting for control. "We shouldn't, Leo. It's . . ."

"It's what?" he murmured into my ear, his mouth so close to my skin that I could feel the warmth of his next rough exhale. I *needed* to feel that five o'clock shadow rake across my body. To feel it burn against my thighs.

The question swam around in my head as I tried to form a coherent answer—it was an easy excuse to blame Larkspur and our professional relationship. But it wasn't like we hadn't already done this before. Was there really harm in doing it again?

Yes, I knew with clarity. And the truth of it had less to do with Larkspur or a flitting attempt at professionalism and more to do with the way my heart splintered into pieces the first time I walked away from him. I gave more of myself to him in the first hours of knowing he even existed than I'd given to anyone in years—and there'd been no consideration of the aftershocks, only of my plan to run. Now I knew I *couldn't* run from Leo because of the business we shared, and escaping from the trenches of this longing was like sawing off a limb with the way it wound itself into the strands of my being.

The truth was, plain and simple, I was scared.

Scared of how much I wanted this.

Scared of the inevitable loss of it.

But I couldn't admit to any of that now without giving him even more of me than he already had. So as I looked at him and forced the words from my mouth. "You're still my boss, Leo. Despite the contract, this isn't a good idea."

I expected to see disappointment flash across his face, but instead he looked even more determined. Like he'd known the excuse was coming, and he was ready for it. A step ahead. "That's too bad, because you look like you could use some relief." His fingers blazed a trail higher to my hip, careful to avoid my panties but not at all retreating. "You deserve to feel good, Mara," he whispered, and then he pressed his lips to my temple with so much tenderness I wanted to curl in on myself, knowing it was a subtle nod to my hurt.

The corner of my mouth twitched, but I couldn't say anything in response. Could only focus on my breathing as it rattled through my chest. We were flying higher with nowhere to go, nothing to aim for.

Leo's mouth moved down to my jaw, like he'd somehow known I wanted him there. His lips skated across my skin—less of a kiss and more of a hunger. "Touch yourself," he breathed, and the words pulsed through me like a beacon.

My eyes snapped to him. The glass of bourbon in my hand trembled and he reached for it with his free hand, slipping it out of my grasp and setting it on the table next to the forgotten bowl of popcorn. As he leaned back into the couch his shoulder pressed against mine, and he looked at me with a quiet resolution. "Mara," he urged, "if you won't let me take care of you, then let me help you take care of yourself." His gaze moved down to the blanket, watching it move as his hand traced a delicious path back to the inside of my thigh. He was teasing me, purposefully turning me on with wicked intent. Winding me so far up I'd have to sink into the pleasure to come back down. "Touch yourself for me, sweetheart."

Goosebumps rose along my body as I trembled with need so big and vast there could be no real relief anytime soon—at least that would be long-lasting. But at this point, I wouldn't be able to rise from this couch without lessening some of the pressure. So when Leo wrapped his hand around my own and guided it under the blanket, I was eager to give up my control —at least for a little while. This was light years beyond what was appropriate . . . but it was safer than giving that power to him.

"Is this okay?" he asked, his eyes black with purpose as he slipped my hand to where I was now aching.

I closed my eyes as my fingers brushed against the fabric of my panties. The thrill was so different than when I did this alone—knowing Leo was right next to me, earnest in his desire for me to let go. It made me feel exposed in a way that I wasn't sure I'd ever been before. I'd never touched myself in front of someone like this. Sex with a partner had always been an expression of mutual pleasure, not just my own. I nodded, feeling his exhale on my cheek as he rumbled his approval.

As my fingers began a slow chase toward my own pleasure he groaned into my neck, and I was suddenly aware of how much this turned him on. With my eyes still sealed shut, I thought about *him*—remembering the way his body had moved with mine, the way he'd edged me higher and higher before tipping me into the best orgasm I'd ever had. The way he'd soothed me afterward as we both came down from the high, whispering praise and adoration before he was winding me back up again.

"Fuck," I muttered.

"Yeah, 'fuck' is right," he responded. He'd taken his hands off of me as I moved on my own, and I quietly moaned when his fingers skated a path down my neck. "Look at how beautiful you are like this. So fucking perfect, Mara. So sweet."

I could feel my pleasure building as my fingers moved faster, and soon I was panting and writhing next to Leo's still and firm body. "I'm close . . ." I managed to say as I reached the tipping point.

His mouth pressed against my neck, hot and wet, and it sent a jolt of pleasure through me. "Come for me, Mara," he murmured into my skin, his voice sinking into my veins like warm, sticky honey. And I did. My climax rocked through me like a bomb detonating, and I rode my own hand through the continued waves of it.

Leo stroked along my shoulder and collarbone, and soon I was leaning into him and his warmth. Not for the first time, I felt . . . cared for by him. A soft smile spread across his lips, his eyes still near-black and glittering with desire. "You're incredible," he whispered, like it was a burning secret he couldn't contain.

"You make me feel brave," I said back through fluttering breaths. He made me feel like I could face anything, as long as he kept looking at me like he was right now.

His smile slipped before he shook his head. "No, Mara. You're the brave one." He pressed a lingering kiss to my forehead, like a bookend on the conversation. Like he wanted to leave it at that.

So I settled deeper into him, my gaze landing back on the movie in front of us, though I hardly knew what was going on in the story at this point. Something about the way Leo shrugged off the positive feedback tugged at me. His earlier words about his music floated to the surface, and I realized it wasn't the first time he'd said something self-deprecating. Maybe the mask he wore so well was more than just for show . . . maybe it was also to camouflage his own walls, his own lines in the sand between him and the rest of the world.

Maybe we had more in common than I thought.

Chapter Twenty-Two

Leo and his parents were both gone when I got home from the gym. He'd texted me about an hour ago to say he'd left to stop in at Larkspur to make sure everyone was okay for the night since neither of us would be working, and that he would be home around six to pick me up for dinner. His parents had apparently gone out for an early cocktail, which was fine by me—I counted myself lucky with how much I'd been able to avoid them since their arrival three nights ago. But I knew that luck would run out with tonight's dinner. If it was going to be anything like our last, I needed to be ready to face Christine-the-Ice-Queen for another round of table sparring.

I shucked my shoes off as soon as I stepped out of the elevator, flexing my toes against the plush rug in the entryway. Training had been especially grueling today as we focused on leg strength, and my feet were killing me, but it was a welcomed distraction from what happened last night with Leo. My gaze shot to the couch as I thought about what I did there, and I immediately flushed. Dolly eyed me with a cat-smirk from her usual resting place on the back of the couch, and I smiled at her with a show of confidence.

Maybe she'd respect me more if I hid my fear.

I had about an hour and a half to get ready, and I'd need to put all that time to good use if I was going to make myself presentable enough for NoMu . . . which reminded me of one sad fact: I needed to find something to *wear*.

I definitely didn't have anything fancy enough, but I hoped to god I had *something* to throw together that would pass the test at the door. Places like NoMu were sticklers about dress code, and I worried what I had wouldn't cut it. I couldn't fathom the thought of being turned away and embarrassing myself and Leo in front of his parents—Christine would have a field day. I marched toward Leo's bedroom and tried to gather myself . . . Maybe I'd have time to run out and buy something really fast. I knew of a few shops down the street that might have what I'd need.

As soon as I walked through the door to the bedroom, I stopped in my tracks. There, resting in the center of the bed, was a beautiful black box with an elaborate golden bow. I stared at it for a long moment before I could get my feet to move, already knowing somewhere deep inside what it was.

Do you have a dress? For dinner?

Leo. Of course he'd already thought of this. I took slow steps to the edge of the bed, reaching down to pick up the box. A folded piece of paper was tucked beneath a section of ribbon, and I pulled it out to find a handwritten note.

Mara,

Wear the dress.

See you soon,

Leo

Something about the masculine curves and swoops of his handwriting felt like an intimate demonstration of *him*. My heart pitter-pattered in my chest as I pulled at the bow, letting the shimmering gold material fall to the bed. Gently lifting the lid of the box, I found delicate red satin, bright and folded in on itself. I let the lid fall to the bed where it landed on top of the ribbon, and I simply stared at it.

I didn't have to inspect it further to know it was nicer than anything I'd ever owned. Nicer than anything that had ever been wrapped around my skin. I couldn't wear this tonight . . . it would be a cherry on top of the already sordid delusion I found myself in each morning I woke up in Leo's bed. I didn't belong here, and soon this little Cinderella story would come to an end.

Surely I had *something* I could wear instead. Though the gesture pierced me in the best way, I couldn't possibly accept. It was . . . too much.

Turning to the closet where I'd tucked away the few clothes I brought for the week, determination settled over me. Last night's dress probably could have worked, even though it didn't hold a candle to the one in the box, but I'd already foolishly worn it. I'd wanted to look good for him, for our date. *Idiot*, I chastised, groaning loud enough that Dolly's ears perked. Besides clothes for work or training at the gym, the only other options I had were a pair of jeans, a pair of faux-leather leggings, and a handful of ratty T-shirts.

There was absolutely no way any of this would get me through the door. I would be a laughing stock to Leo's parents if I even tried. I eyed the box on the bed again, feeling a swirl of nerves running rampant as I considered what it would mean to accept something like this. Once I wore it, he wouldn't be able to return it, right? Unless . . . maybe I could keep the tags on it, and if I was really careful not to stain it, we could pretend it had never been worn and he could get his money back.

It might be a drop in the bucket to Leo, but it wasn't to me. And more than anything else, that fact blazed through me with renewed awareness. I was already gaining a foothold into Larkspur—this felt like way too much.

I walked back toward the box and gently lifted the buttery satin, holding it up in front of me. As the dress slipped down to the floor, I could see it was a gorgeous one-shoulder design with a slit in the skirt on the opposite side. A section of the middle was also cut out, and I gasped at how beautiful it was. The dress was elegant—classic in a way that would stay in style for a lifetime. But also, *so* me.

Shockingly, Leo had known my size—or at least he'd guessed right. A fierce need to put the dress on came over me, but I was still slick with sweat from training. I found a rogue hanger in the closet and hung the dress up on the top of the door frame in the bathroom, hoping the steam from a hot shower would take care of any small creases from the time spent in the box.

I showered in record time, making quick work of shaving my legs and washing my hair. I'd decided to leave my hair down in soft waves and opted for a natural makeup look, hoping to lean into my own feminine elegance to complement the dress. And though I felt exposed at the notion of keeping things more natural tonight, I also realized I *wanted* Leo to see me this way—he'd seen me in looks suited for my place behind the bar, but something about slipping out of that persona tonight felt . . . right.

More so after our kind-of-real fake date last night.

I blow-dried my hair on the lowest setting, finger combing through it to avoid frizz, and I had to admit, the end result looked a lot more like the Mara from *before*. I stared at myself in the mirror and remembered the girl I used to be—the one who ached to fall in love and chase every dream. The one who was confident in her body, in her mind, and in her heart. I lined my eyes with a soft brown pencil and swiped mascara over my lashes. After applying a nude lipstick something still felt off . . . until I realized what it was. My septum ring.

I'd had it in since I got it pierced over a year ago, and I'd loved it every day since, but it clashed against the look I was going for tonight. Before I could think too much of it, I unscrewed the tiny gem that held the thin silver band together and carefully pulled it out of my nose. The effect was . . . dramatic.

It was the first time I'd looked *this much* like my old self again, like I was seeing the young girl who'd been buried beneath the rubble of so much damage. I couldn't deny that this recent time spent with Leo made me *feel* more like her, too. I didn't know what it meant, but I found myself taking shy steps forward and testing the water. Maybe it was time we both put our masks down and show up a little more authentically.

I heard a door shut from somewhere in the apartment.

Shit, I panicked—I wasn't dressed yet.

"Mara?" I heard Leo call out from the foyer.

"I need two more minutes!" I hollered back as I turned to eye the dress that hung from the top of the door jamb. Quickly unzipping the side, I gingerly pulled it off the hanger and stepped into it, slipping one arm through at the top before looking back at myself in the mirror.

The dress was *beautiful* on me. It hugged my body like it'd been made for my curves. And while I felt like an imposter beneath the lush red material, I couldn't deny the excitement and—admittedly—the heavy anticipation for Leo to see me like this.

At the thought, I turned off the light in the bathroom and moved out into the living room with careful steps so as not to step on the hem of the dress with my bare feet. I found Leo standing at the end of the hallway facing the other direction as he chuckled, watching Swift chase after an unamused Dolly.

"Hey," I greeted softly from behind him.

He wheeled around, the casual grin on his face melting and heating into something molten as his eyes found mine. For a long moment, he didn't say a thing as he looked me up and down—making no effort to hurry or hide it—until the corner of his mouth lifted in a drunken smile. "You look . . . wow, Mara. You look absolutely stunning."

My heart glowed from inside of my chest. "Thank you. And . . . thank you for the dress. You really didn't have to do this."

"I wanted to," he insisted, his eyes dropping to my bare shoulder as his throat worked. "You look more beautiful in it than I thought possible."

I couldn't help my own smile from breaking. All my nerves seemed to dissipate as I took in the tuxedo he was wearing, focused especially on the black bowtie at his throat presenting him to me like a gift. His hair was mussed in contrast, and his shoulders were strong and broad, shaped by the lines of his black tux jacket. An urge to slide my fingers beneath the lapels sparked in my fingertips. He looked so clean and polished that I wanted to mess it up. I wanted him disheveled and loose, as untamed and out of control as he'd made me feel.

But then a thought crashed through me, so unexpected I couldn't contain the gasp that burst from my mouth. "*Shit,*" I whisper-yelled, looking down at my bare feet. "I don't have any shoes to go with this!" My mind began racing through the pairs of shoes I knew had made it here from my apartment: black combat boots, leopard-trim Vans, an old pair of rubber flip-flops, the sneakers I ran to the gym in earlier . . . *Nothing* that would be remotely suitable for tonight.

I was instantly mortified, my face hot with shame for ruining all the effort Leo had gone to. Ruining this moment when, for the first time in far too fucking long, I felt *comfortable* in my vulnerability.

Leo gently brushed a finger against my jaw, lifting my face back up to meet his. "Hey," he murmured, "I've taken care of that, too. Come here." Then he reached for my hand and dragged me toward the couch, his dimple visible from the grin he was sporting. And that was when I noticed another black box resting on the coffee table, this one a bit slimmer in width but tied with the same golden bow. "Sit," he directed, and I did so without thought, my mind frozen as I tried to take in what was happening.

Keeping a hold of my hand, Leo lowered himself to the floor in front of me, kneeling on one square knee as it pressed into the rug. He tugged at the ribbon until it pooled around the edges of the box, and my eyes threatened to mist over as he revealed its contents. Inside were a pair of elegantly pointed heels made up of small, golden gems. They sparkled in the sunset glow beaming in from the large windows, making my breath catch. "Oh my god," I whispered.

Leo slowly reached in to grab one of the shoes with his free hand, pulling it out of the box before he turned his long torso toward me. "I picked these up for you, hoping they would pair well with the dress," he explained. He let go of my hand, lightly trailing his fingers down the back of my right calf before wrapping his palm around the arch of my foot and pulling it against the thigh of the bent leg in front of him.

The fabric of his pants *whooshed* against my skin. I could hear my pulse pounding in my ears as Leo lowered the shoe onto my foot, making careful work of getting it into position. His fingers slid around my ankle as he worked to fasten the small buckle of the strap, sparking goosebumps up my whole leg. He must have noticed my reaction to his touch because his eyes met mine, whirling with desire. "I'd say they pair well," I forced out.

He smirked, and it knocked me senseless. "Yes." He nodded, keeping his focus on my face. "So beautiful." My thoughts jilted at the words as my blood simmered. After another moment that seemed to stretch time, Leo cleared his throat and reached for the other shoe. He pulled it out of the box and worked to get it on my left foot with a devastating tenderness. I'd never in my entire life felt so . . . cared for like this.

And the sight of Leo kneeling in front of me . . .

I had to tear my gaze away from him to stop from melting right into the couch—this couch that had already seen so much between us. It felt like my body was heating from the inside out and I didn't know how to stop it, how to let out some of the mounting pressure. Leo finished fastening the second shoe, and his knuckles brushed against my leg as he stood back up.

"One more thing," he said softly, holding a hand out. I looked up at him and found his eyes glinting. I entwined my hand with his and let him help me to my feet, now standing four inches higher than before. Leo smiled. "Are they comfortable?"

Shifting my weight between each leg, I considered. "They're not bad for heels," I jested.

He nodded, his eyes falling down to the sparkling shoes before he looked up toward the kitchen. "Stay here." I watched him move to grab something off the marble island before he was back in front of me, a black velvet box clutched in his hands. "One final touch," he said, and then he opened the box.

Inside was a necklace with stones that increased in size as they dripped down toward the center, where the largest one twinkled brightly against the fabric it rested on. "Oh my god," I whispered, "tell me those aren't real diamonds, Leo."

He huffed a small laugh. "May I?" His eyes blazed in question, and I realized he was nervous. Which had to mean they *were* real. *Real diamonds!* I'd never seen anything so beautiful. All I could do was nod—my throat was constricting with too much emotion to force any words out. His fingers carefully pulled the necklace out of the box and hundreds of tiny rainbows glinted around the room as the glow from sunset shattered through it. My nose stung with tears as Leo moved to stand behind me, gently clasping the chain around my neck and sending a wisp of prickles along my skin. "There," he murmured.

I turned to look at him, feeling wildly out of sorts. "Leo, this is too much," I breathed. "Please tell me everything is returnable . . . I should never have agreed to this dinner knowing I don't own the right attire—"

"Mara," he interrupted me, "I'm quite certain you would have gotten through the door in one of those little bartending outfits I like so much—you have quite the knack for disarming people. Even still, I'm the one who asked you for this relationship. It was my father who made these reservations without much consideration for others. And it happens to please me to do nice things for you. So, please, consider this all a gift. A token of my gratitude."

Heat swirled around us. Leo was stubborn enough that he'd never change his mind to help me return any of it, and the alternative would be to sell the items myself. But the thought of trading any of this for cash behind his back made me feel gross, even if it meant returning the money to him. It was all way too beautiful to pawn off like that.

And deep in my heart, I already knew I'd treasure it forever.

I'd find another way to repay him, I decided. I would make sure Larkspur's revenue continued to grow so that he made ample profits, even with his lowered percentage of ownership. I already regretted asking him to walk away from the day-to-day operations after this agreement was over—he deserved to be a part of the success. To feel as significant as he'd so effortlessly made me feel.

"Thank you," I replied softly, entwining our hands and squeezing lightly.

He swiped his thumb along my fingers as a flush crept from beneath his stark white collar. I felt the sudden urge to press my lips to the spot. "We'd better get going," he said, leading me toward the front door.

Dolly meowed loudly from where she was now sprawled out on the floor. I looked over my shoulder at her, and swore I caught her smiling at me.

Chapter Twenty-Three

LEO HIRED A DRIVER FOR THE NIGHT, WHICH MEANT that instead of riding shotgun in his Bentley we were both tucked into the back seat of a black SUV, intently focused on the view outside of our respective windows. My nerves rattled within me as we got closer and closer to the restaurant, caused by both the intoxicating smell of Leo and this impending dinner.

It wasn't that Alaric and Christine made me nervous—I could handle myself around people like them. But I was supposed to be Leo's girlfriend, which meant I should probably act like I cared what his family thought of me. It would be both impolite and unhelpful to Leo for me to sharpen my weapons and make this any more uncomfortable than it needed to be.

But the way they treated their son irked me beyond measure.

And the way Leo took it, like he might have deserved it, made me see red.

When the SUV pulled up along the curb in front of NoMu, Leo strode around to open my door, then held a hand out for me. The air outside caught me off guard as soon as I was out of the car, but I hardly felt it. I was too focused on ensuring my steps were confident, that I looked the part of a billionaire's girlfriend in more ways than simply what I was wearing.

I caught Leo watching me, the corners of his mouth tugging up enough to indicate his approval. He rocked back on his heels as he swept those bright blue eyes over me with a look like *Now or never*, then said, "Ready?"

I wound my hand around the crook of his elbow and settled into him, grounding myself in the warmth of his body for a moment before looking up at him. A flash of white sliced across his face, and I laughed.

"What?" he asked softly as he leaned a little closer.

"You have a shit-eating grin on your face right now, Leo. It's about as subtle as a brick wall."

His smile only widened. "Hard not to with you on my arm, looking like this."

The words made me feel faint. All I could do was squeeze his arm in return.

Leo steered me toward the door, his shoulders back and his chest puffed with pride. "Let's do this." He gave his name to the striking hostess as soon as we were inside, and I watched her practically drool over him as she checked the screen in front of her. If he noticed, he didn't let on; though it wasn't my place to care about any woman who might be interested in him.

"It looks like the others in your party are already here," she chirped, looking up at Leo with a vivacious smile.

Leo nodded, but I felt his arm stiffen. I laid my free hand on his bicep, doing my best to anchor him. "Great, thanks," he managed to reply.

We followed her into the restaurant and, though we held on to our confidence as much as we could, when our table came into sight we both seemed to make ourselves smaller. Christine was the first one to see us from where she sat between Alaric and another much younger man. She wore a pastel yellow gown and her hair was pulled up in a French twist that radiated elegance. There was no denying it—she was beautiful.

On either side of her, Alaric and the other man were engaged in a loud and animated discussion, both of them breaking into raucous laughter before Christine signaled to Alaric that we'd arrived. Just as we approached the table all three sets of eyes landed on us, and my heart jumped in my throat.

"Leopold." Alaric sat back in his chair and looked up at Leo. "Glad you could finally make it, son."

Leo's eyes narrowed almost imperceptibly. "The reservation is for seven, Father, and it's still ten minutes to. Though, it looks like you and Mom have been able to settle in just fine," he said as he eyed the glass of bourbon his hand was wrapped around.

"Yes," Alaric confirmed, eyes sharpening. "Luckily, we've had great company to keep us entertained. Leo, I'd love for you to meet our new friend, Tanner McCabe. Tanner earned himself some stripes in the tech industry with a handful of merger deals, and I'm looking forward to you getting to know him. Perhaps some of his fire and zest for business will do you some good."

My eyes slid to the young man and found he was looking at me with a curious gaze. His dark eyes moved to Leo as he stood from his chair, reaching a hand across the table toward us. "It's great to meet you, Leo. Your parents are wonderful people. I feel lucky our paths crossed earlier this week."

Leo took his hand and shook it. "Nice to meet you, too," he said stiffly. He turned back to his parents. "You both look lovely. Mom, you are as beautiful as ever. I hope you're enjoying yourself."

Christine's smile was saccharine. "We're just happy you're here, honey." Her eyes bounced to mine. "And you brought your friend."

"Girlfriend," Leo amended, his gaze darting to Tanner before addressing me. "Mara." He smiled, and I could feel it shift from the cool, indifferent one to something real.

I turned to the others, demonstrating my best supportive-girlfriend-smile as Leo pulled a chair out for me to sit in—the one closest to Tanner. "Thank you so much for having us tonight—you've picked a wonderful place for dinner."

"Have you been here before?" Christine asked.

I looked at her, praying my smile wouldn't falter. "No, I haven't. But I've heard wonderful things."

Her lips pressed together and her eyes glinted like she already had me. I did my best not to show I noticed, shifting my gaze to Leo as he sat down beside me. He wrapped one arm across the back of my chair in reassurance, and I settled into his warmth with a level of comfort that was anything but fake.

Alaric swirled the glass of bourbon in front of him before

taking a sip. "I was telling Tanner here about your recent acquisition," he eyed Leo.

"Yes." Tanner nodded. "Sounds like you've got yourself a fun little project! A nightclub?" His smile was wide and wicked as he leaned in closer. "Is it . . . is it like a topless thing?"

Alaric chuckled.

Leo straightened. "Topless?"

"Yeah, you know—" Tanner's eyes bounced to me for a moment before he continued. "Like, strippers?"

Leo's attention shifted back to Alaric. "Well, it looks like you left a lot of details to the imagination, didn't you, Father?"

"Don't be disrespectful," Alaric scolded.

Leo turned to Tanner. "It's not a strip club, it's a nightclub —a very successful one at that. Mara has done an excellent job in creating an environment that attracts hundreds of customers each night." He raised his hand and swiped his thumb lightly against the back of my neck. The next smile he gave me nearly knocked me to the floor. "She's really the mastermind behind the whole operation."

Alaric clicked his tongue. "You credit Mara with your success, then?"

Leo snapped his attention back to him. "Absolutely."

The conviction in that one word made the tips of my fingers hum.

Before anyone could respond, a server came by to deliver a large platter of steamed mussels and two smaller plates of caviar with dry toast and some sort of white cream. Leo and I took the opportunity to order a bottle of white wine for us to share before he served us both some of the hors d'oeuvres while the others did the same for themselves. When he added a small spoonful of the cream on the side of my plate near the caviar, I looked up at him in question.

"Crème fraîche," he murmured softly, and I hoped it was quiet enough that no one else could hear. I'd never had caviar before, and I definitely didn't know the kinds of things it was served with—but I didn't want Alaric or Christine to know that. "It's kind of like sour cream," he added.

I nodded, taking the small plate from him and inspecting it closely. The mussels looked amazing, but I wasn't so sure about the caviar. It looked . . . weird. I watched Leo spread some of his caviar on a small piece of toast before adding a small amount of the crème fraîche to the top. And then he popped the whole thing in his mouth, giving me a sly wink. Looking back down at my own plate, I mimicked what he did on a piece of my own toast before taking a careful bite.

I noticed Christine watching me just as an explosion of flavor enveloped my mouth. The bite was butter, savory, and held undertones of what could only be described as ocean water—it wasn't bad, all things considered. After chewing it down and swallowing the first bite, I made a small show of putting the other half of the toast in my mouth before smiling back at Leo as I chewed.

His eyes danced mischievously, and my body tingled in response.

"So, Leopold, tell me," Alaric said, setting his fork down against his own side plate and folding his hands in front of him, his thick wrists resting on the table linen, "what do you plan on doing in the long-term with this . . . *club* of yours?" His tone was condescending. "What's your end game with it?"

I didn't miss that his eyes flicked to me momentarily before landing back on his son, as if the question pertained to more than just Larkspur. Leo straightened, his pressed dress shirt stretching across his broad shoulders as his face twisted into annoyance and, more subtly, hurt. Seeing him go from playful to defensive so quickly tightened something in my chest—something unfamiliar. It felt . . . protective.

Definitely furious.

"Probably a great way to meet women," Tanner said through a mouthful of food. "Pretty smart."

Leo frowned. "It has nothing to do with women."

Tanner had the decency to look chastised as he glanced my way. "Right."

I wanted to slap him.

"Then what is it?" Alaric asked again.

Leo sighed, sitting back in his chair. He stared at his father for so long I could feel the tension rising between them.

"See," his father continued with a small laugh, "you don't even know how to properly answer a simple question, do you, son?"

Leo's lips pressed firmly together before he finally spoke, his sapphire eyes blazing. "I'm perfectly capable of answering your questions, Father. However, I refuse to partake in your mockery. For fuck's sake, I'm thirty-three years old. I'm not a child."

"You certainly act like one," Alaric replied, his tone dismissive despite his raised voice.

"Alaric," Christine hissed under a sharp breath. "People are looking."

I scoffed. *People are looking?* That's how Christine chose to tame her husband? Not, *You're acting like a bully*, or *Don't speak to our son like that*, or *Leo is perfectly capable of running a successful business.* I felt ready to spew venom at these terrible people.

Leo deserved *so* much better.

Alaric's eyes snapped to me. "Did you have something you'd like to add?"

I glared back at him. "Don't you think you're being a touch unsupportive?"

His eyes widened with a kind of shock that told me he never expected me to actually stand up to him. Leo wrapped a warm hand around my thigh under the table, thumb caressing the side. Tanner cleared his throat before saying, "Now now, sweetheart, calm down—I think Alaric is just looking out for his kid."

I turned my glare to Tanner, noticing a drop of butter hanging from his lip. Disgust rolled through me at the thought of this man—this stranger—trying to keep me quiet in good-old-boy fashion. He literally had no idea what he was talking about and no business interjecting, yet still felt confident enough to tell *me* to calm down? "I'm not your sweetheart," I replied coolly, "and I hardly think any of this is of your concern."

"It's not yours either." Alaric spoke again, his scrutiny of me now out in the open. "I will not have some lowly bartender making any sort of claims against the way I choose to speak to my son."

"*Excuse me.*" Anger smoldered in Leo's features as he glared at his father, his jaw clenching tightly. "You will not speak to her that way, do you understand me?"

Alaric's mouth twisted as he took another drink from his glass. The server came by, completely unaware of the contention at the table as he presented the bottle of Pinot

Grigio that Leo ordered. He gave him a sample in a fresh glass and, when Leo nodded his approval, poured a full serving into two glasses for the both of us. Leo passed one of them to me, and I smiled gratefully. "Thank you, honey," I said, making a compulsive decision to brush some of his disheveled hair off his forehead.

Leo watched me, his skin glowing softly beneath the romantic lighting of the restaurant, before squeezing my thigh again. "Anything for you," he said quietly enough that it felt like it was actually meant for me, and not for show.

"Damn," Tanner muttered on the other side of me. "How long have you two been together?"

It seemed we were dropping the previous conversation.

Leo took charge of responding, his voice losing the warmth it'd just had for me. "Almost a year now."

"Damn!" Tanner said again with more enthusiasm. "That's impressive. I'm more of a one-night-stand kind of guy, you know?" He laughed as he waggled his eyebrows in jest, and Alaric's face broke into a wide grin. It bothered me to see how easily amused he was with Tanner when he couldn't even look at his own son without sneering. I knew it bothered Leo, too, but he did a great job of not showing it.

Christine, who had mostly been quiet on the other side of the table, set down a mussel shell and dabbed her lips with a linen napkin before saying, "You know, Leo was engaged to a beautiful young woman in New York before his . . . *episode*." She looked right at me, as if for emphasis.

Leo was engaged? It felt like a pressure hose being aimed at my face. My expression must have faltered because Christine smirked, and I hated her for it.

Leo tensed beside me. "Mother, I hardly think that's relevant to bring up now." His panic was obvious, but I didn't know if it was the mention of an engagement or his . . . "episode," whatever that meant. Or maybe it was because he knew this was all new information for me.

I tried to ignore the sting of it, of not knowing he'd been engaged only a year ago. Leo didn't owe me his life story, but there was no denying we'd been blurring the lines between what was fake and what was real, and I would've preferred to find something like this out from him instead of his meddling mother. She continued to surveil me, thrilled at her ability to hurt someone who—for all she knew—made her son happy.

I wanted to bite back.

Before I could stop myself, I blurted out, "Maybe she wasn't strong enough to handle the man that Leo is."

Alaric huffed out a laugh, and rage sang in my veins.

Christine looked at her husband and smiled, encouraged by his mockery. "Well, I for one don't pretend to understand my son's type when it comes to women. Rebecca was the picture-perfect bride, and it still wasn't enough to satisfy him."

"Doesn't sound like she was right for him, then," I retorted.

Leo gave my thigh another squeeze under the table. "Mara," he murmured close to my ear. "It's not worth it. I'm so sorry, I shouldn't have brought you here."

I looked at him and found his mouth lined with worry as he studied my face. I gave him a glimpse of a smile. "No, Leo, it's okay. Let them dig themselves into a hole." His scrutiny, even presented through a tightened brow, felt like a warm embrace. He cared about me. I pressed my palm lightly to his cheek, wanting to reassure him we could withstand this. Together.

I wasn't going to back down.

Turning back to his parents, I squared my shoulders. "You're definitely right that you don't understand Leo's type. You've been looking at me like a pesky bug beneath your shoe, and I'm not sure if it's my colored hair or the fact that I'm a bartender—or maybe it's that I've slept with more women in my life than Tanner probably has?" Christine gasped, clutching her hand over her mouth in horror. Next to her, Alaric went as white as the table cloth between us. "He deserves to have a partner who understands his needs and who is invested in helping him reach his own dreams."

"And that's *you*?" Christine spewed.

I shrugged, unfazed. "Maybe. Maybe this doesn't work out, and that's okay." I peered over at Leo, not knowing what I'd find. But he didn't look mad—he looked . . . awestruck. "Or maybe it does. Maybe I contribute to his real happiness." I smiled. "But either way, Leo *deserves* to be happy and supported and fiercely loved."

Alaric's pale face transitioned to red as he glared at me. "You are a disrespectful brat who is clearly only with my son for your own personal gain. If not for you and this sham of a relationship that is *nothing* but a distraction, he probably would never have stooped so low as to buy a fucking *nightclub*. You make a mockery of him and of our family name, and I will not allow it any longer!" If Christine was worried about people looking before, she should be petrified now—everyone around us was gaping at Alaric. He turned to Leo. "And you! You have made a mess of everything! Everything that we worked so hard for!" he thundered. "This is fucking over, do you understand me? You are to return to New York by the end of the month, or I will ensure you are cut off from all of your accounts!"

"You can't do that," Leo argued, keeping his voice low. "Take me off the company payroll, if you wish, but you can't cut me off from what is mine—I have full rights to my own personal accounts. Grandpa made sure of it when he passed. You will learn to speak to Mara with respect or I will make sure you are publicly exposed for far more than your anger and control issues."

Alaric bristled at the threat, eyes dancing in rage. "As if anyone would believe you after the fool you made of yourself, Leo. Give it up, son. You have nothing without me. You *are* nothing without me. I made you, and you *will* fall in line. It's only a matter of time."

Leo pressed his lips together in frustration but stayed silent. I didn't know if it was in an attempt to de-escalate things, or if he really was intimidated by Alaric's words. I prayed it was the former, that Leo wasn't actually scared by anything this sad, disgusting man had to say. But words from last night raced back to my mind . . .

I can't expect to succeed in life on whimsy and foolish dreams.

I'm supposed to take it all over. It's what I've worked toward my whole life—what my father has been preparing me for.

I knew what it was like to exist underneath someone's thumb like this—it felt impossible to get out, to break free. I wanted to climb across the table and strangle Alaric for how easy it was for him to spew vitriol at his own son. I wanted to shake Leo and beg him to leave these terrible people behind. To pursue *his* dreams—like playing and writing music.

I would just have to prove to him that it would be worth it, that he could succeed on his own without any help from his father, no matter what he chose for his life. And I wanted to . . . I *wanted* to make that effort. For him.

He turned to look at me with an expression that was stony and closed off. But his eyes gave him away—they always did. He was in pain. "Let's get out of this dumpster fire of a dinner," I whispered with a small smile, an attempt to show him we were okay. That I had him.

He gave me a tight nod before turning back to his parents. "I hope you all have a lovely rest of your evening . . . Mara and I are taking our leave. Thank you for the hors d'oeuvres—please feel free to enjoy the rest of our wine." He pushed his chair back before standing to pull mine out.

"Leopold." Christine's eyes were wide. "Surely you are not leaving in the middle of dinner? We haven't even ordered our food yet!"

Leo gave her a stiff smile. "I'm sure you'll have a nice enough time without us. You have a guest here to entertain you, after all."

Tanner looked guilty as he picked up his drink, and Alaric rolled his eyes. "Quit being dramatic, Leo, and sit back down."

"No thanks." It was all he said before he hooked an arm around my waist and led us to the front of the restaurant. Both Alaric and Christine gaped at us as we walked away, shocked at his show of defiance.

We stayed silent until we got out the doors and into the cold night air. The sharp bite of a breeze curled around me, and I shivered. Leo didn't miss it, and he shrugged out of his dinner jacket and wrapped it around my shoulders. For a moment, we simply looked at each other—so many words swirling between us. We were teetering on the edge of a cliff as Leo opened his mouth to finally say something.

But then the sleek black SUV pulled up along the curb, its

driver jumping out to open the back door for us. I couldn't help but grin. "I didn't even see you call for it."

He lifted his shoulder, the movement small and restrained. "He never left. I had a feeling."

The admission made my chest ache.

"You hungry?" he asked as he crawled into the back seat after me.

"Starved."

Chapter Twenty-Four

Within twenty minutes we found ourselves back at The Manhole. It was a relief to walk through the doors, to breathe in the stale beer and burned popcorn from their limited kitchen and leave behind the heaviness of disappointment and cheap jabs. My eyes kept gravitating toward Leo's face as we found the table we'd shared last night—as if on silent instinct—feeling my focus sharpen as I kept careful watch of him. I couldn't imagine what he was feeling, to have his own family treat him with such cruelty.

The same ancient bartender made his way out from behind the bar, reaching us with an expression that was neither welcoming nor accommodating. He looked us up and down, taking in our absurd dive-bar attire. Deciding not to try to explain, I simply smiled and ordered two bottles of beer for both Leo and I and a basket of chicken strips and fries to share. He disappeared back behind the bar to fetch them, and when I turned to Leo, I realized he needed to be jostled out of a haze. I reached an arm out through the front of his jacket that I still wore, gently gripping his arm until he looked at me. "Hey," I said gently.

"Hey," he echoed.

"Are you okay?" I asked.

"Yeah." He nodded. "I am." It must've been the steel behind his words because I actually believed him.

The bartender returned with our beer, and we both took a couple heavy gulps. I looked around the bar wondering if anyone from last night was here again, and found some of the same bikers saddled up at the bar. Marge and Otto were nowhere to be found, and my heart sunk.

I wanted to thank her for a successful movie night.

"How you manage to go toe to toe with others is a form of magic I won't pretend to comprehend," Leo said, pulling my focus back to him.

I laughed, and some of the weight that had settled around us lifted. "Good, I like to keep some mystery."

He chuckled. "I can't believe you said you've slept with more women than Tanner. I was simultaneously turned on and mortified that it was in front of my mother."

I shrugged. "I feel like your mom could use some loosening up."

Leo whistled, shaking his head. "That woman is about as stiff as a board."

"She doesn't like me," I said flatly.

"She envies you," he countered.

"*What?*" I exclaimed. I hadn't expected that.

He gave me a pointed look. "She's been bound to my father

for decades, living a life of stifled exuberance that probably feels like a prison. I know what it was like growing up with Alaric Callahan, I can only imagine what it is to be married to him. Having to deal with the financial scandals, the other women . . .” He paused, brushing an imaginary piece of lint off his pants. “I worry about her. But she's too prideful to admit that anything's wrong. She'd rather raze the world around her than put out the fire in her own house.”

His words hit me like a punch to the face. “I might relate to her more than I realized,” I said honestly.

He looked at me with renewed interest. “What do you mean?”

Shit. I wasn't prepared for this conversation—not that I ever was. Though Leo was feeling more and more like someone I might want to share that history with. Just . . . not right now. Not when we had these fresh wounds to lick. “Never mind.”

“Oh no you don't. You don't get to shy away again.” He settled back into his chair—one that definitely looked like it was on its last leg—and crossed his arms over his chest. “Tell me,” he insisted.

I waved a hand. “Just a bad ex. Really, it's old news. We should be focusing on you and your wild-ass family. Has your father always been like . . . *that*?”

Leo let out a breath, no doubt seeing right through my subject change. But thankfully he just said, “I don't know him any other way.”

I snorted. “Well, he could use a good old-fashioned kick in the ass.”

“I've never seen anyone stand up to him like you did. Everyone is always so afraid of him, of the power he has and what he can take away. But you . . . you're so brave, Mara. Like a breath of fresh air after being stuck in that smoke-filled house. I've dealt with a lot of shit from my parents, but tonight it was different. Having you next to me was . . ." He trailed off as he seemed to search for the words. "I felt like I was braver just being near you."

The confession shook the ground beneath my feet. Couldn't he see what a mess I was? I wasn't brave, I just knew how to fight hard enough to make it out of a battle, usually by the skin of my teeth. "Leo—" I started, but he cut me off as he took my hands in his.

"Thank you," he said with so much emotion I thought we both might burst right here at this table.

I nearly jumped out of my own chair to wrap my arms around him, stopping myself with sheer will that was crumbling by the second. "You are literally the perfect man. I hope you find what makes you happy." He looked up at the ceiling to let out a long breath, and I took the opportunity to pull my hands back from his and quickly wipe away a tear that spilled onto my cheek, hoping he wouldn't notice. The last thing I wanted was for him to worry about my emotions on top of everything else.

He *needed* this moment. He deserved to be selfish with it. And I would make sure he understood what real support felt like.

The bartender swooped by to drop the basket of food in the middle of our table, and we both thanked him profusely before diving in. "I can't believe you were engaged," I eventually said between bites of fried chicken.

Leo groaned. "Worst mistake of my life was proposing to that woman," he said through his own mouthful. "No, actually, my worst mistake was listening to my mother when she told me I'd never find anyone better."

I scoffed. After a moment, I dared to ask, "What's she like?"

Leo's eyes snapped to mine with surprise. "Rebecca?"

I nodded. "Yeah."

"She's . . . beautiful. Smart. Her family is wealthy." He shook his head. "Her father is the CEO of a huge tech conglomerate based out of San Francisco—that's where they're from. Rebecca was in New York for school, and we met at a Gala event that her father sent her to on his behalf. My dad's been trying to break into the tech world for years—it's probably why he's so smitten with Tanner. When he realized who she was, he roped my mother in to do what she does best: meddle in my personal life. Next thing I knew, I was on a blind date with her."

I took a long swig of my beer, feeling the carbonation burn down my throat. "What happened?"

"Rebecca can be very charming, and at first it was exactly that. While I didn't love that it was my mother who set us up, I actually liked her. I proposed after six months, which seems much too soon in hindsight, but our families got along well and it felt like the right move for all aspects of my life. I thought she was a good life partner, and she was interested in supporting the business which made my father happy. But . . ." He took a deep breath, wiped at his hand with a napkin. He was stalling. "After I proposed, things became difficult. She spent a lot of money and always wanted *more*. She wanted a vacation home in the Hamptons, and I wanted a small cabin here in Colorado. She wanted to host extravagant parties, and I just wanted to shut myself away and take a break from all that high society bullshit. She wanted to summer in Greece and—"

"Ugh." I smacked my hand over my face. "The way rich people use 'summer' as a verb . . ."

Leo laughed, and it was a sound I craved to hear more of. "Point taken." He smirked. "Anyway, I tried to share my music with her, but she wasn't interested. Much like my parents, she thought it was a distraction from our *real* ambitions. Pressures from the business began ramping up as my father and I worked toward closing a huge deal—one that would have made the company millions. There was a big presentation I'd been working on for months, and it was in my hands to ultimately deliver.

"The morning of the meeting, I fucking crumbled. I . . . I don't even know what happened. I woke up and felt like I couldn't breathe anymore. It was like my brain shut down and I couldn't even process a single thought, so I walked out of the boardroom only a few minutes after the meeting started. My father was furious, and when Rebecca found out she didn't even ask if I was okay—she just threw a tantrum. Said I should have been stronger, that she needed me to be a real man. And that was it. I lost it. I ended things with her on the spot, packed a few bags and bailed. I came out here . . . and I haven't talked to anyone since. Well, until now."

I stared at Leo intently, mind swirling as I processed it all. "Wow," I breathed. "I'm so sorry that happened to you, Leo." It was all I could say that didn't include any of the anger I was feeling toward the people in his life. No wonder Leo struggled to see his dreams as valid.

No one had ever made him feel safe in pursuing them.

He looked resigned when he said, "Yeah, well. It's all in the past."

I shook my head. "No, it's not. I mean, maybe Rebecca is. And good riddance." I scoffed. "But, your *parents*, Leo. They aren't healthy for you. Tonight was proof that they don't deserve to have you in their lives, not if they're going to treat you the way they do, like you're just some resource for their benefit." I suddenly felt like such an asshole for keeping my own parents at arm's length these last couple of years. "Do you even like what you do for your father? Do you enjoy the work?"

Leo's laugh was dry. "I wish I did. It would sure make things easier. But . . . no, I don't. And I'm terrible at pretending I do—my father can always see right through my veiled attempts to please him."

I laughed, and his eyes snapped to mine. "What do you mean, you're terrible at pretending? You've been pretending about our year-long love affair since they got here—and it's been pretty expert-level stuff," I remarked, hoping to lighten the mood a little.

Leo's gaze drifted to my collarbone, where the delicate diamond necklace hung, before moving to my mouth. Something shifted behind his eyes as he considered, but I couldn't put my finger on what it was. Eventually, his eyes caught mine again and he shrugged. "I guess some lies are easier than others."

Warmth spread throughout my body at those words. At the way he was looking at me.

"Look," he sighed. "We don't have to keep doing this. I thought having an elaborate story about falling in love and buying Larkspur for you . . . for *us* . . . would help things. But clearly I was wrong, and you don't deserve to be caught up in any of this."

I straightened in my seat, feeling the shoulder strap of my dress strain from the movement. "Fuck that," I retorted.

Leo's eyes widened. "What?"

"Fuck that, Leo. I'm not bailing on any of this . . . not now. You think I'd be okay with just leaving you in the dust?"

"It wouldn't hurt my feelings," he explained earnestly. "You shouldn't have to subject yourself to this . . . bullshit."

"You shouldn't either!" I exclaimed. "Do you anticipate your parents flying home early after how badly things went tonight?"

"Oh no. My father won't leave until he inflicts enough pain to get what he wants."

I smiled, popping a french fry in my mouth. "Then our mission isn't over."

Leo's mouth tugged up in a grin. He focused on the food, picking out a chicken strip and biting off one crispy end. "You scare me sometimes."

I chuckled. "Good." After taking another swig of the beer in front of me, I felt compelled to say more. "I'm serious, Leo. We go all the way with it. Okay?"

His eyes found a bit of their sparkle in an instant, and it pressed against my throat. "Thank you," was all he said in return.

WE MADE it back to Leo's apartment soon after we finished eating, both of us feeling emotionally exhausted. Leo's parents were still out, confirmed by Georgie downstairs who said he hadn't seen them come in yet. Dolly and Swift greeted us at the door with hungry meows, and Leo found their food container empty in the kitchen.

While he worked to refill it, I slipped into his bedroom to start getting ready for bed. I washed my hands three times first—there was no way I was going to let my greasy chicken fingers anywhere near the beautiful fabric until I could be sure they were clean. Just as I finished washing, I heard Leo walk into the bedroom from outside the bathroom door. "I'm going to change out here, if that's all right?"

"Of course," I said. "I'll be in here for a few more minutes."

After stepping out of my sparkling new heels, I carefully maneuvered myself out of the dress and placed it back on the hanger that was still propped on the door jamb. In nothing but a white strapless bra and matching thong, I looked at myself in the mirror, realizing the diamond necklace still sloped down my neck.

It was . . . breathtaking. I'd never seen myself in anything more beautiful. Thinking about taking it off made me sad, because I never knew when I'd have an opportunity to wear it again. I closed my eyes and remembered what it had felt like when Leo put it on—his warm hands grazing over my skin, sending fire through my body. It had been so obvious that he still wanted more, that his body still yearned for mine the way mine did for him.

It would be so easy to give in. *So* fucking easy.

But what would happen at the end of the week? I'd already asked Leo to disappear once this week was over and his parents went back to whatever hell they came from. Was I really going to let myself fall deeper in . . . whatever *this* was? I thought about everything he'd done for me over the last few days and how it was more than anyone else had done for me in years, and I was still holding him at a distance.

Imagine what things could be like if you actually let him in, I thought to myself.

I wasn't sure I was ready, but I did know one thing: I was determined to making sure Leo knew his worth. Regardless of what might or might not happen between us, if I could use this opportunity to really drive home how important *his* dreams were, I would do it.

I quickly brushed my teeth before giving myself another once-over in the mirror. My hair was still soft and wavy, falling below my shoulders. My face was so much more naturally beautiful. And my body . . . I didn't shy away from how confident I felt like this. Exposed and raw. *Real.*

I wanted to share it with Leo. I wanted to give him a sense of the peace we shared that first night together. So before I could talk myself out of it, I turned the handle and pushed open the door, taking a few steps out into the bedroom.

He was standing on the other side of the room near the lounge he'd been sleeping on all week. His shirt was off, and was bent over, giving me a perfect view of his perfect ass. My eyes roamed the dips and valleys of his back, watching in fascination as the muscles beneath his skin rippled as he pulled on a pair of flannel pajama pants. "Sorry I was just . . ." he began to say, but then he turned around and looked at me through those thick-rimmed glasses I loved so much—he must not have needed the mirror to get his contacts out. I watched as his eyes took me in, from my bare legs and stomach to the white strapless bra, rising up to find the necklace still adorned around my neck. "Mara," he rasped.

It sounded like a plea.

"I was hoping you could help me take it off," I managed to say. I'd meant the necklace, but the way his eyes dipped back down to my panties, I wasn't sure my point had been made. "The necklace," I clarified on a shaky breath. "I'm scared I might break it." It was true . . . I was almost petrified to touch it myself.

His gaze jumped back up to meet mine, and he slowly nodded. "Okay." He gulped, and I tracked the movement of his throat, no longer imprisoned by his collar and bowtie. "Come here."

I stepped forward, and he met the movement with his own. When I reached him, I turned around and reached up to gather my hair, pulling it over one shoulder. His fingertips whirled over the skin of my shoulders, blazing a burning trail until they reached the clasp of the necklace at the base of my neck. Within seconds, it was undone, and I stepped under his arm to turn back to him. "Thank you."

He nodded, turning toward his tall dresser where the velvet box was resting. "I grabbed this from the kitchen," he explained as he gently set the necklace back in, "when I was feeding the cats."

I smiled at him. "Thank you, Leo. It's beautiful." He shut the box and shifted back to me, a lock of his wild hair falling against his eyes. "I think it's time you got your bed back," I said.

His eyes shot to the bed and then back to me. "What about you?"

"I'll sleep there, too. We can behave, can't we?"

He looked back down at my bra before scrubbing his hand over his face. "Are you sure that's what you want?" he asked. "You're probably more comfortable without me."

I hated the way he second-guessed himself. "I'm sure," I confirmed. "It's your bed anyway . . . I've been hogging for long enough."

He grinned for a second before considering. "Okay, I just need to brush my teeth."

Chapter Twenty-Five

By the time I woke up the next morning, the bed was a furnace from the heat of our bodies. Sleeping next to him had been . . . risky, to say the least. I wasn't sure either of us slept much as we both continued to fight for our restraint, but more than once I'd awoken to find a heavy leg or warm arm draped over my body.

After brushing his teeth last night, Leo had stripped down to his usual sleepwear—nothing but a tight pair of briefs—and he crawled into bed next to me. Swift was all too excited to have both of us in one place. She went back and forth between us, kneading her small paws into our arms as she worked herself into a slumber. Dolly, in a wild turn of events, curled up in-between my legs and promptly began snoring.

Seemed to me we were getting closer to that friendship.

I'd carefully unwound my limbs from all other sleeping bodies when I finally woke up for good at about eight this morning. I could hear the clinking of dishes coming from the kitchen and knew Alaric and Christine were up. I had a vision of myself stomping out there and paying them a piece of my mind, but figured it was too early in the day for that particular brutality. So, I decided I would sneak across the hall into Leo's converted yoga room and spend some time working the tension out of my body.

After pulling a sports bra and leggings out from my duffle bag on the floor in the closet, I realized I was down to almost no clean clothes. I'd have just enough to get by for work tonight, but I was in dire need of a washing machine. Now that I thought about it, I hadn't noticed a washer or dryer anywhere in the penthouse. I made a mental note to ask Leo about that later, and quickly slipped out of the bra and underwear I'd worn to bed in exchange for the athletic wear.

It was only a few steps from Leo's bedroom to the yoga room, but they were harrowing nonetheless knowing Leo's parents were out in the common area of the apartment. It would be pretty easy to glance down the hall from the living room and spot me, and I wanted to remain undetected for now. Luckily, I made it across the hall and into the other room without being seen, and exhaled a deep breath once the door was softly clicked shut.

I worked through a longer practice this morning, needing the extra time to feel my shoulders loosen from last night's events. I couldn't quite ease the worry on my mind for Leo, for how he was supposed to move on today knowing that more stilted interactions with his parents were required. I couldn't believe he'd gone through his whole life being raised by such ugly people. It was a wonder that he'd come out the other side so . . . good. So kind and thoughtful and completely wonderful.

Once my limbs felt nice and loose and sweat dripped from my body onto the mat below me, I decided to call it and see if Leo was awake yet. I wanted to stick close to him today—at least until I left for work tonight. I wasn't sure if Leo would be going in too, but I found myself hoping he would.

Before I left the room, I eyed the piano and guitars that were huddled in the far corner and suddenly yearned to hear Leo play.

I tiptoed back across the hallway, quietly opened his bedroom door—and stopped dead in my tracks.

Leo was standing at the edge of the bed, facing away from me, completely naked. His long and strong body flexing in exertion—from what, I wasn't sure. But I couldn't look away from the slope of his back or the way his ass clenched in a steadying rhythm. "Leo?" I whispered, knowing I couldn't just simply stand here and stare.

He twisted around to face me, panic flooding through his flushed face. "Mara," he blurted out, and my eyes dropped to find his hand wrapped around his impressive length, still pumping himself rapidly as if the message of being caught hadn't quite moved from his brain to the rest of his body. On the bed in front of him, laid out perfectly together, was my bra and thong from last night.

"Oh," I mumbled softly before lurching myself toward the bathroom. "I'm sorry!" I called out, covering my eyes with the palm of my hand. "I didn't look! Not really." I stubbed my toe on something hard and cried out with a curse before blindly recalibrating and marching toward what I prayed would be the bathroom door. "Seriously, *so* sorry—I should have knocked!"

Thankfully I made it into the bathroom without further injury and promptly slammed the door shut. My chest heaved as I realized what I'd just walked in on—Leo was fully getting himself off to the sight of my *underwear*.

"Mara." Leo's voice sounded at the door. "I'm so . . . *so* sorry. Please open the door and let me explain."

I shook my head fiercely, as if he could see me. "No thanks!" I blurted. "I mean . . . no need!"

"Mara—"

"It's okay! Really!"

Leo's voice lowered into something stormy. "I'm not going anywhere until you open this door."

God, he was so stubborn. I took a deep breath before twisting the doorknob and opening the door only an inch, peering out at him through the small crack. "Yes?" I asked like a blundering idiot.

His face was still flushed but his eyes were sharp. I couldn't stop myself from looking down, but found he was back in his black briefs; though, he was still fully erect. My eyes were no doubt protruding from my skull as I forced them back up to meet his. "I'm sorry," he rushed out. "I figured you were doing yoga, and I thought I'd have more time . . ." The words poured out of him.

"More time to ejaculate into my panties?" I asked.

He pressed his lips together. "Look, I'm doing my best to control myself and keep everything I'm feeling at bay. But I'd say the effect you have on me is pretty fucking obvious, and the way you looked last night . . . both at dinner and next to me in bed . . . I just . . . I needed to blow off a little steam. Okay?"

"Okay!" I whisper-shouted, doing my best to ignore the heat that was crawling up my neck. I'd wager Leo could undoubtedly see the effect *he* was having on *me*, too. "Got it! Anything else?"

"We're okay?" he asked, eyes searching mine. It was obvious the poor bastard was genuinely afraid he'd done something that might push me away, and with everything else going on, the last thing I wanted him to start second-guessing was me.

"We're good, Leo," I assured. "Promise. I'm just . . . going to take a shower. Okay?"

He gave me a tight nod. "Okay."

I shut the door between us and quickly turned the faucet on in the shower before my limbs went wild in a silent freak-out in the middle of the bathroom. Once I undressed and slipped through the glass door of the steaming shower, I had to work especially hard not to blow off some steam myself.

THE ROOM LOOKED empty when I peeked out the bathroom door, and relief flooded through me. I'd been so hasty in my escape from Leo's elicit self-love time that I hadn't brought a change of clothes with me to the bathroom. I craned my head out further, taking a long look around *just* to make sure, but the bedroom door was shut and not even a cat could be found. Letting out a breath, I exited in nothing but a small towel.

It was safe to assume that, like everything else in this penthouse, Leo's towels were expensive—they were softer than the peach fuzz on a baby's head and felt incredible against my skin. But they'd clearly been designed by someone who didn't enjoy being in one for long. They were so much smaller than the ginormous bath towels I had at my apartment, barely wrapping around my middle. I did my best to keep it sealed shut as I moved toward the closet to pull out the single remaining work outfit, remembering I still needed to ask Leo about how I could do some laundry. I didn't see my underwear—or bra, for that matter—that Leo had been using as . . . *inspiration* . . . so I figured they'd ended up wherever it was that he put his own dirty laundry.

I had to push the implication of that thought away the second it entered my mind.

I made it safely back into the bathroom to change without incident, throwing on my black shorts and a Larkspur T-shirt that said, ALLOW ME TO WET YOUR WHISTLE. The shorts were much shorter than would have been appropriate to wear in front of Leo's parents—the thought of Alaric seeing me so exposed gave me an ick I couldn't shake off, and the last thing I needed was to give Christine any more fuel. So I decided to hunt for something of Leo's that I could wear around the apartment until it was time to leave for work later this afternoon.

I set out to search through his dresser drawers, looking through the perfectly folded clothes as respectfully as possible, until at last I found his stash of sweatpants and pulled on a pair of soft black ones over my shorts. They were a bit too big around the waist and much too long, but after some cinching and cuffing I got them into a wearable state.

When there was nothing left to do but face the inevitable, I sauntered out of the bedroom and down the hall. When I neared the kitchen, I heard some hushed voices and slowed my steps to try to listen in.

"I just don't understand what's kept you away from home this long, honey. It's obvious to us that there's nothing good for you out here," Christine said with a tone that was both admonishing and pleading.

"She's right, son," came Alaric's voice next. "You've had your space, and *clearly* you've had your fun, but it's time to get yourself back on track. Whether you decide to keep ownership of that club or not, it seems to run just fine on its own. Hell, it's not the worst thing in the world to add to your portfolio. But your future is in New York with Callahan Enterprises. It's your destiny, Leopold. Why don't you take a couple of days to get your things in order, and come home with us on Sunday."

I heard Leo sigh, and it sounded so defeated it nearly broke my heart. I waited for him to fight back, to tell his parents to go to hell for the way they treated him last night. But there was only silence.

He wasn't actually considering it, was he?

I rounded the corner into the kitchen, and three sets of eyes snapped to me. I quickly found the pair of warm blue ones that I was growing to be rather fond of, and watched as they fell to the pants I was wearing before a soft smile played on those full, pouty lips. "Good morning, everyone," I greeted, as if I hadn't already gotten *quite* the good morning salute from Leo this morning.

Alaric cleared his throat. Christine turned away from me and opened the fridge, no doubt intending for the dismissal to land just how it did.

But Leo's smile only grew as his eyes found mine again. "Good morning, Mara." He'd pulled on a black crew-neck sweater and gray jogging shorts, and I wondered if he might be planning to go out for a run. He gripped the handle of a black coffee mug, and I flushed at what else I'd just seen that hand wrapped around.

"Hope it's okay I helped myself to some sweatpants," I said, looking down at the black cotton hanging from my hips.

His eyes dipped again, dancing with amusement. "More than okay," he assured. "You know that, sweetheart."

Oh, *right*. I should know that almost a year into dating someone.

"I take it you work today?" Alaric asked dryly as he eyed my shirt.

"Yes," I confirmed with a bright smile. "You know, Leo and I would love to have you and Christine come by and see our lovechild for yourselves."

Christine choked on her own spit from somewhere in the fridge.

"Is that so?" Alaric's eyes focused on me, seeing the challenge for what it was.

"Yep." I popped the *P* with delight. "We even have a DJ tonight. He's an excellent mixer . . . really gets the crowd going." I shot a look at Leo, finding him watching me carefully now. "Hell," I said. "You should invite Tanner. Maybe he'll have more fun surrounded by people his own age."

"I think Leo and I have important things to discuss about his future," Alaric said outright. "But I sincerely thank you for such a warm invitation."

"What about his future?" I countered. "He's building a future here, in Denver. Don't you see that?"

The old man in front of me laughed, and my fists clenched. "You really think a girl like you and that . . . that *bar* are a *future* for my son?"

"Dad," Leo warned. "Enough."

Alaric shrugged. "She's the one poking the bear."

I let out my own sarcastic laugh. "Let me guess, *you're* the bear?" Christine shut the fridge door and moved to stand next to her husband, eyeballing me with disgust. I guess she wasn't used to anyone talking back to Alaric either.

"No," he spat. "The bear is the truth blaring right in front of you. Leo doesn't belong here in this dump of a city. He belongs in New York where opportunity awaits him. You're only holding him back, honey, and the sooner you realize it, the better off he'll be."

Something violent and aching ripped through me. "If you really cared about your son, you would give a shit or two about what *he* wants," I seethed.

His mouth curled with wicked intent. "Sometimes it's the responsibility of a parent to course-correct when our children aren't seeing things clearly," he explained, as though speaking to a first grader. "My son may think that he has it all figured out, that he wants *you*. But he'll come to understand that all of this has merely been a distraction from his real destiny."

I felt hot tears sting in my eyes just as Leo's hand wrapped around my shoulder, pulling me into his chest. I hadn't even realized he'd moved around the island to get to me. My eyes stayed locked on Alaric as Leo's arms wrapped around me—always right there to soothe. "You don't deserve him," I whispered.

This time, it was Christine who clicked her tongue before looking up at her husband. "Come, dear. It's obvious there's no getting through to her. Let's just move on and freshen up, shall we?"

"Of course, my love," Alaric said to his wife, following her back to the hallway that led to their room.

When I heard their door click shut, I finally met Leo's searching gaze. "Your father is an awful person," I whispered.

The corner of his mouth tugged, but it didn't do much to counter the worry in his expression. "I appreciate you sticking up for me, Mara. I really do. But . . . it's not worth it. There's no getting through to either of them. I've been trying my whole life, I'm not sure why I thought anything could be different."

My mind raced with the words that had been spoken before I made myself known, the pressure his parents were putting on him to go back to New York. "You're not going to go, are you?"

He stroked his thumb along my cheek. My breaths were hollow, but the feel of him close to me like this . . . it was everything. "I don't know what I'm going to do," he murmured softly. "I honestly don't know what to do."

I squeezed my eyes shut and buried my face into his chest, knowing that ultimately this was his to figure out. I could only continue to remind him of his worth, of what he deserved—but I also knew what it was like to be disconnected from reality after being so used to hearing the opposite.

It took me years before I could fully grasp that I'd been in an abusive relationship. I couldn't imagine what it was like to have to face such a truth about your own parents.

"I'm here for you," I said into his sweater. "Okay?"

I felt him smile into my hair. "I know, sweetheart."

Chapter Twenty-Six

Leo ended up staying home tonight with his parents, so I walked to work by myself. I hated the thought of him having to go through an ordeal similar to last night's, but he insisted he would be okay, and I needed to be at the club tonight. Of course, he made me promise to text him as soon as I made it here safe, which I did. He'd only responded with a treasured thumbs-up emoji, and I hadn't heard from him since.

I hoped he was okay. I knew it killed him to watch me walk out the door without him. This *thing* between us had been blooming more and more into a crutch, and as I'd made my way to the elevator, he looked at me like I was his life raft, floating away. But as the elevator doors opened, his mother had called his name from the kitchen, and we were forced to part on somewhat shaky ground.

He'd been more quiet today, a little more lost inside his own head. Beyond just the chaos of last night, the pressure had been mounting all week. I considered asking one of the other bartenders to close for me so that I could stay with him, but when I'd voiced the idea during lunch, Leo promptly shut it down and told me he would be fine. He knew how to handle his parents, he'd said.

But I wasn't as convinced. It twisted me up to know that he had to suffer through their merciless critiquing. I may not be as open and honest with my parents as I once was, but that was because of my own fears. They'd always been there for me, no matter what.

Seth had been the force to come between us, driving a wedge in our otherwise rock-solid relationship. But I knew that if I picked up the phone right this minute and finally came clean about things, they'd be there for me. They might be disappointed, maybe a little hurt that I'd waited so long, but they would get past it.

The thought made my chest squeeze—I was homesick. I missed the days when phone calls weren't just a weekly routine, but a near-daily occurrence to share the goings-on in my life. Maybe . . . maybe after this arrangement with Leo was finished and things got back to normal, I could finally find the courage to sit them down.

I always figured it would be easier to let them in once I was firmly on the other side of it all and not still swimming against the current, but as much as I'd accomplished over the last couple years, I still didn't feel like I had anything tangible to show for it. When Larkspur was mine, I hoped the news would counteract some of the pain I'd inflict when I told my parents *everything*. And . . . maybe I would also have someone new to introduce them to, to prove that I really was moving on in my personal life, too.

I knew I'd be devastated if Leo left for New York, but I still hadn't mustered up the courage to tell him I was interested in more beyond this week. It wasn't fair to hope that he stayed without laying all my cards out on the table—and I *wanted* Leo to know how I felt. It was all I could think about tonight while I worked.

He thought I was brave, and it inflated me like a balloon. I wanted to prove him right, wanted to lean into the vulnerability shared between us and give him a little more of it.

The thought made my head spin as I finished counting the cash I'd pulled from the registers behind the bar. I was in the office now, an hour-old cup of hazelnut coffee sitting next to me. I knew I shouldn't finish it, that I'd be up all night if I did. But I hated the thought of dumping it—Leo gifted me this bag. So I quickly chugged the remaining still-delicious coffee before I stood to tuck the cash into the safe.

Larkspur had closed almost an hour ago, yet Frank sat out by the bar like usual, making sure I wasn't left alone while I closed out for the night. Rocco and his team had been in tonight as well, but they'd left once the doors were closed to the public. I knew they would feel like outsiders for a while, but I appreciated their presence.

My eyes moved to the large monitor hanging from the ceiling in the corner of the office, to the visual reminder of Larkspur's new twenty-four-hour surveillance system. I really was thankful for Leo's dedication to our safety here—however frustrating his approach might've been at the time. I almost smiled at the thought.

I shut the heavy door to the safe and set it to lock, listening as the inner mechanisms slid into place. Throwing my empty coffee cup into the recycle bin next to the desk, I grabbed my belt bag from where it hung on the back of the chair and left the room, locking the office door behind me.

Frank was leaning against the bar, scrolling on his phone as I poked my head through the swinging doors. I wondered what a man like him looked at on his phone. As far as I knew, he didn't have any social media accounts. Maybe he read the news, or slinked into Reddit rabbit-holes. Maybe he was talking to a girlfriend—though, I would've bet my tips tonight that he was single.

"Hey, Frank," I called out, watching as he straightened and tucked his phone into his pocket, "you ready?"

"Yeah." He stomped his combat boots over my way.

"Front doors are locked?" I asked.

"Of course," he confirmed, pushing through the batwing doors.

I smiled. "Thanks for staying."

His gaze slid to me as we walked through the stockroom. "I always stay."

"I know," I said, "but . . . thank you. I appreciate you."

He grunted. "Don't go getting sentimental on me, Mara. It's my job."

"Don't get all macho on me, Frank. You go above and beyond, and you know it."

Frank's shoulders slipped up in a small shrug as he opened the back door for me to step through, but the ghost of a smile on his face told me the compliment landed. *Good.* I wanted him to feel appreciated. I wanted *all* of the staff to feel it.

He looked at me again after his eyes swept over the back lot. "You okay getting home? I'm surprised our new boss isn't here to walk you himself."

I gave a high-pitched laugh. I was still so nervous about

people finding out about my arrangement with Leo . . . but I couldn't hide the fact that he'd walked me out of here nearly every night since he'd bought the place. Or that I'd called him my boyfriend in front of the paramedics, though something told me Frank understood I was lying through my teeth to avoid the hospital. "He lives in a building near mine, I guess. I think it makes him feel better." I hoped that was a safe enough answer. While it was technically true that my building was near his, he wasn't *actually* walking me to it.

Frank simply nodded, and the panic in my chest loosened. "All right, you have your pepper spray?"

I pulled the small blue canister out of my belt bag and held it up to him. "Yep."

"And I suppose you won't let me drive you?"

Frank offered to drive me home regularly in the years we'd worked together, and I always turned him down. Partly because I didn't want him to feel obligated—getting me home safe was well outside his job requirement. But also, from the get-go I'd needed to prove to myself that I could keep *myself* safe. Between the pepper spray and the self-defense training, I was now confident that I could. "I suppose you'd be correct." I grinned. "Drive safe, Frank. See you tomorrow."

"See you tomorrow." He stalked toward the only parked car in the lot while I moved in the direction of the busy street that would lead me home.

Home. I almost laughed out loud remembering how that word had felt only a few nights ago. Leo's penthouse was surely *not* my home . . . but I couldn't deny I was anxious to get back there, to see how he was doing. I thought about texting him that I was on my way, but it was nearly three in the morning. He was surely asleep by now—I didn't want to wake him.

I hadn't brought my hoodie with me to work tonight—in the shuffle of leaving without Leo and worrying about him, I hadn't thought to grab it. I wrapped my arms around myself as I walked, feeling grateful it wasn't *too* cold.

It wasn't long before I saw Leo's tall building come into view, just across the street and down a couple buildings from Rudy's Market. I hadn't been back since meeting Leo there, and I knew I should stop in one of these nights to say hi to Rudy. But tonight was *not* that night—I had a man to see. And the closer I got to him, the more anticipation thrummed in my body.

Georgie, of course, was standing just inside the glass doors to Leo's building. His smile grew wide when he saw me, pushing the heavy door open to let me in. "Good evening, Mara!"

"Hey, Georgie. Having a good night?"

"Always, ma'am. Mr. Callahan isn't with you?"

I shook my head. "No, he's upstairs. His parents are still here, so he stayed home to entertain them."

Georgie smiled again. "I see. Well, I imagine you want to get some rest, ma'am."

"Mara, please," I corrected. Georgie's suit was finer than anything in my closet—he surely didn't need to "ma'am" me.

"Of course, Mara. My apologies. Have a great night!" His eyes twinkled in the low lighting of the lobby as he smiled.

I returned a warm smile. "You too. Be safe."

Continuing on through the expansive lobby toward the golden elevator, I pressed the button to go up as soon as I reached it. Thankfully I heard the soft chime within seconds, and the doors opened to let me in. I pressed the access card Leo had given me against the sensor before pushing the *PH* button, and as the elevator whirred with its ascent to his penthouse I could feel the tension almost burst within my skin. Just a few more seconds—a few more seconds and I could lay my eyes on him.

As the elevator doors opened, I found the penthouse dark, save for a small lamp in the entryway that Leo must have left on for me—a gesture that spread warmth through my defrosting limbs. It was the first time I'd entered the apartment without being greeted by at least one of the cats. They must've been curled up in bed with Leo.

I couldn't wait to slide under his heavy covers and watch him sleep until I, too, succumbed to it. Considering I'd finished that cup of coffee, I might end up watching him for a while. I didn't mind the thought of it at all—inviting him to share the bed with me last night had been the right call.

I set my bag down on the console table against the wall in the foyer and soundlessly kicked off my Vans before I moved toward the hallway that led to Leo's bedroom. When I stepped into the narrow hallway, however, I heard a soft melody coming from the room adjacent to his. The door was shut and no light shone from beneath the door, but the sound of music —a piano—was unmistakable.

Was Leo *playing*?

I padded down the hallway until I was standing in front of the closed door. Listening to the music for a moment, I considered what this could mean.

Had he brought up his dreams of playing music to his parents? Had they finally been supportive?

Hope flared within me as I twisted the doorknob and opened the door. Leo was seated at the black piano, its glossy surface gleaming in the moonlight. He was facing away from the doorway, but if I squinted, I could see that his chestnut hair was tousled more than usual. He was wearing a dress shirt, though the collar was uneven and the sleeves had been pushed up his forearms.

His head hung low to his chest as he played a beautiful, melancholic song. The notes swept over the nocturnal scene with a mournful embrace, and my heart clenched in my chest as soon as I realized it—this wasn't a celebration.

Something was very wrong.

I carefully placed one foot in front of the other as I approached him, my heart pounding in my chest with every step. It was clear from the sight in front of me that Leo was hurt. And all I knew for certain was that I would find a way to soothe the ache, to balm over his wounds and do whatever it took to make him smile.

My charismatic, happy Leo.

As soon as he realized I was in the room, his fingers stopped their delicate dance on the ivory keys. He looked up at me with tired eyes, his mouth turned down in the corners. He was exhausted—the proof was written all over his face—and I instantly regretted not being here with him tonight. I should have found a way, should have stayed here where he so clearly *needed* me.

I positioned myself in front of him, my hip lightly brushing against the edge of the piano behind me. "Leo?" I asked, keeping my voice low. "What's wrong?"

He sighed out a long breath as his gaze fell to my legs. After a moment, he opened his mouth to speak, but then closed it again before any sound could escape. He shut his eyes tightly and let his head fall forward, his forehead pressing against my stomach.

My pulse tripped as my hands instinctively rose to his head, my fingers winding through his thick, soft waves. He inhaled, breathing in deeply along my belly as he reached to wrap around my waist. Concern blazed through me. "Leo," I whispered, "are you okay?"

He shook his head, and then mumbled from somewhere in my shirt. "I don't want to talk about it."

I let that sink in. "What do you need?"

He tilted his head up, his blue eyes mere shadows in the dark as they fastened themselves to me. A handful of breaths passed between us. Eventually, his lips parted and the word croaked out. "You."

He swiftly tugged my wrist so I was forced to swing my leg over his lap. His gaze never left my face, watching carefully for any protest. Any sign of hesitation.

But he wasn't going to get any.

The last thing I wanted to do was hesitate—I wouldn't. Not for a second. Because while there were probably a million reasons to stop and consider why this might be a bad idea, a million reasons why letting him in again might only hurt me in the long run, the only thing I could focus on was Leo's broken spirit. I had to find a way to settle his pain, to shine a light into this darkness around him.

So I cupped his face as I lowered myself onto his lap, feeling his stubble beneath my fingertips, and nodded. "I'm here," I murmured. "I'm right here, baby."

My words seemed to snap something loose in him and he groaned, his hands adjusting my hips so that I was pressed firmly against his hard stomach. He closed his eyes as my fingers trailed lightly along his face, and before I let my own nerves sputter through me, I leaned in to kiss him.

I pressed my lips tenderly against the right corner of his mouth. "You are brilliant," I whispered. And then I pressed my lips against the left side. "You are kind and generous," I continued. I tilted my face to reach for his forehead, pressing a soft kiss there as he took in another deep breath. "You are worthy of love and respect."

His eyes opened again, full of so much raw emotion that it sent my heart pounding harder in my chest. And then he lifted a hand to grip the back of my neck and pulled my mouth against his.

It was a kiss dripping in need. Leo's mouth devoured mine with an urgent desperation, a cry to feel anything other than what he'd been feeling. But caught somewhere underneath the surface was also this last week of our crumbling resistance—a different kind of need, born well outside the bounds of what had revealed itself tonight. Whatever it was he'd gone through while I was at work.

The truth was, we both *wanted* this.

I wanted this . . . more than I cared to admit.

My mouth moved against his as our breaths mixed between us, and Leo groaned again as my fingers tugged at his hair. Our movements became frantic, our desire sticky with torment. Leo stood from the bench, holding me to him with his strong arms as he carefully lowered me down onto the cold, hard surface of the piano. His thighs pressed into the keys and a jostle of notes rang out in the air around us.

My legs wrapped around his waist as he drove his hips between my legs, and I could feel how hard he already was. His tongue dove deep into my mouth, curling against mine before he pulled back to look down at me. "Mara," he groaned as his eyes greedily roamed my body, his hands gripping my waist tight as if I might disappear if he let go even for a moment.

"I'm right here," I whispered. "I'm right here, Leo."

"Fuck," he rasped, his voice sandpaper. And then he pushed the hem of my shirt up. I curled my body forward to give him better access, lying back once the material had been pulled over my head and discarded

His eyes continued to graze over me as his finger trailed down my chest and between my breasts. "God, Mara, look at you."

Instantly I was soaring, spinning, weightless.

It was like our first night all over again. He was looking at me like I was . . . real. Like I was *real* to him, and not just some sexy fantasy or splintered version of who I could be that suited him better. And even more significant was that he needed me. He *needed* me like this. All of me.

"I'm right here," I repeated, looking at him intently while also internally relishing the way his hand now gripped lower against my hip, fingers flexing into my skin. "I'm right here, and I'm *yours*, Leo."

The words tasted sweet on my tongue, no bitterness to be found. And though I didn't know what they meant for us, I knew I meant them.

His eyes jumped up to mine, brows knitting together as he took it all in. "Mine?" he asked. As if it couldn't possibly be.

I nodded in earnest. "Yes. Yours." I reached for his hand, the one still gripping my hip, and pulled it up to lay over my overactive heart. "Do you feel this?"

His gaze flitted down to where his palm rested on my chest. "Yes."

"That's because of you, Leo. My heart already knows the truth."

His eyes closed tightly at my words. But instead of pain, there was joy radiating from him. A relief as obvious as the moonlight blanketing the room. And when his lids opened to reveal his blue eyes, pupils blown wide, there was a spark in them that I knew was just for me. "Mine," he committed, hand palming my heart.

I watched as he took another sweeping look down my body, a newfound enthusiasm brightening his features. And then he took a small step back and slid my shorts down my thighs.

He groaned again when he saw I wasn't wearing panties—the shorts were too tight to conceal anything else beneath them. "This is going to be much quicker than I'd normally want, Mara." His voice was gravel. "But I already know I'm not going to be able to control myself with you like this."

If he only knew the way he touched me seemed to piece me back together. "Give me all you got," I said through a smile, my body buzzing with anticipation. "I can take it."

He breathed in deep, tossing my shorts to the ground and sliding a finger along my glistening skin. "Mm," he hummed. But then he hesitated, met my eyes. "I should go grab a condom."

I wound my fingers into the material of his shirt, holding him still. "I get tested regularly—I'm all clear, and I'm on the pill."

He nodded. "I'm clear, too."

I smiled. "I want you, nothing else."

A lopsided grin grew wide on his face, and he refocused on his treasure. "God, you're already so wet for me." He reached to unfasten his belt buckle, and within seconds his pants were undone and around his thick thighs. Pumping himself once, eyes fastened between my legs, he murmured, "I'm going to remember you like this for the rest of my life. I'm going to picture you draped over this piano, so raw and fucking beautiful, until the end of time, Mara."

My mouth went dry as my chest heaved. "Good," I managed to say. "Lock it in while I'm still young and fresh." He smiled, and it nearly killed me. This thing between us was going to screw me up forever. But I didn't care, I needed more. I wanted it all.

He lined himself up against me and drove himself home.

This time, as Leo moved his body into mine with heady precision, his limbs trembled with the effort it took for him to stay calm. Despite his warning, he *was* trying to control himself —he was trying to make this last, the selfless and glorious man that he was. Or maybe it was self*ish*.

Either way, the bold confidence and authority he demonstrated last time was still present in the way he took control of the moment, but it was also obvious how nearly frantic and desperate he was for this.

"*Fuck*," he grunted as he hovered his chest over me, his thighs warm and heavy against mine as he curled in a deep thrust. His teeth skated a shameless path along my jaw before sinking into the skin below my ear. Strong hands wrapped around my hips, holding my writhing body still as he drilled into me again. "This can't be real," he murmured. "You can't be real."

I arched off the surface of the piano as he stretched and filled me with a longing that knew no bounds, and then he met me with a searing kiss. A moan passed quietly between us when he hiked my knee up to gain better access. He was branding himself right into my body, into my soul. I lost all focus on the ways I tried to protect myself from a want as big as this. I didn't let the anticipation of what came next hurl me into any fear-induced delusions—all I could see was the way Leo shined brightly, the way he felt so right against my skin.

"Mara," he murmured through a shaky breath, "tell me again. Tell me you're mine."

His blue eyes were nearly black with desire, and they caught on my mouth as I whispered the words: "I'm yours, Leo." The tension inside of me was pulling taut—he was bringing me higher and higher as he drove me deeper into the piano, and I was so close to tipping over the edge.

His thrusts were wild and feral—he was falling apart at the seams. I ached for more of it. I wanted all of him. "You're mine, Mara," he slurred as he drove his body into mine, and it sent me catapulting right over the edge. The orgasm was loud and bright, like a burning star as it shot across the sky.

Leo broke just after I did, the force of his pleasure hot against my inner walls. I wrapped my arms around his shoulders and pulled him in close as he repeated my name over and over again on his beautiful lips.

Chapter Twenty-Seven

Leo was sprawled casually on the bed with his feet pressed against the mattress, his long legs caging me on either side as I sat cross-legged between them. The early morning light draped his bedroom in a golden glow. His head was propped up on a stack of three pillows, hair wrecked more than usual from winding my fingers through it all night, and there was an undeniable mischief in his eyes behind his glasses as he watched me carefully.

Something about Leo in those glasses nearly dismantled me.

"What?" I asked, feeling my blood heat under his gaze.

His mouth rose in a small smile before he shook his head. "Nothing."

I let each of my hands roam in a lazy trail along his massive thighs, noticing his breathing change as they inched higher toward his briefs. My gaze caught on the tattoo on his left thigh, the ink depicting an arrangement of mountains. "So," I said quietly, knowing his parents were still asleep somewhere across the apartment. "When did you get this?"

His eyes drifted to where my fingertips traced the dark gray lines. "Hm," he hummed thoughtfully. "Senior year of college."

"Were all the boys getting slutty thigh tattoos, or just you?"

Leo barked out a laugh, his smile so wide I could feel it in my stomach. "You think it's slutty?"

I shrugged as I looked back down at it. "I mean, it does have a certain effect. I can just picture a twenty-two-year-old Leopold Callahan banking on something like this to help him pull more young ladies at the country club."

His eyes shone brightly. "While I appreciate the vision you have of young Leopold, I can assure you that I've never been much of a success with the ladies."

I scoffed. "Yeah, right."

"It's true." He reached down to capture my fingers as they made another ascent up the biggest peak, pulling them into his warm hand. Looking up at his face, I found his expression had grown serious. "Senior year of college was when my anxiety got to an all-time high. My body was quite literally breaking down from the inside out because of all of the pressure I felt from my professors and my parents—there was this weight on my shoulders to *succeed*. And I knew it was my last year of freedom before I was fully thrown into the claws of the family business, ready or not. The anticipation became too much because the truth was that I never wanted any of it.

"When I was a boy, maybe eleven or twelve, my grandfather took me on a skiing trip during a particularly hard winter. My father had made a few bad deals and there was significant financial loss. He would come home and just . . . yell. At me, at my mother, at the fucking dog. I think my grandpa knew that things were bad, so he wanted to get me out of there for a little while. He brought me to Colorado, to Durango . . . and it was there that I fell in love with the mountains. I remember feeling so small on those runs, so insignificant. Like the wild terrain didn't care who I was or what I did. It didn't care about my future or what I would make of myself. It was the first time I felt *free*. And I think I've been chasing that feeling ever since."

I squeezed his hand. "Is that why you came here last year? After what happened?"

"Yeah. My grandfather passed on years ago, but I still feel him and that sense of freedom here, so I wanted to be near the mountains again. And I wanted to work on my music. Until recently, those were the only two things in my life that ever made me feel wholly alive."

My breath caught. "And now?"

Leo studied my face for a long moment before he spoke again. "You, Mara, give me that same feeling. You make me . . . You make me want to be braver. You make me feel like I might still have a fucking chance at happiness."

A tear swelled out of my eye, spilling down my cheek. "You can't give up on your music, Leo. Hearing you play the piano last night . . . it was unbelievable. You're afraid to fail, and I get it. I do. But don't let fear win—you're really, *really* good."

He blew out a breath as he eyed me intensely. "What about you?"

My eyes fell back down to his tattoo, skimming along the lines. I knew what was coming. "What about me?" I parroted, buying myself more time.

"Oh, are we going to pretend like I'm the only one who has

a difficult time being vulnerable?" I looked up at him and found his gaze had turned almost expectant, though his tone was soft and comforting as he pressed on. "What happened with your ex?"

The corners of my eyes burned hot as I felt my skin flush. The all too familiar urge to protect myself came rushing to the surface, and I wanted nothing more than to climb out of this bed and run back home to the safety of my own apartment. But Leo had shared so much of himself with me, challenging his ego and fears to open up to me and bring me into his world. Over the last couple of days, he'd become more and more of a safe place, too. He showed me his scars, and in turn, made me feel like I could show him mine. And while both of us still had a lot of work to do in our healing, it felt like maybe we didn't have to do the work alone.

I thought being alone was for the best—was safest. But I was starting to realize that the real healing was in allowing someone in, knowing he could hurt me but having a damn good inkling that he wouldn't.

So I breathed through the panic, taking a moment to collect myself, and then started from the beginning. "I met Seth in college," I began, watching Leo's eyes widen for a moment, as if he hadn't been sure that I would actually share. "I was . . . so different back then. So trusting, and maybe a little naive. My childhood was wholesome and loving, and I just always felt . . . safe. Maybe a little invincible, like no matter what happened I'd always be okay. When I met Seth, I hardly noticed his red flags. I liked the way he made me feel, at first. And that was enough for me to want more.

"He was one of those guys everyone knew. Everyone seemed drawn to him at parties around campus, like he was the nucleus of any fun to be had. So many girls wanted to date him but somehow I'd caught his attention, and when he looked at me it felt like I was the only girl in the world. Now I can look back and see that my lack of experience blinded me from the truth, and that he knew it. I was the perfect blank canvas for him, and he knew I'd let him build me up just so he could tear me down."

I felt Leo's legs tense around me, like he was bracing for the impact of the rest of my story, and I tensed too. This was the first time I'd ever spoken these words out loud, and I worried what Leo might think of me once it was all out. He must have seen my hesitation, because his thumb swiped gently against the top of my hand. "Let it out, Mara."

I squeezed my eyes shut, and kept going. "We got more serious after graduation. We'd only casually dated during school, and I honestly thought that would be it, that I might not see him again once it was all over. But he asked me to take a leap with him, to be with him . . . move in with him. And I was *so* excited.

"Seth loved his *things*, and it took me years to realize I was just something else for him to own. To control. He struggled a lot with insecurity and would always have these ridiculous excuses to explain his failures. He'd find a way to blame other people, and made me believe that his friends were jealous of him, that he had to be careful about who he trusted. He isolated me away from *my* friends, saying that all we needed was each other. That other people would inevitably disappoint us, so what was the point?

"Sometimes I would try to push back and tell him I needed a little space. But that always led to some big dramatic blowout where he'd accuse me of not loving him. I constantly felt like I had to prove that I did, like I was never doing enough to make him happy. During those fights he'd say really awful things to me, like I should feel lucky to be with him, that I'd be nothing without him. That I was weak and foolish and naive. And he was right—"

"Mara," Leo cut in, "no he wasn't."

But I nodded my head. "Yeah, he was. Just, maybe not the way he meant. I felt so . . . alone. He'd made himself the center of my universe, and even though I knew things weren't good between us, I was also way too scared to leave him. I *was* weak, I *was* naive. I was so inexperienced and incapable of seeing how bad things really were, and they just kept getting worse despite thinking I could fix it. He stripped me of every ounce of confidence I had. All my energy went into trying to make him happy, and I never could. I felt like such a failure."

I took a deep breath before the next part.

The worst part.

"The first time he hit me was in the middle of a grocery store. He'd somehow tripped over the wheel of the cart I was pushing, and responded by smacking me across the face so hard I fell into a shelf of canned foods. He thought I'd done it on purpose, that I was trying to make him fall.

"I was too stunned to even cry. I remember just staring at him, waiting for him to laugh it off. Praying it was just a joke. But he looked at me with such hatred before turning and walking away. He walked right out of the store, and I didn't see him until the next day when he finally came home, reeking of alcohol. He broke down crying in the kitchen, saying how sorry he was . . . and I was *relieved*, Leo. I was relieved that he wasn't mad at me anymore, so absurdly happy that the man who'd just hit me in public was finally back home with me and didn't walk away from me for good."

Leo stayed silent, but his eyes had darkened into a deadly storm.

"I let myself believe it was just a blip. That he never meant to hurt me, that it must have been some defensive reaction that I was just unfortunately on the other end of. But then it happened again, and it kind of became a regular thing until he finally scared me so bad one night that I ran. It's taken me a long time to get back to a place where I feel confident in myself again, and I know now that none of it was ever my fault. But I carry so much shame that I ever let someone bring me down so brutally and deliberately. I promised myself no one would ever hurt me like that again."

Leo's gaze was severe, and I realized his hand was sweating over mine. Pain was evident in his features. Embarrassment washed over me.

"I'm sorry, I know that's a lot to dump on you . . ."

Leo pulled me to him, crushing me into a firm embrace against his warm chest. I buried my face into his neck, breathing in the smell of his soap, feeling his hands soothe against my back, along my arms, until the shakiness in my limbs began to subside. "I'm so sorry that you had to endure something like that, Mara. I . . ." He inhaled deeply. "You deserve so much better."

I let out a quiet laugh. "I sort of figured I was done with love—at least for a really long time. And I definitely needed a break from men until I could sort through my fears and heal from some of my internal wounds. I . . . I've known I'm bisexual since high school, but after Seth I kind of thought I might be done with men for good. I haven't been interested in any man in years . . . not until you walked into Rudy's that night."

He tilted my face off of his chest until I was looking at the question shining from his eyes. "I was . . . the first? Since?"

I nodded. "Yeah. I had a brief fling with another ex after— it was more of a comfort hookup than anything. But you're the first new man I've slept with since Seth."

"God Mara, I hope I didn't push you—"

"No, you didn't." I pressed a hand to his cheek. "It was the first time I didn't feel scared, the first time I felt . . . hopeful. I wanted you that night, Leo. You were exactly what I needed."

He let out a deep exhale and his shoulders relaxed. "You were exactly what I needed, too. And, I know we only have a few days left," he said, his tone growing somber, "but if there's anything I can do to help you heal . . . if you can use me in any capacity, Mara, please do."

The pads of his fingers pressed divots against my skin, and hunger curled in my stomach. He was looking at me with so much tenderness and care that it knocked the breath right out of my lungs. But his words sprang wild around my mind.

"Leo," I murmured, sliding my open palm across his jaw. "No. That's not what this is . . . this isn't about using you. I'm *choosing* you, choosing to let you in. To be vulnerable with you. And if I didn't make it clear last night, I've changed my mind about what happens after the week is over. I . . . I don't want you to go anywhere. I want to see this through . . . with you. I said I'm yours and . . . I meant it."

His eyes searched mine, the hope in them shining like a falling star. "You did?"

"Yeah." I nodded firmly. "I did. Please stay." I was no longer frightened. No longer aching to fill the hole in my heart, because it was undoubtedly shrinking by the second—filling with laughter and joy and what felt like a new beginning with him. "No disappearing acts necessary. *Please* don't go back to New York."

His returning smile was boyish, but I could still see the shadows haunting his eyes. "Come here," he said, pulling me closer and shifting our bodies so that I was pinned between him and the soft mattress, his legs still caging around my own. "You are brilliant," he murmured before kissing my cheek. "You are kind and generous," he continued, pressing his warm lips to the other side of my face. And then he looked down at me with such genuine adoration, I felt everything in me shatter apart. "You are worthy of love and respect, Mara."

I tried to stop the tears from falling, but it was no use. "Sometimes I wonder what my life would be like if I never met Seth—what that alternate-universe-version of myself might look like. Is she braver? Stronger? Is she happier because she was never hurt?" I bit my lip, feeling a single tear trickle down my temple. "I've fought for where I'm at. And don't get me wrong, I'm thankful for everything I've built for myself—but I'm also really fucking angry that I had to go through it in the first place. That I had to claw my way back from the depths of hell all because I let some stupid man hurt me. Because I let him *keep* hurting me."

"*Mara.*" Leo's voice was low. He reached his hand up, gently wiping away the next tear that escaped from my eye. "You can dream up that reality all you want. There's nothing wrong with being angry for being hurt, or for wishing it never happened. But . . . I'd like to tell you what I see when I look at you, if that's all right?"

He was looking at me like he *needed* to say whatever came next. I fastened my gaze on his mouth as I nodded.

"You are full of so much fire, so much tenacity that it's nearly blinding. When I look at you, Mara, I see the bravery and strength that you say you yearn for—you already have it. It's in the way you fight for women to feel safe at Larkspur, in the way you fight for yourself and your team there. I see how open you've let yourself become around me, and I don't take that gift lightly because I can't imagine how hard it is to extend that kind of trust after what you've been through.

"You're a dragon, Mara. You show your teeth and breathe your fire when you need to. But it's not the sum of who you are." He swiped his thumb across my jaw, and I leaned my face into his palm. "You're also the most beautiful woman I've ever seen in my entire life. I would find you in any universe, in any reality. I would see you for the devastatingly perfect, sweet woman that you are. And I would do everything in my power to make you mine."

"Leo," I breathed.

"Look at you, my fire-breathing girl." His bright blue eyes were hazy with lust. "Now, open your legs for me, sweetheart."

Chapter Twenty-Eight

"I haven't seen you in days!" Nora squealed, dropping her polishing cloth over the bar top and wrapping her arms around me. It was true—I hadn't seen her since Monday night when we'd last worked together. We normally worked together Wednesdays, but Sam had covered my shift so I could attend the dinner from hell.

"I know, it's been a crazy week. How have you been?"

Nora pulled back, her brown eyes shining in the glow of the neon lights. "So good—Marisela and I almost have our menu nailed down! We still have so much to do, but most of it is just licensing and city approvals at this point. I think we might be open before the holidays!"

"That's amazing, Nor!" I pulled her in for another squeeze, and her tall frame folded over mine. "Although, I hate to ask what that means for Larkspur."

"Don't worry, I'm not going anywhere—not for a while, at least."

Thank *god.*

My phone chimed with a new text, and I untucked myself from Nora to pull it out of my belt bag. Leo's name was written across the screen. "Sorry, Nora, I need to get this. But let's catch up later, okay?" Sam opened tonight, so he would be the first cut once things began to slow down. Which meant Nora and I would have time to talk more when we closed up.

She nodded. "Sounds good!"

"Are we fully stocked back here? Do we need anything prepped?"

"Nope, Sam got it all done before I got here. We're swimming in ice and fresh garnishes," she laughed.

I smiled and headed back out from behind the bar to drop my things off in the office. Frank stood at his usual post by the door to the back, giving me the faintest smile as I passed by. "Evening, boss."

"Frank." I grinned, nodding toward Rocco who stood tall and menacing by the DJ booth. "You keeping that weirdo in line?"

This time Frank couldn't stop the full smile from curving along his mouth. "Fuck yeah."

I laughed. "Good."

After unlocking the office, I tucked my belt bag into the corner of the desk and looked back down at my phone, swiping to open the new text message.

LEOPOLD

> Hello Mara, I hope you're enjoying a wonderful and safe evening. I have some rather important updates, and I'm afraid I can't stand to wait much longer to share them with you. I'm hoping if I give you ample warning before my arrival, I can steal you away from the bar for a few moments. Looking forward to it, Leo

My stomach flipped—this had to be about New York and whether he was going back. After spending most of the morning in bed together, we'd finally forced ourselves out of his sheets so that I could make it to Muay Thai and he could meet his parents for lunch at a local country club that they'd somehow gotten access to during their stay here. Leo wasn't home when I'd gotten back from training.

I couldn't tell from the text what he'd decided, which only plucked at my nerves more. I was terrified that Alaric would get to Leo and crush him in his merciless hold.

But after the night we shared, he wouldn't really consider leaving, would he?

I quickly typed out a response.

> Do you realize that you write text messages like they're emails? You really are such a corporate snob.

A text bubble immediately appeared.

LEOPOLD

> You wicked thing. I'll be there in five.

I decided to wait in the office. There was no use going back behind the bar just to sneak away again. I sat down in the chair at the desk and decided to brew myself some coffee, making a second cup for Leo. True to his word, there was a light knock at the door within minutes before he pushed it open. He immediately moved in to kiss me, his warm hands skating along my face, winding themselves into my hair as his lips took ownership.

He eventually pulled back a few inches and looked down at me, his eyes like twinkling sapphires. "Sorry, I couldn't wait." I took a second to size him up, finding him in jeans and a button-down shirt that was open at the collar. His eyes were bright, his cheeks a little flushed.

"I swear to god if you're about to tell me you're leaving, I'm not going to be able to stand it," I whispered. I didn't mean for the words to spill out, but I couldn't stop them.

He wrapped his arms around me, tucking me in. "I'm not going anywhere, sweetheart."

I pulled back to look at him. "You're not?"

"No. I just spent the last several hours with my father telling him that I was done. I officially resigned from the company and turned over all credit cards that belong to Callahan Enterprises."

I let out a quiet sob. It felt like the entire world had suddenly righted itself, like the ground beneath my feet was no longer in danger of caving in. "Are you okay?"

"More than okay," he assured, pressing a kiss to my forehead. "I called the bank before I met with him and pulled all my own private funds into a new account that he won't be able to find. My grandfather left me a decent amount of money when he passed that has nothing to do with my father or the company . . . so I'll be all right for a while. I want to stay here, Mara. I want to be with you . . . for real. No more pretending."

I pressed my face into his chest. "It's been real for me since that first night, Leo. I was just too scared of the truth."

He squeezed me tighter. "I have something for you," he murmured into my hair, and I pulled back to look at him again. He pulled a rolled piece of paper out from his back pocket and handed it to me.

I reached to take it, letting my eyes fall to the words printed. It was another contract . . . and it took a moment before I realized what it said, that he was giving me the *entire* company. My breath caught somewhere in my throat. "Leo, no, I—" I stumbled over my words. "This is too much."

He shook his head, his sure smile still slicing through his handsome face. "No, Mara. This place has always been yours. It should have been yours the second Robert wanted to sell. I'm sorry I roped you into my bullshit with my parents—it didn't take me long to realize this place was going to be yours no matter what. *All* yours. I'm not going to stand in the way of you having what you deserve."

"But I . . ." Tears clouded my vision. "You can't just *give* me the bar, Leo. I want to pay for it . . . I want to buy it from you."

"Trust me, Mara—"

"No, Leo," I interrupted, voice firmer. "This is . . . this is incredibly kind, and generous. But you bought the bar, with real money. *Your* money. I'm prepared to buy it from you, or . . ." I realized I may not actually be ready to buy the whole thing at this point. ". . . or at least come up with some sort of payment plan. We can figure that part out." His smile grew as I rushed out the words. "I don't want the bar like this. And you just gave up your job . . . I meant it when I said I want to run things together. I could use some mentorship, and more than anything, I *want* you here, Leo. Not just with me, but *here*."

Warm hands cupped my face. "I'll give you anything you want, Mara. Whatever you're comfortable with."

"I want you," I repeated. It was the only thing that mattered. At least for right now.

He looked down at me, emotion shining in his ocean blues. "When I first saw you, I nearly went to my knees for you, Mara. Right in the middle of that convenience store, like a damn fool. I wanted to give myself to you completely without even knowing your name. I wanted to slay dragons for you and shield you from the nasty shit that this world is full of. But you've proven you can slay your own dragons. You are as fierce and bright and fiery as them, all on your own, and you've made me braver just by being around you. Brave enough to finally choose *myself*, and what I want. Trust me, sweetheart—what I want is you."

"Do you want a drink?" Leo asked. We'd just gotten home from a long Friday night shift—Nora caught us making out in the office when she came to tell me we needed a keg change, and I'd had a *lot* of explaining to do. And then the bar got busier than all hell, and I hadn't had the chance to stop moving until we closed. It was a wild night, but the tips were worth it.

Georgie had been waiting with a note from Leo's parents saying that they'd gone home to New York early—it seemed they'd finally understood that they couldn't control their son any longer. I wondered if they'd be back to try again someday, or if this might be the end of their relationship with their son. I supposed it was impossible to know, but one thing was for damn sure—whatever happened, Leo and I would face it together.

I still held out hope that things might resolve themselves at some point, if Alaric and Christine could learn to respect him and give him the unconditional support that he deserved. But I also knew it would take a *lot* of change for anything like that to ever happen. For now, my body buzzed with the knowledge that they were gone, that our agreement was technically over—and I was still here.

That this was really only the beginning.

"No," I said softly. Why drink when there were so many other things we could do? My eyes traced his Cupid's bow, thinking about the shape it took around my breast, and I flushed.

Leo slid his hands into his pockets and watched me with a devilish grin. I tried to force more air into my body, tried to stop my mind from racing. "Then what do you want, Mara?"

My eagerness only grew when his eyes darkened to a deep hazy blue as I pulled off my hoodie. Like the swell of the ocean at night: deep and majestic and full of the best-kept secrets. His hunger was taking hold, fastening itself to my own. I threw him a wry grin. "Wanna watch *The Outsiders*?" I asked. I still technically hadn't seen it.

Leo's laugh boomed through the room with genuine sincerity. That mask of his had been discarded, and I hoped he never wore it again. He stepped forward, pulling me to him and nuzzling his mouth into my neck. "I think Marge was really on to something with that," he said, his voice muffled against my skin.

I smiled. "I mean, you *do* look like a young Rob Lowe—" I

was cut off by Leo's mouth as it pressed against mine to catch the rest of my words on his tongue.

Dolly came racing into the living room from somewhere down the hallway, Swift close at her heels. Swift had taken to chasing Dolly around the apartment in the last few days, and Dolly was anything but pleased. Leo laughed again as I scooped her up—she'd been much more welcoming of my presence lately.

"Dolly Parton, are you being heckled again?" Leo asked her, leaning in and giving her chin a soft scratch.

My eyes shot wide. "Dolly *Parton*? That's her name?" I could feel Dolly's stare as she turned to look at me with those intense eyes, like I should have already known this.

Leo smiled. "Dolly Parton and Taylor Swift—two of the best female songwriters in existence," he said proudly.

I shook my head in disbelief. "You just keep surprising me, don't you?" I was so worried that he'd turn out to be another misogynistic boss when I learned he'd purchased Larkspur—even more so when he asked me to agree to be his fake girlfriend to appease his billionaire father—but it couldn't be further from the truth.

He took the shit I threw at him head on, somehow knowing I desperately needed to let it out to save myself. He never judged me for it . . . he only continued to show up, to remind me that I wasn't alone, that I had permission to fall apart too. That he would be there. And he found a way to render my weapons useless.

The four of us settled into the couch and as I looked around the living room, I realized that manifestations I'd held so closely to my heart the first time I was here were presenting themselves to me like a gift from the universe. I was ending a day of doing what I loved next to the man of my dreams in a penthouse that had begun to feel like a second home. We still had a long way to go in our respective healing journeys, but we'd made strides in the last week—both as individuals and together.

Later, when it was obvious that Leo and I wouldn't be finishing the movie *again* due to roaming hands and whispered praises, we scampered down the hall into his bedroom, my hand held tightly in his. After taking a quick reprieve in the bathroom to brush my teeth and shower, I found Leo already in bed, waiting for me. His long body took up most of the space, and I couldn't help the heat crawling up my neck at the sight of him.

"Mara," he rasped in the dark. I didn't think I would ever get tired of hearing my name from his mouth.

"Yes, Leo?" I answered, slinking closer to the bed.

He reached out for my hand, pulling me to him on the bed so that my legs straddled over his hips. Gently brushing a thumb across my cheek, he whispered, "I'm so happy you're here." I closed my eyes, soaking in the feeling of this, the feeling of *him*. He smiled. "There's nothing in the world I want more than this, Mara," he assured. "Nothing."

His words moved through me like a soothing balm spreading over so many old and tired wounds. I wasn't naive to think that those wounds didn't still exist or that Leo alone would heal them, but I felt safe enough to try and *that* seemed like the hardest part. I bent down to press a kiss against his lips and couldn't help the smile as I did.

Epilogue

Three Months Later

I WAS EAGER TO TAKE ADVANTAGE OF A SUNRISE RUN after a night off from the club in which we spent nearly the entire night curled up in bed together. Leo grumbled as we got dressed, doing his best to convince me to get back into bed with him, pleading that he would make it worth my while. Somehow I'd resisted, and as such was rewarded with the sight of him in jogging shorts.

My eyes helplessly zeroed in on the way the loose-fitting black fabric hung around his muscular thighs, my mouth immediately going dry. His legs were incredible, strong and thick with calves that could have their own zip code. I thought about how those legs had carried my weight numerous times, had supported him as he thrust into me against a wall . . . it was enough to leave me breathless.

When he caught me staring, he threw me a devious grin and a wink that buckled my knees. So I slipped into my shortest spandex as payback.

The January air outside was cold and biting at this hour, but I welcomed the sting of it against my skin knowing the run would warm my limbs in no time. We hadn't had any snow yet besides some flurries that fell just before Christmas, but Colorado weather could be fickle like that. Leo insisted I take the lead, sputtering on about wanting to keep an eye on me to make sure I was safe . . . but I knew he just wanted to look at my ass.

I led him on a long jog around the city that lasted about an hour and a half, stopping only once when Leo began to sputter behind me as he begged for a water break. "How the fuck can you just keep going like this?" he rasped, sweat gleaming on his forehead as he sucked in air.

I rolled my eyes. "Endurance, Leo. Ever heard of it?"

His eyes flashed with amusement as he drank from his water bottle, his chest heaving enough to tell me he was reaching his limit. "I like to save my endurance for better activities than *running*, Mara."

"Oh." I shimmied toward him, watching his eyes bounce to my chest. "Well, we better get going then." And just as he reached for me, I took off again, my waist slipping out of his grasp. He groaned behind me, and I barked a laugh.

We ran the few additional miles it took to get back to his building and both nearly dropped right there on the sidewalk in front of the doors. The daytime doorman, Roger, came outside to inspect us with concern rooted across his face, but Leo waved a hand and told him we were fine, that I might be out to torture him but he was unfortunately a willing participant.

Roger grinned. "I believe the term for that is 'whipped,' sir."

Leo huffed, then shrugged. "Indeed."

We practically crawled to the elevator. But despite our mutual exhaustion, Leo was still somehow able to push me against the wall inside the elevator car with a deep, hungry kiss.

"Leo." I swatted at his chest. "I'm sweaty and gross!"

"No, trust me, you smell like my favorite treat."

"You're a damn liar," I retorted, pushing him back again. But he didn't budge.

His eyes grew darker. "Mara, I have been staring at that perfect ass for eleven miles." He nuzzled into my neck as goose-bumps exploded over my skin. "I need you right fucking *now*."

The elevator chimed as the doors opened to his penthouse, and I pushed past him through the doors. "Let me at least take a shower first," I insisted, walking toward the kitchen to grab a glass of water. But Leo was hot on my trail, chasing me across the living room. I couldn't help but yelp when I felt his hands on my hips, followed by a loud burst of laughter when he cornered me against the island.

He caged me in as he pressed himself against me. "I can't wait anymore," he whispered. And I could feel how hard he was through his shorts.

Anticipation curled low in my belly, watching as a wave of chestnut hair fell across his forehead. He was such a gorgeous man, it almost wasn't fair. "Then shower with me," I breathed. His eyes crinkled in triumph as his hands greedily went for my ass. And before I knew it, he ducked down to wrap a strong arm around my thighs, hoisting me up and over his shoulder as I squealed in surprise. He spanked me once with his free hand as he moved, a growl escaping from his throat as he did, and I felt my own need beginning to roar through me.

As he walked through his bedroom door, he took the

briefest pause to say hello to Dolly and Swift, who were both sprawled at the foot of his bed, eyeing us with curiosity. A small giggle slipped out of my mouth as Dolly let out a quiet meow in response. But then Leo rushed us forward to the en suite bathroom, near desperate with his desire.

He headed straight for the glass shower door and opened it before stepping right in with me still in tow over his shoulder, supporting my weight as if it were effortless. He reached to turn on the shower head above us before pressing my ass against the wall, moving backward to allow for my body to slide down the tiles in front of him.

Warm water cascaded all around us as I wrapped my legs around his waist, soaking into our hair and skin and the clothes we were still wearing. "Leo," I murmured as his hot mouth found my neck.

"Hm?" he grunted, his teeth nipping the skin at the top of my shoulder.

"We still have our clothes on."

He lifted his head to look at me, a dangerous grin spreading across his face. "Fuck the clothes."

His mouth found me in a kiss that left me breathless. My body was pinned between his chest and the cold glass wall behind me—I loved how bad he wanted this. That he couldn't wait.

It drove me wild.

Reaching down, I gripped the hem of his T-shirt and pulled it up his torso, exposing the hard muscle of his abdomen, slick with sweat and water from the wide shower head. He lifted his arms, giving me access to pull the material all the way off of him. As soon as it was off, he pawed at my tank top, lifting it above my head before his lips crashed to mine once more. His hands were everywhere all at once, and I moaned deliriously at the feel of it.

In a frenzy, he focused on my shorts, pulling them down as far as he could while still keeping his mouth fastened to mine. I kicked out my feet around where he stood between them, wiggling back and forth before I shucked them completely. The slap of their impact on the shower floor sounded, and Leo smiled.

He bit my bottom lip hard before kneeling down in front of me, pulling my leg over his shoulder as his mouth landed between my legs. I let out an immediate cry of pleasure.

"Fuck, sweetheart." He groaned. "I cannot get enough of you."

My stomach flipped as his tongue darted out to part me. "Leo . . ." His fingers gripped my ass behind me, pressing me into his face. My heart pounded sharply in my chest as he continued to devour me and soon I was a shaking, boneless mess.

Droplets of water clung to the ends of the hair that I loved so much, in the eyelashes that fanned my favorite color blue. They rolled down his honeyed jaw and neck before nestling into the groove of his shoulder blade, and I was mesmerized. He was a majestic, golden thing of light—so pure and sweet that I wanted to bottle this feeling up forever, because sometimes I still felt terrified that it wouldn't last.

It wasn't long before I was shattering apart in Leo's strong grip, and as I still rode the waves of pleasure that coursed through me, he stood to turn me around, taking me from behind in a single hard thrust. Leo and I fit together perfectly, and as he set the pace to chase after his own release, I felt the unmistakable workings of another for myself.

His mouth crushed against the top of my shoulder as we came together. "Fuck," he rasped. "Fuck, Mara. This is just too good."

"I know," I breathed. And I did. I'd never shared chemistry like this with anyone. As much as I loved hooking up with Charlea before meeting Leo, the high was *never* like this. She must have seen how gone for him I was the next time she came to the bar to visit, because she'd given me a sincere smile before leaving that night, and I haven't heard from her since.

It wasn't until we were drying ourselves off after washing up in the shower that I had the nerve to ask. "Hey, how late do you need to be at work tonight?"

Leo looked at me curiously. "Not late. Why?"

I couldn't explain why I was so anxious about the news I had to share with him. I'd been doing a lot of things behind Leo's back lately, and though I had the best of intentions it still felt like dangerous territory. But I knew that if I told him what I was doing from the start he would have probably tried to stop me—we'd grown a lot in the last few months, but there were still fears that Leo clung to tightly. I did my best to seem normal as I shrugged. "I have something I want to show you, and I think I'll be off early. Can I plan something for us tonight? I'll make dinner."

He grinned. "How about *I* make dinner, but you can still have the rest of your plan?"

I laughed. Though I tried, I was pretty terrible in the kitchen. "Deal."

Leo and I carried our plates of roasted salmon and vegetables up to the roof along with a bottle of Rudy's top-shelf champagne that I'd insisted we pick up on our way home from Larkspur. It felt necessary, considering this was a celebration.

At least I really *really* hoped it was.

He was doing his best to look calm, but I could tell Leo was just as anxious as I was for him to be on the inside of a big secret—we'd shared everything through the progression of our relationship, however tiny or trivial. When I finally went home to my parents and told them the truth about all that had happened to me, Leo was right there, holding my hand through it. My mother cried and my father had been so upset he spent nearly an hour out back working on the shed, hammering into planks of wood with a vengeance I'd never seen from him before. I hated how much I upset them, but Leo was steadfast in his support, even taking the opportunity to go out and assure my father that nothing like that would ever happen to me again.

When Leo continued to try (and fail) to give me the entire club, I resisted. I *wanted* him to be a part of it, wanted him to have legal ties to the place that brought us together again. So, per our contract, he signed over three-quarters of the company to me with a new contract that outlined how I'd pay him for it. And I was a fucking *proud* business owner.

We made it a point to work through all of those hurdles together, to support each other's bravery *and* vulnerability as we faced each one. Tonight, though, I'd managed to set up a little stunt that he had no idea about.

I hadn't been sure what, exactly, the outcome would be when I'd first set out to make it happen. I was just scrolling on my social media feed one night listening to Leo play the guitar and found a viral video of a girl singing a cover of a popular song from inside of her shower—bathrooms, apparently, were great for acoustics. What caught my interest was the sheer amount of people who supported her—the video had millions of views and over seven-hundred-thousand likes.

I remembered looking up from my phone screen to find Leo lost in the song he was playing, his tongue poking out of the corner of his mouth in concentration, and the idea hit me like a freight train. I'd garnered over fifty-thousand followers on my own page, and granted most of them followed me for the content I put out around bartending and Larkspur . . . but people who liked going out and listening to club music probably also appreciated other kinds of music, right?

Leo could play any genre, and though he leaned on playing classical music for a lot of his daily practice, my favorite thing in the world was hearing him play the music that he'd written himself. It was like his body became this fluid thing of beauty as he threw himself into the melodies. It was moody and full of angst, reminding me of some of my favorite indie bands with the way it pierced me like a bull's-eye in the chest.

When Leo came to Denver over a year ago, he put a lot of pressure on himself to record his music and send it out to some of the big players in the music industry, hoping a label executive might like his sound enough to bring him on. Leo didn't sing and had no real interest in releasing music under his own name, but he wanted the opportunity to work with artists as a credited songwriter.

Apparently, he never heard anything back. He knew the likelihood of anything monumental happening were slim, but he'd wanted music to be his escape route from his father and the family business so badly that he was near-desperate for *something* to come of it. When he was only met with silence, he'd been discouraged.

I'd helped him through it, but despite my best efforts, Leo didn't believe he had what it took to be successful with the one thing he loved most about himself. And I didn't like that. Not one bit.

So, I made a social media account for him that I didn't tell him about, and I started secretly recording him while I watched him play. It took a couple of months, but in the last few weeks the videos had gained some serious traction. I also *may* have shared a lot of the videos from my own page to help push them in front of all of my followers, which definitely helped. But then the unthinkable happened.

A small music label from LA messaged Leo's account, asking for a demo.

"So," Leo said as we settled into a cushioned loveseat. His eyes caught mine and harnessed me right to him. "Are you ready to tell me what all of this is about?"

"Almost," I said, pulling the blanket over our legs. "But first, champagne." I pulled the bottle out of the bucket and popped it open before pouring the bubbly golden liquid into two glasses. I handed one to Leo and turned my body to face him—the truth of everything I'd done caught in my throat. "First, I want to say how much I love you, Leo. You're the best man I've ever known, and all I want is for you to be as happy as you've made me." It wasn't the first time I told him I loved him —*that* memorable moment happened the morning of Thanksgiving, before I brought him to my parents' house a second time. I'd woken up with the words burning on my tongue, and nearly tripped over my own feet in my pursuit to the kitchen to tell him.

Leo's brows pinched. "I am happy, sweetheart." He gripped my free hand in his. "You make me happier than I ever knew I could be."

I smiled. "Yes, but love isn't everything . . . You quit your father's company and removed yourself from a terrible situation, and while I love running Larkspur with you, I know it isn't your dream like it is mine. Your music, Leo—that's your passion. *That's* your endgame."

I could almost feel the distance Leo put between himself and the words I spoke. And while I understood his hurt, I wasn't going to let his fears keep him from his dreams. "Mara —" he started to say.

But I didn't let him finish. "I believe in you, Leo. I believe in your music. And based on the response I got from thousands of other people, I think it's about time you start believing it yourself."

His eyes went sharp as he regarded me. "What?"

I nodded. "Thousands and thousands of people, Leo, who all love the music you're writing. They love the way you sound. I've been sharing your music on social media, and—"

"You've been . . . you've shared my music?" he repeated. "You've been recording me?"

"Yes. And I'm sorry I didn't tell you, but I knew you would try and stop me. I knew you would let your fear outweigh the possibilities, and I wanted to prove to you that you have nothing to be scared of."

For a long moment, he did nothing but stare at me, and with every passing second I could feel a growing panic slither through my body. Eventually, he sighed before asking, "Can I see?"

"Oh . . . of course," I said, pulling my phone out of my

sweatshirt pocket. I opened the app and pulled up his account before handing him the phone. Leo took it and curled himself over the screen, looking at the long feed of videos and eagerly scrolling through the comments that people left under each one. I watched as the corner of his mouth tugged up at something he read before he started furiously scrolling again.

It was like magic, watching him realize the impact his music had on so many people.

He looked back up at me, his eyes tender. "Thank you," he said quietly.

I smiled wide. "Leo, this isn't even the best part."

His eyes grew wide. "It's not?"

I shook my head, taking the phone back from him so I could open the message that had come in a couple days ago—the one that changed the whole game. And then I gave the phone back to him and let him read it. "Holy shit," he whispered as he set the phone down and covered his eyes with his hands.

"It's not a guarantee," I said carefully, unsure of how else to put it, "but it's an open door, Leo. It's a *chance*. And I would bet all of Larkspur that it's only the first of many."

He scooted himself across the cushion to get closer to me and I was transfixed as I watched his face transform into something beautiful, something eager and hopeful. My bright and shining Leo—my supernova. His hands etched a path across my cheek. "You wicked woman. You did all this for me?"

Relief flooded in my chest as I wrapped my arms around his neck. "Yes," I breathed. "Of course I did, Leo. You *deserve* this—you deserve to be seen for how incredible you are."

He snaked his arms around me and held me like he never wanted to let go. "I don't even know what to say," he murmured into my hair. "How you manage to be exactly what I've always needed . . . I can't even begin to comprehend it. Thank you for fighting for me. *You* are my endgame, Mara. You're all I see, the only one who really sees me."

I choked on my next breath as a sob ripped through me. I had no idea love could feel like this. There was no longer a clear boundary indicating where Leo ended and I began—we now swirled together into the mists as one. One heart shared between two tired and broken souls who'd finally found the light again.

This kind of love was one I knew I'd never recover from, but in ways so different from what I'd experienced before. I would no longer be able to live my life without the imprint of Leo on my skin, like the sun's kiss on my face.

The traces he left were warm and lively, and the effects of his love would carry me through the rest of my life. He taught me how to love my imperfections, just as I helped him do the same. We honored each other's vulnerabilities and gave each other a safe space to land, no matter how rough the journey.

And for that, I was forever thankful. Just as I was forever his.

Acknowledgments

End Game is quiet and tender beneath the layers of outward fire, and I'm really, really proud of how Mara and Leo overcome so much of their own suffering to find the light in their lives again. I'm especially aware of the strength it takes to dismantle an abusive relationship of any kind, and want to give special acknowledgement to my mother who taught me early on that there is always something warm and bright on the other side.

xo, Michaela

Books by Michaela Jean Taylor

Love In The Rockies

Only You

This Love

End Game

Saddlebrook Falls

Sunshine

Peaches

Sugar

About the Author

Michaela is a hopeless romantic from the western desert who writes grippingly tender romance novels featuring diverse characters and messy, beautifully relatable storylines.

Stay tuned for exciting announcements at
michaelajeantaylor.com